SWIPE BITE

SWIPE BITE

ALEXANDRA VASTI

BERKLEY
NEW YORK

BERKLEY
An imprint of Penguin Random House LLC
1745 Broadway, New York, NY 10019
penguinrandomhouse.com

Book design by Devan Norman

Library of Congress Cataloging-in-Publication Data

Names: Vasti, Alexandra author
Title: Swipe bite / Alexandra Vasti.
Description: First edition. | New York : Berkley, 2026.
Identifiers: LCCN 2026004307 (print) | LCCN 2026004308 (ebook) |
ISBN 9798217189434 trade paperback | ISBN 9798217189441 ebook
Subjects: LCGFT: Paranormal romance fiction | Novels
Classification: LCC PS3622.A8584 S95 2026 (print) |
LCC PS3622.A8584 (ebook)
LC record available at https://lccn.loc.gov/2026004307
LC ebook record available at https://lccn.loc.gov/2026004308

First Edition: November 2026

Printed in the United States of America
1st Printing

The authorized representative in the EU for product safety and compliance is Penguin Random House Ireland, Morrison Chambers, 32 Nassau Street, Dublin D02 YH68, Ireland, https:// eu-contact.penguin.ie.

For my mom, with whom I read the entirety of the Black Dagger Brotherhood while screaming. This is what decades of reading romance together got us—a vampire book!

And for Matt, who has uncomplainingly enjoyed *many* viewings of *Bram Stoker's Dracula* with me over the past sixteen years. Thank you for being the reason all my dating apps are fictional.

SWIPE BITE

CHAPTER 1

Sophronia Vega was in the middle of the most important presentation of her life when the vampire on floor seventeen nearly ate an accountant.

Which, frankly, was ridiculous. It was eleven o'clock in the morning. It wasn't even time for *lunch*.

She'd just finished the slides on global data-privacy regulations and had moved into a persuasive series of remarks on fiduciary duty to shareholders—at least, she thought they were persuasive; she'd practiced them fourteen times yesterday with Delphine—when her phone started to buzz.

She ignored it, which was her first mistake. She should have known the vibration spelled disaster.

Her phone was set to Do Not Disturb. No one should have been able to get through except Del—and Del knew perfectly well that the outcome of this meeting would determine the future of Sophronia's app, her career at HemoCorp Industries, and her entire life.

She wouldn't have called for anything short of bloodshed.

Sophronia flipped the phone over and turned back to the glossy projections that held a year's worth of app data and also her absolute devotion.

"As you can see," she told the HemoCorp executive committee, "Stokr's US rollout has been an unqualified success on every level, from customer satisfaction to month-to-month sell-through. Each of these global territories has been hand selected as the most promising for expansion of the app. We've begun building teams in Singapore, Brazil—"

"What about insurance?" Octavia Pavo interrupted. Her crisp ash-blond hair made perfect arcs where it lay against her silk blouse, and her lilac lips were set in an expression of calm interest.

Sophronia knew better, of course. Octavia had once called Stokr a *breathtaking embarrassment for all vampirekind*, and she hadn't even had the grace to look embarrassed when she'd noticed that Sophronia was in earshot.

Sophronia forced herself to smile back. "We've had minimal insurance claims in the past year, mostly superficial settlements. Unlike the rest of HemoCorp's tech"—her smile seemed to be fixed into place on her mouth now, and she hoped it didn't look too much like a grimace—"Stokr isn't licensed as a clinical-grade product."

"I am aware of that," Octavia said blandly. "Our first dating app. What a shining new horizon for our company."

Sophronia felt a tiny throb of blood rise in the direction of her cheeks. Since she was a vampire and had very little in the way of homegrown blood, her flush was, fortunately, invisible.

Not for the first time in her life, she thanked the spirit of Abraham Stoker that she'd been born a vampire and not a human. She would have rather chewed off her own arm than blush in front of the executive committee. She'd rather print out her slide deck and eat every page individually than reveal a weakness to Octavia and the rest of the executive committee.

To—worst of all—August Vega.

Her father. And HemoCorp's CEO.

"Yes," she said evenly. "Stokr is a dating app. The first human-vampire dating app ever created, using HemoCorp med tech. And within its first year on the market, it's revolutionized human-vampire relations and become the top paid dating app in the country."

Ever since HemoCorp had developed artificial blood a century ago, humans and vampires had lived in uneasy harmony. The invention, which had made the Vega family into a wealthy and powerful dynasty, had eliminated the need for direct human feeding. Vampires could subsist on blood bags rather than people—and their unfortunate reputation as serial killers had slowly faded.

But it hadn't vanished entirely. Some vampires still preferred to drink directly from humans—and the humans liked it too. Enough that they'd risk their own deaths to seek it out.

Luckily, HemoCorp had once again come to the rescue. Three years ago, the company's scientists had developed a simple laboratory test to determine if safe direct feeding was possible by matching vampire salivary enzymes and human blood.

Before hemoenzymatic analysis, direct feeding had been a matter of bloody trial and error. If a human and a vampire were a match, the tiny wounds made by the vampire's fangs closed instantly, with no effect on the human beyond a powerful sense of euphoria.

And if the human and vampire were *not* a safe match—

Well. Thus the vampire reputation for mass murder, et cetera.

"The med tech is sound," Sophronia went on. "We've never once had an error in the lab. And over the past fifty-six weeks that the app has been available to users, its safety record has been perfect."

Happy human-vampire pairs were feeding and frolicking all over the country, and though she knew it was ridiculous—it was a dating app named for Bram Stoker, not dermal grafts and fibrin gels—she was proud of Stokr anyway. Of all the projects under her purview as VP of digital products and solutions, Stokr was the one she was most excited about.

She couldn't help herself. Her eyes shifted to her father, tall and spare and silent in his seat at the head of the table, his blue gaze cool and measured.

This was a *good* presentation. She knew it down to her bones. It didn't matter what Octavia said—August Vega was going to approve the app's expansion, and Octavia and Kriti and Titus and the rest of the executive committee would fall in line.

And though it had never yet happened in the duration of Sophronia's thirty years of life, it seemed possible that this time her father would tell her he was proud.

She felt the bare trace of heat in her cheeks again, and she forced down her stupid childish wishing. Vegas didn't need human things like familial affection or paternal pride. They had HemoCorp; they had *control.* Emotions were nothing more than an invitation to ridicule.

Her phone buzzed again, and her gaze flicked down from August Vega. She fumbled to silence the device, and then—

And then *all* the phones at the conference table were buzzing.

For an instant, Sophronia's mind went blank. *All* the phones—surely Del couldn't be calling all the executives' phones at once.

And then the truth dawned, slow and chilling.

It wasn't a call, this tiny angry buzz that filled her ears.

It was an emergency alert.

She had just a moment to feel a wash of ice down her back, to feel her spine go stiff and straight and her fangs tighten to an ache, when a human burst through the conference-room door.

He had stubble and black-rimmed glasses, and for a split second, she didn't even recognize him as one of her software engineers. His expression was wild, and his dark curls were so disheveled he looked like he'd stuck his finger in a socket. He smelled—

Abraham's eyeteeth. Sophronia felt her fangs tighten further, a hot throb. He smelled *delicious.*

"Ellery Klein," he gasped, "in accounting. She's bleeding out in the conference room."

At his words, Sophronia's whole body went cold.

Before she realized she'd moved, she was across the room, at the door, her fingers around the human's upper arm. She was fast—all vampires were fast—but desiccation could happen in minutes—she'd seen it before.

No.

Not in her office. Not at her company. Not if she had anything to say about it.

"Where?" she snapped. "Show me." And then, behind her, she shouted, "Get a blood patch!"

The human engineer clapped his hand over hers and towed her down the hall—toward comms, not accounting, where the *hell* was he taking her—

"I used the blood patch already," he said. His voice was a rough-smooth rasp. "She'll live. But you can get emergency services up here with a transfusion faster than I can."

He pulled open the conference-room door just as Sophronia made sense of his words. She had top-level security clearance. She could open every locked door from the ground floor up to the seventeenth. With a quick tap into her phone she did it all, then punched the code for HemoCorp EMTs.

As her fingers flew across the screen, her adrenaline-spiked brain took in the scene in the conference room.

On the floor lay Ellery Klein, her red hair pulled back into a high ponytail and a pool of blood rapidly congealing around her. Her head was cradled in the lap of one of the vampires from comms.

The vampire had blood smeared on his chin and a look of gobsmacked horror on his face. His shirt was untucked, the top three buttons undone.

Sophronia quietly thanked the soul of Abraham Stoker that the human engineer had thought to slap a blood patch over the bite. The blood patch—one of Octavia's team's most significant innovations—had been designed for precisely this purpose. As it soaked up freely running blood, the thin fibrin mesh grew thicker and spongier, hastily coagulating into a tough, flexible membrane. The seal it made was perfect: stronger than new flesh.

"Ellery?" the vampire said dazedly. "Oh shit. Oh shit."

Sophronia slapped her phone down on the conference table. Her fingers were shaking. Humans died so *easily*. She knew that they did.

But anger was safer than fear, and so she reached for it like a shield. "What," she hissed, "is going on here?"

The vampire's gaze snapped up to her, and he blanched visibly, the skin paling around his big, dark-lashed eyes. "Oh shit. Ms. Vega. I'm sorry. I'm so sorry. You have to believe that I've never—"

Her gaze dropped to his ID lanyard, tossed on the ground with Ellery's bra, and she found his name. "That you've never *what,* Mr. Helarctos? Decided to dine upon one of your colleagues in the office? Or failed so completely and utterly to take precautions that you nearly *killed* a human?"

"I don't understand," Bastian Helarctos said. His gaze dipped down to Ellery and then back up. "I don't—I don't *understand.*"

People were starting to crowd around the entrance to the conference room—Kriti, Titus, more executive-committee vampires—and Sophronia's gaze flickered to the blood on the ground.

It was an unpredictable combination: vampires and blood and adrenaline.

She knew it was.

"Back *up,*" she snapped at the vampires in the door. Fear cracked her voice, and the sound made her furious. She wanted to tear Bastian Helarctos's throat out with her teeth. "We need space for the EMTs when they get here."

The software engineer—Casey Amato, she thought—moved from her side to the doorway, putting himself between Ellery's body and the vampires. The air beside Sophronia went cold.

"It doesn't make sense," Bastian Helarctos mumbled.

She felt her fangs brush razor sharp against her lower lip as she turned back to him.

"What doesn't make sense?" she inquired silkily. "That you drank from your human colleague and nearly killed her? Or that you did so through sheer mind-numbing carelessness? Truly, Mr. Helarctos, I wonder how it is possible that you secured a job at the most prestigious medical-technology company on the planet and did not think to use its *groundbreaking product*—"

"But I did!"

Sophronia went very still. So did the vampires peering in from the hall.

"What?" she demanded.

Bastian scrubbed the back of his wrist against his bloody chin and gave her a plaintive look. "I *did* use Stokr. We were alone in the conference room—and one thing led to another—but I checked Stokr before I even touched her."

"You used Stokr," Sophronia said flatly. "And Ellery was a match."

"Yes! We paired our apps, and the screen turned green." His lashes came down, and he stared at Ellery's unconscious face. "I've used Stokr a *thousand* times since it came out last year. It's *always* worked."

"It does always work," Sophronia said. "It has to work. Every time. One hundred percent of the time."

That was the only acceptable percentage. Stokr was hers, and it was perfect.

It had to be.

"Not this time," Bastian said. "What the *fuck*."

As if in punctuation, a torrent of HemoCorp medical personnel flooded past the vampires in the door. A handful clustered around Ellery, laying out transfusion bags and plasma kits. One of them tucked a shock blanket around Bastian Helarctos's shoulders.

Another EMT offered Sophronia an emergency single-serve artificial-blood pack, and she bared her fangs so fast the EMT went white and stumbled back.

Bastian's words seemed to revolve in her head, an endless loop of incomprehensible disaster.

I checked Stokr before I even touched her.

What the fuck, her brain echoed. *What the absolute fuck.*

She was still thinking it when the press arrived.

CHAPTER 2

TMZ: BLOODBATH IN INCARNARE . . . HEMOCORP TO BLAME?

Breaking news / July 2 / 8:46 AM PDT

Emergency rooms in Incarnare, California, were on alert last night after eleven—yes, *eleven*—cases of vampire-induced exsanguination were brought in for treatment. All of the humans survived . . . but our sources tell us that one of the cases came from inside HemoCorp itself. Is there trouble in human-vampire dating paradise? Watch this space . . . and your necks.

CNN: SECOND STOKR INCIDENT SENDS FORTY TO HOSPITAL

Updated 5:58 PM EDT, Sat August 7

For the second time in as many months, a glitch in Stokr, the pioneering vampire-human dating app developed by med tech giant HemoCorp Industries, has led to a string of exsanguinations and hospitalizations. HemoCorp spokesvampire Delphine Gaius said in a statement: "I want to assure the public that all humans involved are safe and recovering due to prompt use of HemoCorp's blood patch technology. As always, we urge humans and vampires engaged in relations to keep blood patches with them at all times."

Comment left by @peppermintpattyII: I for one have never deleted an app so fast.

Reply to @peppermintpattyII by @ucialessiab: girl same. fleeing like an h-corp investor rn

CNN: STOKR FIASCO LEADS TO 183 HOSPITALIZATIONS

Updated 12:03 AM EDT, Sun August 29

A complete lapse in functionality for HemoCorp's human-vampire dating app, Stokr, led to chaos across the US last night. Watch NYU student Idrie Yang, 21, describe the scene in the East Village.

Idrie: "The app just started flashing. Normally it turns red if you're not a match—if you could get eaten, right?—or green if you're good to go. But it kept turning, like, blue and purple and yellow, like a kaleidoscope. And then suddenly there were sirens and blood literally everywhere. Thank God my roommate had, like, sixteen blood patches in her bag, or things could have been way worse."

August 30, 7:03 AM
From: Sophronia Vega
To: AllHemoCorpExecCom
Subject: Stokr Emergency Meeting 11AM 17th Flr Conf Room

Please note: executive committee only. Proprietary and sensitive information. Stokr expected to be fully back online by tomorrow night.

TMZ: BAD BLOOD AT HEMOCORP?

Breaking news / August 30 / 11:59 AM PDT

More bad news for Stokr head Sophronia Vega. Rumor has it that the heir to HemoCorp Industries is OUT after a third "technical glitch" led to blood-curdling scenes across the nation. Sounds like Daddy Vega isn't too happy.

Comment left by @norcalwinemom: Good! Kick her to the curb. Jeezus, I was promised hot safe vamp sex, not . . . whatever this is.

Delphine Gaius

12:11 PM

How'd the meeting go?

Sophronia Vega

12:12 PM

Bad.

Really bad.

Delphine Gaius

12:12 PM

Stay put

Bringing gummy worms

The packet of multicolored gummy worms landed with a thump in front of Sophronia's monitor.

She glanced away from the blank email—the blinking cursor—the white screen. "Del. How did you—"

"Get in?" Delphine Gaius kicked off her mules and settled herself into an armless black leather chair: her favorite, the one beside the floor-to-ceiling window. She pulled her knees up and rested her chin atop them. "Wendy."

"Of course." Sophronia's personal assistant was exquisitely loyal—to Del specifically. "I don't know why I asked."

"I don't know why you did either. You know, *you* could bribe her with brown butter frangipane croissants too. I don't have the market cornered on French pastry." Del tilted her head, and blond curls spilled over her billowy orange trousers. "You okay?"

Sophronia swallowed. Her throat felt tight, and she had to stare very hard at her monitor before she could bring herself to answer. "I'm fine."

"You want to come sit next to me?" Del scooched to the side and gestured. "There's room. I can hug you."

Oh Abraham. She felt sixteen again—she and Del in sixth form at Holbeck Priest, her phone locked in her fist after a call with her parents so cold it blistered. Her mother's voice: *Enough, Sophronia. I grow weary of your theatrics. You may not leave Holbeck Priest in the middle of the term.*

Vegas didn't cry. They didn't beg to come home.

But in spite of a hundred years of dynastic history, when Sophronia had slid the phone under her pillow and accepted the hug Del had offered, she'd cried anyway.

"No," she said now. "Only—damn it, Del. They won't let me turn Stokr back on. They said . . . they said three incidents are three too many. They want to shutter it *permanently*. Octavia had a whole file from legal, plus new insurance-premium numbers that can't possibly be right and—"

Del leapt up, half stumbling on her sprawled shoes. "Wait—wait. You didn't get fired?"

Sophronia's lips parted. "*What?*"

"Oh Abraham—I thought I was coming down here to help you pack up your shit. It's all over the news, Soph!"

"*What* is?"

Del yanked her phone out of her pocket and started to tap frantically with both thumbs. "They're saying the committee terminated you. Every shitty excuse for a journalist in the country, pretty much. TMZ broke the story—"

"Damn it"—she snatched the phone from Del's hand—"damn it, damn it. Of course I didn't get fired. The Vega family *is* HemoCorp. They wouldn't dare!"

"Abraham's bloody fangs." Del leaned hard against Sophronia's desk and started to extricate gummy worms. "Soph. I've been out of my mind with worry. I ordered you four cashmere sweaters. And a cat."

Sophronia paused and glanced up from the news apps. "You did not."

"Okay, I just *considered* the cat. Also about twenty-seven different ways to hide Octavia Pavo's headless corpse." Del paused. "I did actually reserve flights and a boutique midcentury resort in Palm Springs, but I'm pretty sure that's refundable."

"Del. It's been"—Sophronia checked the phone—"twenty-one minutes since this story broke."

Del shoved two blue gummy worms in her mouth and slapped a sunset-colored tangle into Sophronia's hand. "It's been an extremely shitty twenty minutes."

Sophronia stared down at the gummy worms, torn horribly between tears and laughter.

"I'm really glad you're here," she got out. And then, before Del's loyalty made her do something hideous like cry, she looked back down at the phone. "Wait. Twenty-one minutes? Abraham's eyeteeth, I was still *in* the meeting twenty-one minutes ago. How could they even—"

Del groaned, then put Sophronia out of her misery by recapturing the phone and shoving it back into her voluminous pocket. "You know this place leaks like a sieve."

"Still." With no loose-lipped employees in her immediate vicinity, Sophronia bit the head off one of the gummy worms instead. "It doesn't make sense. Usually the leaks at least have the general shape of the truth. Why would it leak *during the meeting* that I'd been fired?"

"That's why I thought it was real! Shit, Soph. I'm never

getting those twenty minutes of my life back. Just shave 'em right off the end. You might want to tell Wendy, by the way. She's out there looking like someone's died."

Sophronia took a slightly more aggressive bite of the gummy worm. Vampires might be obligate hemovores, but sugar adulterated by chemical dye was a pleasure unrelated to biological requirements. "No one's died, thank Abraham. Despite the 276 exsanguinations."

Del's brows flew up. "276? I thought it was 234!"

"More reports keep coming in. Unfortunately."

Del sat up straighter. "Do I need to do another press conference? I can—"

Sophronia pinched the bridge of her nose. "I don't know. Probably? We're going to have to—" She blew out a breath and forced herself to say the words calmly and cleanly, like an amputation. "We're going to have to announce that Stokr's shutting down indefinitely."

It hurt. Stupid how much it hurt.

She wasn't developing lifesaving med tech like Octavia's division or spearheading global expansion like Circinus. Her division's products included remote arrythmia detectors, various hemoanalytic-related wearables, and a dating app that, outside her hearing, people called Count Fuckula.

But still: Stokr was *hers*. She believed in it.

She had thought . . .

She had always thought it might do some good for vampires and humans.

Vampires weren't magic. They weren't immortal, and they weren't *made*. They were born and lived and died, just like humans.

But their species was faster and stronger: natural predators to human prey. And though suspicion and strange occult rumors about vampirekind had mostly faded to dark corners of the internet at this point, it was undeniable that humans and vampires living in proximity was risky.

Sometimes—Sophronia knew better than anyone—it could be lethal.

With Stokr, she'd thought, there would be fewer sixteen-year-old vampires weeping in their best friends' arms.

She gritted her teeth at the thought and looked away from Del, scrubbing at the sugar residue on her palm with a Hemo-Corp antiseptic wipe.

Del chewed on her lower lip. "I can make it sound good, Soph." She tested the shape of several phrases on her mouth. "'Extensive safety precautions.' 'A new round of testing and dev from scratch.' Obviously, the loss of public trust is our major issue here."

"*Is* that our major issue?" Sophronia glared hard at the gummy worms still in the bag. "Because I feel like our major issue is the fact that our app keeps almost killing people."

"That . . . is also not good."

Because it was Del, and Del loved her, Sophronia let herself sink bonelessly into her chair. "The worst part is, I'm not even certain the committee's wrong to shut us down. I know the tech is sound. The hemoenzymatic analysis *works.* So what the hell is happening?"

Stokr's rollout had been perfect. Spotless. But Ellery and Bastian's ill-fated hookup in the conference room had turned out to be the first in a string of—

Oh hell. *Bloodbath* was the word the press seemed fond of using.

They were up to three total Stokr-induced catastrophes now, and despite the app's repeated failures, the engineers had been unable to sort out what had gone wrong. Stokr had behaved precisely as it was supposed to on every device, on every operating system. On every hemoenzymatic pair they'd tested.

Sophronia peeled another wipe out of the package and dabbed at her mouth. "The first time, with Ellery, I thought it was some bizarre glitch in the database. There'd never been an error before, and I never thought it would happen again. The second time, I still wanted to believe that. But now . . ."

Del's face was very soft, and so was her voice. "I'm sorry, sweetie."

Sophronia folded the wipe, then folded it again. Neat, precise rectangles, tinier and tinier. "I'm so . . . I don't . . ."

I'm scared. I don't know what to do.

It was impossible to say the words. Even to Del. Failure was a thick black morass she had avoided all her life—a thing she feared so wholly that she couldn't even look at it straight on.

She was a Vega. She *had* to know what to do.

"I know how much it means to you," Del said. "Stokr. HemoCorp. But listen to me—this isn't the end of the world."

Sophronia licked her lips and then touched her tongue to her right fang, just hard enough to feel the bright point of pain.

In the boardroom, she'd stared down a long conference table and felt choked by shame, seared into silence by her father's cold disappointment. Titus Fornax, EVP of regulatory compliance and longtime family friend, had given her half a smile under his beard. *Chin up, kid,* his expression seemed to say.

But Titus's quiet support hadn't been close to enough. Though Titus had tried to speak up for Sophronia and Stokr, the rest of the execs had shut him down.

Octavia, the chief science officer, had wielded data like a cudgel.

Kriti Pillai, HemoCorp's general counsel and the human with the longest tenure on the executive committee, had a sweet, grandmotherly face and no tolerance for fools. When Octavia had insisted on shuttering the app, Kriti had let her glasses dangle on the chain around her neck and said grimly, "Agreed."

August Vega hadn't said anything.

Sophronia hadn't been able to help herself. She'd looked him in the eye and thought, *Please. Don't let them do this.*

She had known better than to say it aloud, of course. Vegas didn't plead.

"I'm going to fix it," she said now. Her voice wanted to shake, and she fought emotion with ice, with cold fury. "I don't care if we have to shut down for the rest of the year, but I *won't* give up on Stokr."

Del tugged the square of polypropylene out of Sophronia's grip, and then she took Sophronia's hand in her own. "Stokr isn't *you*, Soph. And neither is HemoCorp."

Sophronia swallowed.

It was easy for Del to say that. Del had the French bakery, a new dating misadventure every other weekend, a little sun-splashed house with a ridiculous cactus in the front yard. She had a *life* beyond HemoCorp.

Sophronia had the company. And she had Del.

At least one of them loved her back.

Sophronia was still looking down at their interlaced fingers when she heard the whispery sound of her office door coming open.

Her head snapped up. Her eyes flew to the smoked-glass

door, which ought to have been locked, but was opening—again, somehow, damn it, Wendy—beneath a tanned hand.

She didn't need to see his face to know who it was. His scent—the rhythm of his heart—all of it was imprinted somewhere deep in her back brain.

It was the human software engineer who'd broken in on the committee meeting. The one who'd saved Ellery Klein.

CHAPTER 3

Absolutely none of this had been in the HemoCorp job ad.

The walk to Sophronia Vega's office from her admin's desk had felt about a thousand miles long, an interval that had allowed Casey Amato to ponder all his life choices and regret each of them individually.

The ones from today seemed especially catastrophic, in a ghastly death wish sort of way. He'd lied to his junior developers about where he was going, because he didn't want them to worry about their jobs (even though they definitely already were). He'd sweet-talked the admin, with a level of audacity he hadn't employed since he'd been a teenager and had convinced a police officer that he was really, actually supposed to be in a beachside convenience store at three o'clock in the morning.

He'd pushed his way into Sophronia Vega's office uninvited, and . . .

Well. She wasn't actually going to eat him—even though she *could*—because cold-blooded murder was frowned on in corporate America. But she might fire everyone Casey cared about.

And that, he figured, would be worse than death by supervisory exsanguination.

His team hadn't fucked up. He *knew* they hadn't. And he wasn't going to let them lose their positions at HemoCorp.

Not even if it cost him his own.

He gritted his teeth, opened the VP's door the rest of the way, and came face-to-face with a pair of vampires.

The blond one, leaning casually against the huge black desk, was HemoCorp spokesvamp Delphine Gaius. Though she and her brother, another HemoCorp employee, were part of a vampire dynasty almost as ancient and wealthy as the Vegas, they looked more human than most vampires did.

Something about vampires' hemoglobin composition that Casey didn't fully understand meant that they tended to be lean and tall and lightly muscled. But Delphine Gaius was short and almost curvy. Her blond hair curled in every direction imaginable, and, inexplicably, her feet were bare.

The other vampire—he made himself look—was Sophronia Vega.

His boss's boss. HemoCorp's VP of Digital Products and Solutions.

And the most beautiful and terrifying vampire he'd ever seen.

The Vega heir was fine boned, elegant, and probably as tall as he was, which was pretty fucking tall. Her jet-black hair just hit her chin, and beneath her bangs, her eyes were blue.

Her lips were lavender. It meant, he knew, that she was hungry.

"How did you get in here?" she snapped. "Did Wendy let you through?" Her expression looked exactly as it had that day in the conference room: rigid and ruthless and inhumanly cold.

"Um," he said, which was not how he'd imagined pleading for his team and his life.

The problem was, he didn't want to throw Sophronia's admin under the bus. She'd seemed a little frantic, and Casey had lied through his teeth to convince her that Ms. Vega was absolutely expecting him and the calendar invite had vanished in the same technical glitch as Saturday's Stokr failure.

"Was it bichon au citron?" asked Delphine. "I told you, Soph, I don't have the market cornered. If Wendy's the lock, French pastry's the key. Anyone can turn it."

"Damn it," Sophronia hissed. "I'm moving Wendy to sales."

Casey felt the back of his neck heat. He was *not* letting the very nice lady outside get demoted to the worst floor at HemoCorp. "I'm sorry for barging in without an appointment," he said. "It's not your admin's fault. I tried to reach you by email."

"I recall."

Her tone suggested she recalled his emails in the same way he recalled the seagull that had once stolen his fries and then shat in his beard on the boardwalk.

He shoved at his glasses, even though they didn't need fixing. "Right. Well, you asked for a comprehensive analysis of the Stokr backend, so—"

"I *asked* you to deliver any findings to Jackie."

Jackie was Stokr's group chair and Sophronia's direct report. "Yeah. I know. I did that weeks ago, but—"

He thought about Saturday night's catastrophe. Stokr's UI—his project, his *baby*, his and his team's—flashing a dizzy whirl of colors before his eyes. The pictures that had lit up social media: red-streaked walls in an East Village bar, the crumpled remains of a dozen blood patches littering the sticky floor.

"There's more," he said finally. "Something I couldn't bring to Jackie. I needed to speak to you directly."

Sophronia Vega gave him a cool look of dismissal beneath her crisp black bangs. "There is a process. You report directly to Jackie. Jackie reports your findings to me."

"I am aware of that. But if you'd read my emails, you'd know that I—"

"I read your emails, Mr. Amato."

"Well, you didn't *answer* them, so—"

"There is a process," she repeated icily. "Without that process, the company hierarchy descends into chaos."

"The company is already in chaos," he said. "It has been since the day I found Ellery Klein bleeding out in a conference room."

His voice had dropped. He wasn't angry, exactly. He just . . .

It could have been so much worse. It had been a stroke of pure good fortune that he'd gone back into the conference room fifteen minutes after their meeting had ended. That he'd seen Ellery bleeding and Bastian too frozen with shock to use a blood patch.

When he closed his eyes, he kept on seeing Ellery's limp body, her red hair dark with blood.

Kept remembering another hand growing cold in his own.

He had to fix this. He *had to.* He wasn't letting his team lose their jobs, and he was not—*was not*—going to let anyone die.

Behind the desk, the VP's pale face went even paler. Her sharp jaw tightened, and tiny indentations carved themselves into place around her mouth.

She looked elegant and furious and also . . .

And also like she was holding herself together through sheer force of will.

He steeled himself against the part of his heart that wanted to soften at the look on her face. She had ignored him for weeks. She was one of the most powerful vampires in the world. If she plunged her fangs into his jugular right here in her office, her family's money and lawyers would probably save her from any significant consequences, assuming she slapped a blood patch on him before he actually died.

This was no time for misplaced sympathy.

"I have to talk to you," he said, very low. "Not through Jackie or through a report. I need to tell you what I think is going on with Stokr."

She stared him down for several long, silent moments. Her eyes—the precise color and temperature of a glacier—scanned him from the top of his head all the way down past his HemoCorp lanyard and his ancient, battered trainers.

And then her gaze flicked, just briefly, to Delphine at her side.

Delphine was biting her lip, white fangs bright against her burgundy lipstick. Her focus was all on Sophronia, open concern on her face.

"Can't hurt," she said. "Let him say his piece, Soph."

Sophronia didn't respond directly, only pinned Casey with another wintry glare. "Fine. Sit. You have five minutes."

He swallowed hard and sat.

Across from him, separated by the glossy expanse of her desk, Sophronia Vega sat as well.

He paused before he spoke and looked from the Vega heir to Delphine. The blond vampire caught his glance, seemed to parse his hesitation, and then slid her feet back into her shoes.

"Right," she said. "Don't mind me. I've got about sixty thousand emails to answer, judging by the way my pocket's been vibrating for half an hour—"

"No," Sophronia said. "Stay."

Casey took a breath. "It might be better if she—"

"She stays," Sophronia said. "Or you may depart. As you choose."

He winced, but—hell. All right. If she wanted Delphine Gaius here, he wasn't going to argue. He'd gotten inside her office, and he had five minutes. He wasn't about to waste them.

"I'm one of the tech leads for Stokr," he began. "You and I met in July, obviously, but I've been at HemoCorp since the first days of Stokr's development. I—"

"I know who you are, Mr. Amato," she said coolly. "MS in computer science at UC Incarnare, six years at Google in wearables, two-plus in mentoring and coaching junior engineers before you came to HemoCorp."

"Right." He resisted the urge to adjust his glasses again. "I've been in DP&S for two years now, developing the backend for the Stokr UX. The Pillbugs—"

Her nails clicked down on her desk. "The *what*?"

"No, not"—Casey rubbed the back of his neck—"not real pill bugs. The Pillbugs are my team. What we call ourselves. Because we all went to UC Incarnare?"

"*What?*"

"The Pillbugs. That's the mascot of UC Incarnare. It's—never mind." This didn't seem the right moment to discuss the humor inherent in a mascot known as the terrestrial crustacean. "The Pillbugs architect the user-facing features of Stokr. We're the ones who implemented the red and green UI—the tech that communicates as clearly and simply as possible when the app users have made a safe match. Our programming translates from the med-tech backend to what the users see on their devices."

Deep inside the halls of HemoCorp R and D, a team of biologists and material engineers had invented hemoenzymatic matching technology.

But Casey's Pillbugs had introduced it to the world.

"Mr. Amato," Sophronia said, "tell me something I don't already know."

"Okay. I'm getting there. For each of the Stokr incidents, the problem has been on the front end—what the user sees when they interact with the app. As far as we can tell, the hemoenzymatic analysis is still working. The data from when the users first gave their samples isn't corrupted, and the matches are still correct. The problem each time has been that even though the internal data is accurate, the app is displaying misleading outputs."

Sophronia glanced again at Delphine, another quick slash of blue eyes beneath black lashes.

Casey didn't know what that look meant. He spoke faster. "With each incident, the first thing that my team did was to investigate what went wrong with the APIs. Only"—he swallowed—"nothing went wrong."

"Obviously," Sophronia said icily, "something did."

"We checked the error logs," he said. "We ran the reconciliation script over and over, opened a remote connection to one of the nodes in the cluster and—" He bit back the recital. "The point is, we ran every possible analysis. Everything worked. We found nothing that could have led to a front-end failure of any kind, let alone of the magnitude that we saw on Saturday night."

"Then what did cause the fiasco on Saturday, Mr. Amato?"

He exhaled. He thought about Stokr. He thought about his team: Brendan and Mercedes and George, waiting in their shared office, anxious and scared and trying desperately not to show it. He thought about Nonna, who'd be positively delighted to know that she was his last thought before hurling himself into the abyss.

And then he opened his mouth and said clearly: "Sabotage."

The office seemed swallowed up by the intervening silence.

For weeks, Casey had grown increasingly certain that the Pillbugs were killing themselves to find a bug that didn't exist at all—a ghost in the machine. And when Saturday night's catastrophe had burst into the press, he'd known he couldn't wait any longer. The Stokr failures were going to kill someone.

And it wasn't because his team had made a mistake.

Someone had *caused* the Stokr disasters. Intentionally.

Sophronia broke the silence like a pane of glass. "Explain."

"All of the failures have been contained. Limited. The first two were hyperlocal. I think someone pushed a faulty build and then, when they'd wreaked enough havoc, pushed a fix. That's why we can't find anything wrong with our programming—why the app behaves perfectly in every post mortem."

"Who?"

She'd said the word like a whipcrack, but she wasn't arguing, and so he only looked levelly back at her. "I don't know."

Delphine leaned forward, her fangs showing white against her lips. "Beauchene. It has to be." She looked less like a human now—more like the predator she was. "If someone's trying to take down HemoCorp, that's the first place we need to look."

Beauchene Laboratory was a newish med-tech start-up

and HemoCorp's nearest rival in the industry. Though they were young, they were hungry and agile. They'd developed a biodegradable plastic that could be used for blood bags last year, and HemoCorp was still scrambling to produce its own alternative.

But Casey shook his head. "The saboteur might've been bankrolled by someone on the outside. But to deploy a new version of the app, they'd have to have access to our network. Our systems. I can tell you for a fact that whoever's responsible for this is inside HemoCorp."

There was another silence, as tense and charged as the first. Sophronia locked her eyes with his, so deathly earnest he couldn't look away.

And then her pointed chin rose. Her voice came out frozen. "And what do you want in return for this information, Mr. Amato?"

"I—" He frankly goggled at her. "What? I don't want anything except for my team to keep their jobs. For our interface to work the way we designed it."

"Of course. That's why you brought this to me now. Today. At this precise moment in time."

"I don't know what you're talking about."

She scoffed. "Of course not. Tell me, Mr. Amato, is it a promotion you're hoping to achieve from this meeting? More money? Or perhaps merely influence within the company?"

He yanked off his glasses, decided blindness wasn't the way to go, and shoved them back on. "I don't *want* anything. I've been trying to get through to you for weeks, for Christ's sake. You know I have."

"What's changed?" Delphine asked. She looked less coldly livid than Sophronia, but her expression, too, was mistrustful. "Why force your way in here today?"

"After what happened this weekend, I knew I couldn't wait around any longer. Saturday could have been a lot fucking—sorry—a lot worse. Whoever's doing this is smart. Strategic. They're pushing this bug on a weekend evening, when no one is here to see. When it will take us the longest time to fix it."

"When the largest number of people are using Stokr," murmured Delphine.

"Yes." He looked from Delphine back to Sophronia, who was motionless behind the desk, her chin up, her shoulders pinned back. "I don't want anything from you. The only thing I want is to find out who's behind this and make them stop."

Sophronia looked like some classical statue before him: Nemesis, maybe, or one of the Furies. He could hear his own heart beating fast in his ears, and because she was a vampire, he knew that she could hear it too.

But before she could say anything, Delphine broke in again. "You must have realized before you came in here that our suspicion would turn toward your team first."

Her words were directed at Casey, but she was looking at Sophronia when she said it, and so Casey looked too.

Nothing. He couldn't make out anything on that implacable face, couldn't detect a hint of softening in her hard, lavender-tinged mouth.

He blew out a breath. "I realized." He hated that suspicion would turn on the Pillbugs, hated even *thinking* that one of them could have purposely sabotaged Stokr. "I don't believe it. Aside from the fact that I'd trust all three of them with my life, we were together when the second incident happened. It was George's engagement party."

Mercedes had been the first one to see it—a trickle of social media posts that had turned into a fire hose. They'd all four taken an Uber directly from the rooftop bar to HemoCorp, right in the middle of George's fiancé's toast.

"I don't think it's one of the Pillbugs," he went on, "but I want all of us checked out. I want you to put an outside analyst on it—a professional forensic investigator. Someone *not* from HemoCorp. Because if I'm right, the saboteur is someone with access to our systems. And that means someone higher than me in the chain of command."

For the first time, Sophronia seemed to hesitate. She blinked, a heavy fall of black lashes shielding her eyes, and her lips parted for the space of a breath before she spoke. "You—" She paused. "You want me to bring someone in to investigate your team."

"Not *just* my people. Everything. The access logs. The security footage. Anyone with the clearance to get into the system. I'll work with you. I can help you figure out a shortlist. I can—"

"Casey," Delphine interjected, "are you under the impression that Sophronia still works for HemoCorp?"

There was a brief moment of silence while his brain rearranged itself.

Sophronia looked ready to leap out of her chair and tackle Delphine to the ground. Her expression could have curdled milk. "*Del*," she hissed.

Casey was so busy staring at Sophronia that he couldn't tear his gaze away to see how the spokesvamp was reacting. He couldn't stop himself.

She was the *Vega heir*. They couldn't fire her, no matter how bloody the disaster with her division.

Could they?

"I was under that impression," he finally choked out. "Yes."

She turned her furious blue gaze back on him. Her words

dropped like ice cubes in a highball. "Your impression is correct, Mr. Amato. I still run Stokr, despite some risible media speculation to the contrary. Ms. Gaius is suppressing the rumors as we speak."

He had no idea what she was talking about. *Some risible media speculation?* That she'd been *fired?*

He took in the firm slash of her mouth, the thrown-back ferocity of her posture as she sat poised on the edge of her chair—and then, all at once, he did know. His brain gathered up the bizarre moments of this interlude, spun them around like lottery balls, and reassembled them into a shape that made sense.

When he'd forced his way into Sophronia's office to share his suspicions, she'd supposed he'd been motivated by the news of her recent termination. What must she have thought? That he'd come to share secrets with the disgraced former VP so she could use them to win back her job?

What do you want in return for this information? she'd asked. *Money? Influence?*

She'd thought he'd come for a trade.

No. Not a trade. A bribe.

His neck was hot again—all of him felt hot and just this side of pissed as he sat across from her at the desk.

She didn't know him. Of course there was no reason for her to trust his integrity. But still—he knew, even if she didn't, that he wouldn't do anything to hurt her or Stokr or, God forbid, the tens of thousands of humans who used their app.

"I'll work with you," he said again. "I'll work with whoever you want to bring in to investigate. I'll put every bit of knowledge I have at your disposal." He hesitated on the next words before he let them go—then plunged back into speech before he lost his mulish pride. "But know that I had nothing to do with this."

He watched her pale throat bob as she swallowed. It was a long moment before she replied.

"I'll bring someone in," she said finally. "I'll do it today."

And when she tucked a lock of black hair behind her ear, he could see that her fingers were trembling.

For a long moment, he looked back at her—severe and formidable and still as a column of ice—and the lottery balls in his head spun again.

She had no reason to trust him. But then again . . .

But then again, who *could* she trust?

If he was right, someone at HemoCorp had betrayed her. Someone in her inner circle. Someone ruthless enough to sacrifice potentially thousands of humans for whatever they sought to gain.

His revelation was slow. Clear. Pinpoint sharp.

Beneath all that lethal perfection, Sophronia Vega wasn't furious at all.

She was terrified.

CHAPTER 4

Sophronia Vega

2:04 PM

I have a problem.

Delphine Gaius

2:04 PM

I've got gummy worms and haribo watermelons

Pick your poison and give me six minutes to wrap up these talking points for global

Sophronia Vega

2:06 PM

. . .

Both.

Delphine Gaius

2:08 PM

Never mind

Skipping the talking points

Sophronia let Del into her office before Wendy could. "You can't just *skip* the talking points."

Del shrugged and lifted her insulated travel mug to her mouth. "It's Global Affairs. Circinus could ramble for a week without stopping."

"That's why he needs talking points!"

Del laughed and plunked her mug on Sophronia's desk. "I finished them fast. *Both* sounded like an emergency. Here."

Sophronia let her spine bend a little as Del deposited colorful nonfood on her desk and then scooped some emotional-support watermelons out of the bag.

It wasn't an emergency. Not really.

Two weeks ago, she'd sent Casey Amato out of her office and cleared her agenda for the remainder of the day—which, given Stokr's obsolescence, had been considerably less packed than usual. She'd reviewed his notes, all his and Jackie's summaries, even error logs and reconciliation reports that she couldn't make heads or tails of.

She'd spent eleven straight hours watching security footage of Casey's shared office—of his *Pillbugs*, what a horror—and had found nothing but an alarmingly chaotic, brilliant, and close-knit team of software engineers. The three junior developers, Mercedes Obregón, George Chu, and Brendan Bradley, laughed and fought and tossed bat-shaped Stokr-branded stress balls at one another and occasionally played a zombie-killing computer game that Sophronia was relatively certain wasn't allowed on company time.

And Casey . . .

Oh Abraham's fangs. He got there earlier and left later than all the others. She'd never seen anyone so devoted to their job outside the Vegas themselves. He brokered arguments and resolved dilemmas, and when he walked into the office space, every member of his team got happier, like the clouds had parted and the sun shone golden on their faces.

If there was someone sabotaging Stokr, Sophronia had a very hard time picturing Casey as the traitor.

When she'd realized that she'd slowed down the footage to watch him roll his sleeves past the corded muscles of his forearms, she'd clicked off the security app. She'd changed into trainers and tights and gone for a very, very long run.

And then she'd hired the forensic analyst.

But in the days since the cybersecurity expert had arrived at HemoCorp and started her investigation, the human woman had discovered nothing whatsoever. Though her vulnerability assessment agreed with Casey's determination of internal sabotage, she had thus far unearthed no concrete suspects. She'd begun with Casey's team and moved outward from there but had found nothing to point to any particular individual who might've been responsible for the Stokr glitches. Any sign of attack artifacts or anomalies had been wiped from the access logs.

She had no idea who at HemoCorp might have tried to take down Sophronia's app.

Which brought Sophronia back around to her problem.

"I'm not sure what to do next," she said finally. She weighed the merits of each individual sugared watermelon instead of looking at Del as she spoke. "The analyst's come up empty-handed at every turn, and I don't . . . know how to proceed."

"And we're *positive* it wasn't Beauchene? I'm just saying, if we're not getting any clues from inside HemoCorp, maybe—"

"She's positive."

Del frowned down at the gummy worms. "What about non-computer-y stuff? Has this human looked at the security feeds for anything weird?"

"She's analyzed all of the security data we have stored from the last two months."

"What about the ID cards?"

Tracking the use of HemoCorp ID cards to access various offices had been one of Del's suggestions, along with other, more complicated notions involving late-night heists and grappling hooks and elaborate costuming.

Sophronia was glad she'd kept Del in the office the day that Casey had related his suspicions. She'd felt a flare of apprehension when Casey had said the word *sabotage*. Octavia . . . Kriti . . . Titus . . .

Even Del, she'd thought. *Even Del could have done it.*

But her eyes had flown to Del's face—shocked, familiar, so long loved—and she'd known it couldn't be Del. Del would rather pull out her own fangs than endanger a pack of innocent humans. And, equally as true, she would never, ever do something to hurt Sophronia.

She'd cursed herself for suspecting Del, even for a heartbeat.

"Nothing helpful with the ID cards," she made herself say. "There's no record of anyone having used an ID to enter the Pillbugs' office except the Pillbugs themselves."

Del hummed as she took another sip of artificial blood from her insulated mug. "So. Back to Casey, then?"

Closer cooperation with Casey Amato made up most of Del's other suggestions.

Sophronia clenched her jaw and felt her fangs dent her lower lip. "I'm not certain it's wise. To bring him further into this. I would prefer to handle this situation myself."

"Sweetie, you'd prefer to handle everything yourself, but unless you're hiding some previously undisclosed expertise in computer stuff, you're going to need *someone* from Hemo-Corp to help you out here. There's no shame in having another expert on your team."

Unfortunately, it was true. Sophronia could admit it, even if it grated. She had briefly considered trying to get a master's degree in computer engineering in the next few weeks, but it had seemed implausible at best.

"It's not that," Sophronia ground out.

Del tilted her head, a worm dangling between her first two fingers. "Is it because of how he smells?"

Sophronia nearly choked on a gummy watermelon. *"What?"*

"Casey. He smells like heaven in a glass." Del blinked. Her green eyes looked suspiciously guileless. "Don't act as though you didn't notice."

Sophronia took a drink from Del's travel mug and tried to compose her face. It would be ludicrous to pretend she hadn't observed the objective fact of Casey's scent. She had noticed the hot shimmer of his blood before she'd recalled his name from his hiring paperwork, for Abraham's sake.

He smelled like smoky caramel, like wine-soaked plums and black pepper, and beneath it all, something green and wild. His blood—not that she would be sampling it—would be rich on the tongue and just this side of sweet. The flush that had risen on his cheeks as he'd sat across from her at the desk had been almost intoxicating.

But that was *fine*. She had encountered plenty of handsome and toothsome humans in her thirty years of life and had managed to resist eating all of them. She wasn't going to fling herself at his neck and beg him for a taste. Ever since the invention of HemoCorp's artificial blood, several of the oldest dynasties, including the Vegas, had made their independence from humans something of a point of pride—it was why vampires like Octavia found Stokr so embarrassing.

No. The trouble wasn't Casey's outrageous scent.

The trouble was that he was a human.

Sophronia kept thinking about Ellery Klein's unconscious body in the conference room, the pallor of her skin, the blood congealing around her neck. Someone at HemoCorp had done that. Someone Sophronia had trusted.

Humans were so damned fragile. She *knew* that. She could still recall the throb of Izzy's pulse in the dorms at Holbeck Priest.

How quickly it had stopped.

But she couldn't say that, not even to Del. To show one's heart, Sophronia knew, was nothing more than an invitation to be bled dry.

Instead, she swallowed and looked up from the candy, facing Del head on. She weighed her next words before she let them free. "I don't know if I can trust him."

The corner of Del's mouth crimped, doubt and restraint together. "Do you really think he could be involved, Soph?"

"Of course." She sounded clipped. Terse. She tried to soften her voice because it was Del, and Del was only trying to help. "Anyone at HemoCorp could be involved."

"But if he *was* involved, why would he run straight to you to reveal his suspicions?"

Sophronia had asked herself that same question about a

thousand times in the last two weeks. "To make himself look innocent, maybe."

"Innocent of what? If he hadn't come to you, you'd never even know the sabotage had happened."

It was true. She *knew* it was true. She'd run through the same logical progression on her own. Objectively, Casey Amato was most likely innocent of any crime. Rationally, she knew that she needed his help.

She just . . . didn't like it.

"I think you have to trust him, Soph." Del's voice was gentle, as it always was. "I know it's hard for you. But out of everybody in this place, he might be the only person you *can* trust." She grinned suddenly, fangs popping against her immaculate lip color. "And me. Obviously."

Sophronia took another sip from the steaming mug and then made herself speak. "All right," she said. "You're right."

"You'll bring him in, then? You'll ask for his help?"

"I'll bring him in. I'll . . . talk to him."

"Excellent." Del picked up the candy bags and tucked them into her tote. Then she settled herself, ankles crossed, on the very edge of her favorite chair.

Sophronia gazed blankly at her. "What are you doing?"

"Waiting for you to message him!" Del glanced down at her phone. "Don't dawdle. I've gotten forty-three media requests while I've been sitting here."

"Why are you waiting for—" Sophronia narrowed her eyes. "Is this because you want to smell him again?"

"No!" Del paused. "Maybe a little."

"Del!"

Del smiled blithely back at Sophronia's scowl. "Just a sniff. Believe me, I know—no direct feeding until Stokr's back."

Sophronia frowned harder at the reminder. She pulled up

HemoCorp's messaging channel, found Casey's name, and typed: I need you to come to my office.

She hesitated before she hit send. *No.* With the tip of one finger, she tapped the backspace key and deleted I need you. And then to.

Come to my office, she sent, and then, after a brief hesitation, sent a second text. ASAP.

"Do you want to run the messaging by me?" Del asked from the chair. "You pay me an exorbitant salary for this exact purpose, actually."

"HemoCorp pays you," Sophronia countered distractedly. "And no."

The three dots indicating that Casey was typing appeared for the barest moment before his response. On my way.

She felt a pulse of relief at his instantaneous reply, which she squashed with such internal fervor that her fangs stabbed against her lower lip.

She had carefully cultivated her reputation of icy perfection. She was widely regarded as the most terrifying thing at HemoCorp, a company that employed seventy-seven bloodsucking vampires. People called her the Queen of the Damned.

It was, after all, what was expected of her. The Vegas hadn't become one of the most powerful vampire families in the world by indulging in messy, distasteful *feelings*.

"You have a little blood," Del said delicately, "on the corner of your mouth."

Sophronia was still scrubbing it off with an antiseptic wipe when Casey stepped into the office.

He was tall for a human—maybe three inches over six feet—and he carried himself with a kind of lean, slouchy grace that made her think of endurance athletes. His hair was an absolute disaster, and today his shirt was pale stripes, with a cinnamon corduroy jacket rolled up to reveal his forearms.

He looked worried. He smelled unacceptably good.

Sophronia clenched her jaw very tight.

Del grinned at him. “Casey! That was fast.”

“It’s good to see you again, Ms. Gaius,” he said. His eyes—rich, brown, sweet—flicked from Del to Sophronia and paused there. “I was relieved. To get your message. I’m really glad you wanted me involved.”

She touched her tongue to the tip of one fang, hard enough to hurt, before she spoke. “You are already involved, Mr. Amato. I was not gifted with a great deal of choice in the matter.”

“Right,” he said. “All right.” He rubbed at the stubble on his jaw, which was when Sophronia realized she’d started looking at his forearms again.

“What she means,” Del said, “is that her forensic analyst can’t find anything. And Soph needs your help.”

Sophronia sent a murderous glance at Del, who was sidling past Casey toward the exit. “I do not require—”

“Bye!” Del caroled. “Media requests!” Her lashes fluttered blissfully in Casey’s direction, and she tipped a mischievous smile at Sophronia as she shut the door.

Casey had also started to talk, his eyes fixed on Sophronia’s face. “I have ideas. My college mentor was in corporate cybersecurity, actually, before she—oh.” He paused as her words seemed to register. “Did you . . . not want my ideas?”

She forced her jaw to relax, despite a sudden and intense desire to glower at everyone she’d ever met. “Go on.”

“Okay.” He shot her another measuring glance and then sat down on the other side of her desk. “I’m assuming the analyst has done everything she can at the network and data layers, right?" He didn't wait for Sophronia to nod, which was good, because she didn't know what the hell he was talking about. "So I'm thinking we look into the physical layer. The first thing I thought of was to see if any ID cards other than ours accessed the server room these past two months." He sent an apologetic glance her way. "I tried it already, actually. But I can't get into that part of the system without clearance from someone on the executive committee."

"We checked the ID cards already. According to our system, no one was in there who didn't belong."

He ran a hand through his unruly hair, which somehow made it both better and worse, and blew out a breath. "Of course not. I also thought about the security footage. If you give me access, I can try to determine if anyone entered or exited our office—"

"I did that as well."

He searched her face—wondering, obviously, why the hell she had called him in if she'd already done everything on her own.

She thought about humans, and their fragile hearts, and the danger of trusting someone—anyone—when trust was so easy to shatter. When the price was so unbearably high.

And then she pushed the memory of Izzy's freckled face away. Forced herself to look Casey in the eye and tell him the truth. "I do . . . want your help. If you think it would be beneficial, I'll give you access to the security database today."

"Thank you," he said, and his voice was so *sincere.*

Abraham's fangs. He was so nice she wanted to eat him.

She glared at him instead, which he didn't seem to mind. He rubbed his jaw again and considered the middle distance.

"I did have another idea," he said slowly. "I wondered . . . well, I wondered if we might set a trap."

She felt her brows tick up as she regarded him. She hadn't been expecting a frontal assault, but she liked the idea.

She was a Vega. She felt most comfortable on the attack.

"What kind of trap did you have in mind?"

"If we put out a fake report that Stokr's going back online, maybe we can catch our friendly neighborhood saboteur in the act. I can restrict server access to one or two terminals, and we can monitor the security feeds. Or—even better, maybe—I can wait here after hours and watch to see if—"

"No," she bit out.

Casey blinked.

"If you change your team's standard procedure, it will be obvious that you suspect something. Don't stay here by yourself or change the access protocols. Behave as you always do."

Whoever had sabotaged Stokr had already proven that they were willing to risk any number of human lives to take down the app. And Casey—

Sitting across from him, she could hear his blood as it rushed beneath his skin. Could hear his heart—noisy and human and so, so easy to stop.

A stubborn look made itself at home on his face, one she recognized from the last time he'd been in her office. "We can pretend it's something else, then," he said. "Some reason for us to change things around. You could announce a new project for us—a replacement for Stokr, maybe. A new app."

"No. I won't have you exposed."

"*You're* exposed. Whoever's behind this must have noticed your analyst by now. They'll know she reports back to you."

"I am a vampire, Mr. Amato," she hissed. "We are much harder to kill."

"But not impossible."

She hesitated, almost shocked by the fierceness of his voice. He wasn't wrong.

Vampires had compact muscles and tough, nearly impenetrable skin. They had fangs and nails that could tear a human to ribbons. But their vanishingly small blood volume was a terrible weakness. They had to eat often, or else they died, and without blood patches, they could bleed out from a cut that would barely slow down a human. Though they grew stronger as they aged, their vulnerability to injury increased, and so their lifespans were roughly that of humans.

Vampire "immortality" was nothing more than a legend popularized by Abraham Stoker.

Nearly a hundred and fifty years ago, Stoker—queer, Irish, working class, and a vampire himself—had published *Dracula* and transformed the way the public thought of their kind. In one masterful stroke, vampires had gone from craven, bloodthirsty monsters to terrifying, nearly omnipotent ones.

It had been a trade Sophronia had always respected. Who would choose fragility if they didn't have to?

What did it matter if the story of their invulnerability was a lie?

"I wonder," Casey said, and then he paused. His voice was abstracted; she'd heard him sound that way in the footage with his Pillbugs, when he had an idea tumbling around in his brain. "I wonder . . ."

"Yes?"

"Do you have a camera on your analyst right now?"

At his words, Sophronia felt her fangs tighten, alarm and suspicion at once. "Yes. Why?"

He shook his head. "Nothing for certain. I just thought—what if the reason she hasn't discovered anything yet is because she's not *supposed* to discover anything?"

A cool prickle of suspicion crept down Sophronia's spine, raising the hairs on the back of her neck. "You mean—"

"I don't know. But could the traitor have gotten to your analyst somehow? A threat maybe? Or a bribe?"

Sophronia yanked her phone out of her pocket, tilting it to unlock the security app with her facial scan and then holding it out to him. "There's a feed on all the conference rooms. You put her in 17002C when you set her up, right?"

"Yeah." He took the phone, and as he did, his fingers brushed hers.

Warm. Humans were always so warm.

His smoke-sweet scent made her throat feel dry, and her fangs tightened further. She took a breath—*oh Abraham, that was a mistake*—and ignored the pulse of hunger in her belly as his callused fingers tapped at the screen.

He held the phone out for her to see. "Here's the feed."

The image on the screen resolved into the analyst's conference room: the dark walnut paneling, the custom-color-temperature LED lights, the curved-glass monitors Casey had arranged to be there.

And then the analyst. She was . . .

Sophronia's breath seized in her throat. Her heart—a vampire's heart, light and fast—beat one hard, painful thud against her ribs.

The analyst lay face down on the table. Dead.

CHAPTER 5

At Casey's side, Sophronia went bone still.

He'd been right—in her heels, she was exactly his height. His eyes were precisely level with hers, and he was close enough to see her pupils flare, black on blue.

"EMTs," she whispered. "Give—give me the phone. She needs EMTs. A blood patch—a—"

He felt cold all over, his hands barely warmer than Sophronia's as he passed back the phone.

Casey was no stranger to death. He remembered the terrible, blank feeling of a body that had once been alive. He recalled the way grief sucked the sound out of a room.

He knew—they both had to know—that it was too late for the analyst. The blood congealed around her neck was old, her body white and shrunken. Bled dry.

And then—just as Sophronia's index finger swiped the security app away—the corpse on the screen seemed to flicker.

And disappear.

"Wait," Casey said. His fingers cupped Sophronia's elbow before he could stop himself. "Wait. Go back to the security feed."

Her eyes flicked to his, her lavender lips drawing tight, but she didn't argue. She swiped back. In her hand, the screen showed the same conference room as it had before. Dark paneled walls. Three monitors.

Only this time, the table was empty. The analyst's body was gone.

"What?" Sophronia breathed.

"Back it up," Casey managed. His voice rasped on the words. "See if—"

She didn't need him to finish his sentence. She dragged the tip of her finger backward across the screen, and the feed played in reverse.

Nothing. No corpse. No bloodthirsty vampire sinking their fangs into the analyst's throat. Only an empty conference room, the afternoon light slowly fading to the previous night's cool black.

What the hell . . .

Casey tried to force his brain to work the problem. That was what he did—pieced his way through error and catastrophe, sorted through a maze of logs and anomalies in order to set things right.

"See if this is live or on a loop," he said. "The feed ought to show time stamps."

Sophronia flicked a menu, then slowed down the footage to each individual frame as she rolled the images forward and back. As she did, her breath caught in her throat.

Casey made sense of what he was seeing the same moment she did.

The security feed in the conference room was live. As far as he could tell, the table was currently empty of desiccated corpses.

But all the footage between 7:17 a.m. and 3:06 p.m. had been erased.

There *had* been a body in the conference room. They'd seen it, face down in a pool of old blood. But the corpse—and the recording of whatever had happened inside that room—had vanished.

Somehow, whoever had killed the analyst had also gotten rid of the evidence of her murder.

"What," Sophronia grated, "in Abraham Stoker's name is going on?"

Pieces clicked into place in Casey's head on a cold punch of fear.

The conference room. The dead analyst. The deleted footage.

And a traitor inside HemoCorp.

His fingers closed harder on Sophronia's elbow, and before he could think about what he was doing, he dragged her up against him to breathe his next words into her ear. "We have to go. Someone could be watching us here too. We have to take the elevator *right now* and get the hell out of HemoCorp."

She was strong and stiff against him, all elegant planes, and when she pulled back, her face was agonized. "Del—"

He moved his arm to her waist and dragged her to the door, and she truly had a vampire's preternatural grace, because she didn't stumble even in her heels. "Text her from the elevator," he ground out over the terror spiking his bones. "Act normal."

She slapped his arm away from her waist. "There is nothing *less* normal I could be doing than cuddling an employee—"

"Fine—fine—"

She sent a rictus smile to her admin as they passed—"Just stepping out for a meeting, Wendy"—and, God, she was not a good liar. He hoped like hell he was wrong, and no homicidal corporate vampire was spying on Sophronia through the security feed.

In the elevator, she sent security to the conference room with a tap of her finger and then texted Delphine Gaius. Her slim body sagged with relief as she read Delphine's reply. "Del's off-site with Incarnare Medical Center's media team," she said. Her thumbs flew again. "I'm telling her to keep it that way."

He felt a flicker of surprise as he watched her shove her phone into her pocket, then try to force her face back into its usual forbidding lines. Somehow, she couldn't quite manage it—relief and fear still showed in the shape of her mouth.

He'd had no idea, before that first day in her office, that she was so close to Delphine. He'd rarely seen them together in the halls or the HemoCorp canteen.

If he thought about it, he supposed he'd rarely seen Sophronia other than alone.

In the two weeks since he'd confronted her in her office, he'd felt helpless and stymied—as cut off from whatever she was doing to investigate the Stokr disaster as if she'd dropped him inside a box made of six-inch-thick plexiglass. He understood why: She was investigating *him* as much as she was everyone else involved with Stokr's development.

He'd tried to be patient. He'd tried to keep the Pillbugs, restless and brilliant, from going completely off the rails.

He'd tried not to think about the Vega heir: tried, and then thought about her anyway. He'd seen her in the halls twice since then, looking exactly as ruthless and forbidding as she always did. But still, when he sat at his workstation and gazed blankly into the glass, his mind had revolved around her fine-boned hand. The way her fingers had trembled in that immaculate, isolated office. The surprise that had moved across her face as she'd looked at him.

She wasn't quite what he'd thought her to be—that was all. She was exactly the sort of puzzle that caught his brain and wouldn't let go.

Before he realized what had happened, they were outside together in the cool September sun. She looked around, lashes dark against her pale face. "Where—"

"This way," he said, and realized he still had hold of her arm.

He led her down to the Incarnare boardwalk. It was a short walk from the HemoCorp building; Sophronia's floor-to-ceiling window looked out over the shifting blue-gray of the Pacific. Here on the boardwalk, he could smell garlic fries and cumin-spiced chili, cotton candy and axle grease from the old wooden coaster, and beneath all of it the salt scent of the ocean.

At his side, Sophronia was scowling furiously in all directions. "What," she hissed, "are we doing in this—this—" She looked at the corn dog stand over his left shoulder and seemed to grope for words.

"Boardwalk?"

"I *know* what it is!"

She looked desperately out of place in the raucous crowds of tourists and families. Not because she was tall and fanged and obviously a vampire—but because she was the Vega heir.

She wasn't the only vampire on the boardwalk that day. Despite what Stoker's stories had claimed, vampires could stand beneath the sun in the light of day.

They had, for centuries, only chosen not to. Stoker's supernatural myth had disguised a simpler, more vulnerable truth. Vampires hid under the cover of darkness because when they tried to step out into the light, humans feared and hated them.

For the first decade or two after the publication of *Dracula*, humans had argued over whether the vampire story was real. Stoker *was* a vampire—anyone who knew him had known it for a fact. But vampires' tendency to cling to the shadows had given them an air of the occult and obscure.

And then, in the early twentieth century, HemoCorp had changed everything. The company was run publicly by vampires—the cool, practical scientific evidence for their existence couldn't be ignored. When the company had introduced its artificial blood, vampires had become increasingly willing to enter spaces dominated by humans. Vampire children and teenagers had historically been educated at home, but in recent generations, that had begun to change. Casey had had vampires in several of his master's classes at UC Incarnare, and at HemoCorp, he worked closely with more vampires than he'd ever seen in one place before.

And Stokr. Stokr had helped. Had *been* helping.

No—it wasn't Sophronia's height or the razor-sharp points of her fangs against her lip that made her look out of place. She looked that way because she was the daughter of the wealthiest and most powerful vampires in the world. Her sleek jaw-length hair, her pointed heels, that close-cut navy suit made of some shimmering fabric Casey couldn't have identified if Nonna's bungalow had been on the line—all of it screamed *I've never been on a roller coaster in my life.*

"Sorry," he said. "The boardwalk was the first place I thought of. It's easy to get lost in the crowds. We can be sure that no one's watching us here."

And—God.

He hadn't done it on purpose, not really. But the boardwalk, to him, was safety. Was his childhood before everything had gone wrong: his father's hand warm on his shoulder, the sun glinting off the beads his mother wore around her neck.

He cleared his throat. "You contacted security from the elevator, right? Someone's going to check out the conference room?"

Sophronia had set her hands on the boardwalk's sun-weathered wooden railing, and at his words, she lifted her gaze from the ocean to his face. "I did. But"—her lips pressed together, a hint of fangs flickering white—"they won't find anything. There's no body. There's no *evidence.* How can I force them to investigate a disappearance that I can't even prove really happened?"

He thought about the missing footage. The body there and then gone. *Would* anyone believe what they'd seen? The whole thing was so goddamned unlikely, even with the time-stamps to prove that the feed had been tampered with.

Would *he* believe their wild story, if he hadn't seen it with his own eyes?

But no. He shook his head. "Eventually someone will realize she's missing."

Beside him, Sophronia's jaw was tight. "And by then it will be too late."

"I don't accept that. If security won't examine the conference room without hard evidence of a crime, then *we* can. I—"

"*I'll* investigate," she snapped. "I'll . . . contact her family. I will tell them."

He looked at her, the blade-flat line of her mouth, her pointed chin and sharp edges.

He thought about the way her fingers had trembled that

day in her office. The fear on her face in the elevator as she'd texted Del.

"It's not your fault," he said slowly. "You realize that, right? What happened to your analyst. You couldn't have known."

"I could have," she bit out. "I should have foreseen this, after the Stokr disaster. I should never have let anyone else in on the investigation. I should have handled it *myself*."

"You can't handle everything yourself—"

"Why does everyone keep *saying* that?" she demanded. Her hands were locked around the railing now, and her face was angled away from his.

"Because it's true. Because you're not alone in wanting to solve this."

He wanted to find out what the hell was going on just as much as she did. He wanted to find the person who'd sabotaged his app and put thousands of people in danger. Who'd killed Sophronia's analyst and then covered it up. He wanted to protect Mercedes and Brendan and George, and he *did not* want anyone else to get hurt.

"I am," she said, very low.

He looked up. "What?"

"I *am* alone."

He stepped closer to her, set his hands beside hers on the rail. "You're not. Let me help, damn it."

Her fangs were out; he could see them denting the pale purple curve of her lower lip.

But he didn't think she was fighting the urge to plunge those fangs into his throat. It was almost worse—he thought she meant to keep on shutting him out.

He tried to gentle his voice. "You know I didn't have anything to do with this. Do you think I killed that analyst and then showed you a picture of the crime scene?"

"Of course not. But—"

"You can trust me. You can trust my team. You and your analyst have been investigating us for weeks, and I *know* you haven't found anything, because there's nothing to find. My Pillbugs aren't behind this. You need our help if you're going to—"

Something cracked, a sharp pop of wood, and he realized it was the railing beneath her fingers.

"It's not just about trust," she snapped. "You and all your team—you're *humans*. Abraham's fangs, didn't you see that bloodless corpse in the conference room? That could have been *you*!"

She had spun toward him, and her eyes locked with his. Her skin had gone pale; her lips had darkened to violet.

For a long moment, he held her gaze.

"It will be," he said finally. "Us, or humans like us. We know what the traitor's willing to do now. If we don't put a stop to this, more people are going to die."

He watched the tiny muscles of her cheek jump. The sharp press of her fangs against her lower lip. She didn't seem like a cipher anymore, or a statue, or even the Vega heir.

She seemed like a person: real and conflicted. Scared and mistrustful and almost—*almost*—willing to bend.

"Let me get my team together," he said. "Let me tell them the truth. We're humans, I know, but . . . we're not helpless."

She searched his face.

In the gathering dusk, she reminded him of a wild animal—afraid to advance, unwilling to retreat.

So he held himself very still and let her look. He knew

death—and fear—but he knew this, too: the slow reward of patience, of new green leaves cautiously stretching toward the sun.

Whatever she needed to see in him, eventually she seemed to find it. She took a sharp breath and let the railing go.

"Collect your team," she said. "We can talk to them together. *Not* at HemoCorp."

CHAPTER 6

Sophronia had witnessed any number of horrors in her thirty years of life, but a bar named Reverse Cowgirls was swiftly rising to the top of the list.

The music was so loud she couldn't hear her own heartbeat, and the air was saturated with an overpowering aroma of beer-soaked human. She had a peanut stuck to her right shoe. There was *line dancing.*

At her side, Del peered doubtfully up at her from beneath the brim of her cowboy—cow-woman?—hat. A grinning human man at the door had given it to her, and Del, only slightly mystified, had settled it atop her cloud of curls.

The man had turned his gaze to Sophronia next, blanched at the combination of her fangs and her expression, and ushered them both hastily inside.

"Are you sure this is right?" Del asked.

"Unfortunately," Sophronia said, "yes."

They couldn't meet at HemoCorp. It would draw suspicion immediately—the VP of DP&S didn't meet regularly with any of her software engineers, let alone four of them at once. But even so, when she'd told Casey to find another place for them to debrief his Pillbugs, she hadn't been expecting a *bar.*

She'd never eaten a peanut in her life, and she was not prepared to begin tonight.

She and Del moved farther into Reverse Cowgirls' horrifying depths. As they did, a line of high-stepping boots broke and floundered at the sight of their height and fangs. Even with its proximity to HemoCorp, this bar didn't appear to be regularly patronized by vampires.

Despite the invention of artificial blood—since the blood patches, since Stokr—some humans were still afraid of them.

Sophronia understood exactly why. Every time she closed her eyes, she kept on seeing human bodies, cold in a pool of blood.

The analyst.

Izzy.

She tightened her jaw and pushed back the memory. She was in control. She was a HemoCorp VP. The Queen of the Damned.

She wasn't helpless. She would never be helpless again.

They were nearly to the back of the large open room when Casey emerged, as tall and handsome and faintly disheveled as ever. With the aroma of beer and bar nuts in her nose, he was close before his scent hit her.

Bittersweet caramel, black pepper. Sin.

Her knees wobbled.

Del sent her a little tipped-up glance of amusement, and Sophronia frowned harder.

"Hey," Casey said when he saw them. "We've got a private room in the back." He winced a little as he took them in: Sophronia's four-inch heels and vintage drop-waist silk dress, and then the slowly recovering line dance behind them. "I'm really sorry about this. I haven't told them anything yet, and this was the first place I thought of that wouldn't raise a thousand questions. We . . . come here. Sometimes."

"This," Sophronia grated, "is fine."

He winced again.

She and Del followed him in the direction of the back room. The floor was sticky with something that smelled like alcoholic toothpaste, and Sophronia tried not to touch anything.

They were still twenty or so feet away when she realized she could make out the Pillbugs' conversation. Her hearing was sharp enough to pick out their words—their heartbeats—even through the door.

She listened, of course. She'd been listening to them for weeks over the security feed, trying to figure out if she could trust them.

She heard a heavy thump and the sound of something rolling. And then a voice, familiar now from the footage. Mercedes Obregón, UX designer for the Pillbugs, UC Incarnare '24.

"Honestly," Mercedes said, "I'm saving you from yourselves."

"You're not *that* good at pool." This voice, Sophronia knew, was Brendan Bradley's. "Last time George *almost* won."

"Last time," Mercedes shot back, "I was hampered by four rounds of something called the Cow Daddy. Keep your money in your pants, Bren. I'm pretty sure we're all about to get fired."

"We'd better not be. I bought these boots on credit."

The third member of the Pillbugs, George Chu, sounded scandalized. "You bought a pair of boots on credit? Brendan. My lamb. You know Allen's in wealth management, right? Do you need me to set you two up on a call?"

"Where *is* Allen?" Mercedes demanded. "Did Casey tell you not to bring him? Is that why it's just the three of us?"

There was a brief pause before George replied. "Actually," he admitted. "Yes."

Casey pushed open the door in time to catch Mercedes's groan as she ran her hands through her short pink hair. She was perched on the billiards table, a cue balanced on her knees, her back to Casey. Her hair arranged itself in tiny neon tufts, and the cue rolled off her legs and clattered to the floor. "We are so deeply fucked. Will you look over my résumé, George?"

"You're not," Casey said from just inside the door. "Getting fired. At least, not today."

"This is honestly such great news," Brendan said. He was lining up a shot, his tall form bent in half and his boots an implausible shade of blue. "Because we haven't done a single second of work in thirteen business days, and I for one—" He looked up from the pool table, saw Sophronia and Del next to Casey, and broke off abruptly.

Mercedes twisted around, saw the three of them, and blanched. "Oh," she said. "Shit."

Very slowly, she slithered off the pool table and onto her feet.

"Hi," Del said cheerfully.

"I didn't," Brendan said, "mean thirteen. I meant three. No, I meant—uh. None."

Mercedes's face went even more pained. "Please don't judge him by the words that come out of his mouth. I swear he's smarter than he sounds."

"Thanks," Brendan said. "I think?"

"Pillbugs," Casey said, "I know you know Sophronia Vega, VP of digital products and solutions, and Delphine Gaius, from HemoCorp PR." He gestured to the group of humans and looked at Sophronia and Del. "Ms. Vega, Ms. Gaius, this is my team: Mercedes, George, and Brendan."

George seemed genuinely delighted to see them. "Ms. Vega! It's so nice to meet you." He glanced at the pool table, his brow furrowed. "I'm sorry about Casey's bizarre choice of locale."

"If you're here to ask about our unusually heavy load on the network last week," Brendan said, "I swear we were just playing *World of Warcraft*. Not like . . . anything illegal."

Mercedes rolled her eyes heavenward and collapsed back onto the pool table.

Casey broke in with the practiced ease of someone who wrangled junior engineers on a regular basis. "Sorry about the location. And for not letting you bring Allen. I—*we* needed all of you here. Alone."

He hesitated before going on and sent Sophronia a questioning glance. *Are you sure?* his face seemed to say.

And: *Only if you're ready.*

She gritted her teeth. Her fangs had lengthened, biting into her lower lip.

She did need Casey and his Pillbugs. And by virtue of that necessity—and two weeks' investigation and Casey's sheer earnest stubbornness—she had chosen to trust them. Even though it went against every instinct she possessed.

She made herself nod: a sharp, jerky *yes*.

One corner of Casey's mouth tipped up as he held her gaze, and for just a moment—for one delicate vampire heartbeat—she felt warmer than she had in a long time. Less alone.

She scowled at him.

He broke her gaze, mouth still quirked, and turned back to his team. "We're here," he told them, "because we can't have this conversation at HemoCorp, and I wanted somewhere private for us to talk."

"*What* conversation?" Mercedes demanded.

"We believe someone at HemoCorp sabotaged Stokr," Casey said levelly. "And the VP wants us to figure out who it was."

There was a brief silence and then, very fast, an explosion of words from the Pillbugs.

George's face had visibly paled. "Oh shit," he said. "Oh God."

"I knew it," Mercedes said. "Didn't I know it? I fuckin' told you both, didn't I?"

Brendan gave her a doubtful look. "You literally just said we were getting fired."

"*Before* that—I texted you and George *weeks* ago that I thought—"

"Stop," Casey said calmly, and just like that, the three junior engineers closed their mouths. "No texting about this. No *talking* about it, unless you're outside HemoCorp's walls."

"You think . . ." George's skin was taut where it stretched across his angular cheekbones. "You think it was someone at HemoCorp who fucked the app? Not an outside actor?"

"We do."

And then Casey explained. In careful, deliberate language, he told the Pillbugs about his own suspicions, his conversation with Sophronia, and the analyst's investigation and subsequent murder.

Sophronia couldn't help but admire the way he did it. He related the brief, blistering terror of the scene in words calm enough not to scare the shit out of them but firm enough to make them take the danger seriously.

She couldn't help but recall the way his team kept turning

toward him on the security footage, planets pulled helplessly into the orbit of his sun.

"Jesus," said Brendan, when Casey finished describing the analyst's death. "That's scary as hell. Can you—" He glanced at Sophronia, then Del. His eyes were wide; he looked like an anxious, hopeful puppy. "Can you guys *really* move through shadows? Or, like, shift into things? Because that would explain a lot of—"

"No," Sophronia said flatly.

"I am literally begging you to stop going on weird websites, Bren," Mercedes said. "Begging."

George, who'd been gazing blankly down at the pool table, looked up. "It's the most terrifying anecdote I've ever heard, actually, but . . . it's *helpful* too. Someone got into the security system and deleted those files. There'll be a record on the backend, in the access logs."

"There's not," Casey said. "I checked already."

Mercedes blinked. "How? You don't have access to the—"

"I gave him access," Sophronia said. She looked from human to human—wishing, not for the first time in her life, that the stories of vampires' supernatural powers were more than just legend, like Bigfoot or werewolves.

Wishing there was some way to *know* that trusting them wasn't a mistake.

She took a breath, carefully, then let it out. "All four of you can have whatever access you need."

"Whoever's doing this is smart," George said. "It's a vampire familiar with mobile-app distribution. And they have root access to the remote server." He looked cautiously at Sophronia and Del. "Is that . . . Does that describe any vampires at the company?"

"No," Sophronia said. "As far as we can tell, there's no

single person who could be responsible for everything that's happened."

"Someone got rid of the analyst's body," Casey said, "while someone else deleted the footage."

"A team," Mercedes said slowly. "Trying to take down *our* app." She looked up, and though she was the smallest person in the room, there was something ferocious about the set of her shoulders, the tension in her jaw. "Fuck that. I'm not letting that stand."

Very slowly, the corners of Casey's mouth curled up. "Yeah," he said. "I had a feeling you'd say that."

Over the next several minutes, the conversation devolved into sentences that Sophronia only partially understood. The Pillbugs seemed to forget about her and Del entirely; Mercedes pulled her knees up to her chin while George methodically arranged the balls in various geometric patterns and talked with increasing enthusiasm about source control and configuration systems.

"That should work," George said finally. "With the VP's help, we can push that update to the entire HemoCorp network. Gain access to—"

But Brendan interrupted. He'd found a chair and spun it backward to sit in, his elbows resting on the back and his jaw in his hand. "It won't work. Some of the computers at HemoCorp aren't in the network, remember? The C-suite, some of the VPs—they're isolated for security reasons. IT has to update those manually."

"Shit," Mercedes said, "you're right." She looked up at Sophronia for the first time in quite a while. "See? He's not a complete waste of HemoCorp's benefits package."

"Thanks, Mer," Brendan said.

"But it's fine," Mercedes continued. "We can identify the

isolated units and come up with some reason to install the software there—call it a security update or something."

"Why would *we* be doing a security update?" George protested. "We don't work in IT."

"I'm pretty sure the finer points of systems administration versus software development aren't super obvious to the executive committee," Mercedes said.

George tilted his head in acknowledgment. "Okay, that's fair."

But . . .

"No," Sophronia said.

It was her whipcrack voice. All the faces in the room turned toward hers.

"No," she said again and didn't even try to modulate her tone. "Whoever sabotaged Stokr knows exactly who the four of you are. If you're somewhere you don't belong, they'll realize it."

"You think it's someone in the executive committee?" Casey asked quietly.

She hesitated. Octavia, Titus, Circinus—all the vampires on the committee had access to the servers to delete the security footage. Any one of them had enough wealth and power to bribe someone to do the technical parts for them.

Even . . .

Even her father could have done it.

But no. She couldn't believe it. Her father had no special love for humans—or for his daughter's lurid dating app—but he wouldn't do anything that might harm HemoCorp.

"I think it's possible," she said finally. "Yes." She let the tip of her fangs show beneath her upper lip as she stared at the four human engineers arrayed around the pool table, looking focused and earnest and fragile. "I'll do it. Whatever you need me to do, whatever you want me to install on their computers, I'll make it work."

The Pillbugs stared back at her.

"Not to be the asshole here," Brendan said finally, "but . . . do you know how?"

She gritted her teeth. "I assure you, Mr. Bradley, I will figure it out."

Casey was staring at her, an expression she couldn't quite read on his face. Almost . . .

Abraham's bloody fangs. Almost *fond.*

"I'll go with you," he said, and before she could protest, his little half smile widened. As if he already knew what she was going to say. "I know, I know—someone could eat me too."

"You've identified my primary objection, yes."

"I figure," he said, "if we're together, you won't let them."

CHAPTER 7

They were in Octavia Pavo's elegant corner office when everything went to shit.

Casey had been surprised by how easily Sophronia had agreed to smuggle him into the necessary offices at Hemo-Corp. Honestly, she'd surprised the hell out of him several times two nights ago at Reverse Cowgirls, starting with the fact that she'd shown up at all. Somehow, she'd looked even more out of place there than she had on the boardwalk. He wasn't exactly an expert in fashion, despite Nonna's best efforts, but he had the vague sense that Sophronia's elegantly draped ivory dress and spiked heels cost more than the entire bar. By the expression on her face, she'd been entertaining a vivid fantasy of dispatching all five members of the bluegrass band—ideally with her fangs—and between her dress and her shoes and her scowl, she'd looked . . .

Ha. God. He really *did* have a death wish.

She'd looked lethal. Predatory.

Really fucking good.

But it hadn't just been her presence there that had taken him by surprise. It was the fact that she'd trusted them—all of them—with the truth.

His Pillbugs had been exactly what they always were:

George earnestly enthused and Brendan chewing his lip like he was lost. Mercedes, as usual, was so terrifyingly brilliant and assertive he figured she only had another six months or so in her current role before she started quietly taking over things.

But as he'd looked at them, Casey had worried the VP might . . .

He didn't really know what he'd been afraid of. That she'd judge them, maybe. That she wouldn't realize that Brendan's general air of helpless bafflement—just last week he'd messed up his multifactor authentication and somehow lost his personal cell phone somewhere between the bathroom and their office—hid an astonishingly creative brain.

But she was perceptive. She'd let them talk, answered all their questions. She'd unbent a little when the Pillbugs had started to plot and scheme, and then a little more when Mercedes had defended Stokr like a tiny angry terrier.

She'd agreed to the Pillbugs' plan, if reluctantly. They were in it together now.

He didn't know why he liked the thought so much.

He and Sophronia had done six offices before Octavia's without a hitch. Sophronia had access to every HemoCorp employee's calendar, so it was easy to schedule their visits for times when the offices would be empty of potentially homicidal vampire suspects. They'd come up with an excuse for their presence, in case they somehow got caught, but they hadn't thus far had to use it.

Until Octavia Pavo showed up.

Sophronia had positioned herself in between Casey and the door, and Casey was bent over Octavia's keyboard, typing as fast as possible. At the sound of the door's soft hiss, Casey looked up. And froze.

Shit. He could very clearly visualize Octavia's calendar,

which had placed her in Monterey for the rest of the afternoon. But here she was, framed by her office's smoked-glass wall, catching them as red-handed as it was possible to be.

The chief science officer's dark-blond brows drew up at the sight of them in her office. At fifty or so, Octavia was the youngest member of the HemoCorp C-suite. Casey had heard indefinite rumors of vampiric nepotism at play—the Pavos were another ancient and wealthy vampire family.

But if Octavia had been hired due to her family connections, it didn't show. As group chair for synthetics, she'd led the development of the blood patch, which had rapidly become HemoCorp's best-selling product. Her division had lately pushed forward into fibrin gels and other hemostats; R and D teams under her purview were working on intravenous artificial blood products and techniques for rapid tissue regeneration based on vampire saliva. She had her name on more patents than anyone else at HemoCorp, and she could deliver a withering insult without breaking the pleasant expression on her face.

She was equally legendary for both.

Her cool half smile was certainly in place now. "Sophronia," she said. Only the angular arch of her brows implied it was a question.

"Octavia." Sophronia stepped forward, blocking Casey from Octavia's line of sight. "We were just finishing here."

There was a brief silence, presumably for the vampires to size each other up while Casey tried to finish typing as quickly and quietly as possible.

"I assume," Octavia said, "you have some excellent explanation for what you're doing in my office."

He *heard* Sophronia swallow, which didn't seem like a good sign. His fingers flew.

"Security upgrades," Sophronia said, which was the lie they'd concocted.

"Security upgrades?" Octavia repeated. "I can see how those would be necessary, considering this door was locked when I left."

"We had to access some of the workstations directly," Sophronia said, exactly as he'd coached her that morning. "I didn't think you'd mind. While Stokr's shuttered, I've tasked my teams with upgrading the database encryption to protect user privacy."

"Privacy?" There was a hint of a laugh in Octavia's voice. "No doubt your users are very concerned about privacy when they're lying ice-cold in a morgue."

There was a small, thick silence.

Oh shit, Casey thought. This was where Sophronia leapt across the room and put her teeth into Octavia's throat.

She wouldn't actually do it. He didn't think so, at least. Octavia was about twenty years older and thus physically stronger than Sophronia—plus, murdering a colleague was definitely illegal and probably bad for one's career trajectory. It was more that . . .

Sophronia cared about Stokr. He knew she did. She wouldn't let Octavia's mockery stand.

But to his surprise, he heard Sophronia swallow again. Her words came out tight. "We haven't—no one's in the *morgue*. The press release made it perfectly clear—"

Now Octavia did laugh, a cool sound that bore no real resemblance to amusement. "The press release, yes. I read it. It remains impossible for me to understand why you'd trust your reputation to a publicist who wouldn't even have a job at HemoCorp if it weren't for your influence on your father."

Sophronia took a step back. Casey winced and set one

hand atop his thumb drive to hide it from Octavia's line of sight.

"I didn't—I don't have anything to do with the hiring at HemoCorp," Sophronia said. "You *know* I don't. I recused myself years ago so that no one would say that about Del and Hugo. I—"

Casey's fingers closed over the thumb drive, and he wondered what the hell was going on. Why was she on the defensive? Surely she could see that Octavia was just trying to get a rise out of her—digging her fangs into Sophronia's vulnerable flank.

"Please," Octavia said. "Spare me. Everyone in Northern California knows the Gaius girl is your pet. What baffles me is why your father continues to allow the two of you to stumble around making messes that the rest of us have to clean up."

Again, Casey expected . . . something. For Sophronia to slice her hard, sharp vampire's nails across Octavia's smirking face, maybe.

For the Vega heir to *fight*.

But instead she took another step back. "I—" she said. "I don't—"

His heart did something funny at the thin, undefended sound of her voice. A little unexpected throb of protectiveness.

He slipped the thumb drive into his pocket and rose smoothly to his feet. "All done," he said and stepped, smiling, toward Octavia Pavo.

She was tall, like most vampires, but she still had to crane her neck to meet his eyes. He figured she didn't have to do that much—she looked awfully pissed about it, beneath that chilly veneer.

Her expression probably shouldn't have amused him as

much as it did. He stifled the desire to laugh, and then he also buried the urge to set his hand to the curve of Sophronia's lower back.

"We'll get out of your hair," he said to Octavia. "Thanks. Ms. Vega"—he turned his smile on Sophronia—"I appreciate your helping me out with the door access. Your office is next, I think."

She blinked at him. Her face was paler than usual, and if he looked very closely, he could see her pulse flutter in her neck.

"My office," she said finally. "Yes."

They had almost made it out the door when Octavia's voice stopped them. "Sophronia."

Sophronia didn't turn. Only stopped, motionless, an ivory statue except for the small quick throbs of her pulse.

"I can't see any reason you should have unlimited access to my office," Octavia said. "Let's be certain that's addressed in your security update. In fact, I'll bring it up to your father."

Sophronia didn't say anything back. She moved into the corridor, and Casey followed her. When she would have turned in the direction of her own office, Casey put his thumb and forefinger to her elbow. With a firm, careful grip, he guided her to the elevator instead.

She let him do it. But when the elevator doors had fully closed, she shook him off.

She scowled ferociously at him, hot blue eyes and taut lavender lips. "If you can't remember the way to my office," she snapped, "I'm sure I can find you a map. I believe we pass them out at onboarding."

His smile, which had faded at Octavia's parting words, was back on his face before he could stop it. He thought: *There she is.*

"I know where your office is. I'm taking you down to my car."

"To your *car*?"

She looked so appalled that he almost laughed outright. "Vampires have those, right?"

Her lips parted, but the sound of the elevator doors coming open onto the parking garage cut off whatever answer she'd meant to give.

"Here's the thing," he said as he led her out. "I have an idea."

•••

Sophronia felt . . .

Shaken wasn't the word. She refused to be shaken.

Surprised, maybe, was okay. She hadn't expected Octavia, that was all. When she'd heard the vampire's cool voice, the hair on the back of her neck had prickled and her fangs had tightened to an ache. She'd leapt in front of Casey without a thought because even if Octavia *wasn't* responsible for the Stokr sabotage, Sophronia didn't want Octavia any closer to him than she had to be. She didn't want any vampires to touch him.

Except then Octavia had started being . . . well, being *Octavia*, and it had the same general effect on Sophronia's composure that it always did.

She pressed the tip of her tongue to her fang. Why—*why* did she let Octavia affect her that way? What was it about Octavia that turned Sophronia into a pathetic teenage version of herself?

It wasn't just that Octavia reminded her of her mother. They didn't really resemble each other, other than their vampire's height and lean build. Octavia had strong features, a sharp aquiline nose, ash-blond hair. Fidelia Vega had been softer in her beauty, her black hair always pulled back in a low twist to hide its tendency to curl. But they had the same sharp elegance, an air of command that was bred in the bone.

Before she'd died, Fidelia had always been exceptional at forcing Sophronia to confront things about herself she didn't want to look at too closely.

Octavia seemed to have the trick of it too.

Was Sophronia's friendship with Del a weakness? Did she really overlook Del's flaws because she couldn't see past how much she loved her best friend?

Was it possible that by allowing their friendship to continue, Sophronia was *hurting* Del? Ruining Del's chances for professional advancement because people thought Del didn't deserve her job?

Abraham's fangs, she *hated* this. Hated relationships and vulnerability and love most of all.

She heard a little *pop* and realized she'd been gripping the seat belt so hard she'd put a hole in the fabric with the tip of her nail.

"Oh—Abraham," she said reflexively and looked over at Casey. She'd been breathing shallowly because in close confines his caramel-and-black-pepper scent made her fangs ache. "I didn't mean to—"

He didn't look over at her—his eyes were on the road and both his hands were on the wheel because of course he would be a careful, law-abiding driver—but his mouth was still doing its soft, amused thing. "No worries. This car's really old. Terrible gas mileage."

She glanced around at the sedan's interior, which appeared to have a cassette-tape player installed in the dash. "Do we not compensate you appropriately at HemoCorp?"

"No—no, it's not that. I just . . ." He hesitated. Nudged at his glasses. "This car was my dad's."

Oh for *Abraham's* sake. She smoothed the seat belt carefully with the tips of her fingers, locked her hands in her lap, and made a mental note to find the best antique-car restorer on the West Coast and fly them to the HemoCorp parking garage on Monday.

"Really," he said, "don't worry about it. I did way worse when I was a kid."

She gave him a doubtful glance. "Goldfish crackers? Crayon on the glove box? What could you possibly have done?"

"Stole it." His mouth curved up higher. "A few times."

She blinked. Absolutely nothing in her experience with Casey Amato suggested he was the type of person who might *steal a car.*

But before she could figure out some socially acceptable way to say *I beg your fucking pardon*, he kept talking. "It'll get us to the university, though. It's made this drive a couple hundred times, I'd estimate."

She recognized that quick instinct to turn away from the past, and so she let him change the subject. "You said there's a professor you want us to speak to?"

"Dr. Zélie LeBlanc. She was my mentor back when I was in school, and the Pillbugs' too. Did cybersecurity for a bank in New York for a decade before she quit to come teach. If we need fresh ideas, Dr. LeBlanc will have them."

Sophronia hesitated. "You don't think what we planned with your team is going to work?"

He gave her another one of his quick, earnest looks. "I think it could. But—Octavia saw us in her office. If she's the one behind the sabotage, her guard's going to be up."

"You think she'll uninstall your software?"

"Maybe, if she can figure out what I did. But it'd be way easier for her to just stop using her computer for anything incriminating."

Damn it. He was right. She gritted her teeth. Her fangs bit down into her lower lip, just short of drawing blood. "She shouldn't have been there. She was supposed to be in Monterey."

"Maybe her meeting got canceled?"

"Sure. Maybe. Or maybe someone told her we were there."

Casey's fingers flexed on the wheel. "You think she's the one, then? Who sabotaged Stokr?"

"Of *course* I do," she snapped. "She hates Stokr. Thinks it's tawdry and humiliating."

He hesitated. "And that's motive enough to take it down? Why would she, when it was making so much money for HemoCorp?"

"I don't know. I . . ."

"What about Titus Fornax? He's the vampire with the longest tenure at the company, other than your father. He'd have the influence and the access. Can you think of any reason why he'd go after Stokr?"

She felt her jaw tighten. "It's not Titus."

"What makes you so sure?"

She thought of the way Titus had come to her defense. The only person on the executive committee who had. "He doesn't mind Stokr. He doesn't . . ."

Stupid, stupid to say it. Of course it could be Titus. It could be any of them.

It was only that, whenever she thought of HemoCorp, of her family, she thought of Titus too.

When she was a child and her father had brought her to the office, he'd permitted her to sit in on his meetings as long as she didn't interrupt. Someone had had the bright idea of giving her a legal pad, and she'd taken such diligent notes that Titus had started to bring her an extra pen.

Make a carbon copy for my secretary, he'd said with a wink. *Your notes are twice as good as his.*

When she'd been nine or so—long before Holbeck Priest—Titus had let her spend a whole summer in his office. He'd called her his intern, and it had been years before it had dawned on her that he hadn't really needed her around. That it had been a kindness.

"You don't want it to be Titus," Casey said finally.

She blew out a breath. "I guess not. But still, I can't help thinking that Octavia makes the most sense. You saw her in the office today. She knew we were up to something."

"I saw her," he said. "She's . . ."

Sophronia waited for him to finish, but he didn't go on. "Awful?"

He laughed. "That's not really the word I was searching for, but yeah, she's pretty awful."

She watched the taillights ahead of them, the white-painted lines of the freeway and beyond it, the sky. "People always say we're . . . similar."

There was a pause. A charged silence.

She stared furiously out the windshield and considered whether her skin was durable enough to survive flinging herself out of the moving car. Why had she said it? Did she want him to contradict her?

This was why talking to Octavia rattled her. Because when she looked at the older vampire, part of her saw her mother.

But part of her—a little fearful part, one she tried viciously to bury—saw herself.

Reluctantly, she glanced over at Casey. He wasn't looking back; he was focused on the freeway as he signaled for the exit ramp. But his mouth was still curved in that little half smile, beautiful and terrible and fond.

"Do they?" he said finally. His eyes caught hers and held them for the space of a heartbeat before he looked back to the road. "I don't see it."

CHAPTER 8

The UC Incarnare campus was home to twenty thousand students, which did not in any way square with the fact that everyone there seemed to recognize Casey.

To be fair—which Sophronia could be, even though she'd gotten her heel stuck between the planks of a wooden walkway that might generously be called rustic, and also Casey's scent was slowly killing her—it hadn't been until they'd gotten to the computer science building that Casey had transformed from "handsome-if-poorly-coiffed member of the public" to "beloved community celebrity."

The computer science building was an exquisite glass-fronted structure tucked between soaring redwoods, and they hadn't even made it halfway up the bustling steps before someone stopped them.

"Casey?"

The speaker was a dark-haired teen with braids and enormous glasses, and when Casey pulled her into a hug, her toes left the ground. "Ana! How's school?"

Returned to earth, the girl smiled up at Casey like he was her own personal sun. "Good! Actually, no, Quintero's class is a nightmare, and I sort of live in his lab, and my lab group thinks I have shit taste in music, but—" She rolled her eyes.

"Give me until December. Death metal is so much more compelling during exam season. I'll get 'em."

Casey was grinning. "Ana"—he gestured—"this is Sophronia Vega, one of the VPs at HemoCorp. Sophronia, this is Ana."

"Oh shit," Ana said. "Hi! It's so extremely cool to meet you."

"A pleasure." Sophronia looked at Casey. "How do you two . . ."

"You remember Mercedes from my team? Ana's her sister."

Sophronia could see the resemblance now that she knew to look for it—the casual insouciant set of their shoulders, their pointed chins.

"Plus," Ana said, "Casey tutored me for the ACT."

Sophronia blinked.

Casey blushed—a throb of blood that made Sophronia's fangs ache. "It was nothing. You didn't need me."

"Sure I didn't," Ana said agreeably. "I'm a natural genius." She made eye contact with Sophronia and mouthed, *He's lying.*

Casey made a valiant attempt to change the subject. "Listen, Ana, we're here to see Dr. LeBlanc. Do you know if she's in her office?"

"Pretty sure," Ana said. "Put in a good word for me?"

"I told you—you don't need me."

"Yeah, yeah." Ana hugged him again, quick and light, then dashed off, shouting, in the direction of a clump of undergrads.

Sophronia gave Casey a sidelong look as they entered the building. "Do you tutor all of your junior engineers' baby siblings?"

He scratched at his stubble, which mostly served to waft

around his agonizingly delicious scent. "I didn't really . . . it was just a few pointers."

"That you delivered twice weekly in one-hour increments?"

It was a palpable hit; even his ears were pink now. Hunger knotted her belly, and she vowed to the soul of Abraham Stoker not to make him blush again.

In the halls, more undergrads recognized him. Apparently he came to talk at various career showcases, and mentored several teams for some sort of mysterious programming competition, and was currently in the process of organizing a computer science internship program across Northern California.

She took in this information.

It felt dizzying, although that might've been due to the fact that she was trying her hardest not to breathe in his vicinity. How did he even have *time* for it all? She'd seen the long hours he put in at HemoCorp when she'd tracked him on the security feed. The early mornings and late nights, his glasses crooked and his hair wild and his thumb rubbing absently across his jaw.

In the suite of offices, more people spilled out to embrace and coo over him. One of the junior faculty showed him a flower blooming on her window cactus. Another—a suntanned blond man—said something about rock climbing, which Sophronia supposed explained the calluses on the tips of Casey's fingers that she'd felt when he'd taken her arm. Casey grinned and promised to drop a pin for the new beach bouldering spot he'd found a few weekends back.

He made it seem effortless: all those friendships, all that easy warmth.

Somehow, it made Sophronia think of the first time she'd spent a school holiday with Del's family. Her mother hadn't been overly keen on her friendship with Del, or the Gaiuses in general, whose well-known affection for humans was considered distinctly outré by most of the other vampire dynasties.

But Fidelia Vega had been in Switzerland, and so Sophronia had gotten to spend the school break at Del's. The Gaius family had two kids—twice as many as was typical for vampires—and they never sat down for formal dinners, just waved their mugs of artificial blood and shouted at each other over something called Monopoly that Sophronia didn't at first understand and then became obsessed with.

She could remember it all: the pottery Del's mother made herself, the slick feeling of the glaze beneath her fingers, the plastic dice in her hand. The way they'd laughed—Del and Hugo and their parents—and shamelessly cheated, and roasted one another when they landed on the dangerous-seeming dark-blue squares.

The way they'd hesitated, not quite sure how to react, when she'd obliterated them all with ruthless efficiency the third time they'd played the game.

She'd clenched her jaw tight. She'd thought . . .

That was the point, wasn't it? She'd thought they would laugh.

And then they had: Hugo winging a utility card in her direction while Mr. Gaius roared with amusement. Del had pushed at Sophronia's chair with her bare foot, groaning, *I should've known the capitalism game would be your favorite.*

She would have killed for them, after that.

That, she supposed, was what she was feeling now, as she looked at Casey: that same sense of longing for the sun.

She ground her teeth and tried to stop *feeling.*

Eventually, Casey managed to shed his admirers and lead her down to Dr. LeBlanc's office, where he rapped lightly on the open door. Inside, Dr. LeBlanc looked up. She looked startlingly young for the career she'd had—her mid-fifties at most—and was wearing a glossy aubergine lipstick that Del would've cheerfully committed crimes for.

She grinned at the sight of them, which at this point Sophronia had come to expect. "Casey!"

"Dr. LeBlanc. You have a minute for us?"

"For you I do." Her voice was low, a buttery rasp of New Orleans on the vowels.

He dropped himself into a chair across from her desk and gestured for Sophronia to sit next to him. "Dr. LeBlanc, this is Sophronia Vega, from HemoCorp. Sophronia, Dr. LeBlanc, my mentor here at UCI."

"Before you left me for the filthy lucre of industry," Dr. LeBlanc said—by her tone a familiar, affectionate barb. But as her gaze shifted to Sophronia, her expression cooled. "Ms. Vega. Of course. I recognize you from the press conferences."

Where she'd been standing silently while Del publicly defended their app in the face of outright disaster.

Excellent.

Sophronia tried not to grimace. "Thank you so much for seeing us without an appointment."

"Casey has a standing appointment here at UC Incarnare. That's how he's managed to lure away three of my best and brightest to join him at HemoCorp straight out of school."

Yes, she recalled that now. That was where his Pillbugs had gotten their name—the mascot of the university, which seemed both baffling and unpleasant.

Though what did she know about human universities? Maybe they were all represented by arthropods.

"HemoCorp is exactly why we're here," Casey said. "Stokr, specifically. It's my app that's failed so . . . dramatically, these last few months." He glanced at Sophronia. "Ours."

She hated that she liked the word so much. She glared at him.

His mouth quirked in return for half a second before he kept going. He didn't tell Dr. LeBlanc everything. They had decided in the car what could be related and what—like the analyst's murder—needed to be kept quiet for Dr. LeBlanc's safety and the integrity of their investigation. Carefully, precisely, he outlined what they'd mutually agreed to disclose: their suspicions that Stokr had been sabotaged and their investigation inside the company.

When he finished, there was a brief, vehement back-and-forth between the two engineers, littered with so much jargon that Sophronia only understood one word in five. Dr. LeBlanc seemed to be grilling Casey on what he had done to search out failure points that could have led to the summer's bloodbaths. Apparently Brendan had "merged a pull request without rebasing"—a bad thing, Sophronia suspected, based on Dr. LeBlanc's wince and Casey's affectionate amusement as he described how he'd fixed it.

Eventually, the professor seemed satisfied. She sat back in her chair and toyed absently with a fountain pen. "You know," she said, "I never really thought you'd made this kind of blunder. Once, maybe, I could've accepted. But three times?" She shook her head. "It didn't seem like you."

"We know sabotage seems like a pretty wild suggestion," Casey said, "but trust us when we tell you—"

Dr. LeBlanc waved a hand. "Not wild. In the corporate world? Cold-blooded murder wouldn't surprise me."

Casey, who'd been halfway through running his hand

through his hair, froze. He coughed, then seemed to remember that his hand existed and put it back in his lap. "Right."

"I told you before you took the job at Google what it would be like." She gazed at him. In the afternoon light, her deep-brown skin looked glazed by gold. "Are you still sure this is what you want, Casey? You don't have to give your life away to a corporation just because you think you're supposed to. Teaching—I've said from the start that your heart's in teaching."

Sophronia looked from the professor to Casey. She felt . . .

She didn't know what she felt. Ridiculous, to feel jealous—to want to throw herself across him, to want to flash her fangs and tell Dr. LeBlanc that *no one* was taking him away from Stokr.

Stupid, most of all, because Dr. LeBlanc was right. He'd be a really good teacher.

His wide mouth came up on one side. "Maybe someday. But I'm happy where I am. I like what I do. I like Stokr."

Dr. LeBlanc raised her brows. "You like designing a dating app?"

"I do, yeah." He didn't look at Sophronia when he spoke, but she could hear the way his heart picked up, the sudden mouthwatering rush of his blood. "I think it's really important, actually. I think it's—" He broke off to laugh. "I almost said, *an instinctive human need for connection*, but it's not just humans, is it? It's all of us. We're all looking to find another person to talk to, to hold on to. Someone who sees us. Someone who makes the world feel brighter and sharper and more profound, just because they exist in it. And even if—"

He paused. Looked cautiously at Sophronia.

There was no power on earth that would have made her interrupt him.

"Even if it's just for a day," he said finally. "A night. Even if that's all they get out of Stokr—it still matters to be known like that."

His earnestness—his sheer breathtaking honesty—stunned her.

Stokr was what it was. She wasn't ashamed of it. Vampires and humans couldn't interbreed without IVF and gene editing; most diseases weren't cross-communicable between the two species. Without the possibility of pregnancy or STIs—and with the euphoria of blood drinking in play—the app attracted a lot of people looking for short-term hookups.

And yet . . .

Even if it's just for a day. A night. It still matters to be known like that.

It was what she wanted for Stokr too. Only she'd never tried to put it into words.

She looked at Casey: his long callused fingers, the easy set of his jaw.

In that moment, he felt more foreign to her than any human ever had. She couldn't imagine what it would be like to plunge so fearlessly into vulnerability. Didn't he realize how dangerous it was to leave his heart open for the taking?

Had no one ever taught him how easily he could be torn apart?

Dr. LeBlanc sat forward. "All right," she said. "I get it. There's no talking you out of this, is there?"

Casey pulled his gaze away from Sophronia's. "Not today."

"In that case," Dr. LeBlanc said, "I have something I've been working on that might be able to help."

She withdrew a slim tablet from her desk, flicking past security screens with quick gestures, and then handed it to Casey. He nudged up his glasses and took it, brow furrowed.

Dr. LeBlanc turned one of her monitors toward them, gesturing as she explained. "I think you're right that accessing the servers from inside HemoCorp is a dead end. But at this point, you don't need to track their workstations. You need access to their personal devices. You need app activity logs. Browser history."

"I don't understand," Sophronia said. She looked from the curved monitor to the professor and then to Casey, who was tapping diligently at the tablet's screen, his eyes narrowed.

"Do you have a list of suspects?" Dr. LeBlanc asked. "All the people at HemoCorp with motive and access to the network?"

Sophronia thought about the HemoCorp executives. She thought, with a little twist of pain, about her father. "Yes."

"And can you get them all into one room?"

She blinked. She looked again to Casey, who was now staring at the tablet in front of him with something approaching ecstatic devotion. "I suppose. If I needed to. Why?"

"If you can get close enough—to their devices, I mean, not their useless physical bodies—my program can get you inside. Every app. Every activity log."

"This shouldn't be possible," Casey said softly. "Without touching the devices—without their credentials—"

"This is why you came to me, isn't it?"

"And with this root certificate, you can redirect and decrypt the secure traffic to the . . ." He looked up. "You are a genius. And this is *illegal*."

Dr. LeBlanc smiled, slow and feline. "Not yet. Legislation always takes a while to catch up to the tech."

Sophronia leaned forward. "I don't understand. This program—what does it do?"

"It's spyware," Casey said.

"Technically," Dr. LeBlanc said, "yes. The program uses something called peer-to-peer connection to insert itself into devices within a certain radius and determine what those devices have been up to. There's no need for Wi-Fi sniffers—my program circumvents the server and the network entirely. I've set it up in such a way that the install is invisible on the device by bypassing their security measures."

Sophronia blinked. "I don't . . . Why do you have a program that can do all this?"

"Part of cybersecurity work is identifying vulnerabilities that can be exploited by threat actors," Casey said. "Dr. LeBlanc employs a hands-on approach." He looked amused and impressed and the faintest bit alarmed. "For your situational awareness, we may be violating several federal statutes just by hearing about this tech."

Dr. LeBlanc waved a hand. "Thought crimes aren't illegal in this country."

"Oh, good." His mouth curved. "I'll tell them I was just thinking about treason when they haul us away."

Sophronia looked from Dr. LeBlanc to Casey to the mysterious diagrams on the tablet. "You said—all we have to do is get everyone in the same room? They just need to be there, and your software will tell us if their devices have accessed the Stokr server?"

"That's right. Casey's team can perform a remote install—that's the beauty of the program. If the Stokr server or its database appears in their recent access history, you'll be able to find out." Her gaze had gone sharp as she looked at them. "Or—more importantly—if they try to sabotage Stokr again in the future, you'll be the first to know."

Casey set the tablet back on Dr. LeBlanc's desk and

turned to Sophronia. "This could definitely work. I knew Dr. LeBlanc would have something for us."

She felt the tug of his enthusiasm like a tide. Relief like a gravitational pull. She'd been right to trust him. She never would have known about Dr. LeBlanc or had access to this tech without Casey on her team.

"Do you have any ideas for how we can get them all together?" he asked. "The whole executive committee?"

Her gaze fell to the desk as she considered the question. She drummed her nails on the arm of her chair.

She could call a committee-heads meeting, maybe—although that might raise some alarms after today's run-in with Octavia. Some announcement regarding a DP&S product? A fake security training? But how could she make certain everyone was present, without raising their saboteur's suspicion?

The low slant of the sun through the window tickled at her mind. The days were growing shorter with the approach of fall, and the creamy light made her think of golden sandstone walls.

Of grapes. Of wine mixed with blood.

The fragmented images resolved abruptly in her head, and suddenly—

She knew where they could go to install the program.

She looked up and met Casey's gaze. "The HemoCorp executive summit. It's at Titus's family vineyard, the first weekend in October. Can we be ready by then?"

"Absolutely." His eyes were amber in this light, and his voice, low and steady, scraped against her nerve endings. "We'll do whatever it takes."

CHAPTER 9

The luxurious Fornax vineyard was a place Casey could've appreciated more readily if he hadn't first seen it from the inside of a rented white van with TICKLE YOUR TASTEBUDS CATERING stenciled on the door.

"Holy shit," Mercedes said. She'd taken shotgun and was seated next to Rick Tickle—family friend of George's fiancé, Allen, and owner and operator of the Tickle van. "Holy *shit*. They have their meetings here? I swear to God, as soon as we get back, I'm finding that spreadsheet with everyone's bonus structure. And changing mine." She glanced at Casey. "I'm just kidding. Don't tell the VP I said that."

"I don't think this is part of HemoCorp," George said. "Allen's company manages the investment portfolios of at least half of the big vampire families. They just *have* stuff like this. One piece of their diversified assets."

But to Casey's eye, the Fornax family vineyard didn't look like an investment strategy. It looked beloved. Treasured. They'd passed half a dozen sprawling fields of vines, green on gold, and at the top of the hill found the vineyard's headquarters. There were several low-slung buildings of rustic sandstone and plate glass: home to wine production, offices, even an ivy-drenched pool house.

It had taken them over an hour to drive to the vineyard from Incarnare, on top of the ten full days of planning that had been required for the Pillbugs, Sophronia, and Delphine to get their scheme off the ground. While the HemoCorp executives met and chatted over dinner—artificial or real blood for the vampires, according to their preference, and wine and elegant farm-to-table canapés for the humans—Casey, Mercedes, and Brendan would be hidden in the kitchen, presiding over the technical aspects of Dr. LeBlanc's soon-to-be-illegal software.

But they couldn't all stay tucked out of sight. Someone had to be in the room with the VIPs in order to activate the installation—and George, to his infinite dismay, was the only one of the Pillbugs who'd ever worked as a server.

Which meant that, at the moment, George was dressed in Rick Tickle's best catering outfit and looking faintly green.

But George was going to be fine. He wouldn't be alone in there. Sophronia and Delphine would be with him.

They'd met up six times for slightly raucous planning meetings over coffee and pie at the Flying Sausage, a bafflingly UFO-themed diner ten blocks from HemoCorp. The coffee was terrible, and the pie wasn't much better, but it was always empty. Chronically so—Brendan was convinced it was a front or possibly some kind of extraterrestrial hideout.

Casey had been secretly amused to discover that Del and Sophronia were willing to indulge in human food as long as it was mostly processed sugar. They'd been extremely impressed by Reddi-wip.

Three other times, he'd met with Sophronia alone. She'd secured a tiny unused custodial office at HemoCorp, which she'd verified wasn't visible on any security cameras. They'd arrived ten minutes apart and had spent hours reviewing

Dr. LeBlanc's software, the list of executives and VPs who would be at the summit, and the precise machinations by which Casey and his team would sneak into the vineyard undetected.

She had a dazzling brain. As far as he could tell from googling her—which he had done an embarrassing number of times, in various and increasingly arcane formulations—she didn't have a postsecondary degree. Most vampires didn't. But what she lacked in academic credentials, she more than made up for in curiosity and willingness to learn. She'd had him explain Dr. LeBlanc's software in layman's terms, and then she made him explain it again, in more and more specific engineering terminology, until she had the concepts backward and forward.

He'd suspected at first that she meant to teach herself enough about software engineering and cybersecurity that she could kick him off the project and do it all herself. Eventually, though, he'd realized she just wanted to understand. She was a perfectionist, but most of that ruthless rigor seemed turned inward. If she was going to do something, she wanted to do it *right*.

She was forbidding. Stern. So fucking lovely she made his head spin. She moved with graceful, precise efficiency, and she parceled out her words with equal crisp reserve. If she'd been someone else—and not one of the most powerful vampires in the Western world—he would have called her shy.

He'd wondered, as he'd sat beside her, if the tension in her jaw ever relaxed. If there was ever a time when she was just Sophronia, and not the Vega heir.

He'd imagined . . .

Hell. It didn't matter what he'd imagined. They had a job to do, a murderer to catch, and if he wondered, sometimes, whether the two of them would be a hemoenzymatic match, well—if he wanted to find out, the first thing he had to do was fix Stokr.

The van unloaded them—along with chafing dishes full of computers and keyboards—at the kitchen's rear entrance.

Brendan had suggested they wait in the van for George to reemerge, but Casey hadn't liked the idea. He'd wanted to be as close as possible in case anything went wrong; if George needed to be extracted, he wanted to be on hand.

Del had agreed. "I'll get you a place inside," she'd said. "No one will bother you."

Casey had started to ask for more details, but Del's lavender mouth had curled up. "Leave it to me. I've got this."

Somehow, she'd done it. When Casey and his Pillbugs strolled into the bustling kitchen from the rear, they were ushered to a small table set up behind an industrial refrigerator. On the table, Casey identified a handful of power strips, a cable modem, and several bottles of Fornax Vineyards pinot noir.

Brendan was looking around with an expression of bemusement. "Can vampires even drink wine?"

"Sure they can," Mercedes said. "Ethanol poisons humans and vampires equally. It doesn't discriminate." She sat down at the table and started to unpack equipment from the chafing dish. "Can I just say that this is unexpectedly cool? I feel like a spy. But also like . . . one of Brendan's frat brothers, kind of?"

"We say *fraternity*," Brendan said.

George's teeth were chattering. "Cool. Yeah. Spies. Assuming we don't get *eaten*, it'll be great."

Before Casey could say something reassuring, Sophronia swept into the kitchen. She had on one of her intimidating work outfits, all luxurious fabrics tailored to her tall, slim body. This time, her jacket and skirt were a deep glazed red, and her little shirt thing underneath was lace-edged ivory. Her legs were a mile long above the straps at her ankles, which he—

Wasn't noticing. Was absolutely *refusing* to look at.

He considered taking off his glasses for the rest of the summit. He considered, briefly and futilely, going outside, finding the pool they'd passed, and tossing his glasses into the turquoise water.

Unfortunately, he needed to be able to see. He kept his glasses on.

Sophronia's face was set—apparently he was still looking at her—and her lips were a darker purple than he'd ever seen on her before.

Blood hunger, that color meant. There was a faint but discernible coppery scent in the kitchen as the staff loaded trays with heavy crystal tumblers full of blood.

"Is this good?" she asked Casey. "The space, I mean? Del got you everything you need?"

"It's great," he said. "How did she . . ."

Sophronia looked torn between anxiety and amusement. "When we were nineteen or so, I got Del invited to the summit as my guest. And instead of sitting sedately at the table like I always did, she snuck off to the kitchen and—well, I don't know, honestly. Something about a luge? And vodka? She said she learned about it from her brother."

Sophronia looked like she was trying to make sense of the sudden existence of some obscure winter sport here in the Diablo foothills, and Casey had to bite the inside of his cheek to keep from laughing. Maybe Hugo was one of the rare vampires who'd gone to college.

"Anyway, whatever she did must've been pretty memorable, because even after a decade, the chef agreed to look the other way."

"That makes sense," Mercedes said. "I've only known Del for like two weeks, but I'd let her step on me if she asked."

"Mer!" George hissed.

Casey gave in and laughed.

Sophronia didn't. She only looked at them, severe and—he knew her subtle expressions now—worried.

And then she did something that stunned him. She reached out and put her hand on his arm.

He had on a jacket. He couldn't feel her skin against his. But still—his pulse leapt.

He knew she'd be able to hear it.

"My priority is keeping you safe," she said. "All of you. If there's the slightest sign of trouble, I want you all back in the van and halfway to Incarnare before anyone at HemoCorp catches sight of you. I don't—"

She broke off. Her eyes were exactly level with his. So blue he could feel it, like the breathless gut punch of cold water.

"We can install Dr. LeBlanc's software another time, if we have to," she said finally. "Don't get hurt."

"I won't." He put his free hand on top of hers—a cool silk sensation, a thrill like an electric charge—and, as he watched, her pupils flared. "You too, okay? Be careful."

She let him hold her there, her hand trapped beneath his, her eyes locked on his face.

And then she pulled free. "Don't do anything stupid," she said.

He took a breath as she turned—deep enough to catch the faintest hint of her perfume. He kept on watching until she was out of sight and looked, even then, at the door through which she'd vanished.

He was always looking at her.

Mercedes nudged him with one very sharp elbow. "Did you hear her? Don't do anything stupid."

He blew out a breath, then rubbed a hand across the back of his neck.

Dragged his gaze away from the place where Sophronia had been.

Too late, he thought. *Way, way too late.*

CHAPTER 10

The summit wasn't usually death by slow torture. In fact, most of the time Sophronia loved the biannual meetings because they involved endless obsessive discussion of HemoCorp (her favorite thing) and also because if she and Del snuck into the kitchen after the dinner ended, Titus's chef invariably produced tiny handmade gummy roses dusted with pink champagne sugar.

But this year, she couldn't concentrate on Circinus's rambling discussion of regional differences in digital marketing or even her father's surgical inquiries into the projects of three different R and D group chairs. She mingled, as was expected of her, and made polite conversation—but as she strolled across the glass-walled solarium, she kept looking for George among the servers. Her phone was in her bag, and it was taking all her considerable willpower not to drag it free and try to somehow identify the progress of Dr. LeBlanc's invisible spy program.

She didn't do it. She had to act normal—and normal, for the Vega heir, meant paying close attention to HemoCorp and HemoCorp only.

She crossed toward one of the servers bearing a tray of faceted tumblers of artificial blood. Like all Vegas, and most of the upper crust in vampire society, she didn't partake of real human blood, even when it was donated and placed in a glass, the way it was here at the summit. She'd never even wanted to—had been cured of any lingering curiosity after she'd watched her closest, most trusted vampire friends accidentally murder a human in their dorm room.

Drinking from a human might taste better than artificial blood—she'd heard it did, at least—but doing so was also tantamount to admitting vampires' dependence on the other species. For dynasties like the Vegas' and Pavos', who cherished their own wealth and power above everything, humans were a weakness they rarely indulged in. Sophronia had wondered, sometimes, if she ought to use Stokr herself just for the optics.

But after Izzy, she couldn't bring herself to do it.

Sophronia reached for a crystal tumbler just as Del appeared at her side to do the same. The Gaius family wasn't nearly so obsessed with vampire superiority, but Del, too, hadn't touched real human blood since that night at Holbeck Priest.

Sophronia wondered, sometimes, if Del felt the same hideous guilt that she did. The same awful responsibility. They had brought Izzy to the party; they'd both believed she would be safe.

They never talked about how wrong they'd been.

Del tipped her head so that her blond curls brushed Sophronia's shoulder. "How are you holding up?" she asked under her breath.

"Fine."

"I saw you come in. Figured you'd be over here by the blood pretty soon."

"What? Why?"

The corner of Del's mouth tipped up, familiar mischief in her green eyes. "You looked . . . thirsty."

Sophronia gritted her teeth, and Del laughed into her cup's scarlet depths.

It was, unfortunately, true. The HemoCorp artificial blood smelled perfectly fine. Like food. But Casey, back in the kitchen, had smelled better than food. Better than *anything*.

She *was* thirsty—his sweet spiced scent had gone straight to her head. But it wasn't all blood hunger, this heat in her belly.

She thought of the way he'd looked at her: the heaviness of his eyes, his callused hand spreading wide over hers. The thrill that had skimmed across her skin. The sudden throb of his pulse.

She moistened her lips and raised her glass to her mouth.

But before she could drink, she noticed a tiny knot of H-Corp execs heading toward them. Kriti, Octavia, Titus. Her father.

She set the glass back on the tray and swallowed against the sudden tightness in her throat.

"Uh-oh," Del muttered. "Tell me why they look like the Vampire Inquisition."

Kriti, the only human in the group, was the first to speak. Her eyes didn't flicker down to the carmine liquid in the glasses; HemoCorp's human execs learned pretty quickly to ignore the sight of blood. "Sophronia. We were just discussing you. Tell us about the Stokr division's progress in resolving the app's failures from this summer. August said you'd moved to a new round of testing and development, but it seems to me it's been several weeks since we've had an update."

Sophronia stifled the urge to glance at her father. "We're

in the middle of a ground-up redesign of the app. When Stokr goes back online, it'll be after extensive restructuring of both the user experience and the backend services."

Octavia arched a single brow. "And something about privacy, is that right?"

Sophronia took a breath. "Yes. The database security has been upgraded to conform to—"

"That sounds expensive," her father cut in.

She paused. Swallowed again. "Not necessarily. I've been able to redirect the workflows of some of my software engineers—"

"Thrifty," Octavia said. She made the word sound like an insult. "But reasonable, under the circumstances. They don't have anything else to do."

Titus raised his glass—a red blend, Sophronia was pretty sure, not blood—in the direction of August Vega. "She's put together a good plan, your girl. We've met a couple of times to ensure regulatory compliance for the user data as she upgrades."

"I'm sure our shareholders will be pleased to know we're in compliance when the stock tanks again," Octavia said pleasantly.

Titus smiled right back. "I'd think you'd be more appreciative, Octavia. Regulatory compliance is pretty damn important when it comes to winning those lawsuits you keep talking about."

"I hear there are eleven now," Octavia shot back. "That name Stokr specifically."

"Anyone can sue," Sophronia said. "That doesn't mean they'll win. Legal tells me that the waivers they sign when they drop off their samples for the database are airtight. Not to mention no one's been seriously injured."

Octavia sent her a slow, predatory smile—a full baring of her fangs. "Not seriously injured? In my lab, Sophronia, when we see exsanguinated humans, we call that an unacceptable risk."

"Stokr is still shut down," her father said mildly. "If you have additional concerns, Octavia, perhaps you can put them to Holmwood. I believe he's one room over, fighting off over-eager new legal hires with a stick."

Octavia raised her chin in acknowledgment of August's words. Her gaze flickered over Sophronia and Del—that self-satisfied curve still in place on her mouth—before she turned to seek out the chief legal officer.

Kriti murmured something to the other execs about fibrin gels, and she and August both moved in the direction of some R and D vamps tucked around a tower of imported champagne.

"I'll be right behind you," Titus said.

But instead of walking away, he looked at Sophronia.

He dropped his voice, low enough that only a vampire could have heard him. "Don't let Octavia intimidate you."

Sophronia's fangs dug into her lower lip. "She doesn't."

Titus paused before replying, long enough for Sophronia to feel a twinge of embarrassed heat.

She *refused* to be intimidated by Octavia. Octavia was wrong about Stokr. It wasn't a *breathtaking embarrassment*, and it wasn't a dangerous vulnerability either.

Sophronia just needed to prove it.

"Her bark is worse than her bite," Titus said finally. "She doesn't mean half of it. Claudia says . . ."

He hesitated, his mouth going firm beneath his white beard, his fangs almost invisible.

Claudia was Titus's wife.

And Octavia's sister.

Two children were rare in the vampire dynasties due to inheritance concerns. In earlier and more sanguinary centuries, vampire teens had had an unfortunate habit of murdering their siblings for precedence.

But Claudia had been gentle, retiring—almost, some vampires scoffed, human in her ways. She'd been ten when the Pavo family had given in and produced Octavia, who'd turned out to be precisely the ruthless, bloodthirsty heir they'd been looking for.

Claudia hadn't minded. She hadn't wanted to be the Pavo heir anyway. She'd been eighteen when she married Titus: a practical marriage to unite the two dynasties that had turned into a devoted love match. And though she spent a great deal of time in their quiet cliffside house these days—after a slow, painful recovery from the same rare vampire virus that had killed Sophronia's mother—Sophronia knew that Claudia and Titus were happy.

"Claudia says—and I repeated this to August—that if we leave Octavia to her gels and her dermal patches and whatever else she's working on down on her floor, she'll forget about Stokr eventually." Titus shot a glance in the direction of August and Kriti. "Your father . . . He can't say it, Sophronia, but he's proud of what you've accomplished."

Sophronia's lips parted, but before she could speak, Titus gave her hand a quick squeeze. "Fidelia would have been too. Stay the course. I'm going to go see what Novinus and the rest of R and D have done to my champagne."

He turned, leaving Sophronia with her hand half raised and her heart in her throat.

Proud.

She thought about it, sometimes. Wondered what her mother would have thought. Fidelia had been nurtured in the same dynastic system as Octavia and Claudia—had believed that nothing was worse than weakness. She'd been cruel sometimes, and yet there had been a ruthless logic to her exacting demands. She'd wanted Sophronia to be the best, because only at the top would she be safe.

When Sophronia had been eighteen and fresh out of Holbeck Priest, she hadn't even thought to look for a job that wasn't at HemoCorp. Titus had been the sole vampire who'd tried to convince her to do something different. His own daughter, ten years older than Sophronia, worked in venture capital for clean-energy start-ups.

Take a year or two before you come to HemoCorp, he'd told Sophronia. *Give yourself time to be you, before you're the Vega heir.*

But Sophronia had never wanted to be anyone else. She *loved* HemoCorp—cared endlessly about every tiny detail, from the architectural lighting she'd commissioned for the lobby to the precise thickness of the ID cards she'd tested in her hands before she'd let them get printed.

She was at the dazzling beginning of what was sure to be an illustrious career. She was everything her mother had wanted her to be. And . . .

Proud.

Maybe, if Fidelia hadn't died, she would have been.

It felt . . . cold. That word. It didn't matter the way she'd thought it would.

"Soph," Del murmured.

She breathed in the scent of Del's shampoo, the artificial blood she'd forgotten to pick back up. Flexed her fingers. "It's okay. I'm fine."

"No, I—" Del's voice was tight. "It's Octavia. She's not going in the right direction."

Sophronia felt her fangs punch down, ice skittering across her nerve endings. Her gaze shot to Octavia, who'd just passed in front of the doors to the solarium.

She wasn't headed toward the next room, where Holmwood and the legal team had congregated around the bar.

Her phone was in her hand, and the cool mask of her face was taut with . . .

What was it? Surprise? Alarm?

Sophronia yanked out her own phone. Was something happening with the Pillbugs' install? Was it—Abraham Stoker forbid—visible, somehow? Could Octavia tell that something malicious was happening on her device?

There was nothing to see on the phone's screen: only the glassy reflection of Sophronia's own face. Her gaze flicked to the exits, automatically searching for threats, for lines of attack.

When she glanced back, Octavia was gone.

"I'll follow her," Del whispered.

"Wait—don't—"

"Stay here. Text me if anyone else leaves."

Sophronia gritted her teeth and watched Del dart out of the room.

Del was smart and strong and too damned impulsive for her own good. She looked like a human, but she wasn't—she was a vampire, with a vampire's speed and fangs and near-impermeable skin.

But still. Sophronia felt her own fangs descend farther, digging needle sharp into her lower lip. Del was six inches shorter than Octavia, twenty-one years younger, and about a thousand times less lethal.

Sophronia's fingers tightened around her phone. She

searched the room, watching for threats, for signs of anything abnormal, but there was *nothing*—

And then the dark glass of her phone screen lit up with a text.

Delphine Gaius

6:42 PM

Octavia's heading for the kitchen

Sophronia felt her heart stutter—a missed beat, and then a painful, heavy throb.

The kitchen.

The Pillbugs. Alone and undefended and terribly, fatally human.

For the space of a single breath, she thought of the analyst's body in the conference room. Of Izzy, cold already, and René sobbing in hysterical horror: *I didn't mean to, I didn't mean to, I'm sorry.*

Another message appeared on her screen, and then another.

Delphine Gaius

6:43 PM

I'll slow her down

GET YOUR HUMANS OUT OF THERE

CHAPTER 11

She was running before she was fully out of sight of the solarium.

Her blood felt hot, her fangs agonizingly tight—every muscle in her vampire's body coiled and ready to hunt. She was fast, even in her heels; she nearly ripped the door off its hinges as she raced outside to the kitchen's rear entrance.

SOS, she texted Casey, and by the time she was inside the kitchen, they were all in frantic motion. His team was hastily shoving computer equipment into what looked like a rolling industrial freezer.

Casey was still sitting in front of his laptop, his expression grim and his fingers flying.

"Let's go," she said. "Time's up."

"Hang on," he said, "hang on, I'm almost—"

"There's no *time*—"

"Take the team," he said. "Get them in the van. I'll be right behind you."

She gritted her teeth. Mercedes and Brendan pushed the freezer into a shadowed corner where it wouldn't be noticeable, and George tore out through the back to get the catering van. Sophronia followed him, holding the door open for Brendan and Mercedes as they hurried out.

"Is everything okay?" Brendan asked.

She didn't answer, because she had no fucking idea. "Did you finish the install?"

"I think so. But Casey—" Brendan looked anxiously from the van to the kitchen door. "He's still in there."

He hesitated, then started to step back toward the kitchen, but she stopped him with a lethal look. "Get in the van," she snapped. "If we're not out in thirty seconds, don't wait for us."

"But he's—"

"I'll get him," she said, very low. "He's going to be fine."

Behind her, she heard the van's engine turn over, but she was already moving—back inside the kitchen, back to where she'd left Casey.

He wasn't there.

For a moment, her heart tripped over itself in pure animal terror. The table was clear: no computer, no suspicious cords. Adrenaline punched into her veins, lighting up her body, sharpening her senses.

It wasn't hard, then, to find him, tucked into the shadows behind the standing freezer. She could hear his rapid heartbeat. She could smell him: his painful, familiar, unbearable scent.

Octavia would be able to smell him too. Octavia would know his scent instantly—it was impossible to disguise.

She slipped silently across the kitchen and pressed herself into the shadows beside Casey. His pupils flared; his lips parted as if to say something, but she shook her head.

Her hearing right now was keen enough to pick up Del's voice in the hall outside the kitchen. That proximity meant Octavia was close.

Too close.

They weren't going to make it out to the van in time.

Silently, unbreathing, she nudged Casey deeper into the shadows. Just here, in the back of the kitchen, there was a door—she remembered it, from all those years ago with Del.

She opened it. And then she pulled him down the stairs into the darkness.

•••

When he'd gotten Sophronia's SOS, he'd lost time.

He couldn't quite remember what he'd said to his team, what urgent words had crossed his lips. All he could think was that they were his people, and he'd brought them out here to this beautiful, treacherous place, and he could not, *could not* let them get hurt.

When he'd heard the van's engine start, relief had pulsed through him, so strong his head spun. *They're safe*, he'd thought. *Thank Christ—they're all right.*

And then Sophronia had come back, her face like marble and her eyes hot and blue.

She'd come back for him.

He didn't know what to do with that fact or with the strange flame it sparked in his chest.

He let her lead him silently down a set of stairs he hadn't known existed. Tiny golden lights, dim and flickering, were tucked into walls around them. It was a tunnel, designed to look rough hewn, as though it had been cut straight into the sandstone. Slowly, it dawned on him that this was where the Fornax vineyard's wine was stored: casks and barrels left to age deep in this cool subterranean space.

At the base of the stairs, they stopped, positioning themselves behind a shelf of rock where the shadows were deepest. He opened his mouth to speak, but Sophronia cut him off.

She leaned closer to him, her hand on his shoulder, her mouth at his ear. She breathed her next words almost soundlessly. "Octavia's in the kitchen. She can't know you're here."

He felt—

God. His heart was still pounding, but his body didn't seem to know the difference between fear and relief and his sudden physical awareness of her.

Her lips—her breath on his ear—

He put his hand on her waist. Felt her sharp inhale as he did.

It was impossible not to be transfixed by the contrasts of her: the taut muscular power of her body, the fluttering beat of her pulse at her neck.

"It's okay," he murmured. He moved his mouth closer to her ear and shaped his lips around the words, letting them free as softly as she had. Softer. "We're okay."

There was a tiny pause, a moment of hesitation. And then, to his surprise, her fingers fisted in the fabric at his shoulder, a sudden clutch that drew him nearer. That brought them face-to-face.

This close, he could smell her faint perfume. She smelled like . . . like redwoods after the rain, wet bark and thick leaves and shade.

She looked down at his hand, spread wide across her waist. And then she lifted her eyes to his.

In the dim gold light, he could see that her eyes had gone unfocused, her pupils huge. Her lips were a darker purple than he'd ever seen them, almost indigo.

And Casey realized with a strange heady thrill that he knew what that color meant on a vampire's mouth.

She was hungry. She needed to feed.

He'd thought about it. God, he'd wondered about all of it—if she ever used Stokr. If she ever drank from humans.

What it would feel like if she drank from him.

His pulse throbbed in his ears.

Her lips parted. Her lashes dropped, and her gaze fell first to his mouth.

And then to his neck.

He could feel his blood beating, hot rhythmic throbs beneath his skin. He knew she'd be able to see it. To feel his heat. There was something riotous in his veins—yearning—a yank that pulled his body taut.

He wanted her. He wanted to feel her body, know that she was safe. Spread his hand across her belly and relish the cool-silk sensation of her skin.

He wanted to let her put her fangs to his neck and drink deep—wanted it with a wildness that surged in his belly and sang along his skin.

"Soph," he breathed.

She looked up. Her eyes were glassy; he could see the edges of her fangs. He could *feel* her body beneath his hands, tense with want, held back by the thin shell of her restraint.

His fingers bit into her waist, pulling her closer, and her lashes fluttered: up to his face and then back to his throat.

He tipped his head back.

Do it, he thought. *I want you to.*

In his pocket, his phone buzzed.

It felt like an electric shock. Sophronia gasped, and his head spun. His fingers slipped away from her body as she shrank away from him, pressing her shoulders against the tunnel's sandstone wall.

Jesus. *Jesus.*

He fumbled for his phone, his heart thudding. Sophronia

breathed in tiny, shallow pants, like she'd forgotten how to fill her lungs with air.

His fingers felt clumsy, his mind not altogether there. He squinted at his screen in the dim light and tried to peel his brain back from whatever precipice he'd just been ready to fling himself over.

George Chu

7:04 PM

Kitchen's clear. We're out back in the van. There's something you need to see.

He looked back up at Sophronia and kept his voice low. "George says we can come up."

Her eyes were closed, her lashes black against her cheeks. Her lips were still dark with blood hunger.

When she opened her eyes, her pupils were still blown wide. "He's right." Her voice sounded blurred at the edges. "They're gone. The kitchen's empty. I can hear—" She broke off. Looked down. "Go ahead. I need a minute."

"Soph—"

"Just." She took another shallow breath. "A minute. I'll be right behind you."

He looked at her—God, he wanted to look and look and . . .

More than look. He could still feel the span of her waist beneath his hand.

He swallowed and went back up alone. He took the stairs two at a time, and when he emerged into the kitchen's cool fluorescence, he felt briefly dazzled by the light.

The catering van was idling behind the building, and as

he stepped outside, the van door slid open. He ducked inside, and Rick peered back at him from the driver's seat. "Ready to go?"

Casey looked to George, whose face was bright with eagerness. "You found something? Already?"

"Oh yeah."

"Then we'll wait for Sophronia."

It was exactly a minute before she stepped out into the twilight—she was nothing if not precise. Her lips had faded to pink, and he knew she'd used the sixty seconds to find a cup of artificial blood to take the edge off her hunger.

He couldn't—

God. The ache that had risen in him when he'd held her in his arms was still there: shaky, needing.

He took off his glasses. Rubbed his hand across his mouth. He couldn't think about wanting her right now.

Impossible, when he looked at her, to think about anything else.

She slipped inside the van, her eyes on his face. "Is everything okay?"

He let George answer. The black sleeve of George's fake catering uniform fluttered as he held out the tablet in their direction.

"We looked at Octavia Pavo's phone first, like you asked us to." George's voice sounded anxious, and his hands were shaking, but he was certain of what he'd discovered. Dr. LeBlanc's program had worked exactly as well as Casey had known it would. "And we found something immediately. Octavia doesn't have the Stokr app installed on her phone, but listen to this. She accessed the Stokr database. Where the hemoenzymatic data is stored."

Sophronia leaned forward, her gaze skimming the tablet's

screen, which mirrored everything the Pillbugs had found on Octavia's device.

"When?" she asked. "Over the summer, when the app went down?"

"Not over the summer." George looked up. Met Casey's eyes: nervous and exultant at once. "Yesterday."

CHAPTER 12

Sophronia had six minutes to get to her father's office, or else she was going to be late to the meeting she'd scheduled with his admin.

Six minutes. The elevator would eat up at least two and the walk down the hall a third—which meant she had a hundred and eighty seconds to stare at her reflection in the fifteenth-floor restroom.

One hundred eighty seconds left to *get her shit together.*

Three days ago, she'd almost put her fangs in Casey's neck. She couldn't stop reliving it: her body pressed against the solid wall of his chest—his hand spread wide across her ribs—his voice murmuring in her ear: *We're okay.*

She was not accustomed to relying on anyone's strength but her own.

The temptation had been instantaneous. Overwhelming. She'd wanted to lean into him, to let him hold her. She'd wanted to feel his hands on her skin, hot where she was cool.

She'd wanted to drink. Desperately, single-mindedly—her thoughts had been saturated in wine-drenched plums and smoky caramel and that tiny hint of wild green vines. She'd felt uninhibited and ravenous, her throat burning, her belly tight.

He'd turned his head. She'd seen his pulse throbbing in his neck, and she'd thought: *He wants this too.*

She had almost, almost done it.

She took a luxurious white paper towel from the stack, ran it under the faucet, and pressed it to the back of her neck as she stared at her own face in the mirror. Her eyes looked bruised.

She hadn't been sleeping well. She'd started every day with a long, punishing run, hard enough to push the fear and recrimination from her mind.

But eventually she had to stop, lungs burning, sweat stinging her eyes—and everything came flooding back.

Direct feeding from a human was said to be almost ecstatically satisfying. It wasn't always part of a sexual act—sometimes vampires just wanted to eat—but between two willing adult partners, it often was. Intentionally or not, there was something erotic about the plunge, the suction, the vampire's pull and the human's slow willing surrender.

And humans liked it too. People said—

People said there was nothing like sex with your fangs in a human's neck. People said that sometimes humans came just from the pleasure of the bite.

But without Stokr—without hemoenzymatic matching—putting your fangs into a human's neck could kill them in minutes. She'd seen it happen.

It was the bite that was the problem. A vampire's stomach couldn't hold more than two or three pints of blood—it was virtually impossible to drink a human dry. But enzymes in vampire saliva thinned human blood catastrophically, removing its ability to clot and keeping the wound open.

She'd watched René's teeth break Izzy's skin, so fast and sudden none of them had been able to stop him.

She'd watched Izzy go cold before the paramedics had arrived.

It was why HemoCorp's hemoenzymatic analysis had the capacity to change the world. If Sophronia's saliva was a safe match for Casey's blood, she could drink from him without fear. When she pulled her fangs free, his skin would heal quickly beneath her tongue. He'd be left with nothing worse than lightheadedness and euphoria.

But if she'd taken blood from his neck and she *wasn't* a match—

He could've died right there in the tunnel.

She couldn't stop the old terrible memories from coming back, from transforming her nebulous fear into a visceral, crisp-edged nightmare: her shoes soaked and sticky with blood, her throat raw as she'd screamed for help.

They didn't have Stokr. She *could not* drink from Casey. Even if she'd wanted to check the data logs directly to see if they were a hemoenzymatic match—if Casey's blood was even *in* the database—she knew now from Dr. LeBlanc's program that Octavia had accessed the server. The data was compromised. She couldn't trust the hemoenzymatic pairs anymore.

She couldn't trust herself.

Her time was up. She had to go, or else she was going to be late, and her father hated tardiness. She rubbed the back of her hand across her mouth, crumpled up the paper towel, and threw it in the trash as she left.

The smoked-glass walls that surrounded her father's office were opaque, so he couldn't see her coming. She had to wait for his admin to call him, then wait longer for him to unlock the door and let her in.

His office looked a lot like her own. Fidelia Vega had favored antiques—refined Georgian lines, rosewood and polished ebony. But Sophronia and her father tended toward clean, spare interiors: glass and light and the shimmering expanse of the ocean outside.

She didn't know . . .

Sometimes it was hard to know what things she cared about for their own sake and what she loved simply because her father had loved them first.

August Vega sat behind his desk. He didn't say anything when she came in, only inclined his head in the direction of a chair.

She took it. She moistened her lips, locked her fingers together in her lap, and sat forward. "I'm sorry for leaving the summit so abruptly. It was—"

The rhythm of Octavia's footsteps above their heads, Casey's hand on her waist, his scent, his scent, his—

"—an emergency."

Her father raised his brows. "I trust you have the matter under control."

Abraham's eyeteeth, she'd never felt less in control in her life.

She gritted her teeth. "It's about Stokr. That's why I scheduled this meeting with you."

"About Stokr?" He paused, surveying her. His eyes were a clear, pale blue—lighter than hers. He'd been forty-seven when she was born, and now, at seventy-seven, his hair had faded almost to pure white. But vampire strength belied external appearances—he could crack the marble of his desk with a single well-aimed blow. "I understood from your comments at the summit that the Stokr division was in the process of a complete rebuilding."

"It is. It—" She broke off. She'd rehearsed this, plenty of times, and still she found it hard to push the words past her lips. "I brought in a forensic analyst to look into what happened over the summer. A Caltech PhD—someone smart and unbiased."

"And what did she discover?"

"I don't know," Sophronia said. "She's dead."

There was a cool space between them: a palpable hush, like a wall of ice.

"Explain," her father said.

She knotted her fingers harder together and did what he'd asked. In careful words, she told him about the analyst's death, her own recent work with the Pillbugs, and what they'd uncovered at the Fornax vineyard.

It was a calculated risk. Despite the evidence of Octavia's intrusion into the database, they couldn't be certain she was the Stokr saboteur. It was still possible that her father was behind everything that had happened.

But she'd never believed her father had anything to do with the Stokr sabotage. And she needed him.

He was the only person who could have Octavia removed from her position at HemoCorp.

Sophronia had spent three sleepless nights debating with herself about whether confessing everything to August Vega was the right next step. She'd even, in a moment of weakness, pulled out her phone to call Del and ask for her opinion.

But she'd thought better of it—had gritted her teeth and set the phone carefully back on her nightstand.

If she was wrong about her father, then the guilt would be hers and hers alone. She didn't want Del to know the crushing weight of failure.

She took a measured breath and brought her recital to a close. "What happened to Stokr wasn't just a glitch. Someone—most likely Octavia—took it down intentionally."

Her father hadn't said a word. He had always been sparing with his speech. Fidelia's lectures—*You continue to disappoint us, Sophronia*—had forever gone uninterrupted.

"I see," he said finally. "And your evidence for this accusation is—what? That she accessed the Stokr database a few days ago from her phone?"

"That's right."

"But you cannot say what she did with that access? What information she might have attempted to procure?"

"No. The spyware program doesn't show that level of granular detail. But she had no reason to be there at all. Stokr isn't hers."

"To be sure." Her father paused. Laid his hands on the table. "I begin to think it shouldn't be yours either."

She paused. Blinked. "I'm sorry?"

"I've been considering this for some time. I'd like to move you out of Digital Products and Solutions. Perhaps into Global Affairs with Circinus."

Her heart couldn't remember how to beat correctly. It had stopped at his words, and now it began again in dizzy fits and starts, punching double time against her ribs. "You want to take Stokr away from me?"

"Sophronia." He turned his hands over on the table, palms up. Almost an appeal. "Before this Stokr fiasco, you were thriving here at HemoCorp. You're very good at what you do."

Her lips parted.

"But since this summer," he went on, "you've buried yourself in a project that has no discernible end game. You have no evidence against Octavia, only a vendetta."

"I don't have a *vendetta*. I—"

"Sophronia."

Her name in his quiet voice silenced her. She sucked in a

breath and tried to slow her heart. Tried—desperate and frantic—to stop *feeling*.

"You cannot let yourself become overcommitted to any one project," August said. "You have to be flexible. Agile. I know you can be ruthless when you need to be, and this is an opportunity to exercise that skill. For the good of the company, you have to learn to let things go."

She took another breath before she spoke. The air was cool in her nose; her father's office smelled papery and clean. "I can't just let Stokr go. There are people involved. My employees—"

"Can find other positions. You can cover their transition services, if you like."

"But Stokr—"

"Is a dating app. An interesting use of HemoCorp technology, to be sure. But not a profound loss."

She felt frozen. Struck by a sudden ice-edged terror: She was going to cry in front of her father.

She bit down hard—harder—until her fangs dug into her lower lip and pain distracted her from the sting at the backs of her eyes.

Stokr *was* a loss. To her, it was.

"You seem unhappy," her father said. "Let me talk to Circinus. We'll find you a place there. Another VP position—a lateral move."

"I don't—"

"This is a good thing, Sophronia. It's important for you to engage in as many different divisions of the company as you can."

His hands were still open on the desk. It was strange to look at them—the tapered elegance of his fingers, the blue veins beneath his thinning skin.

Looking at her father's hands felt like some strange double vision. She could remember the way his hands had looked when she was a child: deft and powerful. A memory so vital that it almost overwrote the evidence of her eyes.

Her father was strong, like all elder vampires, but he wasn't immortal.

He couldn't run the company forever.

Someday, he was telling her, *HemoCorp will be yours.*

"Take some time to consider," her father said. "You'd be excellent in Global Affairs. Smart, efficient. Better than Circinus. Let's meet again before the end of the fiscal year."

Let's meet again before the end of the fiscal year.

They would, of course. She'd schedule it with his admin.

She thought, absurdly, of Monopoly. Of handmade pottery, and Del's bare feet, and the way the word *family* had shifted in her head, complicated and radiant and painful—like learning a new definition for something you'd always thought you'd understood.

She swallowed once before she stood. "I'll think about it."

"Good. And, Sophronia?"

She paused at the door. "Yes?"

"Don't antagonize Octavia. It's in your best interest to leave her alone."

She nodded once and left the office.

She couldn't make herself smile at the junior employees in the hall. They shied back a little at the expression on her face.

Queen of the Damned.

It was, she supposed, who she was.

There had been no family dinner, no vampire gathering or HemoCorp event, that hadn't begun and ended with a reminder from her mother that Sophronia was the Vega heir.

That any crack in her composure was an embarrassment, that any hint of weakness would be blood in the water for their enemies.

Her father had always been more restrained. She could count on one hand the number of times in her life that he'd told her exactly what he wanted her to do.

But he'd told her today. He wanted her to drop the investigation, move on from Stokr, let the app remain shuttered. For the good of HemoCorp.

Her stomach churned. She felt her jaw pop and realized she was gritting her teeth almost hard enough for her fangs to puncture her skin.

Would it be better if she stopped investigating the Stokr sabotage?

She wanted answers. She wanted *justice*, damn it. But then again—

There was no way she could tell herself that she'd made the Pillbugs safer, not after the escapade at the summit. She hated to quit—absolutely loathed the idea of giving up. But maybe it *would* be for the best. Now that the app was shuttered, maybe whoever had sabotaged Stokr had gotten what they wanted.

She thought of Casey in the wine cave, Octavia a handful of feet away. His luscious, wild scent, as easily recognizable as his face.

She'd brought him into Octavia's office. She'd taken him to the Fornax vineyard. She'd told herself she needed his help to stop a cold-blooded murderer, but in the end, *she* was the one who could've killed him.

It was only when she heard the familiar rhythm of his heart that she realized she'd gotten off the elevator at the wrong floor.

She'd meant to go to her own office. But instead, she was standing outside his, staring at her own reflection in the smoked glass.

She knew he was inside. She could tell from the sound of his heartbeat that he was there and that the rest of the Pill-bugs weren't.

She stared at the door for a long moment and then pulled out her phone. Found her brief, professional text chain with Casey and typed: Are you busy?

She regretted it the second she hit send.

Maybe he wouldn't answer. Maybe he wouldn't even see her text. Maybe he was in the middle of a very important computer thing that required all his attention, and before he finished she could somehow drive to UC Incarnare, find Dr. LeBlanc, and get the professor to hack his phone and remove all traces of any text messages Sophronia had sent, ever, in her entire life.

Unfortunately, his response was almost instantaneous. Nothing I can't put on hold. Everything ok?

She didn't know how to answer. She didn't know why she was even *here*.

Are you in your office? she typed, which seemed considerably less creepy than *I'm standing outside your door listening to your heartbeat. Do you mind if I come in?*

Yeah, he said. Meet me here?

Be there in 5, she sent and then stood in front of the glass, feeling ludicrous, for four minutes and fifty-nine seconds.

He opened the door before she could, and when he saw her, idling in front of the glass, he smiled.

He was so . . . he was *so* . . .

She scowled at him. "Shut the door."

He was still smiling as he closed it behind them. "We can

talk in here," he said, once they were concealed. "At least, I'm pretty sure we can. Dr. LeBlanc and Mercedes spent about an hour testing something out this morning, and now Mer says the security feed is looped until"—he checked his watch—"forty minutes from now, I think. They said they could do longer, but I thought people might start to wonder why none of us had moved."

"Where are they?"

"The Pillbugs?" His gaze flickered across their desks in the shared space: Brendan's spider plant, George's stack of hand-calligraphed wedding invitations, Mercedes's haphazard array of colorful mugs and bat-shaped stress balls. "They said they were going to the canteen, but to tell you the truth, I think they might be trying to steal back Rick Tickle's van. George said he thinks better in there."

She *hated* how this human slipped beneath her defenses. The way he made her feel like it was okay to laugh.

"Do you think this is a mistake?" Her voice was abrupt. Terse. She hadn't even realized she was going to say it.

He stepped a little closer to her. "I think kidnapping Rick Tickle and stealing his van is a mistake, yeah." His eyes were soft. "I'm guessing that's not what you meant."

"All of this." She was clutching the edge of one of the desks, and she made herself loosen her grip before she cracked it. "This investigation. Do you think it would be better if we left Stokr shut down?"

Only the subtle tightening of his shoulders told her that she'd caught him by surprise. "I don't think that would be better. No."

"But maybe"—*I'm putting you in danger; my father's right; I have to be ruthless*—"the saboteur got what they wanted. Maybe by drawing all of this out, we're only prolonging the risk. Maybe if we left Stokr alone, we could move on from this, and nobody else would get hurt."

"Soph," he said. "Whoever did this *killed* your analyst."

"You think I don't know that? Do you think I've forgotten the way—the way she—"

He put his hand over hers on the desk, and as he did, his breath hissed through his teeth. "Jesus. Your skin's like ice. Are you all right? What happened?"

She yanked her hand free. "Nothing happened." And then—oh for Abraham's sake, what was it about this human that made her lose her mind—she heard herself say, "I met with my father."

He took her hand back. Held it, gently, between his warm, callused palms. "You told him what we found? About Octavia?"

"He told me to leave it alone."

"Soph." His thumb brushed against the bones of her wrist. "We can't leave it alone."

"I keep thinking maybe Stokr . . ." She looked at his fingers enveloping hers. Let herself, just once, breathe deep. "Maybe all of this was a mistake."

"It's not a mistake. Listen—let's say you're right and Octavia was the one who sabotaged Stokr. That still doesn't explain why she was in the database four days ago. We don't know what she's after. If her end game was to take down the app, then why is she still accessing the hemoenzymatic data? There's something more going on here. And no one at HemoCorp is safe until we know what it is."

He made it sound simple. Awful, exasperating *human*—he made impossibilities feel easy.

She gritted her teeth and looked down at their hands. "I don't want your people to get hurt."

"I know." His thumb pushed into the center of her palm. "We won't let them."

Her chest ached. His hands were so warm, and he was so close, and she felt it again—the terrible, heady temptation to lean into his strength.

And then the door came open.

She yanked her hand out of his grasp and leapt backward. Because she was a vampire, she didn't trip—instead, she launched herself across the room and pressed her back against a wall before the Pillbugs at the door could open their mouths.

Which, obviously, made her look extremely guilty. They probably thought the Vega heir had been about to eat their boss.

Which was great. Excellent. She hated *everything*.

"Uh," Brendan said. "Hi."

George grinned blissfully at her. "Oh good. Now I don't have to have Casey text you from the Flying Sausage."

Her heart was still beating too hard as she looked at the junior engineer. "Did you find something?"

"A lot," Mercedes said. "And not enough. Get Del to meet us there, and we'll explain everything."

CHAPTER 13

"You can squirt it directly in your mouth," Brendan said helpfully.

Mercedes choked on her coffee. Casey rubbed his hand across his mouth and tried not to laugh.

Del, who'd ordered an entire can of Reddi-wip and had been dubiously pondering its steely underside, looked up. Her green eyes gleamed. "I don't know why I didn't think of that." She turned to Sophronia. "Open up. I'll do you first."

"I will disembowel you," Sophronia said.

Casey gave up on suppressing his laughter and nudged an empty, vaguely-UFO-shaped dish in Del's direction. "You can put it in here and eat it with a spoon. Also"—he indicated the glass pillar beside her—"that's granulated sugar in there. In case the whipped cream isn't enough."

Del closed her eyes and sighed. "I love human restaurants."

The first time they'd gone to the Flying Sausage, Sophronia had looked almost as guarded and out of place as she had at Reverse Cowgirls. She'd watched Del slide into the silvery booth like she was trying to memorize the action for a test. It had taken Del a good hour of persuasion to get her to taste the whipped cream, and only a visible flare of her pupils had suggested how much she'd liked it.

But by now she looked, if not quite like one of them, then not on the outside either. She was sandwiched in between Del and George, her hands wrapped around a hot cup of terrible coffee that Casey knew she wouldn't drink. Her bangs had gotten windblown on the walk to the diner, and she looked less like the Vega heir when she was mussed. More like one of them. More . . .

He stifled whatever word his brain had been trying to supply, which seemed to be *touchable* or possibly *sweet*.

God help him, he was soft over her. It had been impossible not to take her hand in his office, not with that stricken expression peeking out behind the implacable chill of her eyes.

He liked her stern competence, her ferocious sense of right and wrong. And he liked this, too: the hints of *her* beneath the cool-glass surface. The way she trusted him enough to let him see.

He realized he was watching her hands around the mug—wondering if they were warmer now—and made himself stop.

He turned to Mercedes. "What did you guys find?"

Her face lit up. She peered behind her, but the Flying Sausage was as empty as ever. Still, she lowered her voice. "A lot. Maybe too much? We divided up the data from the phones at the summit, and we've been running a bunch of different analyses. No one's been into the Stokr server since Octavia four days ago, but there was other stuff that leapt out at us. Other people."

"Kriti Pillai," George said. "She's the human who's been on the executive committee the longest, right?"

Sophronia nodded.

"I asked Allen to look into Kriti's financial portfolio"—he gave a slightly guilty wince—"because she's been using a *lot* of personal finance apps on her own device during work hours. He said she's restructuring her holdings or something? Liquidating her assets. For whatever reason, she seems to think she's going to need a lot of cash on hand. Soon."

Casey felt his brows rise. "Suspicious."

"Also," Brendan added, "we figured out from his call logs that Circinus Ossian, in Global Affairs, is in the middle of a divorce."

Del's mouth dropped open. "That's . . . what? Vampires don't get divorced."

Brendan shrugged. "Apparently they do."

"Abraham's balls," Del said. "Good for him, honestly. Too many high-profile vampire couples sticking it out for the sake of the dynasty, even though they hate each other."

She deliberately didn't look at Sophronia as she said it.

"That *is* interesting," Sophronia said. "My father . . ."

She trailed off. Casey realized he'd tensed.

"He offered me a position in Global Affairs," she said finally. "I wonder if he knows what's going on with Circinus. Maybe he thinks Circinus needs help."

Del made a face. "Circinus is going to be a pariah in some vampire circles when this news gets out. Would your dad fire him over it, do you think? Reputation is everything to . . . some vampires."

Sophronia shook her head. "I don't think so. He specifically said that he'd talk to Circinus about finding a place for me. It didn't sound like he planned to force Circinus out."

"But," Casey said, "Circinus doesn't know that. Maybe he thinks he needs some inside pull at HemoCorp because he's afraid of losing his job. If he controls whether Stokr is functional, that could give him some leverage over you and your father."

"Maybe." Sophronia put down the mug, rubbing absently at a tiny smudge across the words MAY THE FORCE BE WITH BREW. "But we don't have anything concrete. You couldn't find any traces of Stokr-server access on the devices? No one's tried to get into the database again?"

Mercedes drummed her fingers on the table. "No. But, uh . . . we did have one idea."

Sophronia leaned forward. "What is it?"

"Okay, so we've been cross-referencing everybody's work calendars—thanks for giving us that access by the way, super useful—and it looks like Octavia, Circinus, and several other exec-level vampires are all going to be at the same event next week. Not at HemoCorp."

"What event?" Casey asked.

"A really fancy fundraiser." Mercedes shot a single hasty glance in Casey's direction and then hurried onward. "Some celebrities going, lots of rich vamps. We're thinking we go to the site early, maybe pose as waitstaff, and then circulate a rumor that Stokr has come back online."

"You know how much I hate this kind of thing," George said, "but I think Mer's right. It's kind of perfect. If our bad guy hears that Stokr's back online, there's a good chance they'll dip into the server to see what's going on. And since they're not at HemoCorp, they'll have to do it on their personal devices."

Mercedes grinned. "Which, obviously, we have access to."

"Oh Abraham," Del said. "I *love* it. Could we . . . what if we got there early? Maybe we could plant a few recording devices in key locations?" She gave a low whistle through her fangs and turned to Sophronia, face alight. "Your dad will have to kick Octavia out if you have a sound file of her mid-freak-out because her sabotage has been unsabotaged."

Casey felt his mouth tug up at the expression on Del's face. In their planning meetings the last few weeks, no one, not even Mercedes, had been as enthusiastic about the possibility of covert ops as Del.

Sophronia looked taut, predatorily alert—but she'd been won over by the idea too. Casey could tell. "It's better than sitting around waiting for the other shoe to drop. This way, we control the narrative. Put our saboteur on her back foot for once." Her sharp gaze found Mercedes. "What kind of event is it? How do we get inside?"

"Grappling hooks?" Del offered. "Or—I saw this thing on the news about using an angle grinder to cut through plate glass—"

"I, uh," George said, "don't think that's going to be necessary."

Sophronia fixed him with a cool blue stare. "Why not?"

"So here's the thing," Brendan said. "The event is a two-thousand-dollar-a-plate benefit, and it's already sold out. But I'm pretty sure we can just walk right on in."

"What? Why?"

Mercedes darted another look at Casey. "It's a film foundation. In Parce Domine."

He set down his mug on a sudden, deeply unfortunate intuition.

"That sounds fun," Del said. "Glam. Can I raid your closet, Soph?"

"You are seven inches shorter than me." Sophronia was looking intently from Mercedes to Casey and back again. "Why are you so confident we can waltz straight in?"

"Because," Mercedes said, "it's the Greenbrier Foundation."

Casey took off his glasses and pinched the bridge of his nose. "Oh hell."

The Greenbrier Foundation was a well-known arts nonprofit in Northern California, devoted to the preservation and restoration of classic film. Their star-studded events raised hundreds of thousands of dollars every year to support museum archival projects and to recover lost and damaged work by underrepresented filmmakers.

They'd been a regular part of Casey's childhood, those $2,000-a-plate dinners—because his grandmother was on the Greenbrier Foundation board of directors.

"Nonna Amato can get us in to the benefit," Mercedes said cheerfully. "She can probably find us a secret hideout and waitstaff outfits too. She'll love it."

Casey mumbled something he wouldn't have said in front of Nonna.

The worst part was, she probably *would* love it. A clandestine caper that involved her grandson in a tux, with the most beautiful vampire in the entire world on his arm?

"Oh God," he muttered and put his glasses back on. "All right. How long did you say we have? A week?"

Mercedes was visibly smothering her amusement now. His whole team had met Nonna, and as a general rule they seemed to relish her ruthless torture of their lead engineer. "You've got it."

"I'll drive up this weekend then. I'll explain the situation to Nonna"—*somehow*—"and find a way to get us into the benefit."

"I don't understand," Del protested. "Your grandmother works for the Greenbrier Foundation?"

"Sort of. It's . . . a long story."

Beside Del, Sophronia set down her mug. She straightened the edge of her knife so that it lay exactly parallel with her spoon and didn't glance up when she said, "How long does it take to get to your grandmother's house?"

"Two hours or so, depending on traffic. Why?"

But as he looked at her, he realized he already knew why she was asking. He knew her now: strong and delicate at once, guarded and intense and fiercely protective.

If there was information hidden, she wanted it revealed. If there was a chance that someone new might be drawn into their small, dangerous inner circle, then she was going to want to be there to make sure that person was safe.

He already knew what she was going to say.

"Enough time for a long story, then." She looked up and met his gaze: windblown bangs and tense mouth and cool blue eyes. "I'm coming with you."

CHAPTER 14

They were going to die on the way to Parce Domine. Two hours in Casey's ancient sedan was exactly two hours too many, and Sophronia had spent the past week repeatedly regretting the fact that she'd accepted his offer to drive. *She* should've driven; her car had a backup camera and power windows and never seemed to smoke slightly when she got above fifty-five.

She ran her fingers gently over the seat belt as she slid into the passenger seat. It was perfect. Seamless. She'd seen the pictures the car restorer had sent her from the HemoCorp parking garage—she'd *known* it was fine.

But she'd wanted to see it for herself.

His gaze settled on her fingers, cautiously testing the fabric, and he smiled at her, so damn fond, like he knew she'd had it restored.

Like he knew that was the reason she'd agreed to let him drive.

She scowled at him until he turned back to the road, his mouth still set in that expression she knew by heart.

Deliberately, she removed her gaze from his face and glanced behind his seat at the plastic bag he'd resettled from the front to the back when she'd gotten into the car. The sack had the name of a local liquor store emblazoned on the side, which seemed a little concerning for eleven o'clock in the morning.

She recognized the whiskey bottle, just visible through the plastic. And . . .

"Sour . . . mix?"

The back of Casey's neck went pink as he engaged his turn signal. She'd forgotten—intentionally erased from her mind, maybe—how maddening his scent was in the car like this. She'd *just* eaten, and still, her stomach flipped.

"It's my grandmother's favorite," he said. "The mix specifically."

She gazed dubiously at the bag. "I've never heard of that."

He rubbed his hand across his mouth—to hide, she suspected, that terrible smile. "God, she's going to love you."

It felt like a shock of cold water.

Sophronia had dated before. Several carefully selected male vampires from families her mother had approved of. Once, disastrously, at Holbeck Priest.

This wasn't the same. Casey wasn't bringing her home to meet his family—this was professional; it was *work*. And still, her chest felt tight. Crushing.

She's going to love you, he'd said. Like it was easy.

She'd started to bounce her foot, the sole of her shoe slapping against her heel. She made herself stop. "That's not my primary concern."

He *was* smiling, because he was a monster. "I don't think there's much you can do about it. There's really no stopping Nonna once she gets going."

"You mentioned that her relationship with the Greenbrier Foundation is . . . complicated?"

He nudged at his glasses and kept his eyes on the road.

"I—well, not really, I guess. She's—" He paused. "Have you ever heard of Lola Lovell?"

The name seemed vaguely familiar. "The actress?"

"Yeah. A human actress in the '60s."

In its earliest days, film had been dominated by vampires. Vampires were tall and graceful and excellent at dancing, and no one had loved the stage like Abraham Stoker. But plenty of humans had found their way on screen as well, especially after the middle of the century. Sophronia could call Lola Lovell to mind, if somewhat fuzzily: strong features, a pile of curly dark hair, a liveliness and energy that fairly crackled onscreen. She'd been a major Hollywood star until she'd married a director and retired at the height of her popularity.

"I recall her," Sophronia said.

"Well." Casey adjusted his glasses again. "That's Nonna."

Sophronia blinked. "I'm sorry?"

"Nonna—my grandmother. Her name is Dolores Amato, but her stage name was Lola Lovell."

She stared at him. She could see it, kind of—the height, the hair, the easy long-limbed grace—but at the same time she absolutely could not. Casey was quiet in his confidence. He *blushed*.

On the other hand, Sophronia was fairly certain Lola Lovell had posed nude on a French beach. She'd fallen off a horse playing polo with a British prince and once, famously, punched an insolent reporter in the mouth.

"Ah," she managed.

"Yeah." His neck was still pink. "She's on the Greenbrier board. She's passionate about the golden age of cinema, and she's *really* invested in supporting young female directors. I'm pretty sure she raises about eighty percent of their funds herself, when she gets her Rolodex out and starts making calls. She's like a tidal wave. You can't really stop her."

Sophronia's imagination, which had filled in the picture of this visit with cookies and lemonade and other grandmotherly things vaguely drawn from human sitcoms, began to build a new vision around whiskey sours and high-waisted bikini bottoms. "You're . . . close?"

"Yeah." His smile was still there. Softer now. "Yeah, we're really close. She raised me after my parents died."

Her fingers passed over the seat belt again, carefully, cautiously. She couldn't even feel the seam of the repair. She'd expected it to leave a mark. "You were a child?"

"Not really. Fifteen." He slanted a glance at her. "You?"

She pressed her tongue to the tip of her fang. "I was twenty."

It was . . . nice that he'd asked. He could look it up easily enough—the death of the Vega matriarch from a rare vampire illness had made national headlines. It had seemed impossible: the press, the news cameras. She'd kept on looking up the stories on her laptop, as if seeing it in black and white might make her mother's death feel real.

The morning sun made strands of Casey's hair gleam red, like bits of flame. "That's a tough age."

"I don't think any age is easy."

Her voice had come out sharp, but he didn't scare easily, this human. He kept his hands on the wheel, that faint, soft curve still touching his mouth. "No," he said. "You're right. But still, twenty seems hard. You're just figuring out who you are as an adult, and then you have to do it all over again without them."

She ran her fingers along the seat belt. Pressed her other palm against her knee.

"Tell me something about her," he said suddenly. "Something that wasn't in the news."

She looked over at him, but his eyes were on the road. And that made it easier, somehow.

"I bought her perfume once."

As soon as the words left Sophronia's mouth, embarrassment struck her, an awful, uncomfortable warmth. She didn't even know why the words had leapt to her mouth.

Only . . . maybe she did know. She still had the bottle on the corner of her vanity. It had been there so long, she'd almost stopped seeing it.

But as she'd crossed to her closet that morning, the sun had caught on the faceted glass, tossing rainbow spangles across her bedroom wall.

She'd looked at the bottle as she'd dressed to go meet Casey's grandmother.

She'd remembered.

"I was little," she said. "Probably seven or eight." It was loud on the freeway, a muffled roar of wind and passing cars. She could almost pretend he couldn't hear her. "Titus took me shopping—it was my mother's birthday, and she and my father were out. The bottle was made of the prettiest pink crystal. I thought . . ."

Out the window, the sky was blue and cloudless; the sun was bright enough to make her eyes burn.

She could remember how proud she'd felt when Titus had dropped her back off at the house. He'd had the perfume gift wrapped; the ribbon had been gold, and the whole thing had smelled of lilac and sun and snow.

She cleared her throat and went on. "It was some cheap thing. I realized that later. Some department store scent she never would've worn. I don't know why Titus even let me get it. I guess he never would've . . ."

She broke off.

Fidelia hadn't wanted the perfume. It hadn't been up to her standards, even then. Sophronia had realized her mistake instantly, the moment her mother had seen the gaudy gilt department store paper and reached out to take it between finger and thumb.

But Titus . . .

He was the kind of vampire who put messy tempera paintings from his granddaughter on his $20,000 refrigerator. It wasn't his fault that he hadn't understood.

Casey reached out and captured her hand in his. "Soph," he said softly.

"No, it's—" She shook her head, trying to make him understand. "It's not about that day. She never brought it up, and neither did I. I just tried to do better the next year. But after she died . . ." She cleared her throat again. "After she died, I found the bottle with her things."

It made her feel fragile—unlike herself—to think about that perfume, wrapped in tissue and set in a drawer.

"All that time," she said, "I didn't realize she'd kept it."

Sophronia had never really known what had driven her mother. Vampire families like theirs were accustomed to conflict, to the constant struggle for power. The Vegas had been at the top for decades, and Fidelia had wanted to keep it that way.

Had it been a desire for power? Or—as Sophronia sometimes wanted to believe—a bone-deep need to keep her daughter safe?

Both, she'd thought that morning, as the sun glanced iridescent off the crystal that her mother had kept.

It could have been both.

Casey still had his fingers wrapped around hers. He had a pale white scar across his knuckles—long healed.

"And you?" she said. "Your parents? What were they like?"

His thumb skated across her skin, warm and fleeting. There was a smile tucked into his voice when he spoke. "When we get to Nonna's house, I'll show you."

•••

Dolores Amato's bungalow was a mid-century architectural jewel box, nestled into a hillside and surrounded by spilling green ferns and ruby bromeliads. The steps up to the front door were worn smooth with age, and before they went inside, Sophronia looked over at Casey. He had the liquor bag in one hand and the door knocker in the other.

He smiled at her—easy and crooked, all confidence in the corner of his mouth. "You've got this."

She glared at him. Ridiculous, unbearable human. He . . .

What would make him think she'd been worried? They were here for *work*. This wasn't—*she* wasn't—

She was so flustered that she couldn't come up with anything to say before Lola opened the door.

Casey's grandmother was somehow even more than everything Sophronia had expected. She had to be close to six feet tall, and her hair was an unlikely jet black, trimmed into a curly pixie cut. She was dressed in a plunging teal jumpsuit, and her arms jangled with bracelets.

"Come in," she said, "come in, come in—oh good, Casey, my sour mix." She peered into the bag. "And those chili-lime chips I like! Good boy."

He was grinning down at her. "Hi, Nonna."

"Hello, baby." Her eyes fastened on Sophronia. "And you

must be Ms. Vega. My, my. Casey has told me so much about you, and yet I can't help but feel he's left out everything I need to know."

Casey blushed, unfortunately. Sophronia felt her knees wobble.

"This is Sophronia Vega, yes. One of the VPs. At my *job*." He said it in a vaguely chastening tone, which Lola did not acknowledge in any way. "Sophronia, my grandmother Dolores."

"Thank you so much for letting us stop by, Ms. Amato."

"Call me Lola." She gave a little breezy wave. "Or have a couple of whiskey sours and call me Grammy. I don't mind."

"That's—" Casey said. "Uh. You don't have to—"

Lola laughed. "Stop standing on the doorstep, or the neighbors will think I forgot to invite you in. Shirley down the street already told Una that I'm too old to host mah-jongg night. I don't need to give her any more ammunition."

"Shirley's going to regret that when she's iced out of celebrity-memoir book club."

"Trust me, precious—she already does."

Lola led them both into the house. It was filled with light and sun and lush plants—huge windows lit the creamy walls and wood trim. The hallway was crowded with pictures, and to Sophronia's amusement, a good two-thirds of them were of Lola herself, on red carpets and embracing presidents and slathered with some glistening oil on a beach that looked like the French Riviera.

Some of the pictures—Sophronia slowed helplessly—were of Casey.

He followed her gaze. He must have been six or so in the photo she'd stopped in front of, sandwiched between a lanky man with a familiar head of curls and an exquisitely beautiful woman in a long, straight skirt. They were on the boardwalk; she could see the roller coaster in the background. There was a shy smile on his little-boy face and a smear of something pink on his cheek.

"That's them," he said. "My dad, Michael—he was a film professor. My mom was an engineer, and then she had me and got really into homesteading. She kept goats." He laughed softly. "God, she fucking loved those goats."

Lola had paused at the entrance to the kitchen. "I must've told Rachel a thousand times that they'd eat her out of house and home, and what did they do? Ate her *hair.*" She shuddered. "Worse than rats. Worse than a *horse.*"

Casey laughed again. "They didn't eat her hair, Nonna. I think she cut it."

"Because they were constantly chewing it! I remember."

He grinned at Sophronia. "She remembers everything. It's the worst."

There was something so—

Lovely. Unbearable and lovely, the way they were together. The ease with which they spoke of the ones they'd lost—Lola's son, Casey's dad. The soft familiarity of the memory, like a coin gone smooth at the edges.

She didn't know how to guard against the sudden desire to weep.

Lola brought them into her big sunny kitchen, where she'd put out a tray of olives and cheese and, incongruously, a little glass cup filled to the brim with jelly beans.

She took Casey's bag out of his hands and started to mix up drinks. The bracelets on her arms winked in the sunlight, and the crystal glasses she pulled out of her counter were exactly the same ones the Vega family had in their house.

She grinned at them both. "Drink?"

"It's 1:00 p.m., Nonna, and I've got to drive us back to Incarnare."

"Hmm," she said and plunked a glass in front of him. "We'll see."

She looked at Sophronia, who shook her head. "No, thank you."

Lola took her own glass in one hand and picked up the jelly beans in the other. She set them in front of Sophronia. "Please. Have these, at least. I won't eat them."

Sophronia looked down at the jelly beans. "Oh. Thank you. I—"

"Casey said this sort of thing is your favorite."

Sophronia blinked.

Casey took off his glasses. "Nonna." He pinched the bridge of his nose. "I'm not sure I—"

She cackled. "You *did.* How else would I have known to get them?" She pulled out one of the kitchen chairs and seated herself between Casey and Sophronia. "Now. As delighted as I am to see my favorite grandson and his extremely tall and beautiful colleague—"

"Nonna."

"—I understand you're here for a reason. Something about Greenbrier? How can I help?"

They'd discussed it all in the car—what Casey could tell his grandmother, what information wouldn't endanger her. She already knew about the Stokr disasters from the news; Casey had told Sophronia that Lola was a voracious consumer of TV media, despite being relatively fuzzy on the concept of apps.

Even so, Sophronia had to push back the protective instincts that sharpened her fangs and tightened the muscles of her thighs. Lola—for all her vibrant laugh and glittering, boundless energy—was eighty-four years old. A human.

Humans, Casey had said. *Not helpless.*

She tried to hold on to that.

When he was finished, he sat back in his chair, rotating the glass in one hand. "We're hoping you can get the two of us into the benefit early. We'll conceal recording devices in various locations throughout the facility and then circulate the rumors about Stokr going back online between the guests and the waitstaff. Meanwhile, our team will keep an eye on the suspects' devices and an ear on the bugs."

The Pillbugs had already planted several bugs in various likely locations throughout the HemoCorp building, although the ones in the executives' offices seemed to be put out of commission on a regular enough basis that Sophronia suspected someone was doing periodic sweeps of the whole C-suite. Their team had the expertise and materials and strategy—they just needed Lola to get them inside.

Sophronia hoped they wouldn't have to resort to Del's angle grinders.

"Hmm," Lola said and passed a hand across her mouth.

The familiarity of the gesture caught at something in Sophronia's chest and pulled tight.

Family. This was what it looked like.

"Let me think about it," Lola said finally. "It might be possible. I'll need some time to consider."

Rather than looking relieved, Casey set down the glass. "Nonna," he said warningly.

"What?" She grinned at him, all gleaming innocence, and then stood abruptly. "Oh my, is that someone at the door?"

She vanished, only to emerge moments later with a pair of women in tow. The two newcomers looked to be in their sixties or so; neither rivaled Lola for glamour, though the smaller, buttoned-up one did have a pair of rhinestone cat's-eye glasses magnifying her curly lashes.

They were both carrying grocery bags of food and looking slightly beleaguered.

"Mrs. Harrison," Casey said resignedly. "Dr. Harrison."

"Casey, beloved," said the bespectacled one, "how many times have I told you to call me Mindy?"

"*What* a coincidence," Lola said. "Mindy and Eve happened to pop by for dinner."

Casey looked over at Sophronia. *I'm so sorry*, he mouthed.

Lola thrust Casey's untouched whiskey sour into his hands. "Might as well have this! Eve, you want a whiskey sour too? Mindy, a double?"

"Of course." Mindy settled herself beside Casey. "I brought handmade manicotti. Isn't that your favorite?"

"Handmade by Whole Foods," Eve put in.

Sophronia didn't totally understand what was happening. "Manicotti?"

"It's pasta," he said. "Nonna—Mindy, I'm so grateful for the dinner, but we really have to get back to—"

Lola pinned him with an expression of earnest devastation. "You're not going to leave without eating, are you?"

"And your favorite meal too," Mindy said. "Who would've guessed that you'd be here?"

Casey looked helplessly over at Sophronia. "I guess—if you don't mind?"

"Of course she doesn't." Lola leaned over the butcher-block island and twinkled at them both. "Stay for dinner. Chat with Eve about computers."

"Eve's an astronomer. That's not really the same—"

Lola reached up to her cabinets to pull out plates, rattling them loudly enough to cut off Casey's protest. "Dinner will give me some time to think about this favor you asked me for. I'm sure I'll figure something out eventually." Her brown eyes—a sharper, more devious version of Casey's—glinted. "By morning, at least."

It finally dawned on Sophronia what was happening. It might've been quicker, except she had never been subjected to such a ruthless and good-natured effort at matchmaking in her life.

Lola wanted them to stay the night. Together.

CHAPTER 15

I am so sorry about this," Casey said.

It was almost midnight. Dinner with the Harrisons had been followed by a few more neighbors appearing in succession with champagne and tiny Italian cookies and a HemoCorp artificial-blood bag from the corner pharmacy for Sophronia, carefully packed in a cooler and served with a straw. Lola had brought out photo albums, and Eve Harrison had tried to convince her to upload the pictures to the cloud while she'd flipped each page and talked vividly and comically about her career and her son and her beloved Casey.

Sophronia had . . .

Honestly. It was horrifying how she'd devoured the photos. She'd had to clutch her hands together in her lap so she didn't reach out and brush her fingers across baby Casey's sweet flushed face, his round cheeks. He'd carried goats and worn Spider-Man pajamas and looked miserable at basketball. In his teens, he'd gotten glasses, and one photo—he'd been perhaps twenty—had caught him in the act of some sort of outdoor rock climbing. A trail of winding floral tattoos had spilled across his bare chest and abdomen, which was unfortunately something Sophronia was now going to think about every fifteen to twenty minutes for the rest of her life.

Currently, the tattooed computer engineer in question was leading her up the stairs to where Lola had indicated the guest bedrooms were.

At least, Sophronia thought she'd said bedrooms. It hadn't been *bedroom*.

Had it?

"I probably should've seen this coming," Casey said. "Only I forgot she texts now. It gives her an unfair advantage."

"It's fine." She had—Abraham save her—enjoyed the evening more than just about any night in recent memory, a fact that she would sooner pull her fangs out than admit.

He paused at the top of the stairs. "Do you have everything you need? Do you—are you hungry?"

She wasn't. The blood bag had been fine. Plenty. But the thirst that always simmered beneath the surface when he was around flared to life at his words, and her gaze fell to his neck.

He saw it happen.

His lips parted, and a flush heated his throat.

His smell hit her hard then. The air seemed saturated with rich caramel and wild plums—with some smoky, intoxicating liquor a thousand times sharper and hotter than Lola's whiskey.

His pulse beat harder. Helplessly, she watched the quick throb of his blood. At his side, his hand twitched, as if to reach for her.

Her head seemed to swim a little, inundated with wanting. With Casey.

Would it be so bad to touch him? To feel the rough press of his fingertips against her skin, heated and urgent and—

Lola's voice emerged from the stairs behind them, and Sophronia jumped like she'd been caught.

"My babies. Did you find everything you need?"

Casey dragged his eyes away from Sophronia's face, then cleared his throat. "I think we're good, Nonna."

Lola moved around Casey to indicate one of the hallway doors. "I made up your old bedroom for Sophronia while you two were busy chatting after dinner. I took down the posters on your walls ages ago, Casey, so don't worry."

"I didn't—" He rubbed the back of his neck, his expression wry. "I never had any posters, Nonna. I'll take the guest room down the hall."

"Of course you will," she said agreeably. "It wasn't posters? Of that vampire actress from the teen show you liked so much?"

He went even redder; Sophronia's fangs throbbed. "I don't know what you're talking about."

"Your phone screen, maybe?" Lola waved a hand. "Oh well. It doesn't matter." She was grinning shamelessly when she turned to Sophronia. "I put everything you need on the dresser, precious. Toothbrush, towel, pajamas. There's just one bathroom on this floor—right at the end of the hall."

"Thank you," Sophronia said. "It's been—" She hesitated. "Lovely. I had a really nice evening."

Lola reached out and squeezed her hand. "Come back anytime you like." She turned and made her way down the stairs, descending carefully in a swirl of fragrant green tuberose.

Casey breathed a laugh as he watched her vanish at the landing. "I know she's a lot."

"I like her."

There was a tiny pause. When she looked up at him, his eyes were soft. "Yeah," he said. "Yeah, me too." He hesitated. "You didn't answer before. Is there anything you need?"

To fix Stokr. To keep you and Lola safe inside this perfect jewel box house.

To know if you and I . . .

She shook her head. Swallowed. "Good night, Casey."

"Night, Soph."

She waited until he'd shut the door to the other bedroom, and then she carried the things Lola had left out for her down to the bathroom at the end of the hall. She showered in a steamy swirl of jasmine bodywash, brushed her teeth, and went to put on the pajamas Lola had left for her.

It was only then that she was confronted by the full scope of Lola's machinations. Instead of pajamas, Lola had set out . . .

What *was* it? Sophronia picked up the thin brick-red T-shirt—*Only* a T-shirt, where was the *rest*?—and gazed at it. PARCE HIGH CROSS COUNTRY, it said, with a little design of galloping wild mustangs.

Casey's . . . high school sports-team shirt?

She shrugged into it, feeling absolutely ridiculous. He was tall for a human—six three, maybe—but that only put him a few inches taller than she was. The worn cotton shirt barely covered her underwear. She could see her hip bones right through it, for Abraham's sake—it was indecent. It was soft as butter and clearly beloved, and it was *Casey's high school sports shirt.*

It was adorable and intimate, and if he saw her in this shirt, he was going to think that it—that *she*—

She turned on the faucet and splashed some cold water on her already-damp face. When she was done, she looked up and met her own eyes in the steam-streaked glass.

You, she told her reflection, *are the Queen of the Damned. Calm down.*

This was fine. She was a vampire—cold-blooded and silent on her feet. She just needed to sneak across the hall and into the bedroom. There was no reason for Casey to ever know that she'd slept in his high school shirt. It wasn't like she was going to bring it home with her or spend the night sniffing it.

It didn't matter anyway. It didn't smell like him.

She stifled the sound that wanted to emerge from her mouth—she feared it was a whimper—and twisted the faucet closed. And then, before she could convince herself that sleeping on the floor of the bathroom was a perfectly fine and normal thing to do, she yanked open the door.

On the other side was Casey, directly in front of her, his hand lifted like he'd been about to knock.

She froze.

They both did, at first. And then, almost unwillingly, Casey's gaze dropped. His thick dark lashes covered his eyes, but she could *feel* the hot path of his gaze sliding down her body: his thin shirt, her breasts, her legs.

She slammed her eyes closed, which regrettably did not make her disappear. "Um," she said. Her skin was prickling all over, like electricity sparking along all her nerve endings. "I—this is what Lola left out for me to wear to bed. Is this okay?"

She couldn't see him, but she could feel his warmth. Hear the soft groan of the floorboards as he took a step closer to her. "Yeah," he said. There was a faint laugh in the words, scratching against the hoarse sound of his voice. "Yeah, Soph. It's okay."

She made herself open her eyes. "I don't have to—"

He reached out and took the bottom edge of the shirt

between his thumb and forefinger. Whatever she'd been about to say vanished: a candle blown out.

The back of his knuckles brushed the top of her thigh. She hadn't been able to make out his heartbeat over the tap, but it was all she could hear now. His pulse pounded. His scent had changed: greener now, more spiky and wild.

He didn't have his glasses on. Steam from the bathroom pearled on the tips of his eyelashes as he looked down at his own hand. Slowly, his thumb rubbed along the hem of the shirt.

It might as well have been her own skin for the way her body reacted—went tight and sensitive and aching all over. Her breath hitched.

"I'm, uh." He twisted the edge of the shirt around his fingertip, pulling it taut against her bare skin. "Having a hard time remembering why I came down the hall."

"The—bathroom," she got out. "Did you need the—"

"Yeah." His knuckle brushed her thigh again. His skin was so much warmer than hers. "That was probably it."

She couldn't make herself move. She stared at his fingers—long and tan and callused. Pictured them wrapped around the pale skin of her thigh.

When she looked up, he was already looking back. His voice came out gritty. "Soph."

Her head spun. She felt like she couldn't get enough air; every lungful was all Casey—pure, glittering temptation.

She breathed—shaky, hot, so *hungry*—and then pulled herself free of his gentle two-fingered grip. She almost stumbled as she moved down the hall. "Good night," she gasped and didn't even wait for his reply before she closed herself in the bedroom.

She flattened her back against the door and then slid, very slowly, down to the floor. She stared at the patchwork quilt covering what had once been teenage Casey's bed.

Oh fuck, she thought dizzily.

She *had* to fix Stokr. Fast.

CHAPTER 16

"I feel like this location is a serious downgrade from the last time we did spy stuff."

Casey couldn't actually see Mercedes, but he could hear her plaintive voice and the soft scrape as she adjusted one of the temporary monitors they'd set up in a humid laundry room at the Golden Palm Hotel.

George's voice rose over his rapid typing. "I love this laundry room, actually. I'm going to tell Allen we should consider laundry rooms for the wedding venue. We're like . . . four floors away from murderous vampires this time, instead of right next door."

"Okay," said Brendan, "but have you considered the lack of snacks?" His morose question was slightly muffled by the rattle of an industrial washing machine. "No one is bringing craft mocktails with crystallized sage leaves to a laundry room."

"Hang on," Mercedes commanded. "Let me get my phone. Okay, say 'mocktails' again. I'm gonna text a video to your frat brothers."

Brendan's voice was vaguely offended. "That's just . . . what they're called. Everyone calls them that."

"Do they though?"

Casey emerged from the linen closet in which he'd been changing.

Mercedes looked up, took him in, and threw down her phone in disgust. "Oh come *on*."

Casey glanced down at his tux. "What?"

"This is so unfair. You get to go be James Bond while the rest of us are in the *laundry room*?" She ran her hands through her hair. "I'm quitting."

"Proximity to murder," George said. "Just keep that in mind if you get jealous."

True to her word, Nonna had managed to figure out a way to get them all into the benefit's elegant venue. Sophronia was far too recognizable to the HemoCorp vampires in attendance to pose as waitstaff, so Nonna had procured a ticket to the sold-out event for her. *Two, actually*, she'd informed Casey, so blithely that he'd instantly felt suspicious. *One for each of you.*

In the preceding week, Nonna had also managed to meet with the event manager at the Golden Palm to secure a floor plan of the hotel, as well as a hiding place for the Pillbugs, who would be listening carefully to the night's events. Casey and Sophronia, for their part, would be using Nonna's two tickets to dine, dance, and try to activate the scheme they'd come up with.

Tonight, anyone close to Sophronia's and Casey's devices would see an app available to download that looked a hell of a lot like Stokr.

Del, who was staying with the Pillbugs for comms support, had taken charge of circulating the story of Stokr's fake reactivation among the waitstaff. She'd bribed, cajoled, and otherwise influenced a pair of her brother's former college friends into signing up to serve drinks and spread rumors with enthusiasm.

Within a few hours, everyone at the party would hear that Stokr was back online—that the "glitch" had been resolved. Del had even mixed in some juicy bits of gossip suggesting that someone at HemoCorp had been responsible for the app's catastrophic failures.

She'd grinned at them. "Comms is my specialty, remember? Listen, if Octavia hears a rumor someone's been fired over Stokr, there's no way she's going to ignore that."

They had carefully placed recording devices all over the hotel to catch any secret phone calls. And if the saboteur didn't react immediately—in case it *wasn't* someone at the party—they had Dr. LeBlanc's program to tell them if anyone accessed the server over the next few days to try to figure out what the hell was going on.

The door came open, and Casey tensed—it was meant to be locked—before he realized who it was.

Del looked vaguely like Catwoman, for some reason, in a stretchy black jumpsuit and bloodred lipstick even though she was supposed to stay out of sight with the Pillbugs. And Sophronia—

Sophronia was wearing a long green dress that shimmered even in the bright fluorescent lights of the laundry room. Every time she took a step—which she was doing now and also scowling—the dress's heavy fabric parted to reveal her left leg up to her thigh. He could see a mile of cool-silk skin and taut muscles, and her shoes had a tiny little black strap around her ankle, which he thought was probably illegal.

Oh hell, he wanted her.

He'd wanted her for weeks. And ever since the night he'd seen her in his goddamn cross-country shirt, all legs and sweet heat-flushed mouth, he hadn't been able to pretend otherwise.

Even to himself.

He wanted to curl his palm around her ankle. Slide his finger between that strap and her skin. He wanted to be closer, as close as it was possible to be, wanted to feel—

Mercedes coughed loudly and then kicked him, which made him wonder how long his brain had been offline.

He cleared his throat and looked, with as much dignity as he could muster, at George's screens.

He and Sophronia stood quietly while George reviewed the floor plan, identifying the locations of every bug they'd planted earlier that day. Del was in a fever of envious excitement; she kept talking about alternate routes down to the ballroom and asking hopefully if there were any more of the tiny microphones "just, you know, in case."

When they were ready—twenty minutes until the dinner started, by Casey's watch—they made their way out of the laundry room. Instead of going toward the elevator, Sophronia headed for the stairs.

"It's four floors," he said. "Are you sure that . . ."

She pried open the door to the stairwell. "I don't wish to take the elevator right now."

"You—" He paused to recall the locations of the recording devices—none in the stairwell—before he spoke. "You look really beautiful."

She frowned harder and kept descending.

He skipped a couple of steps to catch up. "Are you—"

She stopped to glare at him over her shoulder. Her hair caught in her glossy lipstick, and she swiped at it angrily with one scarlet-tipped hand. "Did you just *have* that tux? It's—I'm—just looking at you is actually making me . . ."

He felt amusement tug at his lips. "Furious?"

"Yes!"

He pushed her hair behind her ear. It curled up a little, touching the blade-sharp line of her jaw, and he brushed it back with the tip of his finger.

She swallowed. He'd paused one step above her. Bare inches between their bodies.

"Sorry," he said, very low. "About the tux."

She sucked in a breath. And then, lashes falling over her eyes, she whirled back around and headed for the ballroom.

He rubbed his hand across his mouth. And then he exhaled sharply, straightened his glasses, and made an effort to *get his shit together*.

It was difficult. He'd been frayed around the edges for days now. Weeks. And it wasn't just that charged moment in the hall at Nonna's or his worries about Stokr and his team's safety.

It was Soph. Her long fingers stroking the seat belt in his car, which he knew perfectly well she'd had fixed. The way she'd said goodbye to Nonna the next morning—shy, almost yearning. Like she wanted to stay.

He'd pictured her at Nonna's over breakfast. God help him, he'd imagined her there over Christmas, Nonna's multicolored lights shining like stained glass on her hair.

He hadn't stopped picturing her, in a thousand different incarnations that all made him ache. Slow mornings in his bed at home, her pale body dawn tinted. Her hand in his on the boardwalk. A kiss pressed into the bare skin of her shoulder.

He took the stairs two at a time and tried to stop thinking.

•••

Per their plan, they emerged a few minutes apart into the sea of black-tie guests. Casey recognized a number of West Coast vampires who'd attended these benefits for as long as he could remember, including Circinus Ossian from HemoCorp. He could pick out a few celebrities in the crowd, including a well-known female director who was married to a historian from UC Incarnare. The Golden Palm was only twenty minutes or so from the university in one direction and the Incarnare boardwalk in the other.

He didn't see Novinus, from R and D, or Titus's wife and daughter, all of whom had appeared on the guest list.

Or Octavia.

He and Sophronia mingled separately for a few minutes—Nonna saw Sophronia first and descended on her in a swirl of glittering purple gemstones—but they were ushered on to dinner before Del's humans on the waitstaff could properly circulate any rumors about Stokr.

They were seated next to each other: no doubt another one of Nonna's little coincidences. Casey looked around the large room, tipping his head in Circinus's direction when he spotted him next to a serious-faced vampire whose fangs were visible against her dark lipstick.

"Do you know who that other vampire is?" he asked in an undertone. He had a call open on his phone with the Pillbugs; he knew they'd be listening in. "The one Circinus is sitting next to?"

Sophronia followed his gaze. "That's Titus's daughter, Livia."

Casey supposed that meant that the delicate blond vampire across the table was Claudia: Livia's mother and Titus's wife. Based on what Dr. LeBlanc's program had pulled from his device, Titus was in near-constant contact with both of them.

Circinus, seated beside Livia, seemed to have enjoyed

several rounds of the benefit's wine-spiked blood. His cheeks were pink, a rarity for vampires. He leaned in and murmured something in Livia's ear.

She smiled tightly at him and nodded.

"Are they . . . friends?" Casey asked.

Sophronia was looking coolly at Circinus, who had to be at least twenty years older than Livia. "We're all in the same circles. I don't think they know each other especially well." She pinched her lips together. "Livia's a single mom. I guess it's possible that Circinus is looking for a new young vampire wife."

A wife. Or . . .

Casey drummed his fingers on the table and said, very quietly, "I wonder if Circinus used Stokr."

There was no way for Sophronia to know, but the question wasn't really for her—it was for the Pillbugs. In moments, his phone buzzed in his pocket with the answer. He tipped the screen so Sophronia could read it too.

Looks like yes, George had sent. I see his hemoenzymatic info in the database.

Sophronia's expression iced over. "Of course."

Circinus's divorce, Casey knew, was not even close to being final.

For privacy reasons, the database didn't record the results of any matches, only the data from when each user gave their initial hemoenzymatic samples to the lab. There was no way to tell how often Circinus had used the app or whom he might have matched with. But still . . .

Getting caught using a dating app couldn't be good for his divorce case.

Was it possible that the Stokr sabotage hadn't been intended to destroy the app or harm its users but merely erase some embarrassing history?

Keep an eye on Circinus's call logs, Casey texted back. If there's anyone he's been spending a lot of time on the phone with, we need to know who it is.

He spotted Nonna, who was sitting one table over from Circinus and the HemoCorp vamps. Seated with them were a few humans he recognized from local universities. In fact—

Casey blinked. Glanced at Sophronia and then back at Nonna's table.

Said softly: "Is that Dr. LeBlanc?"

It was. The other humans at the table were primarily UC Incarnare and Caltech faculty, many of whom had come from industry. Dr. LeBlanc was dressed in a gleaming white pantsuit, lights sparkling off the glass in her hand.

At the sight of her, Sophronia tensed.

His phone buzzed with a text from Mercedes. Holy shit. Her name wasn't on the guest list last week, but it's there now. She must've been a late add like you two.

"That's odd," he murmured.

Not necessarily, George texted. Plenty of UC faculty here. Could Nonna have gotten her in?

"I guess. I'll ask her as soon as I can pull her aside."

George was right. It wasn't necessarily suspicious that Dr. LeBlanc was here unexpectedly. This wasn't a HemoCorp event; there was no reason for her presence to be anything other than a coincidence.

But his skin prickled with unease. And by the ferocity of Sophronia's upright posture—the way her gaze kept returning to Dr. LeBlanc—he knew she felt it too.

Something wasn't right.

And they still hadn't found Octavia.

After dinner, the benefit moved into the ballroom. He and Sophronia circled the dance floor, moving to the bar, where Casey ordered bourbon and Sophronia accepted a thin-stemmed glass of HemoCorp artificial blood.

He'd just raised the glass to his lips when he heard it: the first faint whisper of "Stokr" from one of the other party guests at the bar.

The bartender—one of Del's brother Hugo's many friends—had his phone extended, their dummy app visible.

"They're talking about it," Casey murmured to the Pill-bugs. "Stay alert."

We're on it, sent George. Start circulating. The more devices you're in range of, the more people will see the invitation to install our tricky little baby.

The fake version of Stokr didn't actually function. Its only purpose was to get people talking—if anyone attempted to use it to make a match, it would return nothing but a 404 error. But it *looked* real. Real enough, they hoped, to lure their saboteur into making a mistake.

They moved cautiously in opposite directions. Casey saw another black-coated waiter gesturing with his phone, and a tiny clump of vampires in expensive outfits whispering something he couldn't make out, devices in hand. He circled past them, slowing, but they shoved their phones into their jackets and broke apart.

And then, across the room, he spotted Octavia.

She was dressed in floor-length black lace, a pink-tinted champagne flute in one hand and her phone in the other. She was frowning ferociously down at the screen.

Casey's gaze darted toward Sophronia. Half a ballroom between them and he still knew exactly where she was.

She'd seen Octavia too. He watched her freeze, glance at him, and then cautiously move in Octavia's direction.

He shot off a text to the Pillbugs. Octavia has her phone out. Anything happening in the servers?

Nothing of interest, Mercedes sent back. We're watching.

And then, from behind him, he heard a familiar voice, low and smooth on the vowels. "Casey?"

He half turned. Dr. LeBlanc stepped forward, her brow creased, a tiny purse clutched to her chest.

"Dr. LeBlanc." He tried to keep Octavia in sight, and Sophronia. "I didn't expect to see you here."

"I could say the same."

"My grandmother is on the Greenbrier board."

In his peripheral vision, he saw Octavia drop her champagne flute on the tray of a passing waiter. Her black-tipped nails flew as she typed something into her phone.

"Is she?" Dr. LeBlanc's voice was even. "I hadn't realized."

Octavia's fingers stopped moving. She punched something in with her thumb, tightened her fist around the phone, and lowered it to her side.

And then Casey heard it: a single vibration from Dr. LeBlanc's bag.

The sound a phone made when a text came in.

He stood very still.

It was a coincidence. The sound *must* be a coincidence.

And yet, from the corner of his vision, he saw Octavia glance, just once, at Dr. LeBlanc.

His pulse picked up, alarm and disbelief together. It couldn't be. Octavia—and *Dr. LeBlanc*?

His head spun out the possibilities as he watched Dr. LeBlanc pull her phone from her bag and read whatever was on the screen. If Octavia was texting Dr. LeBlanc, that meant they knew each other. Knew each other, and yet Dr. LeBlanc had sat across from Sophronia and Casey in her office, listened to their story, and never once mentioned Octavia's name.

The crease between Dr. LeBlanc's brows deepened as she looked up from her phone. "I had wanted to speak to you about your app," she said, "but—another time. I'll be in touch."

He nodded as she turned away, and kept his eyes on her back as she headed for the door.

And then several things happened at once. Octavia moved into a cluster of vampires, vanishing from sight before he could track her. And Sophronia took a handful of steps, so lithe and graceful he barely realized how fast she'd moved, and then was at his side.

"Did you see that?" she hissed.

"I saw." He held his phone to his mouth, speaking softly to the Pillbugs. "What app was Octavia in about sixty seconds ago?"

Not the Stokr server, George texted back instantly. Looks like she was in her messaging app?

His skin went cold. Sophronia's whole body seemed to vibrate. "What did she send?" Sophronia asked. "Who did she text?"

Can't pull up the content, George sent. The app tracks signatures for the actions only. But we might be able to mirror it so we can see the number . . .

Ten digits flashed across the screen. Casey recognized them instantly.

Holy fuck, Mercedes sent. That's Dr. LeBlanc.

Casey looked at Sophronia. Her blue eyes were huge and stunned, and she looked—

Betrayed.

His throat was tight. "I didn't know," he said. "I didn't know they knew each other. I didn't—"

Jesus Christ. He never would have brought Dr. LeBlanc into their investigation if he'd thought she might be acquainted with Octavia. He'd known the professor for more than a decade. It was impossible to believe that she could be involved in the sabotage.

"Where did they go?" he got out. "Del, can you see if the waitstaff knows—"

Already on it, she texted. Octavia's in the Abstract Expressionists gallery.

"Do we have a recording device in there?" Sophronia murmured.

Yep. But Dr. L's heading out, I think.

"Not fucking yet," Casey muttered and pulled up a new text thread.

Can you meet me in the Abstract Expressionists gallery? he sent to Dr. LeBlanc. Sorry to do this now, but it's urgent. You know why.

"Casey," Sophronia whispered. Her hand had come to rest on the sleeve of his tux, her fingers long and pale against the black fabric. "What are you doing?"

"Hopefully getting them into a room together so we can figure out what the fuck they're up to."

"Dr. LeBlanc will know you sent the text. What's she going to think when she walks in and sees Octavia in there? She'll know you orchestrated the whole thing."

"Soph." He turned, his hand coming to her shoulder. "If Dr. LeBlanc's been in on it the entire time, then *all* our data is compromised. Everything. If she tells Octavia to shut up and stop talking about crimes, then at least we'll know for sure she's part of it."

His phone buzzed before Sophronia could reply. Her fingers tightened on his arm, almost hard enough to hurt.

On my way, Dr. LeBlanc said.

Shit, Del sent, Hugo's friend says Octavia's leaving the gallery.

"We can't let her." Casey moved quickly toward the door that led to the galleries. "I'll stop her if I have to."

No, Del sent. Wait, give me a second. I've got this.

Sophronia caught his arm and dragged him away from the galleries and in the direction of . . .

He'd memorized the floor plan. She was towing him, quickly and deliberately, toward an industrial-cleaning-supplies closet.

We're good, Mercedes texted. Octavia's staying put. Del's got her on the phone with a fake H-corp emergency.

"Good work," Casey muttered.

She's taking one for the team. Told Octavia she thinks the synthetics lab is on fire.

More texts from Del popped into life in quick succession.

I'm really good at comms actually

Soph, about that raise?

"You know I'm not in charge of that," Sophronia murmured, and then opened the door to the closet.

The small space was neatly organized, stocked with industrial-sized toilet tissue and rows of grapefruit-and-sea-salt-scented cleaning products. Sophronia shifted a mop bucket out of the way, and Casey squeezed in, then shut the door behind them both. She yanked her phone out of her clutch and found the app with the audio feeds for their recording devices. "Abstract expressionists," she muttered and punched a button. "Got it."

In the silence of the supply closet, Octavia's coldly irritated voice emerged from Sophronia's phone's speakers.

"—definition of an emergency, Delphine, is both embarrassing and inadequate. I—"

Casey breathed.

A text from George came in: You two hearing this?

Loud and clear, Casey sent back.

There was another sound—a scrape? a door being opened?—as Octavia ended the call with a curt dismissal.

And then—in an altogether different tone—she said: "Zélie?"

"Octavia."

It was, undoubtedly, Dr. LeBlanc's voice.

Fuck me, said Mercedes on the group chat. They do know each other.

Casey felt a pit of ice open up in his stomach. He didn't want to believe that Dr. LeBlanc could be working with Octavia. He shot a glance at Sophronia's stricken face, and he—

Goddamn it. He didn't want to be the reason all their brand-new evidence was useless. He hated the idea that he could've been the one to lead her wrong.

"I'm so pleased you came to the benefit," Octavia said. "I've been hoping to hear from you."

"To the—" Dr. LeBlanc broke off, and when she spoke again, her voice was noticeably cooler than it had been. "Did *you* send the comped ticket to my department? I was told it came from Greenbrier directly."

"You mentioned a fondness for film that night at the wine bar. When I never heard back from you I . . . got creative."

"Octavia—"

"Zélie." Octavia's voice dropped, and Casey leaned in to listen, his breath ruffling Sophronia's hair. "We had a really good time that night. I was surprised you never replied on the app."

Casey's brain, which had been operating under duress ever since he'd gotten into a closet with Sophronia, began to experience a bright, blazing revelation.

The group chat was having one, too, apparently.

Delphine Gaius
8:46 pm
Wtf?!

Mercedes Obregón
8:46 pm
OH OKAY DR L CAN GET IT

"We did." Dr. LeBlanc's tone was clipped. "And I meant it when I told you I didn't intend to repeat it."

"I see. Well. A coincidence that you're here in this room with me, then?"

Dr. LeBlanc paused—recalling, no doubt, the fact that it was *Casey* who had sent her into the abstract expressionist gallery. When she spoke again, her voice was pitched just slightly louder.

She was the smartest person he'd ever met. She knew they'd be listening.

"We met once," Dr. LeBlanc said, "before I knew who you were."

"Surely my role at HemoCorp doesn't preclude me from—"

"I appreciate the ticket to the benefit," Dr. LeBlanc said.

"But if you're looking for someone to spend the evening with, Octavia, I suggest you look elsewhere."

There was a brief, frozen pause and then an echoing sound, as of footsteps receding. A door scraped, and Dr. LeBlanc's voice came again, more distant. "I hope you have a pleasant evening."

Rapid-fire texts filled Sophronia's screen:

Delphine Gaius

8:47 pm

Going to decapitate Octavia

Talking about how Stokr is so embarrassing and here she is down bad for a HUMAN

Actually no

Going to BLACKMAIL HER

Are these texts admissible in court?

Sophronia spun to face Casey. "So Dr. LeBlanc—"

"Hasn't been working with Octavia," he said. "I guess not." He was almost dizzy with relief. He hadn't led Sophronia straight into a trap by taking her to Dr. LeBlanc. Sophronia had been right to put her trust in him.

"When Octavia accessed the database," Sophronia said slowly, "could she have been trying to find Dr. LeBlanc's personal information?"

His phone buzzed, and they both glanced down.

Delphine Gaius

8:48 pm

You think she was looking
for Dr. L's number???

To text her tonight???

"Yeah," Casey said. "Yeah, I think she might have been."

Delphine Gaius

8:49 pm

Abraham's balls. I almost
feel bad for Octavia

Hacking a database because
she got ghosted

Ouch

Across from Casey—inches from his body—Sophronia took a little shaky breath.

His eyes shot to her face. Her expression was intent, her eyes a clear, cool blue. This close, he could smell her deep forest scent beneath the citrus cleaning products—green plants, sunlight falling through leaves.

Soft. She smelled . . . soft. Touchable.

He put his hand to the wall beside her head. When he spoke, his voice grated a little on the words. "I'm really glad Dr. LeBlanc wasn't working with Octavia. I wouldn't—"

He paused. Swallowed. Watched her eyes track the movement of his throat.

She drew in another breath, and as she did, her pupils flared.

He closed the channel to the Pillbugs.

"I wouldn't disappoint you," he said, very low. "Not if I could help it. I would never let you down."

Somehow, his hand was on her face. He could feel the flutter of her breath across his fingers. The slow silken brush of her hair.

"I don't—" She looked at his mouth. Down to the pulse at his throat. "I can't do this, Casey. I don't want to hurt you."

"You won't." He stroked his thumb along her jaw, and she made a small sound. Her skin was cool beneath his hand, and he wanted to drag his palm down her neck. Down between her breasts.

"You don't know that," she whispered.

"I do. You're not going to hurt me, Soph."

"I might," she said. Her voice was thick, her consonants blurred and breathless. "You have no idea—how close—"

His phone buzzed.

He didn't move. He didn't take his eyes off hers.

And then her phone buzzed too: once, twice, a third time.

She broke his gaze, breathing shallowly, and pulled out her phone.

There were half a dozen texts already, from Mercedes and George and Brendan.

Something's going on at
HemoCorp

Security cams down, no clue
who's inside

LOTS of activity in the Stokr servers, but none of it's coming from the ballroom

Casey, where the fuck did you go

Are you seeing this???

The slow daze of his arousal shifted. Adrenaline shot into his veins; his vision seemed to go sharp around the edges. His fingers flew as he reopened the voice channel with the Pillbugs. "I see you," he said.

Sophronia leaned in, speaking directly to the phone in his hand. "I've got a driver waiting outside," she said. Her voice was crisp—no trace of the soft slurred consonants from moments ago, the whispery breath across his fingers. "I can be at HemoCorp in ten minutes."

George Chu

8:51 PM

I don't know if that's going to be fast enough.

"Maybe not," Casey muttered, "but it's worth a try." He caught Sophronia's hand in his and shoved open the closet door. "Mer, keep me updated with whatever you're seeing on your end. Del, can you make sure Nonna gets out of here safely?"

Delphine Gaius

8:53 pm

You got it. I'll tell her 007 sent me to whisk her away.

"Thanks."

For a split second, Sophronia didn't move. She was staring down at their interlocked hands, her lips parted as if to speak.

And then she looked up. Her jaw set; her grip tightened around his fingers. "Let's go," she said.

They ran.

CHAPTER 17

Sophronia should've been able to lock down the building from her phone. She spent the whole ten-minute ride from the Golden Palm trying to do it, frantically, while the Pillbugs texted moment-by-moment updates of whatever the hell was going on inside the Stokr server.

It should've been easy—the security app, her facial recognition, a quick emergency passcode.

But it didn't work. The app was down, and then it didn't recognize her face, and no matter what she tried, she couldn't get *in*.

When the door to the HemoCorp building came open beneath her hand—without her ID, without anyone at the security desk to buzz her in—her skin felt like ice.

She and Casey plunged through the darkened lobby and into the elevator, and she pressed the button for the twelfth floor, where the Pillbugs' office was located.

"What are you seeing?" he said into his phone as the elevator doors slid closed—so slowly, so *painfully* slowly. "Anything on the feeds?"

"We still can't get in," came Mercedes's steady voice. "And we can't get in touch with HemoCorp security, either, but

I've got a private fleet headed your way. They're about"—a pause—"four minutes behind you, I think."

"Good."

"But, Casey," broke in Brendan's voice, "the activity in the server stopped six minutes ago. Nothing new since. I think you guys might be too late."

"Damn it," Sophronia hissed. If she had missed her chance to catch whoever this was in the act—

"It'll be all right," Casey said. "I swear, Soph. It's going to be all right. We'll figure it out."

He caught her gaze, and she realized he'd entangled their fingers again.

Or she had. She didn't know. She pressed the tip of her tongue to her right fang and nodded once.

"I'm closing this channel," Casey said into the phone as the elevator crept toward the twelfth floor. "I'll call you back as soon as we know anything."

"Don't do anything stupid," Mercedes said.

Casey ended the call as the elevator came to a halt, and Sophronia felt a spike of anxiety.

"Stay behind me," she whispered as the doors slid apart.

Even in the dim lighting, she could see the exasperated glance he sent her way. His hand was still on hers, and he squeezed tight as they stepped out of the elevator.

She held her breath, listening for any heartbeats other than their own.

But there was nothing. The office *felt* empty—no soft rustle of breath or noisy thump of a human heart.

Damn it, she thought, *damn it, damn it.* They *were* too late.

She pushed ahead of Casey and moved down the hall

toward the Pillbugs' office. There was no one inside; when she slipped past the door, the room was dark and the office was in its usual state of disarray. Nothing appeared to have been touched.

Casey moved around her to one of the workstations, but she caught his arm and shook her head. *Fingerprints*, she mouthed and gestured toward the desk's glossy surface.

He nodded and stepped away, then pulled out his phone to snap photos of the scene.

She'd just tugged open the door, intending to head down to the server room, when she heard it.

A quick, light heartbeat. More than one. Coming fast.

And she knew why she hadn't heard them before.

They were vampire heartbeats. Vampire hearts—smaller than humans' and so much quieter.

Fast. Strong.

Deadly.

Her own heart seemed to stop in her chest as she spun toward Casey. "Stay here," she hissed, almost silently. "I hear—"

He looked up, saw whatever expression was on her face, and then promptly ignored her words by vaulting across the room to her side.

And oh, *fuck*, the vampires were coming closer, and he was a *human*, she couldn't let him—

She stopped thinking coherent thoughts.

She hurled herself into the corridor ahead of Casey and ran in the direction of the vampires. She was close enough to identify two distinct heartbeats now and to make out the direction of their flight.

They were heading for the stairwell. They were trying to leave—she could cut them off. She just needed to catch a glimpse of them—find out who they were and *keep them away from Casey—*

But if she could hear them, that meant they could hear her too. Their heartbeats sped up—a rapid, fear-fueled gallop—

And then they came around the corner, right in front of her.

She heard the sound before she even took them in.

A thin pop. Another.

The glass wall to the office beside her shattered.

She stared at the vampires—dressed in black from head to toe, professional, neat black shoulder holsters and black masks and—

Gunshots. That's what the sound had been.

Casey caught her arm and dragged her backward, into one of the empty offices, shoving her down beneath the desk. "Soph," he gasped. "Jesus Christ—are you okay?"

She struggled back, trying to pull herself out of his arms. Her head spun. There was glass—oh Abraham, there was glass *everywhere*, but she didn't think Casey was bleeding. She would've known that scent anywhere. "I'm fine, I—

"Hold on for a second—"

She yanked herself out of his grip on a white blossom of pain. "I'm *fine*. I have to get back out there."

"The fuck you do." The words snapped out of him, so grim and unexpected that she froze despite herself. "They were shooting at you, Soph. You're not going anywhere."

"I don't *care*." She forced herself to push back, to stand, and when she spoke, her voice was hoarse. "You have no idea how much this matters to me. I *can't* just let them get away."

His eyes were hot and intent as he searched her face. There was something in his expression that made her tremble, suddenly. Some bleak terror—an old fear that he held back with a clench of his jaw.

"All right," he said. "But—goddamn it, Soph. You matter a hell of a lot more than Stokr does."

She looked at him—the shape of his mouth, the tight arc of his jaw. His eyes.

He meant it, she thought.

She squeezed his hand for one quick, shaky breath—and then she was running again, back out into the corridor, sprinting in the direction the vampires had gone.

Abraham's fangs. Adrenaline had made her unsteady. She wobbled in her heels as she tore down the hall.

She was fast—usually much faster than a human—but somehow Casey stayed right behind her. She thought, a little dizzily, of a brick red T-shirt with a herd of wild mustangs on the front.

He followed her all the way to the bank of elevators.

"This should be faster," she gasped. "It's twelve floors." She must've been more afraid than she'd realized—she couldn't catch her breath, and she could hear her own pulse pounding harder and harder in her ears. "We might be able to beat them."

Inside the elevator, Casey yanked out his phone. "Where's security?" he bit out—to Mercedes, maybe, or George—she couldn't hear the human voice on the other end.

That was—strange. She could usually . . .

"Thank Christ," he said and then turned to Sophronia. "Security's here. Downstairs in the lobby."

"Tell them"—she sucked in air—"there are vamps with guns up here. Tell them . . . if they're humans, tell them to be careful."

"Got it," he said, and then—

And then the lights went off.

Beneath their feet, the floor shuddered. There was a horrible sound—grating metal, a scream of gears—and then the elevator ground to a stop.

"What the hell," Casey said under his breath. And then, into the phone: "The elevator just stopped with us inside. Everything's gone dark. Mer, can you still hear me?"

In the sudden silence, Sophronia could just make out Mercedes's voice, thin and tinny: "The—I think the power's out at HemoCorp. Shit, *shit*—Brendan, did you lose the security guys?"

"Mer," Casey said, "what's going on out there?"

"I—" Her voice shook. "We've lost everything. The security channel, internet, even the internal H-Corp phone lines. HemoCorp's a big fuckin' black hole right now. What can you see from where you are?"

"Not a lot. The elevator tripped the emergency brake—I think we're between four and five, but I'm not one hundred percent."

"Shit," Mercedes said. "All right, all right. You guys—you guys stay put, okay?"

Casey breathed a laugh. "Pretty sure we can do that, yeah."

"All right. Just hang in there. We're coming to get you out."

Casey ended the call and turned to Sophronia. He looked rumpled—his hair had beaten back whatever he'd done earlier to tame it, and his glasses sat crooked on his face. There were shards of glass on his black jacket.

He put a hand to her shoulder, bare except for the thin, beaded strap of her dress. "You okay?"

Somehow, the trembling she'd heard in Mercedes's voice seemed to have taken up residence in her own belly. In her lungs, which worked and worked and still couldn't pull in enough air.

"Yeah," she said.

Or—tried to say. It came out a wheeze.

Casey's whole body tensed. His gaze sharpened on her face. "What's wrong?"

His voice sounded strange. Everything sounded strange—a shimmering haze seemed to have settled over her senses, white sparks at the edges of her vision. "I don't . . ."

He put his hand to her waist and then, almost instantaneously, yanked his hand away with a hiss.

She looked down, following his gaze.

His hand was covered in blood.

Her lips parted. It didn't . . . make sense. She should've smelled his blood, she should've *known*—

But he wasn't looking at his hand. He was looking at her waist. At the ragged tear in the fabric of her emerald dress. At the place where the fabric had darkened: a slow spreading patch of damp.

He wasn't bleeding. Relief was cold and heavy, a wave that blackened her vision as she leaned hard against him.

It wasn't Casey's blood, pooling at her side, running slow and thick down her hip.

It was hers.

CHAPTER 18

Soph," he said. "Hey, Soph, listen. Listen to me. You're going to be fine. Just—breathe, okay?"

He didn't know what he was saying. She was sitting on the ground, leaning heavily back against the elevator's metal wall. Her hands—her skin—her whole body was ice-cold. Like she was already dead.

His hands shook as he tore open the blood patch. He had one in his jacket—he always kept one on him; everyone who worked at HemoCorp was supposed to—and then he ripped open the tear in her dress to find out where the blood was coming from.

It was smeared on his fingers. His palm. A darker red than a human's and tinged with blue, but still it made him think—

It made him think of—

He shoved back the memories of his mother's hands through sheer force of will. He found the raw furrow on Sophronia's side and slapped the blood patch over it. "How the fuck—"

It shouldn't have been possible. Vampire skin was tougher than humans', stronger and far more durable. It was difficult to pierce: a natural defense given the fact that vampires had so little blood volume. Shattered glass shouldn't have been able to cut her like that.

"I think"—she was wheezing; her lips were indigo—"it must've been a bullet."

"Jesus *fuck*. You were hit?"

"Grazed, I think. Didn't"—another gasp—"feel it."

"Okay," he said. "Okay." The blood patch had thickened already, gone opaque and spongy as her blood filled it, sealing the wound. "You're all right. Anywhere else? What hurts, Soph?"

"Chest," she gasped. "Can't breathe."

He pulled down the straps of her dress, revealing her sternum, her black strapless bra. There was no blood—no wound. No sign of trauma except the traces of blood his hands left, blue-red against her ivory skin. "I don't see anything."

But even as he said it, he knew what was wrong.

It wasn't her chest or her lungs. She couldn't breathe because she needed oxygen.

Needed blood.

Vampires had so little. Their bodies made almost none; it was why they needed human blood to survive.

He peeled off his jacket and put it over her shoulders. "It's okay. You're going to be fine, honey." He opened the call with Mercedes, and when she answered, her voice frantic, he cut her off mid-sentence. "How long till you get here?"

"I don't know—we're here, Casey, but we can't get to you. The elevators are down, and those vampire fuckers put some kind of smoke bomb in the stairwell so we couldn't see them. We couldn't stop them, Case. We tried—but it's pitch black down here, and everything's full of smoke."

"Break a goddamn window," he snapped. "We need you. Soph got grazed by a bullet—"

"*What?*"

"She's okay." God, he hoped she was. "I had a patch with me. But we're stuck in this goddamn elevator, and she's lost a lot of blood. We've got to get her out of here."

"We're trying."

"Mer—"

"I know. I *know*." Her voice cracked. "We're *trying*."

He cut the call and checked the blood patch again. It looked good—it covered almost all the wound on her side, and the edges he could see beneath the patch were clotting. She wasn't bleeding anymore, but—

Fuck. How much blood had she lost? Human bodies had nine pints of blood, and vampires had an eighth of that, and . . . And how much had pooled beneath her on the elevator floor?

His brain tried to work out volume and surface area, but the numbers kept on slipping away, like water through a fist. He couldn't think. Her face was white, her lips a deep bruised purple, and her eyes were closed, her lashes heavy on her cheeks.

He pulled the edges of his jacket tighter around her. "You're going to be okay. All right? Do you hear me, Soph? You're going to be fine. Mercedes is here—the Pillbugs—they're going to get us out."

She didn't react. She didn't move at all, except for the painful, labored way her chest rose and fell.

"Soph?" He bent forward, low and urgent, and cupped her cheek in his palm. "Sophronia."

Her lashes fluttered and then went still.

The bottom dropped out of his stomach.

Fuck it, he thought. *Oh fuck it.*

He yanked at his sleeve. His cuff link popped free and

landed on the floor with a tiny metallic clink. He pushed the fabric up past his elbow, then held his bare wrist to her lips.

"Drink."

That seemed to penetrate. She pulled away; the back of her head hit the elevator wall behind her. "No," she said hoarsely.

"Goddamn it." He got down on the floor beside her and pulled her back against his chest, one arm wrapped around her waist and the other at the level of her mouth. "*Drink*, Sophronia."

"No." She turned her head away. Her voice sounded thready, raw: a seam being pulled apart. "I could kill you."

"You're not going to kill me."

She twisted to look up at him, and the anguish in her eyes felt like a blow to his solar plexus. "You don't know that," she wheezed. "Even if I don't . . . take too much . . . you could bleed out."

"I don't fucking care, Soph."

"It's not"—she gasped again—"worth the risk."

Her words made him furious. Helpless. He wanted to shake her, and instead he pulled her tighter. She felt so strong beneath him—strong and delicate and terrifyingly fragile.

She was so *cold*.

"Of course it's worth the risk," he hissed into her ear. "*You* are worth the risk. You think I'm going to sit here and watch you die?"

He had done it before. He had waited, helpless, in the rain and the cold and watched his mother stop breathing.

Sophronia didn't say anything, only reached up and brushed her fingers through his hair. Glass fell tinkling around them, a shower of iridescence. Her chest heaved as she tried to breathe, and her eyes looked . . . fogged. Faraway.

"No," he said. "No. I'm not goddamned losing you." He pressed his wrist to her mouth again, but she clamped her lips closed, refusing to put her fangs into his skin.

His body was a black hole of memory and panic—of grief and fidelity and sudden, furious purpose, scored along his bones.

She was ready to court death?

Well, so the fuck was he.

He fumbled along the floor for one of the shards of glass that had fallen from their clothes and hair. He picked one up—tiny, almost too small for what he meant to do—and then dragged it across his palm. He barely felt the blood that welled up, that dripped hot and scarlet onto his thigh.

He held his hand up to her mouth. "Drink," he said.

Her pupils went instantly huge and black. Her hand shot out—faster than he would have imagined—to grab his wrist.

She froze, her back against his chest and her fingers locked around his arm. Holding him still.

"Drink," he murmured into her ear. "I want you to."

He could see the tips of her fangs denting her lower lip as she gritted her teeth. Slowly—agonizingly slowly—she pulled his hand to her mouth.

He braced himself for the sensation of her bite, only—

He felt a sudden dizzy wave of pleasure, a slow smooth glide.

Something stuttered in his brain. His breath caught, then dragged as he gulped air, and he looked at Soph, at her face, at his hand—

She hadn't bitten him. Goddamn stubborn self-sacrificing vampire, she'd licked across the thin cut. His blood was on her lips, in her mouth, and she shook with the effort of her restraint, fighting the instincts that told her to take more.

And then—and then—

The cut on his palm sealed itself.

As he watched, the edges of his skin knit themselves back together, leaving a neat white line.

And then even that faded.

"Soph," he breathed.

She twisted to meet his gaze. Her lips were parted—stunned understanding on her face.

She knew what it meant: his palm suddenly clear and unmarked.

The enzymes in her saliva had healed his cut, not prolonged the bleeding. The two of them were a hemoenzymatic match.

If they'd had Stokr, it would have lit up green. She could drink from him, and no one would get hurt.

He didn't need to explain. Wordlessly, he pressed his wrist against her lips, and she clutched his forearm, hard at first and then gentler as she forced her grip to relax. Her freezing fingertips skated over the muscles of his forearm.

"I won't—take too much," she vowed against his skin. "I won't hurt you, Casey."

"Jesus fucking Christ," he said. *"Drink."*

She bit him.

It felt—

Unbelievably good.

His eyes slid closed, his breath hissing out without his conscious intent. He'd done this before—not often but occasionally, in his misspent adolescence—but nothing had ever, *ever* come close to how good it felt to have her drink from him.

She swallowed again and again, long, slow waves of suction that he felt through his whole body. His head spun. His veins felt like honey, his muscles taut and his limbs heavy.

He couldn't think. He didn't know what he wanted—but, oh fuck, he wanted it bad. His free hand splayed across her belly, and he pulled her back against him. Closer. Harder.

She shuddered, and then she broke the seal between her mouth and his wrist. Her tongue passed across the tiny bite wounds, closing them, and *Jesus* that felt good too. He heard himself make a sound—a little raw, desperate breath, just this side of a groan.

She stiffened, and her hands fell away from his arm. "Casey." Her chest was still rising and falling too fast, but as she twisted to look at him, he saw—with a pulse of relief stronger even than the pleasure of her bite—that her lips had already flushed to pink. "Are you okay?"

"Am I okay?" He almost laughed. He felt lightheaded, dazed with pleasure. Dizzy with arousal. Freed from her grip, his hand had found its way into her hair, cupping the back of her head. "I'm not the one who got shot."

"I didn't take too much?"

"I'm *fine.* Do you need more?" She turned fully to face him, and he ran his hand down her neck, her collarbones, her chest—Christ, her skin felt good, warm everywhere he touched. At her side, where her dress was torn, he could see that her wound was healing already, the blood patch peeling away to reveal new skin.

He felt . . .

Proud. The pink flush on her mouth, the heat of her body—*he* had done that.

"I don't—" She licked her lips. Swallowed. "I'm afraid to—"

Her hands came to his biceps. His jacket slipped down, baring her shoulder. He reached for her—meant to tug the jacket back up.

His hand didn't cooperate. He found the thin strap of her dress and then, helplessly, slipped his index finger beneath it.

He couldn't get enough of the feel of her. Couldn't lift his palm away from her skin.

"Don't be afraid," he murmured. "You're okay, honey, I promise."

"It's not that." Her hand slid up to his neck, into his hair, and she made a tiny hungry sound. "Casey. You can't imagine how good you taste."

Oh Jesus. He was all hindbrain now, all stupidity and devotion and lust. He touched her mouth with his thumb, and then, when her lips parted, slipped between them.

Somehow, his thumb brushed one of her fangs. Her pupils flared at the light touch, and she whimpered, a soft, hot sound that lit up his veins. He wanted her—oh hell—consumingly.

He wanted to be consumed.

Her gaze fell to his mouth, and that was it. The last fucking straw.

He yanked her closer and kissed her.

She kissed him back. Her lips parted—she gasped a little as he licked and sucked, as his tongue slipped into her mouth. God—oh *God*, he'd wanted this for so long, and she was here, and she was safe.

His tongue slid against her fang, and she groaned, shuddering at the sensation, her grip tightening in his hair. He reached up and pulled off his glasses—he didn't see where they went; he didn't care—and then caught her face in his hand, his thumb caressing her jaw, her throat, the unbearably soft skin behind her ear.

She kissed him harder, pushed closer, her knees pressed to either side of his hips, and oh God, it felt good—she felt *so good*. He couldn't stop touching every part of her he could reach, palming handfuls of her skin. He loved the shape of her body, all taut elegant lines—he loved the way her hair brushed his cheek—he loved the sounds she made when his tongue was in her mouth, hungry and wanting.

He broke away but only to take her hand and press her palm against his neck. "Take more."

"I—" She ran her tongue along her fang, and the sight made his body go tight, need like a punch in the gut.

"You're not going to hurt me." He brought her fingertips to his pulse.

She liked that. Her eyes went glassy, and her knees tightened against his hips—and—hell. He was so turned on he couldn't see. Couldn't think of anything except Sophronia above him, her scent of cool shade and wet earth, the impossible feel of her body under his hands.

"I won't hurt you," she said: a whispered repetition, a low, steady vow.

She stroked his throat, a slow drag of her fingertips that made his eyes want to roll back into his head. And then she leaned forward and pressed her mouth against his neck.

Not a bite. A kiss.

He palmed her thigh—bare from where the slit on her dress had ridden up—and pulled her closer.

This time, it was slow. A sweet, hot burn as her fangs broke his skin—a deep, deep drag as she sucked, swallowed, sucked again.

His brain shut down. There was nothing in his head but pure white-hot pleasure—no thoughts except everything he wanted to give her. Everything he wanted to take.

He couldn't track the individual sensations—everything was tight and soft, aching and hungry. His hands were on her hips, her ass—she was *perfect*; she was so fucking good, and he was telling her so, in soft filthy words as he held on to her, as he rocked against her. He found the tips of her hair—her back—he could *feel* her skin grow hotter beneath his hands, and the sensation made him out of his mind, made him—

The lights in the elevator came on.

His brain was slow to make sense of what was going on. It took a dozen thudding beats of his heart for his mind to catch up, as Sophronia whimpered and pulled away, licking a hot stripe across his neck to close her bite.

Her eyes looked bright, lust glazed. Her hair was mussed from his hand, and the slit on her dress was hiked up nearly to her pelvis, and he wanted—

"Casey," she said. Her voice held the faintest trace of a slur. "I think—I think the power's back."

The elevator didn't move. But he'd just managed to struggle to his feet—to find his glasses and wrap his jacket around her, to resist the urge to take her back into his arms and kiss her gloriously carmine mouth—when the doors ground open.

From half a floor above, Del peered down at them.

"Hi," she said. "Please tell me no one's dying."

CHAPTER 19

"I'm just saying I wouldn't judge you."

Sophronia looked up from a very intense focus on the weave of her pants. Del's gaze was fixed on the road as she drove them up to Lola's house in Parce Domine, but her mouth was doing something smirkish.

"You wouldn't judge me for what?"

"If you . . . you know. Did it with your software engineer last night in the elevator."

"I—" Oh Abraham. It had been about twelve hours since she'd taken Casey's vein, and his blood was still hot inside her body. Her cheeks burned when she blushed. "I've told you like a hundred times that we didn't—"

"And *I* am telling *you* that I wouldn't judge you. I would say *Congratulations, sweetie, you deserve it*, and also, *Please tell me you got back into your clothes before the security cams switched on.*"

"We—my clothes were never *off*—"

"You know that makes it hotter, right?"

"Del!"

Del glanced over, saw how red Sophronia's face was, and cackled.

Sophronia considered climbing into the glove box. "It's

not . . . first of all, we *didn't*. And second of all . . ." She gritted her teeth, the points of her fangs digging into her lower lip. "I shouldn't have taken his blood without Stokr. I could have killed him."

"Okay, but can I point out the obvious fact that you *didn't*? He's fine, Soph." Del didn't seem to be trying very hard to repress her amusement; she was smirking again. "But even if you had—have you seen the way he looks at you?"

"How does he—"

"Like he just woke up from a fantasy about being suffocated by your thighs."

"Delphine."

"Like he's drowning and your pussy is oxygen."

"I am going to *push you out of this car*."

"I'm just saying." Del's laughter broke out around the edges of her words. "If you killed that man, he'd die happy. You know he would."

Sophronia scowled down at her lap.

She had spent all night simmering in guilt and self-recrimination and—Abraham save her—sexual frustration.

Nothing in her life had prepared her for what Casey had done in the elevator: for the jagged cut he'd drawn across his palm, the hot, sweet smell of his blood.

A vampire in the grip of blood hunger was dangerous. Casey *knew* that. He'd known that the moment he opened his vein, every lethal instinct of her oxygen-starved body would light up, urging her to bite. To drink deep, regardless of the cost.

And Casey—awful, courageous, reckless, self-sacrificing Casey—had sliced his hand open anyway.

Though she'd been half conscious, barely aware of anything beyond the cottony whiteness of pain, the scent of him had still gone straight to her head. One second she'd been ravenous, and the next, his blood—so rich, so *right*—had saturated the air, overwhelming her.

Yes, some ancient vampire instinct had hissed. *Take it.*

But she hadn't. She *hadn't*—she'd resisted, no matter how good he smelled, no matter how fast the world had compressed to the agony in her chest and the red salvation of his blood.

All she'd been able to think was *No* and *No* and *I'd rather die than hurt you.* When she'd licked across the cut on his palm, she hadn't even thought about it as a way to test their hemoenzymatic compatibility, even though of course she'd known it could be. That was how vampires and humans had established the safety of feeding before Stokr—a risky, dangerous game, especially with hungry vampires who had a tenuous grip on their control.

She'd seen it happen. She'd seen it go fatally wrong.

But with Casey . . .

Abraham's fangs. She'd watched the cut on his palm heal, and it had felt like a miracle.

She'd wanted to bite him—she'd wanted to *devour* him—and she *could*, and she wouldn't kill him.

She hadn't fully understood what would happen next. She'd had no idea how hard his blood would hit her—surely direct feeding couldn't *always* be like that, or vampires would never do anything else. Her body had gone feverish, some strange combination of giddiness and power and breathtaking arousal. Every touch had felt magnified: like her skin was somehow attuned to his, to the brush of his callused fingertips. To the singular rhythm of his heart.

No. It wasn't always like that.

It was Casey.

She'd spent the entire night awake, her body electrified by the heat of his blood in her veins, her brain buzzing with desire and tormented by guilt. She'd stared at her messages app, typed and deleted a number of increasingly unhinged apologies and confessions, and then switched to googling things like *Can a human die from blood loss even if they seem fine* and *How to tell if your human feeding partner is okay.*

Eventually, with a little throb of shameful desire, she'd searched *How often can a vampire drink from the same human?*

But even that wasn't what she really wanted to know.

Why? she kept thinking.

Why had it been so unbearably good between them—and why had he risked his life like it was *nothing*—and why did the thought of it make her want to cry?

And why did she want so badly to do it again?

She hadn't managed to calm down in the slightest by the time they made it to Lola's house in Parce Domine. Casey had driven separately—his car was full of Pillbugs—which had seemed like a good thing when he'd texted her earlier that morning to plan their meeting. She didn't think her tenuous self-control could've withstood two hours in a car with him, slowly succumbing to the temptation of his blood.

She hadn't accounted for the fact that the first time she saw him after she'd had her fangs in his neck, she wouldn't be able to think about anything else. She hadn't realized a tortured flare of heat and hunger and shame and arousal would hit her, all at the same time, right there on his *grandmother's doorstep.*

His hair was wild, and his jaw was thick with stubble, and in between his T-shirt and his sweatpants, she could see a tiny half inch of lavender and green ink.

The only good thing about her current ability to blush was that it seemed distantly possible she might burst into flames before Lola answered the door.

Lola was wearing teal again—some kind of linen separates that Del went into raptures over—and the bracelets on her wrists glittered as she ushered all of them inside.

In the hall with the family photos, Casey fell back. He linked his fingers with Sophronia's—all unhesitating ease, that terrible confidence that made her want to believe impossible things.

"Hey, you," he murmured. "How are you feeling?"

He'd asked her that in a text, too, but she'd pretended not to see it. It felt too vulnerable—Abraham's fangs, about seventy-five percent of her brain wanted to pretend the elevator had never happened.

Except that was impossible. With his blood in her veins, he smelled even better than he had before.

He smelled like *hers*.

She looked down at their linked hands and tried to remember what he'd asked.

"I'm fine." The furrow across her waist left by the bullet was gone, a thin pink line all that remained. She felt stronger than she ever had in her life: no blood bag had ever worked on her that fast or that intensely. "And you?"

His gaze dragged from their hands up to her face, and he blushed a little.

Somehow, the sight and scent of his flush was another relief. She hadn't taken too much of his blood.

"I feel, uh"—his voice grated on the words—"really good, actually." He swallowed, and she was briefly hypnotized by the bob of his throat. "Listen, Soph, I want to—"

Whatever he wanted was drowned out by an exasperated

voice from the kitchen. "Jeezus, Casey. Get in here for the debrief, or I'm going to stuff you two back in the elevator and leave you there."

His gaze shifted in the direction of the kitchen and Mercedes's voice. He blew out a breath, rubbed his thumb across Sophronia's knuckles, and smiled.

Her heart felt like a lightning rod: electric and singing and dangerous.

"Later," he said and led her into the kitchen.

At the long wood table, Brendan nursed coffee and Lola scooped cut fruit out of Whole Foods containers. George was fishing through a whole faceted crystal bowl of sugared gummies, and Del and Mercedes had their heads together over something on Mercedes's tablet.

Beside Lola—to Sophronia's shock—sat Dr. Zélie LeBlanc.

"Hi, baby," said Lola. Her grin took in Sophronia and Casey both.

"Nonna." Casey sat down beside her, some leftover tension in his shoulders easing as he took her in. "I'm glad you made it home safe."

She grinned hugely at him. "And with all my blood still in my veins. Unlike some people I could mention."

Casey cleared his throat. His ears were pink.

Sophronia pondered whether her cardiovascular fitness could sustain a sprint out the front door and then all the way back to Incarnare.

Luckily, Dr. LeBlanc interrupted before Sophronia could flee the scene. She looked more casual this morning than Sophronia had yet seen her, glasses framing her deep-brown eyes. Her gaze skipped over the Pillbugs and then settled on Casey. "I'm glad you're all here. I'm sure my presence this morning is unexpected—and thank you, Lola, for letting me drop by. I wanted to apologize to you directly, Casey, Mercedes. All of you. I should have mentioned that I had used Stokr myself. That I had encountered Octavia Pavo in the past."

"You're entitled to your privacy," Casey said, "as much as anyone else who uses Stokr."

"Of course." Dr. LeBlanc tipped her head in acknowledgment. "But I understand why your trust might have been shaken when you learned that Octavia and I had been in contact. I'll admit that I didn't foresee that possibility when I gave you my software. I did not expect to see her again."

"It doesn't really matter now," Mercedes said. "Right?" She drummed her fingers aggressively on Lola's kitchen table. "We know for sure it wasn't Octavia. She was busy chatting up Dr. L. *while* the raid was going down over at HemoCorp."

In the frantic debrief they'd all done with HemoCorp security and Sophronia's father, who'd been on the scene within minutes of their emergence from the elevator, there had been no mention of the news they'd circulated at the party about Stokr going back online. As far as Sophronia could tell, it had been put aside as another nonsensical rumor, like the leak that she'd been fired.

There was no way that the raid on HemoCorp had been a spur-of-the-moment reaction to their scheme. It had been elaborate. Thorough. Professionally planned.

"I think you're right," Del said. "If we assume the saboteur was the one who organized this raid, we can eliminate Octavia from our list of suspects. Circinus, too, and any other exec-level vamp who was at the Golden Palm last night."

"I'm not certain it entirely eliminates them," Sophronia

said. "Someone could have planned the raid first and then gone to the benefit for an alibi."

"Sure," Mercedes said, "but you have to admit, they all seemed pretty distracted."

It was true. Sophronia had been thinking the same thing, in the tiny portion of her brain that hadn't turned to self-recrimination soup.

Circinus and Octavia, at least, had seemed far more involved in their interpersonal dramas than in masterminding a technical raid on HemoCorp.

And . . .

What Sophronia had assumed to be Octavia's motive—her highly public disdain for Stokr—no longer seemed quite so convincing. Apparently, Octavia's disparagement of the app stemmed from her own ambivalence about using it, not some deep-seated opposition to the project. It wasn't hard to believe—Octavia dating a human would shock the fangs off the elders in the Pavo dynasty. Sophronia wasn't surprised Octavia's private interest in the app didn't match her public-facing perspective.

No. Octavia's general awfulness about Stokr didn't mean she was the saboteur.

Someone had attacked HemoCorp directly. And Sophronia had the evidence of her own eyes that Octavia had been busy in an abstract expressionist gallery at the time.

"I'm cross-referencing the guests now," Mercedes said, her face still buried in the tablet. "Novinus, Circinus, Octavia . . . moving them to the bottom of our suspect list, at least."

"I agree," Del said. "I have to think whoever planned the raid would've wanted to oversee what was going on."

"It's worth noting," Dr. LeBlanc added, "that this is a massive escalation. The sabotage to Stokr was covert. Easy to explain away as a failure in the software. But there's no way any of this can be hand-waved."

Casey scratched at his stubble, a familiar faraway look on his face as he considered Dr. LeBlanc's words. "You're right. They've put themselves squarely in our crosshairs now. Why would they do that?"

"I suspect," Dr. LeBlanc said, "you've got them running scared."

Beside her former mentor, Mercedes looked up from her tablet. "Good." She smiled a little, slow and dangerous. "They should be."

Sophronia leaned forward, eyes on the junior engineer. "What do you mean? Do you know something?"

With one finger, Mercedes tipped up the corner of her tablet. "Let's just say those vampire fucks aren't as clever as they think they are."

Casey's gaze sharpened as he looked at Mercedes. "What did you do, Mer?"

"I bugged the server room."

Sophronia felt her fangs tighten. *Yes.* She knew they'd planted bugs, how could she have forgotten—

But George sighed and shook his head. "We did it together, remember? I checked the program's database last night before we even left HemoCorp, but there was nothing there. No stored audio. The vamps must've found and destroyed the recording device we left."

"You're right," Mercedes said. "I checked the database too. But"—her expression went smug—"there was more than one device in the room."

"*What?*" That was Brendan, his boots dropping down to the floor as he leaned in to look at Mercedes's tablet. "You planted another device? Mer, *when*? You didn't tell us?"

"You sneaky little genius," George breathed. "They must've seen us place the bug—I *knew* our patch to the security feed was porous. But once they found and destroyed the device they knew about—"

"They weren't looking for a second. I know." Mercedes preened. "I couldn't talk about it—I didn't even want to *text* about it, just in case. But I have crystal-clear audio from the server room last night."

"Holy shit," Del said. "Did you play it? What did they say?"

Mercedes's ebullient expression dimmed slightly. "Unfortunately, not that much."

"What—"

"Here." Her fingers danced across the tablet. "Just listen. It's not that long."

The sounds that emerged from the tablet's speaker were hushed. Almost inaudible. A hiss of doors, the scrape of something being carefully moved. The soft tapping of computer keys.

Eventually, they heard a low female voice: *Upload's complete.*

A second voice, louder, male: *Corridor's clear. Which one of these doors is their fucking office?*

Blueprint's on your watch, remember?

Yeah, yeah. Don't tell [unintelligible] *I'm shit with maps.*

"What?" Del broke in. "What name did he say?"

Mercedes hit pause, but Sophronia shook her head. "Play it through to the end. Then we'll listen again."

Mercedes nodded and let the recording play. There were only a few more sentences—confirmation of the office's location and then a furious command to abort mission when the vampires realized they weren't alone.

And then gunshots. Glass breaking.

The recording hadn't picked up Sophronia's voice or Casey's. But she could remember what came next, blade sharp and clear in her mind.

Casey's arms around her. His voice, low and rough, gasping her name.

Mercedes paused the recording and then backed it up to the beginning and let it play through again.

When it was done, Brendan rubbed the back of his neck, his face pale. "They uploaded something. Some virus, maybe? Or a connection to an encrypted communication channel? Shit, Casey. It could be *anything*."

"We'll figure it out," Casey said. "I'm more interested in what they said next. Was it an acronym? *Don't tell RWR I'm shit with maps*?"

Mercedes played it a third time, and Sophronia felt her skin prickle.

Casey was right. Her brain had wanted to interpret the acronym as some word or name she didn't recognize, but it had been letters.

RWR.

Del already had out her phone. "I've never heard of RWR. Do you want me to look it up?"

"In an incognito browser, maybe," George said. "In fact, you might—"

But he broke off. Lola had replaced her teacup in its saucer with a delicate ceramic clink. A ripple made its way across the surface of her coffee. "If vampires are involved—perhaps vampire private security—then I have to think that RWR is Raymond Winterburn-Ross."

Sophronia's lips parted. She stared at Lola, whose familiar brown eyes shone, keen and bright, in the morning sun.

Raymond Winterburn-Ross. *Of course.*

"Who?" George said. He looked helplessly from Lola to Sophronia to Casey. "I don't know who that is."

Mercedes ran her fingers through a pink tuft of hair. "Raymond Winterburn-Ross was a vampire film star in the . . . '40s, maybe?"

Lola looked vaguely pained. "His first leading role was in 1959."

"Right, okay. The '60s. He was a huge, *huge* star—everything he was in broke out, studios clamored for him, that kind of thing. Toward the end of his career, he built himself a castle in Northern California and retired from public life. He's famously, uh, a little weird."

"A paranoid billionaire," Lola said, "with a wildly inflated sense of his own importance."

"Did you ever work with him?" Del asked Lola.

"No." Lola's expression went deliberately bland. "He did not act with humans."

"They say he doesn't associate with humans at all anymore," Sophronia said. "All the staff at the castle—they're all vampires."

"Wait," George said. "You think this random vampire billionaire sabotaged Stokr and then ordered a raid on HemoCorp? Why would he do that?" He looked at Sophronia. "Is Winterburn-Ross some kind of silent partner in the company?"

Sophronia shook her head. "Not as far as I know, unless he's investing through a shell company. But a lot of the vampire families know each other. It's . . ." She trailed off. Felt her belly grow cold. "My mother definitely knew him. My dad—I'm sure they've interacted before."

She didn't want to believe that her father could be behind the sabotage. She couldn't imagine he would intentionally hurt HemoCorp.

But she couldn't look away from reality. She'd stared at the wall of her shower last night, the hot spray against her shoulders, the last of the dried blood washed away, and put the pieces together, one by one.

The analyst's desiccated body. The vampires roaming their office's darkened halls. Her father's attempt to remove her from DP&S.

Now this connection to Raymond Winterburn-Ross.

Whoever had done this was a powerful, well-connected vampire with the highest levels of clearance at HemoCorp.

The evidence kept on pointing back to August Vega.

Her fingers curled into fists, her nails digging into her palms.

Lola seemed to understand Sophronia's internal conflict. Her face softened. "Winterburn-Ross may not be involved directly," she said. "As I understand it, he operates an entire heavy security fleet at his estate. It's possible he hires them out for the right price."

Sophronia swallowed. Nodded. "We have to talk to Winterburn-Ross. Figure out who at HemoCorp he's been in contact with."

"I wonder . . ." Lola tapped one teal nail thoughtfully against her teacup. "Perhaps I could invite him here to discuss the Greenbrier Foundation. Tell him we're naming an award after him." She smirked. "He'd like that."

There was a brief clamor around the table, from which Casey's voice emerged the loudest. "Absolutely not. Nonna. There were vampires with guns at HemoCorp last night. They *shot* Sophronia. We're not inviting them to your house."

"I doubt Winterburn-Ross was at HemoCorp personally," Lola said dryly.

Sophronia shook her head. "I agree with Casey."

At Lola's words, images had invaded her mind. Lola alone at the table. Enemy vampires shattering the front door. Glass in shards and blood on the sun-drenched wooden planks.

No. She wouldn't let that happen. She *refused.*

"Plus," Del added, "if he doesn't talk to humans, Winterburn-Ross won't come here."

Lola sniffed. "To his own detriment, I'm sure."

"I'll do it," Sophronia said. Her nails were still pressed into her palms, small painful arcs. "I'm the Vega heir. If I show up at his house, he'll see me."

Casey's response was instantaneous. "I'll go with you."

She hesitated. Searched his face: stubble-rough, soft-eyed. Determined.

"Casey," she murmured.

"You'll need me there," he said. "To take care of the tech."

She didn't know what to say back. She wanted to put him in a box, keep him safe here at Lola's house, and never, ever let anything bad happen to either of them.

But she couldn't do that. He was as invested in uncovering the Stokr saboteur as she was—she knew he was. He'd shown her in the elevator exactly how much he was willing to risk.

And she—

Oh Abraham help her. If they could make it work, she wanted him by her side.

"Perhaps," Dr. LeBlanc said, "we can take a day or two to regroup. Plan something a bit more strategic than simply showing up at Winterburn-Ross's doorstep. If you give me a little time in my office, I suspect I can outfit you two properly to overcome whatever technological defenses Winterburn-Ross has at his disposal."

Casey's gaze dragged away from Sophronia's. His expression went from affectionate and exasperated at once as he looked at his former professor across the table. "Are you implying that you can help us hack into Winterburn-Ross's home network?"

One corner of Dr. LeBlanc's mouth tipped up. "That wasn't a hint, child. It was a statement of fact."

CHAPTER 20

"Rebrief time."

Mercedes's voice sounded crisp and clear as it emerged from the speakers in Sophronia's dashboard. Casey had kind of forgotten cars could *have* Bluetooth; it was extremely convenient.

Brendan's voice broke in. "I don't even know what that means. Did you say 'rebrief'?"

"It means we go over the plan again. I read it in a Stucky fic."

"I don't know what that is *either*," said Brendan plaintively.

Casey had to bite the inside of his cheek to keep from laughing. "We're good to rebrief, Mer."

They were four hours into the six-hour drive from Incarnare to the Winterburn-Ross compound. Sophronia was driving—she'd insisted on it, and Casey didn't mind. It gave him time to look out the window and admire the patches of ocean view from the cliffs, the lodgepole pines and the sun glinting off the waves and—

Well. Okay. That was bullshit. He was admiring exactly *one* view, and it was the place where Sophronia's silky dress rose higher and higher on her slim, muscular thigh every time she hit the gas or brake.

She knew it too. She'd glanced over at him, and he'd let himself smile at her, hungry and shameless. He'd brought his hand over to her side of the car and pressed his knuckle to the place where her dress stopped and her skin began.

Her breath had hitched. Her skin was colder than it had been the last time he'd touched her.

He wanted to tell her she could drink from him again. He wanted to tell her to pull the car over somewhere in the woods; honestly, he was still so wound up from the elevator that he wanted to beg her to take his neck and then sit on his face.

Their texts over the last five days had been mostly professional—who was driving to Nonna's, what time they were meeting at the Flying Sausage.

Except for once. Two days after the elevator, she'd asked him how he was feeling. *Your blood should be fully replenished by now,* she'd said. *But tell me if you're having any symptoms.*

I've never felt better, he'd sent back.

There had been a long pause. Dots appearing, vanishing. Starting again.

Me too, she'd said finally. And then, after another hesitation: *I'd never done that before.*

He pictured her face: the tension in her jaw, her eyes dark as she stared at her screen, her hands clasped around her phone as if she might snatch the words back.

He felt—oh God, completely stupid over her. So pleased and proud it was almost embarrassing.

Part of it was that she'd drunk from him and nobody else. But that had been need: the demand of biology, the twist of fate that had made them a hemoenzymatic match.

No. What really had him tangled up in knots was that she'd told him so. That she'd let him see that tiny vulnerability.

Can we do it again? he'd sent.

There hadn't been any dots that time. Just silence from the phone, for long enough that he'd thought she wasn't going to reply. And then, an hour later, a single text that had made his teeth ache.

I'd like to.

He tucked the very tip of his finger beneath the hem of her dress and forced himself to listen to Mercedes as she recapped their plan for the hundredth or so time.

"Casey and Sophronia, you're visiting Winterburn-Ross on Greenbrier Foundation business. You're looking to secure funding for a new grant, focused on the restoration of vampire-directed silent films. You're hoping Winterburn-Ross will be interested in the project."

"But you don't actually care," George added. "All you have to do is get into his house and talk to him for twenty minutes or so. Dr. LeBlanc thinks we can get into his home network via the app we installed on your phones."

Sophronia's gaze had flicked down to Casey's hand on her leg, and she moistened her lips before looking back to the winding highway. "And it doesn't matter if we're near his office or his computer, right?"

"Nope. Anything connected to his Wi-Fi will do." Mercedes paused, and Casey heard the brief clicking of keys through the speaker. "Remember, you don't need to confront him directly. We don't want you two trapped in his scary vampire nest. Get in, talk to him about the grant, get out. We'll take care of the rest."

Unlike at the Golden Palm, they'd decided it was too risky to keep a line of communication open with the Pillbugs. They had no wire or bugs—nothing on them that might arouse Winterburn-Ross's suspicions. Even bringing Casey along was fraught, but they'd decided to lean on his connection to Greenbrier to justify his presence.

He hadn't wanted Sophronia to go alone.

"We've got this from our end," Mercedes said. "Don't do anything stupid."

"I'll text you when we get there," Casey said and ended the call.

There was a brief silence—Casey pondered the wisdom of sliding his hand down and indulging in a palmful of her thigh—before Sophronia said abruptly, "Are you hungry?"

He blinked.

"I just—" Sophronia gritted her teeth, and her eyes flicked down to his hand again. "I can stop at a gas station and get you something. Winterburn-Ross isn't going to have human food on the compound. I barely convinced his secretary to let *you* in. I thought maybe you—"

"I'm fine, Soph." He had no willpower when it came to her cool-silk skin. He splayed his fingers over her thigh. "Are *you* hungry?"

"Of course not. It's just—it's very difficult." She scowled at the road. "To be in the car with you. Especially when you're doing that."

His index finger was making a little circle over her knee, but he paused at her words. "Do you want me to stop?"

"I—" She was still staring straight ahead, her jaw tight. "No. I don't."

"Soph?"

"Yes?" she bit out.

"Do you want to see a movie with me?"

She glared harder at the road, her fingers locked around

the steering wheel. "That's not . . . you can't just . . ." She clamped her mouth shut, her fangs digging so hard into her lower lip he thought she might draw blood.

"Hey." He settled his hand more firmly on her knee, heavy, soothing. "What's wrong?"

There was a brief, taut silence. And then—

"What were you thinking?" she said tightly. "In the elevator. When you cut your hand." She darted a quick glance at him, and beneath her bangs, her blue eyes looked—wounded, almost. "You do realize that you could have died?"

"You wouldn't have hurt me."

"It's not about whether I would have wanted to, Casey! It's biology. If I'd bitten you, and we hadn't been a match . . . we didn't have another blood patch. You could've bled out on the floor."

He leaned back. Blew out a slow breath. "I know."

"Why would you do it?"

He didn't totally know what to say. He hadn't been thinking clearly. The past and the present had been inseparable: his fear for her; his old, old grief. "I couldn't just sit there and let you gasp for air. Not if I could help you."

"And you think it would've been easier for me? If you'd given me your blood and then died because of it? Do you think I would've been *glad* to survive, knowing what it had cost?"

"No," he said quietly. "No, I don't think that."

Silence shifted between them as they wound up another foothill, away from the ocean. He watched the trees: Douglas fir, incense cedar, knobcone pine. His dad had loved to hike—had taught Casey the names of trees and shrubs and tiny bugs in the palm of his hand.

Sometimes it still seemed impossible that all those trees should still be on the earth, when Michael Amato wasn't.

"I was there," Casey said finally, "when my parents died."

He could hear the quiet breath she drew, but he didn't turn. He kept his eyes on the forest, his hand on her knee.

"I was at this stupid coding camp. In Seattle. It was the summer. I was staying in a dorm." He breathed, a little almost laugh. "I fucking hated it. I was shy. Anxious. I was six one already and amazingly awkward, and anyway, when I got appendicitis, I was thrilled that I got to go home. My parents came to pick me up."

He felt something cool brush across the top of his hand, then settle. She'd rested her palm atop his.

He licked his lips, looked out the window, and went on. "My mom was driving. It was raining when the other car hit us."

Casey had been asleep. His parents had picked him up from the hospital, where the junior professor who'd been leading the camp had held a faintly panicked vigil throughout his appendectomy. Casey had been so tired, so relieved. His mom had brought him a pillow for the car, scented with the lavender oil she'd been trying fruitlessly to infuse that summer, and his dad had winked and pointed to a spare pillowcase he'd tucked into the back.

When he'd woken, it had been all terror. Rain, screaming, lights. Cold.

"My dad died instantly," he said. "He was thrown from the car. I couldn't even see him. His body. But my mom—she was still awake. She got herself unbuckled, and she was trying to get me out of the car, but she couldn't get my seat belt undone."

It had been too dark to see what was happening. He hadn't known she was bleeding, hadn't been able to see the extent of her injuries.

She'd held his hands. *It's okay, baby*, she'd said, over and over. *It's okay, baby, you're going to be fine. Everything's going to be fine.*

"It was quick. She wasn't—in pain. She died before the paramedics got there."

His mother's fingers had gone stiff beneath his, and he'd . . .

Known. Fifteen and a stranger to blood, to death, and he'd known instantly what that blank stillness had meant.

"Casey," Sophronia whispered. "I'm so sorry."

He let himself look at her. Her cheeks were pale, her lips a rose-tinted lilac.

Her black eyelashes were spiky from damp.

"The thing is," he said, "I figured it was my fault. Because they had to come and pick me up."

Sophronia's grip went tight, almost painful. A vampire's cool strength. "No," she said. Her voice was sharp. Definite. "No, Casey. It wasn't—"

"I know." He turned his hand over and linked his fingers with hers. "I know it wasn't. That was half a lifetime and a shit ton of therapy ago, and I don't think that way anymore." He took a breath. Focused on the shape of her fingers in his, the cool forest scent of her perfume. The way the sun shifted through the trees and left dappled patterns on the dash. "But I was messed up for years after that. Wild. Self-loathing. Angry at everyone whose lives seemed perfect and normal the way"—another breath—"mine had been."

Her fingers squeezed against his. Holding on. "That's when you went to live with Nonna?"

He felt his mouth tug up at the memory—painful and

familiar and sweet. "She had to basically kidnap me, but yes. There's no one else in the world, probably, who could've survived me at that age. She kept buying me things—plants, a cat—I don't know, parasailing lessons—because she knew I needed something to do with all that self-destructive energy. And eventually I started . . . to care. About things. To want to be alive again."

"Casey," she murmured.

He cleared his throat. "Anyway, the reason I'm telling you all of this is because I know I hold on. Too hard, sometimes."

He'd meant what he'd said to her in the elevator—meant it beyond all shadow of a doubt. She was worth the risk.

But it hadn't all been about her. He'd been caught up by fear, blue-black memories etched into his ribs, tucked in between the rhythm of his heart.

He had fucked things up in the past by clinging too tight. Stupid shit—lab work that he couldn't let go of, spreading himself too thin with extracurricular tasks he'd chosen to take on. Not sleeping because he was afraid of missing something he'd promised to do.

His only serious relationship had started his senior year of college and ended the following year. When Madison had moved to Switzerland for grad school, he'd been overwhelmed by throat-clogging anxiety because he couldn't be there. Because if he wasn't there to make her coffee in the mornings—to take care of her oil changes and put together IKEA furniture—then he felt . . . superfluous.

He pressed his thumb against Sophronia's wrist. Felt the smooth sensation of her skin and, beneath it, her pulse.

"You're so careful," she said. Her eyes were on the road, and the soft swing of her hair shielded her face. "With your team. With . . . me."

"I don't want to lose anyone else." He breathed in: deep shade and Sophronia. "I know it doesn't work like that. Hypervigilance doesn't keep bad things from happening, no matter how much I wish it did. But I haven't figured out how to stop myself from trying."

"I wish . . ." Her voice was barely audible. "I wish you were that cautious with yourself."

He tugged her hand toward him. Pressed his mouth to her fingers. "When it matters, Soph, there's nothing I wouldn't give up."

There was a brief silence, charged with tension. He couldn't see her expression.

When she spoke, her voice sounded like it was being pulled through metal. "I'm not going to let anything happen to you. Not at Winterburn-Ross's. Not anywhere."

"Soph." He breathed a laugh against her skin and then kissed her knuckles again. A third time. "Maybe I haven't been obvious enough. But if I'm being honest, I'd feel a lot better if you could promise that nothing bad is going to happen to *you*."

She didn't tug her hand away. She let him hold on to her—let him unfold her fist and trace the lines on her palm with his mouth.

"You," she said finally, "make me feel . . ."

Her voice trailed off. He listened to the low roar of the wind, to the slow exhalation of her breath. Felt her fingers curl cool around his.

"Safe," she said.

•••

The Winterburn-Ross compound was massive. The first guardhouse was occupied by two armed vampires dressed in unrelieved black, who confirmed Casey and Sophronia's appointment via earpiece and picture ID before waving them through. After that, they still had about a mile of twisty forest road to traverse and then a second gatehouse—and an eight-foot bramble-covered stone wall—to pass through before they caught sight of the mansion.

If *mansion* was even the word. Casey had looked up the place before they left Incarnare, and a not-inconsiderable number of breathless *Architectural Digest* pieces referred to it as a "churrigueresque castle." The exterior of the main house dripped with stucco ornament, and massive stone fountains flanked the enormous doors.

There were at least two more members of the black-uniformed security squad milling around the property. He assumed they were vampires too: They were tall and lean, although he wasn't close enough to pick out the tips of their fangs. Judging by the tension in Sophronia's jaw—which redoubled when she had to relinquish her car key to a valet—he figured he was probably the only human here.

Casey was expecting a butler, or at least more armed security vamps, when the castle's massive gilt-and-mosaic door swung open before them. Instead, they were greeted by Raymond Winterburn-Ross himself.

Casey had looked him up too. Winterburn-Ross was ninety-one years old, a fact that probably kept a lot of conspiracy podcasts fed when it came to rumors about vampire immortality. He looked thirty years younger, at least, with his thick head of black hair and broad shoulders; in the right light he could probably pass for forty-five.

He was sharp featured, with black eyebrows that arched demonstratively over pale-blue eyes. His gaze passed over Casey without even a trace of condescension: as though Casey simply weren't there.

"Sophronia Vega," he said. His voice hinted at his age more than his face—a faint, raspy mid-Atlantic accent marked his words. "Welcome to my home."

Sophronia had her shoulders thrown back and her chin lifted. Casey could just see the edges of her fangs. "Thank you for seeing us, Mr. Winterburn-Ross. This is my colleague from HemoCorp, Casey Amato—although today he's here on behalf of his grandmother, Lola Lovell."

"Indeed." Winterburn-Ross still didn't look at Casey, an impressive snub given Sophronia's direct introduction. "My secretary mentioned the connection to the Greenbrier Foundation. I'll admit that I do not typically favor navel-gazing do-gooders with my attention or my funds. But—for Fidelia's daughter—I am willing to consider an exception."

Sophronia nodded tightly and didn't say anything.

Tension radiated off her, as apparent to Casey as a cloud of mustard gas. He wondered if Winterburn-Ross could feel it too.

The elderly vampire stepped back, gesturing for them to enter. "Come. Let's find somewhere more comfortable to discuss what it is that you want from me."

Though Casey had grown up with old-Hollywood celebrities and black-tie benefits, it was still hard not to gawk at the inside of the house. The castle was immense—built on a scale totally unnecessary for human or vampire habitation. The tiles were gold-veined marble, and the walls arched in vast stone buttresses overhead.

Eventually Winterburn-Ross led them to a cavernous room lined with books and elaborate jewel-toned mosaics. He gestured for them to enter and then paused, his hand going to his ear, where Casey belatedly noticed an earpiece roughly the same shade of bluish ivory as Winterburn-Ross's skin.

"My apologies," Winterburn-Ross said to Sophronia. "A call from my secretary. I'll join you in my office momentarily."

He stepped aside, and Sophronia and Casey made their way into the "office." Casey paused to eye the books on the shelves, which were all bound in matching bloodred leather.

But Sophronia caught his hand and pulled him forward, as far from the entrance to the room as they could get. She paused in front of an enormous black marble fireplace and hissed, "Casey. Look."

He glanced down. She was holding out her phone, and his eyes darted to the entryway. They couldn't risk drawing Winterburn-Ross's attention—

But the vampire wasn't within their line of sight.

Casey looked back down at Sophronia's phone, expecting to see a text from the Pillbugs or some email from HemoCorp. But instead he saw . . .

Nothing. The phone was black.

"I don't know what's going on," she whispered. "It went dead as soon as we walked through the front door. I can't get it to turn back on."

What the . . .

He pulled out his own phone, but it, too, was black and unresponsive.

"Your grandmother said he's paranoid," Sophronia whispered. "Could he have done something to make our phones stop working?"

It was . . . not impossible. Not even unbelievable, for a well-connected vampire with effectively infinite resources. There was bleeding-edge technology, mostly illegal, that could create a tight perimeter to block any cellular network and drain the batteries on their devices almost instantly. The so-called Faraday nets used intermittent mini voltage surges—the same kind of technology as an EMP blast—to fry devices in their immediate vicinity.

"Shit," Casey muttered. It was *exactly* something a security-obsessed vampire might do to anyone entering his compound. Without their phones, there was no way they could take photos or make recordings of anything they saw inside his house.

No way they could contact the outside world.

Sophronia looked up and met his gaze. There was a frozen, fixed look on her face, and he knew she'd realized the same thing he had.

Without their phones, Dr. LeBlanc's program couldn't be activated. There was no way for their team to access Winterburn-Ross's home network.

They were on their own.

CHAPTER 21

Sophronia watched Casey's face change—transform from shock to sudden, fierce focus. He slid his useless phone back into his pocket. "Okay," he said. "Okay. This is going to be fine."

"I think we need to get out of here." Unease had been building inside her since they'd first driven past a gatehouse full of armed guards who might as well have been twins to the vampires they'd seen during the HemoCorp raid. "I don't like this. We're completely isolated."

Without their phones and the solid, reassuring certainty of the Pillbugs on the other end, they were at Winterburn-Ross's mercy.

"I think we should still do the meeting."

She gritted her teeth. "Why? Without Dr. LeBlanc's app—"

"I know. I know. But"—his gaze flickered to the door—"I'm not willing to give up. You keep Winterburn-Ross busy, and I'll see if there's a phone I can use to make contact with the Pillbugs. A laptop, a tablet. Anything."

"Are you *serious*?" she hissed. "You want to roam around a giant vampire lair by yourself—"

"I'll say I have to go eat a protein bar or else I'll die on the spot. I'm guessing Winterburn-Ross doesn't have a great grasp on human metabolism."

"No," she bit out.

His hand was on hers. "Soph. We've come this far. I don't want to give up."

Damn it, *damn* it. She didn't want to give up either.

She stared at him: the disheveled sweep of his curls, his unbearable, encompassing focus on her face.

If anyone could do this, it was Casey. He had the expertise, the quiet competence, the easy self-assurance to talk his way out of danger if someone found him where he wasn't supposed to be.

But still—oh Abraham, she recognized his reckless determination. It was the same stubborn, noble, idiotic bravery that had possessed him in the elevator.

When it matters, Soph, there's nothing I wouldn't give up.

"What are you going to do if they bite first and ask questions later?" she ground out.

The corner of his mouth tipped up. "You're here. I know you've got my back."

There was no more time for arguing. She heard the faint sound of Winterburn-Ross's heartbeat grow closer, his cultured voice ending the call with his secretary. She gritted her teeth and sent Casey a single jerky nod.

He brushed his fingers against hers, just once.

And then they went to meet with Winterburn-Ross.

The vampire ushered them to a trio of chairs, where two squat crystal tumblers of blood waited on a tray. Sophronia picked up hers, but her heart was beating too hard, her stomach roiling. She could only pretend to drink.

She *had* to calm down. Winterburn-Ross would be able to hear her heartbeat.

She took a breath and tried to pretend she was nervous about asking him for money.

They'd fleshed out the idea of the grant with Lola, who apparently had been waiting for only the slightest pretext to articulate a ten-year film-restoration program with a mission statement, annual deliverables, and a theoretical board of directors (chairwoman: herself).

August and Fidelia Vega hadn't been as devoted to film and theater as some other vampire families, but Sophronia had been raised with a healthy appreciation for the art form. Her years of saturation in HemoCorp financial modeling had helped her fill out the precise fiscal details of their fictional proposal, and it wasn't hard for her to talk fluently about the imaginary project. Casey's occasional charming childhood anecdotes about celebrities in Nonna's kitchen and helicopter rides to silent auctions added exactly the right note of personal familiarity with the Greenbrier Foundation.

They made a good team.

Winterburn-Ross continued to ignore Casey with a kind of deliberate effort that grated on Sophronia's nerves. While it wasn't unusual for the scions of the most powerful vampire dynasties to think themselves superior to humans—they were stronger, quicker, and usually extremely rich and famous—Winterburn-Ross's outright refusal to acknowledge Casey's presence was bizarre. Infuriating.

And, honestly, somewhat convenient. When Casey politely excused himself fifteen minutes into their pitch, Winterburn-Ross didn't even bat an eye. He tapped his finger against his earpiece, and a female vampire in a tailored charcoal suit appeared at the door to escort Casey wherever he wanted to go.

Sophronia strained after the sound of his heartbeat. It was

much louder than a vampire's—in this near-silent house, she would be able to hear him from yards away.

She'd memorized it instantly: the precise hiss of blood and thud of muscle that made up Casey's heart. She'd known his scent and his pulse from the day he'd burst into her meeting and saved Ellery Klein.

Nothing had changed. His heartbeat was still the same—steady and rhythmic, uniquely his own, and at the same time as fragile as any human's.

And yet . . . everything had changed.

She knew him now.

She thought of Casey at UC Incarnare, tutoring Ana Obregón, and coaching competitions, and organizing an internship program across half the state. The late nights and early mornings at HemoCorp. His little gifts for Nonna. The way he'd stayed behind at the Fornax vineyard to finish the install, even after he'd made his team get to safety.

He gave and gave and gave, and part of it was his nature: all that generous confidence in himself and his place in the world.

But it wasn't all simple or easy. He had lost his parents, his childhood, his security, all in the space of a single night. And she could see now, in every action he took, in every risk and plunge, the desire to do *enough* this time so that he never lost anything again.

There was some astonishing courage in it. He had lost. He feared losing more. And despite it all, he didn't shy away from love and affection.

He knew exactly how much it could hurt. And still, he'd pressed a kiss to her knuckles and willingly let her in.

She looked up. Winterburn-Ross had asked her something, and she hadn't been paying close enough attention to know how to respond.

She cleared her throat and set down the tumbler of artificial blood. She still hadn't tasted it. "I apologize, Mr. Winterburn-Ross. I was thinking about the grant program's budgetary projections. Can you repeat the question?"

His pale-blue eyes rested on her face. She couldn't hear Casey's heartbeat anymore, and she knew Winterburn-Ross would've noticed it, too—that Casey had vanished out of earshot. "Interesting," Winterburn-Ross said.

"What is?"

"That you brought a human here. I wonder what need you could possibly have of him. Why a Vega vampire would bother."

A ripple of cold passed over her skin. Her ears strained for some sound: a heartbeat, the throb of blood through human arteries. "Mr. Amato and I became acquainted through HemoCorp, and he introduced me to Greenbrier's mission. He and his grandmother are very persuasive."

Winterburn-Ross took a slow sip of blood. "I see. And yet there are several vampires associated with Greenbrier, as I understand it."

"Yes." Her voice was cool. Steady. She breathed slowly and kept her pulse under control.

"Fascinating, then, that you chose to bring a human here. To my home. When my predilections are so . . . well known."

A paranoid billionaire, Lola had called him, *with a wildly inflated sense of his own importance.*

Perhaps that was all it was. He was offended she'd brought a human to his castle; he thought she should have known better.

And yet the words felt ominous. The tension in the room notched tighter, and she still couldn't hear Casey's heart. Her muscles felt coiled tight; her body screamed for action.

Enough, she thought.

She wasn't leaving Casey alone any longer.

She rose, smoothly, to her feet. "Excuse me. I wonder if I might give some documents to your secretary for you to review later. I have some forecasts you might like to see—estimates of the program's timeline both with and without your contributions—"

Winterburn-Ross rose as well. "I take it," he said, with a brief ironic twist to his mouth, "that your humble supplication is at an end?"

"I won't—"

"Take up any more of my time?"

She was moving—slowly, casually—toward the door that Casey had left from, and Winterburn-Ross was keeping pace with her.

Her fangs were tight. Adrenaline had leaked into her bloodstream, sharpening her hearing, her eyesight. Her back brain did a rapid assessment of Winterburn-Ross's height and age and general physical condition. At ninety-one, he'd be far stronger in a hand-to-hand fight—but she could outrun him, if it came to that. She could get to Casey first.

She didn't think he would kill Casey in cold blood right in front of her. That would be murder, and vampires were subject to the same laws humans were.

But then again . . .

It didn't matter that Winterburn-Ross was a vampire. He was a *billionaire*. Here on his own property, surrounded by his loyal staff, she could imagine why he might think himself invulnerable to consequences.

Her fangs pressed against her lip, and it occurred to her that she didn't care, right now, about laws. If Winterburn-Ross threatened Casey, she would tear his heart out with her teeth.

They'd reached the door. She made herself pause and meet Winterburn-Ross's eyes. "Perhaps you might call your secretary back? I'd like to leave our projections in her capable hands."

Winterburn-Ross inclined his head, watching her carefully. He lifted a hand to tap the earpiece and then paused, his fingers going still.

Sophronia froze too.

Faint—faint but getting louder—was the rapid sound of a human heart.

Excitement. Agitation. Fear.

She stepped into the hall and turned in the direction of the sound. She didn't let herself display alarm—she didn't run.

But, oh, she wanted to. Her fangs ached, sharp, agonizing—her blood rushed in her ears, her stomach knotted, her brain was screaming at her to *go*, to *chase*—

Casey's heart pounded harder—louder—

And then he came around the corner. His hands were open—his palms empty—his face set in smooth, unworried lines.

His pulse raced, a frantic *throb throb throb* that she felt in her belly.

"Mr. Amato," she said coolly. "Time to go."

His gaze flicked from her to Winterburn-Ross and back again, a quick flutter of his curly lashes. "Sure. I'm ready."

Winterburn-Ross was stone-faced. This close, Sophronia could hear his heart, too—precisely as calm and unruffled as it had been throughout their meeting. "I'll walk you out."

"That's not necessary—"

"Please." For the first time, his gaze shifted to Casey: cold and assessing. "I want to."

He raised his hand and tapped at his earpiece. He didn't say anything—but somehow, a pair of black-outfitted security vampires materialized in the hallway.

Casey's heartbeat hadn't slowed. She had to stop herself from reaching out to take his hand.

It went against her every instinct to put her back to Winterburn-Ross and the other vampires after she'd placed her proposal in the secretary's hands. But she had to—she made herself turn and walk calmly outside. Wait for the return of her SUV, the key ring cold and hard in her palm.

The doors to the SUV slammed shut, sealing them in. Winterburn-Ross's spare form vanished behind them as she slowly accelerated down the driveway and past the first gatehouse.

"Casey," she said breathlessly. Her fingers were locked around the wheel, and she was afraid to look away from the twisting road. "Are you—"

"Wait." His voice was terse. A quick, firm command. "Nothing until we get off the compound."

In minutes, they should be out of whatever technological isolation Winterburn-Ross had plunged them into. Back into contact with the Pillbugs and safely out of the elderly vampire's reach.

"Can you do something with the phones?"

He hastily attached them to the magnetized charger in the dashboard, but neither of the devices responded.

"Shit," he muttered. "I think they're bricked."

"That's okay—you should be able to pull up my contacts

in the car—it works even if the phone's not charged. A safety feature."

"Good." He squeezed her knee, gave her a hasty crooked smile. "Thank God we took your car and not mine. As soon as we get off the property, I'll call Mercedes and explain everything."

She nodded. She eased the SUV down the rest of the winding forested road, exhaling hard as they passed the second gatehouse.

"We're out," she said. "Another couple of miles and we'll be back on the highway."

Casey was already tapping at the touchscreen on the dashboard. "Good. Give me one second to—"

A tree next to them exploded.

"Jesus," Casey said reflexively. "What the hell—"

She heard it then: the crunch of tires behind them, the whistle of a bullet. The thud as it hit another tree.

She stomped her foot down on the gas pedal as hard as she could. "They're after us," she gasped. "Casey—those were gunshots."

CHAPTER 22

A bullet tore through the passenger mirror. Casey twisted to look behind them, where a black Escalade plunged down the narrow road in their wake.

"Jesus Christ," he grated. "Soph—get us out of here—"

"I'm trying!" She swerved as the road angled hard to the right. "Abraham's fangs—Casey, get *down*—"

He was already leaning forward, punching Mercedes's number into the touchscreen.

Mercedes answered in seconds. "Casey?"

"Mer—"

"Oh my God, Casey!" Her voice went muffled. "He's here—we've got him. Holy *fuck*, Casey, we've been out of our minds! You've been out of contact for forty-three minutes, do you—"

"I know—Mer, listen—"

The SUV's wheels on the passenger side spun free of the ground as Sophronia took a sharp cut to the left. A heartbeat later, a bullet shot wood chips off another tree, inches from where their car had been.

He realized that she could hear the bullets in the air. Her hearing was more sensitive than he could've imagined—her reaction time was faster than he would've dreamed possible.

"Casey?"

It was Brendan's thin, terrified voice from the speaker this time. Casey had never heard him sound like that before.

"We're okay," Casey got out. "We're in the car, but Winterburn-Ross's security vamps are chasing us."

"*What?*" demanded Mercedes. "Why did they let you go, if they were just going to chase you down?"

"I have no idea. Plausible deniability?" Even Winterburn-Ross would have a hard time ducking a murder investigation if they'd never emerged from his house. But if they careened off the road and over a cliff . . .

Sophronia's knuckles were white where she gripped the wheel. "Maybe if we live, we can ask him. *Shit!*"

Another bullet whizzed past, and one of the passenger-side tires burst. Casey swore, and Sophronia barely kept the SUV from spinning out.

"Can you guys see them?" Casey asked urgently.

"Trying," came George's voice from the speakers. "Trying, trying, give us a second—"

They plunged down the twisting road, and every time Casey looked behind him, the Escalade popped in and out of sight behind the thickly forested curves.

When Sophronia spoke, her voice was low and vibrating. Her fangs were out, white and razor sharp. "I am not going to crash this car."

She didn't look over, but he knew—he *knew*—that she'd said it for him. Fear—single-minded protectiveness—all of it pulsed through him, a thin, high buzz in his brain. Dizziness, like the quiet after an impact.

They weren't going to crash. They were going to get out of this.

Casey leaned closer to the dash, biting out his words. "We

lost comms as soon as we went inside the castle. I accessed the network manually through a goddamned wireless printer. Winterburn-Ross must've found out somehow."

"Did you find something?" Sophronia didn't take her eyes off the road. Her voice was tight. "Is that why he's chasing us?"

"I got into his secretary's inbox. Dozens of emails to and from Kriti Pillai."

"*Kriti?*" Sophronia demanded. "About Stokr?"

"I didn't have time to look at them all. I didn't see Stokr, but—Soph, there was a hell of a lot there about HemoCorp. Internal reports from R and D about fibrin gels and tissue regen. Financial models. Lots of dates and times. I don't know what they were for."

"I thought"—Mercedes's voice was overlaid with the sound of frantic keystrokes—"Winterburn-Ross doesn't talk to humans."

"Apparently he does."

"Okay." George's voice was thready but audible. "I've got eyes on you now. Holy *shit*, they're close—two vamps in the vehicle behind you and—and another black SUV about a mile back."

"How can you see us?" Sophronia's knuckles were white on the wheel. Her jaw tense.

"We have a drone—contingency plan—you're gonna see a gravel path in about a hundred yards. Take it—take it *now*—"

Sophronia yanked the wheel hard, and the SUV's tires spun in the gravel.

"They're going to see our tracks," Casey gritted out.

"Not if I—ha! Fuck yeah, motherfuckers!"

A cloud of smoke erupted behind them.

"Smoke bomb," George said. "I got the idea from the bad guys at H-Corp. Put one on the drone a week ago, just in case. Sophronia, this is going to sound nuts, but do you see that embankment coming up? Where the trees break?"

"Yes."

"Go over it."

"Yes, you're right," she said thinly, "that does sound nuts—"

"Do it," George said. His voice was steady. Confident. In this moment, watching from his screen, George was utterly focused, intensely in control.

She shot a single heart-stopping glance at Casey, who jerked his head in a nod. His heart was in his throat, but he trusted her—he trusted the Pillbugs—George wasn't going to lead them wrong.

She jerked the wheel, hit the gas, and plunged over the embankment.

They skidded down soft earth—a too-close pine snapped the driver's side mirror off—and then they were back out onto another road. The wheels spun, grabbed traction, and launched them forward.

"Right!" shouted George through the speakers. "Go right!"

Sophronia yanked the wheel to the right. The SUV tore around the curve, and George cackled. "Good *fucking* job, Sophronia! They're confused as hell—one of their vehicles is going about eighty miles an hour in the wrong direction. If you can get out onto the main road, I think you can—"

He broke off.

Sophronia's fangs made white points against her lower lip. "We can *what*, George?"

This time it was Mercedes who responded. "They're—I don't know how they—they're turning around. *Shit*, they're heading right toward you. How do they know where you—"

"Did you take something from the house?" George demanded. "Something they could be using to track you?"

Sophronia looked down at their phones, which were still nothing more than dead hunks of metal attached to the charger. "We didn't take anything! The phones, maybe? GPS?"

Casey's brain spun, spun—

Stopped.

"It's not the phones," he breathed. "It's the *car*."

"What?"

"They had the car the whole time we were inside—plenty of time for them to plant a tracking device."

"What—" Sophronia looked down at the wheel as though it were suddenly an enemy. "What do we—"

"Pull over," George ordered. "Get out."

"We'll lose you if we do," Casey warned. "Our phones are dead."

"You're going to lose a lot more if those vamps catch you! Sophronia, take the car into the trees up ahead. The woods are thick there—drop the SUV and run like hell. Can you guys go about . . . four miles? You'll hit the main road—I can try to send an Uber—"

They plunged forward into the trees, and Sophronia threw the car into park. "Don't call an Uber. Don't call *anyone*. We're going to be fine."

Mercedes's voice was a terse command. "Leave your phones. Don't take anything with you, and *do not* do anything stupid."

"Run," George said urgently. "I'll use the drone to distract them."

It was the last thing Casey heard him say. He unfastened his seat belt and hurled himself out of the car, and Sophronia was there beside him, kicking off her heels and plunging barefoot between the trees.

He breathed deep, filled his lungs with air, and opened his stride to keep up with her.

"Casey." She was running flat out, mud flicking up to spatter her bare legs. "Are you—"

"I can do four miles." He was scared shitless—he wanted to press her down to the ground and cover her with his body—but he made himself send her the ghost of a grin. "Parce High Cross Country, remember?"

"Oh for Abraham's sake—"

He pushed harder, drawing past her so he could be first around a blind curve, just in case something was waiting for them. "Keep up."

"Save your breath," she got out. Her chest was heaving already; vampires were built for speed but not necessarily endurance. "You're going to need it."

He did need it. Ten minutes into their dead sprint, he was panting, too, his glasses peeled off and shoved in his pocket because they kept steaming up.

But if Winterburn-Ross's security vamps were still hunting them, they'd been thrown totally off track. Casey didn't hear any more bullets or the sound of wheels crunching on gravel. He didn't hear a single thing besides the pounding of their feet on the dirt and the rasp of Sophronia's breath at his side.

She didn't flag, and neither did he, though the punishing pace she'd set had them flying downhill.

Three miles or so in, he looked over at her: long legs eating up the ground, bare feet in the earth, and dirt spattered up her calves. His glasses whacked the side of his thigh, and between breaths, he got out: "You—run?"

The corner of her mouth twitched up as she looked over at him. "Most days."

"I figured."

He'd let her pull ahead, just a little bit, just for the pleasure of watching her, when she turned hard past a thick stand of trees and slid right off a slope.

He was behind her in a second, clutching her to him, pulling her up from where her knees had hit the ground. "Shit. Soph. Are you—"

She turned into him, her arms coming around his waist. "I'm fine. I'm *fine*, Casey. Just muddy."

He held her against his body for a long breath anyway.

Jesus. He felt himself shudder as adrenaline leaked away, as the sense-memory of their panicked drive slowly faded.

"Mud's fine," he muttered into her hair. "I love the ground, actually. I'm—God, Soph. That was . . ." He took another breath: her deep woods scent, cold air, earth. "I'm really glad you're okay."

She twisted back to look at him. "We're safe," she murmured. She was so tall; her mouth was an inch from meeting his. "I promise."

When they finally found the highway, he felt almost drunk on relief. His head seemed to float, a strange unsteady sensation, like silence after an impact. Like the first painful breath after surfacing from too long underwater.

They'd made it. They'd gotten away clean.

A car whizzed past and then another. Sophronia hesitated, her body angled toward his. She was still breathing hard, her hands on her knees. "Should we . . . Do we try to hitchhike?"

He put his glasses back on and gave her a quick once-over. Her bangs clung damply to her temples; her throat and chest gleamed with perspiration, and her dress was slick with mud.

She was six feet tall, barefoot, and very, very obviously a vampire.

"Uh," he said.

She looked down at herself and then at him. She reached out—he thought she was going to straighten his glasses, but she only plucked a pine needle out of his hair. "I guess we look a little disreputable."

"I wouldn't pick us up." Somehow—God, endorphins and safety had his head spinning—laughter seemed to be lurking in his voice. "Why did you tell the Pillbugs not to call an Uber?"

"I have no idea!"

Now he did laugh.

She set her hands to her hips, but her attempt at a scowl was too relief blurred to stick. A smile kept breaking out around the edges of her mouth, and he noticed that her nail polish had chipped.

He liked it like that—imperfect and real. He liked everything about her.

"I guess I was trying not to get some innocent Uber driver murdered if vamps with guns were right behind us," she said.

"Come on." He took her cool hand in his and tugged her across the highway and into another deeply shaded stand of trees. "If we keep heading downhill, eventually we'll get to the coast and civilization."

"That could take hours, Casey."

"Probably, yeah." His mouth tugged up as he pulled her into the woods, their feet sliding through more damp earth. "Want a piggyback ride?"

Her lips parted. And then, to his surprise, she laughed, just a little. It was the first time he'd ever heard the sound: scratchy, breathless. Hers.

His heart made a dizzy revolution in his chest.

"Oh Abraham," she said. "Maybe. Mostly because I can't stop slipping."

“Whatever you need, Soph.” He paused, his eyes on the chipped green polish. The place where her fingers tangled with his. “Anything.”

He looked up, and she was already looking back. Her gaze caught his and held, and her fingers tightened in his grip.

And though she took a breath and looked away as they picked their way down the rock-strewn slope, she didn’t let go.

CHAPTER 23

It was full night by the time they broke into the surf shop.

Sophronia supposed the hour and the cloudless dark were fortuitous, because nobody was around to notice when Casey picked the shop's ancient lock.

In response to the look she sent his way—presumably something like *What the hell, Casey?*—his mouth curled up. A little crooked, shameless grin. "Misspent youth, remember?"

"I remember."

They'd spent a good two hours discussing the emails that Casey had seen between Kriti and Winterburn-Ross's secretary. Kriti couldn't have killed the analyst—that had been a vampire—but her connection to Winterburn-Ross could perhaps explain how the woman's body had vanished so quickly. The attack on their SUV had shown that the billionaire wasn't above murder.

Casey hadn't been able to access Winterburn-Ross's email account, but he had scoured the secretary's inbox for names and numbers he recognized. There hadn't been anyone else from HemoCorp there, and no mention at all of Stokr specifically. But the fact that Kriti had leaked internal HemoCorp documents to Winterburn-Ross was hard evidence against her.

For Sophronia, it was a relief so strong it hurt.

Her father hadn't been the one in contact with Winterburn-Ross. August Vega hadn't sabotaged Stokr or paid the vampires who'd nearly killed her during the raid at HemoCorp.

It had been a long walk down into the foothills and then—furtively, ridiculously—barefoot through a suburban neighborhood. She kept flinching when motion-sensor lights went off, and one distant siren had her vibrating, ready to break into a sprint.

But they both recalled the sleepy beachfront motel they'd seen on their drive up from Incarnare. Somewhere in their postadrenaline comedown, they'd decided it seemed like a decent spot to wait out the night until they could go back to Incarnare in the morning.

The surf shop had been a bonus.

"Here." Casey tossed her a pair of black flip-flops, which smelled strongly of rubber and did not resemble anything she'd ever worn in her life. "Now you don't have to explain to the front-desk clerk why you're barefoot."

"I think you're overestimating the level of scrutiny we're about to face at an establishment that charges by the hour."

"They do not." He finished unbuttoning his mud-flecked shirt and then peeled it off. "Would it be weird if I left this shirt here? Like . . . reverse stealing?" He grinned at her. "Maybe they'll hang it up and sell it."

"As—bonfire fuel, maybe."

It was difficult to talk. She'd seen the floral tattoos that wound around his chest and side in the photo album at Lola's but . . .

Well. Photographic evidence paled in comparison to the real thing. In the dim neon light from the street, his skin looked silvery, the tattoos rippling dark and light, like shadows painting his lean, muscled body. Her gaze skimmed across his pecs—she recognized poppies, lupines, and, trailing down his ribs, a tracery of lavender.

His hands paused on the button of his trousers. His fingers were long and deft, and the white scar stood out against his knuckles. And she was . . .

Staring. She was staring, and he must have noticed by now.

His scent had gone spiked. All green and wild, beneath the smoky caramel and the brandied fruit.

She dragged her gaze back to his face. There was a flush high on his cheekbones.

"Soph," he said thickly.

She felt hot. Hungry. Just this side of panicked.

She grabbed the first bathing suit cover-up she could get her hands on and spun. "I'm going to—I'll just duck back here. And change."

Her stupid shoes flipped and flopped as she ducked behind a rack of postcards. She had to crouch to fully conceal herself as she changed, and she found herself face-to-face with what appeared to be a tank of live hermit crabs.

She pressed her forehead to the cool glass and ordered herself to get her shit together.

A hermit crab clinked its tiny shell beside her ear.

She shrugged out of her dress, and a thousand dollars of silk charmeuse—which she'd stained irremediably and also torn at the ribs when she'd gone ass over teakettle in the woods—puddled at her feet.

Reverse stealing. Oh Abraham's eyeteeth, he made her want to laugh.

She pulled on a bikini from the nearest rack—even her underwear had mud on it because vintage silk wasn't made for a four-hour hike—and then slipped the beach cover-up over her head.

It unfurled to her hips, and—

BEACH GIRLS GET WET FASTER, it read. In neon pink.

She stared down at the letters printed across her tits.

She couldn't move. She *refused* to turn around. She was going to stand here until she died and her bones turned to dust, or at least until the sun came up and she was arrested in the surf shop. She—

"Soph?" Casey said. "Everything good over there?"

She gritted her teeth. "I'm fine."

She emerged, stone-faced, around the postcard rack, to find Casey in a pair of perfectly normal black swim trunks and a shirt with a sailfish on it. He had a pen in one hand and a roll of receipt paper in the other, the end of it covered in his messy scrawl.

He blinked once as he took her in.

"Don't," she ground out.

He tore off the receipt, stuck it in his pocket, and wrestled back the amusement breaking out around his mouth.

And oh for Abraham's sake, his smirk only made him *more* delicious and charming and stupidly, miserably hot.

She hated everything. She spun away from him, and her flip-flops slapped her heels as she strode across the shop.

"I was just going to say," he said from behind her, "that I like your shirt."

"I already knew that's what you were going to say." She'd grabbed her wallet when they'd fled the car, and so she peeled some bills out and stacked them on the counter.

"I was also going to say"—his scent was everywhere, muddling her head—"that you're about to be the best-dressed vampire at our pay-by-the-hour motel."

She turned. He was right behind her. She could feel the weight of his gaze, heated and heavy, and the sensation made her belly turn over. "I thought you said it wasn't pay by the hour."

His palm ghosted down her arm, then wrapped around her fingers. "Did I?"

He pulled her closer, and she let him—let him close the distance between them until it was nothing. Until she breathed his air, and when he moved his lips, she felt them brush against her own.

"I forgot," he said, low and rough. "Good thing you're here."

And—oh. There was no will left in her to resist. She tipped her head up, and he tipped his down, and then they were kissing.

His mouth was hot. Every brush of his lips, the slow pressure of his tongue—all of it was sweet and hot, and when he wrapped his hand around her hip, her thighs went loose. She tilted into him, her pelvis canting toward his.

He groaned a little. His tongue brushed the sensitive edge of her fang, and she whimpered against his mouth.

His breath hitched. His hand slid up beneath the soft cotton of her cover-up, and his thumb nudged the knot where her bikini tied at her hip. Slipped underneath. "I haven't been thinking clearly," he muttered. "For a while."

She pushed her fingers into his hair. Her breath shuddered out, and when she inhaled again, everything was Casey. He was warm, his blood throbbing in his veins, and he smelled so unbearably good, and they were safe.

She let herself relish it all. She let herself drown in pure animal pleasure as he put his mouth to her neck, as he sucked at her skin, as his thumb played along the edge of her bikini bottoms. Her skin felt tight, her nerve endings reacting to every glide of his tongue, of his callused fingers. When he slid his hand around to cup her ass and pull her into him, the sudden contact made her gasp.

"Soph," he said hoarsely. He rocked, just a little, against her, and she could feel him through the thin material of his bathing suit. Her body felt soft and unsteady, her brain hazed. "I want you. Do you—can we go somewhere? Can we—"

"Yes," she said.

The word was out of her mouth before she knew she was going to say it.

He paused, as if startled by the speed of her reply. His curly lashes came down, and then back up, and he looked her in the eyes as he said quietly, "Are you sure?"

One of his hands framed her jaw. The other was still settled around her hip, firm and grounding.

She had time to think it through, then. She had so much time; his eyes were patient and encompassing as they rested on her face.

But she didn't want to change her mind. She had decided days ago, weeks ago. She just hadn't let herself admit it until now.

"Yes," she said again. "Right now. Let's go. I don't want to wait."

His lips tugged up. He stood there motionless, staring at her, for long enough that she might have started to feel anxious, except . . .

Except he looked at her like he was staggered by her.

Like she made him happy.

He kissed her on the mouth, once, hard, and then he dragged her by the hand out the back door.

On the street, as they made their way toward the motel's

dim neon light, he said, "Soph. Did you leave like . . . five hundred dollars on the counter?"

"I—that's how much a locksmith costs, Casey!"

He was laughing, soft and unhurried, and right there in the motel parking lot, he wrapped his arm around her waist. He yanked her to his chest and kissed her again.

•••

They had to ask the desk clerk to borrow his phone. The kid, who definitely had a joint concealed somewhere, was engrossed in something on his Switch and probably wouldn't have noticed if they'd come in naked.

Casey watched as Sophronia's thumbs flew over the screen. He couldn't see what she was typing, and her dark lashes covered her eyes. Whatever it was, it took a lot longer than a quick text to let Delphine and the Pillbugs know they were safe.

He didn't mind. He was content to watch her. He would've been happy to stand there until the sun came up.

She always looked beautiful, but right now—her nails chipped, her bangs mussed, and every inch of her long, long legs visible, *touchable*—

She looked like she'd just rolled out of bed.

His bed.

His girl.

"One room?" the desk clerk asked the Switch.

Casey met Sophronia's eyes. "Yeah," he said. He had his hand on her back, and his fingers found the thin bikini tie there, a tiny ridge beneath her cotton shirt. He didn't take his eyes off her as he spoke. "One room."

She licked her fang, and—Jesus—he could practically feel it along his skin.

He didn't know how they got down the hallway. He barely saw the inside of the room—little and worn, a dim warm lamp, rosettes of sand on the tile—before he was spinning her, pushing her back against the door and his body into hers. His glasses clattered to the floor.

Her hair was like silk—he was grabbing it by the handful, gasping out her name as he touched the back of her neck. The taut muscles of her waist rippled under his other hand, and he realized he had his fingers up under her ridiculous shirt, his palm coasting along her belly, her skin cool and soft under his hand.

His tongue was in her mouth. He licked along her fangs—felt her moan against him, and oh fuck, he loved how tall she was, loved that when he pressed his hips forward, she responded with a little breathy sob.

"Soph," he muttered. He had a palmful of her breast now—he swore when he felt the tight point of her nipple. She was so gorgeous—so turned on—and he—

"Wait," she gasped.

He froze. Made himself take a shuddering breath and drop his hand.

"Absolutely," he said. "I'm here for whatever you want, Soph. I don't want anything you don't want to give me."

"No—no." Her fingers were wrapped around the back of his neck. "It's not . . . I don't want to stop. I just—" She hesitated. Her eyes were very blue, and her lips were darker purple now. She was hungry.

"If you need to drink from me, Soph, you know I want that too."

"I—" She licked her lips. "Do. But first I wanted to tell you that I resigned from my position."

"*What?*"

He couldn't . . . he didn't understand.

She'd left HemoCorp?

The floor felt unsteady under his feet. Sophronia—and HemoCorp—somehow they had become the bedrock of his world. Stokr was the reason they were together in the first place. The reason they were right here, pressed thigh to thigh in a motel room on the beach.

"I left Digital Products and Solutions," she said. "Not the company. Jackie will take over DP&S, and I'm moving to Global Affairs with Circinus."

"When did you—"

"Just now. That's what I was doing on the desk clerk's phone. It'll be official tomorrow morning, but I put the wheels into motion tonight." Her lips parted, and she tightened her fingers in his hair, hard, then visibly forced herself to relax her grip. "It's . . . I was your boss, Casey. When I headed DP&S. And now I'm not."

Oh Jesus Christ. He understood, all in a rush. His head felt light—he had to lean forward and brace his palm against the door beside her head. "Soph. You scared the shit out of me."

"No. Casey. That's not . . . I've been thinking about it for weeks. I just didn't want you to feel like . . . I don't know, like you had to—"

His breath ruffled the dark sweep of her hair. "You didn't want me to feel like my continued employment was contingent on being your personal blood bag?"

"Yes—I don't know." She sounded agonized, and her hand was still on the back of his neck. "I was your *boss*."

He almost laughed, a little helpless exhale against her ear. "You recused yourself from hiring decisions at HemoCorp years ago because of Del."

"Salary adjustments too." He felt her start to relax beneath him, now that she realized he wasn't going anywhere. "But I didn't want you to feel obligated or—or pressured to—"

He hooked his finger through the tie of her bikini bottoms, then slid his knuckle along the top of the thin spandex. "Do this?"

Her voice scratched over her reply. "Exactly."

He knelt down, shoving her cover-up high enough so that he could put his mouth where his hand had been—the soft ivory skin just above her black bikini. "Hmm," he muttered. The sound came out rough: a small vibration. Her hips jerked. "Let me think." He kissed her lower, warm over the fabric. "Do I still want to do this, now that our corporate hierarchy has been restructured?"

He pressed his tongue flat against her. Her knees wobbled—his hands on her ass held her up.

"Yeah," he said. "Yeah, Soph. I really fucking do."

He hooked his finger under the bathing suit and shoved it to the side and then listened to every tiny gasp and whine she made as he licked her. He—oh hell—he felt the same hot dizzy pleasure that he had when she'd drunk from him, when his tongue had slid along her fangs. His brain went white. He tried to focus on what she liked, how she responded, but she was so wet, and her knee was over his shoulder, and his fingers were inside her, and oh *fuck* if he kept on doing this, she was going to come on his face.

He didn't stop. He held on to her and relished her taste, her whimpers and sobs, the way she . . .

Oh God, he was losing it. He was drowning in her, in the sounds she made as she fell apart. He wanted to watch her next time—wanted to see her eyes, her mouth, every part of her wrecked and ravished. He wanted—

He didn't know what he wanted. Only more. Only everything.

When she stopped shaking, she pulled him up, and he stumbled backward to the bed, taking her with him, dragging her down to straddle his hips as he sat on the edge.

"Do you want to drink?" he got out. Jesus—her fangs scraped against the thin skin of his neck, and the pressure against his cock was too goddamn good, he needed to *calm down*—

"Not yet," she gasped. "Casey—I want—"

She stroked him—two hands—he felt like the top of his head was going to come off. Her bikini bottoms were still on, shoved to the side, but he managed to peel her shirt over her head and—

He sucked in a breath.

Her thighs were spread, her knees pressing into his hips. Her body was seashell luminous in the moonlight, and he could see the scar on her waist that his blood had healed, the swell of her breasts and the points of her nipples beneath the thin fabric of her bathing suit.

Her pupils were wide and dark, and her lips were wet, and she was as ravenous as he was. As desperate.

As unmoored.

He watched her face as she lifted her hips, then eased herself down to take him in.

"Slow," he ground out. "I don't want to hurt you, honey."

Oh Jesus—he had to—he couldn't think—she was so wet, and unbearably tight, and *cool*.

She had to go slow. He knew she'd need a minute to accommodate him, and he knew he couldn't thrust up into her yet, but—fuck—he *wanted* to—

Her thighs trembled, and his palm was on her back, which

shuddered with each uneven breath. She whimpered as she took him deeper, and it shouldn't have turned him on so much, but God, it fucking did.

"Now," she whispered. "Can I drink now? It'll be easier for me if I—"

"Please."

She buried her fangs in the side of his throat.

Pleasure. Pure, blinding pleasure tightened his muscles, shot through his veins. Emptied his mind of everything but Soph, Soph, Soph.

He didn't know what was happening. He didn't know where he was. His hands were full of her—she was grinding down or he was pressing up, deep and slick and—and he could feel each pulse of her throat as she swallowed, her skin warming beneath his hands, the incomprehensible clutch of her body around him.

She sucked hard—and then she tightened around him—another pulse, another, all pressure and bliss.

And he came, too—hard, in waves—seconds after she had, his cheek pressed against her hair and his hands gripping her hips.

"Fuck," he got out. "Oh fuck. Soph."

She broke the seal—licked across his throat—he shuddered, thrusting up into her again. Again. Her forehead pressed against his neck, and her breath came in quick, hard pants, her body still trembling in jerky aftershocks.

He withdrew—slippery, agonizing, decadent—then flipped her over and laid her on her back in the bed. She made a tiny sound in her throat—a husky, sultry little whine that popped like sparks in his brain.

"Holy shit," he muttered and shifted down between her

legs. He pulled hard at the tie on her bikini bottoms. "I've never come so fast in my life."

"It's the bite," she gasped. Jesus, she felt hot to the touch now. Fevered. He loved it. "But it's not—I mean, you should still be able to . . . that is, people say that—"

He had her bathing suit off now, so he grabbed her hips and yanked her, laughing, down to his mouth. "You're the Stokr expert."

"I'm—"

He pinned her legs to the bed, and whatever she was going to say was swallowed up by a single choked breath.

He looked up at her. Even in the dim light, he could see that she was pink-cheeked. Her hair was a wild snarl of black, her bangs heavy over her eyes. She was looking back at him—soft, wrecked. Happy.

He'd never seen anything that he wanted that much.

"I promise you, honey," he said. "I'm not fucking done."

•••

They showered. Dozed. Shared a bag of M&M's from the vending machine and then had sex again. The moon was out, and it shone on her skin. Painted her silver, glistened in the sweat-damp place between her breasts.

It was easy this time. Languorous. Chocolate sweet.

When dawn brightened the small room, she had her head on his chest. His fingers were tangled through her shower-damp hair, and she was tracing the lavender tattoo on his side with slow, warm fingertips.

"Soph," he murmured.

She looked up.

She was so beautiful. The blue of her eyes reminded

him of the ocean under the sun, clear and shifting and endless.

"I don't think we're getting the grant money from Winterburn-Ross," he said. "You're going to have to be the one to break it to Nonna."

She turned her face into his chest and laughed.

He tucked the sound away: a little memory to be taken out later. To be cupped in his palm like a gemstone, faceted and rare.

Twice, she'd laughed. This time, he'd felt it on his skin, a soft hum over his heart.

It felt good. Sweet.

Terrifying—like leaping off a cliff and waiting for the cold weightless plunge of the sea.

It felt like falling in love.

"I have no idea how we're going to get back to Incarnare," she said. "We don't have phones. Or a car. Do you think that desk clerk kid will let me borrow his phone to call a really expensive Uber?"

"I think you could convince him." He pressed a kiss to the top of her head. "We don't need an Uber. I have a better idea."

"Will it get us back to Incarnare today? I want to go straight to HemoCorp to tell my dad about Winterburn-Ross and those emails with Kriti." She hesitated for the space of a breath, then flattened her hand against Casey's chest. "I want to tell him everything."

"I think it'll get us home pretty quick, yeah." Casey felt his mouth tug up, and he spread his hand over hers. "How do you feel about helicopters?"

CHAPTER 24

Lola, it turned out, had a lot of friends. The helicopter arrived not an hour after Casey made the call to his grandmother.

Lola's neighbor's personal pilot took the two of them all the way down the coast. The water burned with the sun's reflection, a shimmering, painful sort of beauty. Sophronia couldn't tear her eyes away—not even when Casey put his hand over her thigh and she tucked her cheek against his chest.

She didn't regret anything.

Not taking him with her to Winterburn-Ross's estate.

Not relinquishing her role as head of DP&S. She'd thought about it for weeks, ever since her father had suggested the move to Global Affairs. After the elevator—when Casey had texted to ask if she wanted to drink from him again—she'd resolved to make the transfer. Yesterday, with the evidence they'd found in Winterburn-Ross's network, it had felt almost easy to let Stokr go. Casey and his Pillbugs would be safe.

And she didn't regret a single second of the night they'd spent together—even if now, as she breathed him in, she felt off balance. Almost afraid.

He made everything seem so simple. So *easy*.

But it wasn't, not for her. Emotion overwhelmed her. Gentleness, she'd always been taught, was a weakness. An invitation to be ridiculed.

But he hadn't. He never would.

The brightness stung her eyes. She inhaled: black pepper and caramel, a profusion of tangled green.

They didn't go back to her apartment to change, only had the helicopter drop them off as close to HemoCorp as possible.

She needed to talk to her father. She wanted Stokr fixed, the leaks and sabotage under control. She might be at Global Affairs now, but she needed to know she'd left DP&S set right.

She had extra clothes in her office, fortunately, although walking through the HemoCorp lobby in a lewd T-shirt was an experience nothing in her life had prepared her for. Her cheeks were hot, flushed with Casey's blood in her veins, and she absolutely refused to look anyone in the eye.

The Queen of the Damned, on a workplace walk of shame.

Shit.

She met back up with Casey outside her father's office, and—

Oh Abraham, it was like she could breathe easier just because he was near her. Relief pierced her the moment his scent was in her nose. It hurt and felt good at the same time, like blood rushing back into a compressed vein.

She knocked on the door to her father's office. She should've made an appointment with his admin, but there hadn't been time. She could still feel the tiny impressions the bikini's knots had left at her hips.

"Enter," her father said.

The door unlocked with a hiss, and she and Casey slipped inside.

Her breath snagged, and her pulse skipped at the sight of Titus Fornax across from her father at the glossy black desk.

She hadn't heard another heartbeat from outside the office's smoked-glass walls—hadn't even been listening for one. She'd been too wrapped up in thinking about Casey.

But Titus was all right. She made herself inhale and tried to force her heartbeat to slow. It was Kriti who'd worked with Winterburn-Ross. Not her father. Not Titus.

She hadn't been wrong to trust them.

"Sophronia," her father said. His voice was even. "I've put through your transfer request to Global Affairs. I'm pleased you'll be moving in a new direction. And . . . surprised." His eyes shifted to Casey. "To see the two of you here."

"Dad," she said. "We need to talk. Casey and I—we have information about who was behind the raid on HemoCorp."

Her father's pale brows drew up. "Do you?"

Titus cleared his throat and moved to stand. "Let me—"

"No," her father said sharply. "Stay. Sophronia, Mr. Amato, sit down. Tell us what you've learned."

She sat. She wanted to take Casey's hand, but she couldn't. A lifetime of training had taught her not to reveal herself that way. Especially not in front of her family.

Instead, she leaned forward and, quickly, tersely, told her father and Titus everything. When she got to the part where she and Casey had split up inside the castle, Casey took over, describing what he'd done in quick technical jargon that she suspected her father didn't understand any better than she did.

"I found dozens of emails between Ms. Pillai and Winterburn-Ross's secretary," Casey said. "Initiated by both, though more frequently on Winterburn-Ross's end. I didn't have time to read every email, but what I saw was pretty damning."

"Winterburn-Ross must have known we found something," Sophronia said. "Or suspected it, at least." She described their wild flight down the mountain, and her father's expression tightened. His cheekbones were sharper than hers, and his face seemed gaunter than the last time she'd seen him. "Winterburn-Ross didn't mean for us to get down that mountain alive."

"Sophronia," August said, "you shouldn't have gone to that place without talking to me first."

She fixed her father with a level look. She'd learned that impassive gaze from him; she wondered if he recognized it. "I couldn't speak to you first. Someone inside HemoCorp took down our security before Winterburn-Ross initiated the raid. And we didn't know who it was."

There was a brief silence as her father absorbed her words. His lips pressed together. His head tipped back, just a bit, as though he'd taken a blow.

The sight made her chest hurt.

Despite everything, she didn't want him to know that she'd suspected him, even for a moment. She didn't want him to think she'd betrayed him.

But he only nodded. "I understand. That was . . . reasonable, given the circumstances."

She sat forward. Her bangs fell into her eyes, and she shoved them back. "All of this—the raid, the sabotage—it must've been Kriti. I don't know if you want to confront her directly or just pass our suspicions on to the authorities, but we need to get her out of HemoCorp. Today, if possible."

She wasn't optimistic enough to think that they could turn Stokr back on. Not yet, at least. Not until they'd confirmed Kriti's involvement and identified anyone at HemoCorp she might've worked with. But with Kriti out of the company, the Pillbugs could perform a full forensic analysis on her workstation—access her emails, her Slack chats, everything.

It would be a step forward, at least. A slow shift back to the way things had been, even if she wasn't the one overseeing DP&S.

But her father was shaking his head. "Sophronia. For many reasons, I wish you'd spoken to me first."

"What do you—"

"I already knew about Kriti and Winterburn-Ross."

The air in the room went still. The only thing she could hear was the familiar rhythm of Casey's pulse: a throb in her ears that echoed with her father's words.

"What?" she breathed.

"I already knew. Kriti came to me—oh, nearly a month ago now."

A month ago . . . that had been *after* the analyst's death. After the Stokr sabotage. "It could be a trap. A deception. She could've—"

"Sophronia. Listen to me." Her father's voice was very quiet. Almost gentle. "Kriti had nothing to do with the Stokr fiasco or with the raid on HemoCorp. Winterburn-Ross reached out to her first. He discovered that Kriti's son was involved in an embezzlement scheme and attempted, with some initial success, to blackmail Kriti by promising to keep his knowledge secret."

Sophronia stared blankly at her father.

Kriti's son—Sophronia recalled him, if vaguely, from Kriti's stories over the last decade. He worked in finance in New York. He had four or five little girls, and Kriti liked to fly them all out to California because they were so fond of the beach.

He had been . . . embezzling money? And Winterburn-Ross knew about it?

"What—" Her voice came out choked. "What did Winterburn-Ross want from Kriti?"

Her eyes flew to Casey. Could this be why the Pillbugs had seen Kriti moving around her personal finances? To help her son? Or to pay off Winterburn-Ross?

"Not money," her father said. "He has more than he could need in ten vampire lifetimes. He wanted information. Access to HemoCorp's internals." His face was pale, and his mouth looked serious. Dark with blood hunger. "Kriti planned to give it to him at first. And then, instead, she came to me."

"So you've been involved? All this time?"

Her father inclined his head. "I have. I worked with Kriti to buy time—to develop fake documents we could pass to Winterburn-Ross while she extricated her son from a mess of his own making."

It made sense. All of it made too much sense. Her father valued fidelity; duty was to be rewarded. He would have helped Kriti, if she'd come to him. If it meant protecting her family.

He had always been good at staying quiet.

All her life, her father's silence had been a tangible thing, filling the room, pressing the air out of her lungs.

Memory seemed to choke her. She could still see the sapphire birds on the wallpaper at their house. Remember the way she'd stared down at her hands. It had been two weeks after Izzy's death, and she hadn't been able to stop picturing the blood crusted around her nails, dried into the lines of her wrists.

You are a Vega, her mother had hissed. *You don't apologize, and you don't make a scene. And you do not drag our family's name through the dirt because you cannot control your pathetic desire to be just like the rest of them.*

At her mother's words, she'd looked up.

Not at Fidelia. At August.

Was it true? Had she really gotten Izzy killed because of her own weakness? Let a girl die because she wanted to be accepted more than she cared about doing the right thing?

She couldn't judge. Couldn't tell what was true and what was just a tempting lie. She'd wanted someone—some adult that she trusted—to tell her what to believe.

Her father hadn't said anything.

She pushed the memories back. Her fingers closed into fists as she focused on August.

"No," she said. "It doesn't make sense."

"Sophronia. I've borne witness to every phone call—every demand that Winterburn-Ross made. I—"

"So you're saying that Kriti passed fake information to Winterburn-Ross, and then he managed to get into Hemo-Corp's security system during the raid anyway?" She shook her head. "It's too convenient. Maybe Kriti was playing you—or Winterburn-Ross somehow realized that she was trying to mislead him—"

"Winterburn-Ross isn't responsible for the raid on Hemo-Corp."

Her breath hissed through her teeth. "Yes, he *was.* Those vamps mentioned him during the raid—"

"His name?"

"Well . . . no, but—"

RWR, they'd said. Surely that was enough.

She shook her head, frustrated, disbelieving. "I know they

were his vamps. I saw them. The way they moved, their uniforms. Even the way they spoke—"

"Let me guess. Dark clothes, earpieces. Sophronia, that's all hired mercenaries."

"Dad. You can't be serious. How many vampire mercenaries are there in the continental US? And we already know—*you* just confirmed it—that Winterburn-Ross has some kind of interest in HemoCorp. And you want to try to pretend they're not connected?"

Her father's face was very still. He looked . . . tired. Old. "Sophronia. I am asking you for the last time to let this go."

"Or what?" Her heart was beating hard, pounding against her ribs, drumming like she was running from some larger predator. "You're going to take me off of Stokr? Well, surprise, Dad—I already quit."

"Yes." Her father brought his hands together on the desk. "You did." His gaze flicked to Casey. "And I find myself wondering what precisely your motivation was."

Blood rushed to her extremities. She'd fed from the vein recently enough that the sensation was warm. Hot. Her fingertips burned.

"August," Titus said mildly. "Don't."

Her breath snagged in her chest.

That—*that* was what her father had never done. He'd never spoken up for her like that. It was Titus, always Titus, his lined face gentle, his guidance soft and unfaltering.

She could still remember it: her mother's birthday, her hand small in Titus's larger one. The awful cheap perfume he'd let her buy—because who would criticize a gift from a child?

He hadn't even been able to imagine it.

"Don't take this further than you mean to go," Titus said. His eyes were on August. He didn't look toward Sophronia.

Didn't, she thought, want her to feel his pity.

Her father's cool gaze shifted to Titus and then back to her. "Humans," he said softly, "are a weakness, Sophronia. This paranoid conviction that there's some hidden plot against you—this *obsession* with Stokr—all of it is a weakness. And Vegas—"

"Don't have weaknesses." Her throat felt raw. "I know."

"Don't approach Winterburn-Ross again. Leave Stokr shuttered. And—"

He betrayed himself then. His eyes flicked again to Casey, like he couldn't help himself.

"Remember," he said. "What can happen."

She rose. Her legs were shaking. "I remember." Her voice cracked. "I remember everything. That's *why* I'm trying to figure out what the hell happened. I'm trying to do better this time, Dad. I'm trying—"

"It's not your responsibility anymore. None of this is."

She held his gaze for a long, long moment before she turned away.

She was still shaking—a deep vibration, fear and memory and suffering cold in her belly—when she pushed through the door and out into the hall.

Casey was behind her. She could hear his heartbeat; she breathed his scent into her lungs with every trembling inhalation.

And in front of her, at the end of the hall, was Octavia. Walking briskly, her ash-blond hair in place, her lips painted a cool dark burgundy.

When Octavia saw Sophronia—disheveled, bloodless, unsteady—her brows rose.

"What happened?" she murmured as they passed. "Did Daddy take away your favorite toy?"

Sophronia's muscles tightened. Her nails dug into her palms.

Octavia was *wrong*. Stokr wasn't a toy. Sophronia wasn't some spoiled scion angry because her pet project had been thrown out with the trash.

Stokr *mattered*.

She wanted to claw Octavia's eyes out—she wanted to fling open her father's door and tell him he was wrong. She wanted him to *listen*, and she didn't want him to betray her, not even through inaction.

But Vegas didn't plead.

She walked to the elevator.

And when Casey came in behind her—when he wordlessly pressed the button for the parking garage instead of her floor—she let him.

CHAPTER 25

Casey took her to his house.

He didn't tell her where they were going. He only opened the car door for her. Watched her as she clipped her seat belt and ran her fingers silently across the invisible repair. Reached out and gripped her knee, a quick tight squeeze, before pulling back and setting his hands to the wheel.

She didn't say anything either. She felt—

Torn up inside. Angry and frantic and betrayed. She knew they weren't wrong. She *knew* Winterburn-Ross had something to do with the raid on HemoCorp.

What she didn't know was why her father had denied it.

The fear that had sunk its claws into her ribs weeks ago was back, digging deeper, piercing her lungs so that she couldn't suck in enough air. Why had her father pressured her to leave DP&S? Why would he insist that Winterburn-Ross was innocent?

Unless her father was behind it. Behind all of it.

It made too much sense. If August truly believed that Stokr was a weakness that HemoCorp couldn't afford, he would want to separate his daughter—his *heir*—from the project before he took it down.

But could he truly be so ruthless—so willing to endanger thousands of humans?

To endanger *her*?

She shied back from the thought. Spun away, like a horse in a pen, checking and checking for a place to break out.

She had to think about something else. She couldn't let herself dwell on her father.

Vulnerability meant that when you were attacked, you died—and so you were never vulnerable. You never showed the soft places: You hid them. Buried them deep in the dirt, beneath razor wire. Beneath thickets of thorns.

She stared straight ahead and didn't look at Casey until he pulled into his own driveway and put the car in park.

His house was a little white stucco bungalow with a tiled roof, tucked into a stand of scrubby pines. When he took her to the front door, all she could see were plants. They spilled from pots and barrels—tiny bromeliads tucked in between grasses, big red blooms she didn't know the name of hanging heavy from vines.

When he opened the door, a pair of tuxedo cats greeted him, twining around his ankles.

He knelt, scratching one beneath its chin and murmuring little soft words. The other retreated, a look of cool disdain crossing her feline face, as though she couldn't care less that Casey hadn't petted her first.

"I didn't know you had cats."

He looked up, then stood, smiling faintly. "I don't really know how it happened. They started showing up on my terrace about a year ago. Deckard—that's this guy—forced his way through the door, pretty much. I took him in, got him fixed. Pris, the little prickly one, was harder to get to the vet. There was a lot of blood." His smile broadened as he looked at the smaller of the cats, who'd retreated to a bookshelf and was flicking her tail menacingly at him. "Mine, obviously."

She felt her body go hot, a spiked tangle building inside her, tightening instead of unfurling here in the sun-drenched softness of his living room.

It was just like him—to find some needy thing and lavish his care and attention on it. Even if it cost him. Even if he had to bleed.

He was still looking at the cats. "I meant for them to stay outdoors, but . . ." He turned to her, a little sheepish. "Well, anyway, somehow now they have a pet sitter who comes by every day at noon to check on them in case I stay late at H-Corp. Two really fancy cat beds George and Allen got them, which they don't deign to use."

He must've seen something in her face: the snarl of emotions she couldn't pick apart or name.

"Come on," he said and took her hand. "Come sit down."

He led her into the kitchen, where he went to work fixing a pot of coffee. This room, too, was filled with sun and plants: fat succulents in pots and probably a half dozen different types of orchids, all blooming away on the sill of a huge picture window.

She didn't sit down. "I should go," she said stiffly. "I need to . . . order an Uber somehow. Buy a new phone."

"Yeah," he said. "I get it." He crossed to the fridge and pulled out a single-serve artificial-blood pack, the kind they sold at the pharmacy with the straw built in. "Do you want to eat before you go? You can take a minute, Soph. As long as you need."

She blinked at the blood bag and then at him. She *would* need a blood bag, if she stayed too long. She'd taken his vein last night—it was too soon for her to drink more than a few swallows from him.

And yet—why did he have a blood bag in his fridge? She'd never been here before.

Did he . . .

Her throat burned.

Were there *other* vampires who came to his house?

She hadn't pegged him for a suckboy. She hadn't . . . when he'd told her to drink from him, she'd thought . . .

She ran her hands up her arms; her skin felt sunburned, too sensitive. She hurt.

The sensation made her even more angry. Why *shouldn't* Casey be a suckboy? They hadn't promised exclusivity. They hadn't promised anything.

Her stomach roiled. She wanted to curl her shoulders down and press her elbows over her belly, and she absolutely *refused* to do it.

The only answer to the horrible rawness inside her was offense. Was never letting him see.

She raised her brows. Cast a derisive glance at the blood bag. "That's convenient."

He didn't seem to catch the sneer in her words. Or didn't entertain it. "I picked it up a week or so ago. I thought it would be good to have around just in case." His lips curved. "'Best By' date's in December, so no worries there. I checked."

She felt hotter. Colder. Her jaw clenched. "Did you?"

"For you, Soph. In case that wasn't clear."

So he *did* understand her. But, oh Abraham, that didn't make her feel better. She felt *worse*, her blood buzzing in her ears, her stomach muscles clenched.

What did he see when he looked at her? Her fears—her

open wounds? The charred and blistered corners of her heart?

She couldn't let him. She *could not.*

When she spoke, her voice came out cold and scornful. Exactly like her mother's. "Bold of you, Casey."

He hesitated. "What?"

"To assume I was such a sure thing."

He put the blood bag down on the kitchen table, carefully, the way he did everything. "That's not—"

"No, it's fine. I get it." She gritted her teeth hard; her fangs stabbed at her lip. "Let's just fuck. We can skip the dinner date."

"Soph—"

"That's why you brought me here, isn't it? We don't need to pretend otherwise."

It wasn't. She knew it wasn't. But the words were there: a lifetime of poison in her veins just waiting to be surfaced.

He drew closer to her—*closer*, after what she'd just said. His eyes rested on her face. "I know you're upset," he said evenly. "What your dad said back at HemoCorp was shitty. It wasn't fair to you, and it wasn't right, and if you want to talk about it, I'm here."

"I *don't.*"

He set his hand to the place where her shoulder curved. His palm was callused and warm, and he smelled like smoky caramel, like black pepper. Like cheap coconut shampoo from a beach motel, where he'd made her come so hard her vision had bleached white.

She grasped a fistful of his shirt and yanked him closer. His hand tightened on her shoulder; his mouth came to hers, separated by a breath.

He didn't kiss her. He only cupped her cheek in his palm. Gently. Like she was fragile.

"Don't," she hissed. Her fangs were out—anger, adrenaline. Arousal. "I didn't say you could touch me like that."

She wasn't an alley cat, hungry for his affection. She was a vampire. She could kill him where he stood.

But he didn't flinch. He didn't step back.

"Soph," he murmured. And then he brushed his thumb across her lower lip.

She closed her teeth over it, pressing her fang into his skin.

His eyes locked with hers, but even still he didn't move. Only breathed deep, watching her face.

It made her furious. Didn't he realize she could cut him to ribbons?

Didn't he see that she could break his heart?

She tightened her jaw. Her fang bit down, almost piercing his skin. She could feel the warmth of him, the heat of his blood, and still his expression didn't change.

It was his scent that betrayed him. It spiked green: a deep forest tangle of brambles and vines.

Not fear. Desire.

His voice came out gritty. "Spoiling for a fight, Soph?"

She was. She *was*.

She scraped her fang along the pad of his thumb, a slow glide that made them both shudder.

But he didn't run. He only slid his thumb free, dragging along the sensitive surface of her fang. As her breath hissed out, he stepped into her space, pushing her back hard enough that her ass hit the kitchen table. Her knees parted, her skirt shifting up her thighs, and he settled between them. He was taller, hotter—when he reached up to take her jaw in his hand, his grip was firm.

"If that's what you want," he said, very low, "I'll give it to you."

She still had a handful of his shirt, and she tried to yank his mouth down to hers, but he resisted. He made her work for it—made the muscles in her forearm burn as she pulled him down.

When he kissed her, it was hard. Rough. He held her jaw, positioning her how he wanted, his teeth scraping her lip. She could've broken away easily, but she didn't. She let him hold her because it felt like he was the only thing keeping her body—every raw burning atom of her—from flying apart.

She kissed him back. His free hand skated up her ribs to cup her breast through her thin blouse. He breathed deep—almost a groan—as he felt the tight point of her nipple through her lace bra. His touch was bright, electric. A charge that skimmed the surface of her skin. That pulled low and deep between her legs.

Her knees dug into his hips. She reached for him, palming his erection through layers of fabric.

He made a hoarse sound against her mouth and tried to pull back, dropping his grip on her jaw. "Oh God," he muttered. "Soph."

She pulled at his shirt. A little white button popped free, rolled along the terra-cotta tile. Her fingers dropped to the metal of his belt buckle.

He thumbed her nipple through her bra, almost reflexively, and he swore. "I don't want to hurt you."

"You're not." She arched into his hand, dragging herself against lace, against his palm. "Harder."

She wrapped her fingers around his cock through his pants, and he swore again, pinching her nipple like he couldn't stop himself. It felt—oh Abraham, it felt good, pleasure flooding her, driving out the thoughts that wanted to suck her down.

He brought his mouth to hers, tipping her head back as he kissed her, as his tongue slid against her fangs. He shoved up her skirt with his free hand, stepping closer, forcing her to relinquish her hold on him so that he could press himself against her.

And then he—

He shifted his hand to the nape of her neck. Gentled the hard press of his mouth. Kissed her slower. Deeper.

He rocked against her, hot through the fragile lace of her underwear. Pleasure hit her nerve endings like a drug, and with every tiny thrust, every hint of friction, he kissed her more softly. More sweetly.

No. *No.* She didn't want sweet. She didn't want him to hold her like this: all tenderness and comfort. She wanted to be cold steel. A wall. A knife.

But instead of pulling away, she reached for his neck. Beneath her fingertips, his skin was warm. With his blood still in her veins, her body recognized him in some impossible, intimate way.

He smelled like her. Her own.

Let go, she told herself.

And held on tighter.

She let him kiss her, lingering and thorough. Sweet as honey, spilling from the comb in a languid golden ribbon.

More than that. She kissed him back the same way.

She tasted salt. He pulled her tighter against his chest with one hand, and with the other reached up to brush against her lashes.

She was crying. She hadn't realized. Hadn't even felt the dampness on her cheeks.

"Casey," she said thickly. "I—"

He didn't let her finish. He kissed her instead, featherlight brushes against her eyelids. The corner of her mouth. Her cheek. "It's okay."

"I don't want to—"

"You can push, Soph," he murmured. "As hard as you want. I'm not going anywhere."

It was a revelation so clear and cold that it seared her. Tore open some old wound and cauterized it clean.

He was right. She was an animal in a trap, senseless with fear, turning her teeth against an open hand. If she pushed so hard that he fled—if she *drove* the loss she feared—was that not some final protection? Her actions. Her choice.

Except she didn't want that. She didn't want to open her mouth and hear her mother's voice. She didn't want to hold herself so tightly that she drove her own shattering.

She wanted Casey the way a plant wanted the sun. She wanted to curl around him, put down roots. Bend.

She exhaled hard, a sensation too much like a sob.

"We're not going to give up," he said quietly. "All of us—the Pillbugs, and Del, and me and you. Even if you're not at DP&S. Even if we have to do it all on our own time, out of Rick Tickle's fucking catering van. We're not going to stop until we find out the truth."

"And what if . . ." Tears were hot and unfamiliar on her cheeks. "What if the truth is something I don't want to hear?"

He breathed out, very softly. And then he wrapped his arms around her. His cheek pressed into the top of her head.

And though it went against every instinct of her body to

drop her guard, she did it anyway. Let her muscles go loose. Breathed his scent deep into her nose and accepted his comfort like the gift it was.

"I promise you, honey," he said finally. "You'll survive it. And you won't be alone."

CHAPTER 26

He saw her every day.

The morning after their confrontation with August Vega, Casey and the rest of the Pillbugs were reassigned to develop the UI for HemoCorp's new wearable arrhythmia detector, while Sophronia threw herself into her role in Global Affairs. But he'd promised her they wouldn't give up, and they didn't. In every spare minute, the Pillbugs analyzed data from Dr. LeBlanc's spyware, ran forensics on their own workstations, and tried fruitlessly to get more information on Raymond Winterburn-Ross.

It wasn't working. The vampire was a fortress. Whatever network Winterburn-Ross used was completely insulated from outside threats, and he didn't respond to any of the various email probes that the Pillbugs tossed out into the ether. In the surf shop, while Soph had been changing, Casey had snagged the roll of receipt paper and jotted down all the phone numbers he could remember from Winterburn-Ross's secretary's inbox. In the past two weeks, he'd cross-referenced them with the contact details of every HemoCorp employee and had found no overlap whatsoever.

He'd even, in a moment of weakness, called Nonna to see if Greenbrier had any possible connections they might exploit—maybe some friend of Winterburn-Ross's who might be willing to take their calls. But Winterburn-Ross didn't seem to have friends: only lackeys and occasional business partners.

Sophronia and Del hadn't found much out from the vampire side either. At Casey's house, over pizza and beer, Del had described an extremely disappointing vampire-scion dinner party, with hand gestures wild enough to nearly knock over her glass of pink lemonade.

It was *probably* not blood that made the lemonade that color, but Casey hadn't asked.

The six of them had gotten together at his house, at the Flying Sausage, even twice at Reverse Cowgirls. They'd formulated and discarded plans, exchanged data and ideas—nothing sensitive was getting put into writing these days—and every night, Casey had waited for Sophronia to step away. To pull back.

He steeled himself to have no expectations of her. They hadn't had any kind of conversation about their relationship, and if he tried, she shut him down. The closest she'd let him come to any admission was that day in his kitchen, when he'd told her the blood bag was for her.

And still, at the end of every day, she kept on turning back to him.

He let himself relish the nights of Sophronia in bed: sometimes his, sometimes her own. He memorized the shape of her as she stepped into his shower, the sight of her hair, black against his white cotton sheets. The way her hands wrapped around the hot mug she wouldn't drink from.

She wore his UC Incarnare sweatshirts all the time, and she fed from his wrist, the inside of his elbow, his throat, as often as he could persuade her to. Often enough that her lavender lips seemed permanently tinted pink.

I don't like to be defenseless, she'd whispered late one night. His arms had been around her, her breathing so slow and light he'd thought she was asleep.

His mouth had curved. He'd traced the vulnerable expanse of her back. *I know, honey.*

She'd turned her face. Her cheek had pressed against his heart. *But you make me feel like I don't need defenses. Like all the walls I've tried to build don't matter, because you're here inside them. With me.*

She'd let him hold her—let him keep his palm between her shoulder blades until her skin warmed beneath his hand.

He'd forced back the desire to hold her tighter. To demand something she wasn't ready to give.

It was enough. It had to be enough.

She'd spent the previous night—Friday—at his house, and they'd wandered, slow and dreamy, down to the Incarnare boardwalk after the cats had woken them up at dawn for breakfast. The wind had mussed her hair, and it felt easy to wrap his arms around her from behind. To press his palm against her chest and feel the steady beat of her heart.

"The donut stand's open," he murmured into her hair. She liked the cinnamon-sugar ones the best, donut holes dropped hot and freshly sugared into a waxed bag.

She smiled at him and let him buy the donuts. She had on something silky and ribbed: a pajama set? Some yoga . . . thing? The little Nonna had managed to stuff in his head about women's fashion didn't extend to soft, clinging lilac blue that outlined every curve and plane of Sophronia's body.

God. It was bliss to be with her like this—away from

HemoCorp, together in the sun. To slip his finger beneath the strap of her tank just to feel a little more of her skin.

They shared the donut holes and watched a family make their ponderous, overly burdened way down the beach. The dad had four or five kid-sized coats—impressive, since there were only three children—and a handful of Popsicle-colored beach toys. The mom was chasing the kids in a sort of maniacal way with a towel, and the oldest one tickled the toddler until he screamed with laughter.

"They're vampires," she said softly.

He blinked. Looked down at her. "Really? I thought vampires usually only had one kid."

"The kids are vampires, and the dad. The mom's a human. I can . . . hear it. In their heartbeats."

He felt his mouth curve up as he looked out at the family. He could see it, he supposed. The dad was tall and thin, though at this distance Casey couldn't make out fangs against his deep-brown skin.

"It's—" He paused. Tried again. "I used to love to see that. Human-vampire families."

She shifted, tilting her head to look back at him. "You don't anymore?"

"I still do. It's just . . . I used to think 'That's what we're doing with Stokr. We're helping make that possible.' I know all the Count Fuckula jokes, believe me. But I guess I was really in it for *that*."

"Casey," she said softly.

He shifted his hand across her chest, tucking his thumb into the notch of her collarbone. He had a little sugar on his fingers; the grains rubbed against her skin. "We'll get it back. We just need a little more time."

"I believe it. I believe *you*." She tipped her head back

against him. Her eyes closed, her lashes dark against her cheeks. She took a slow breath. "I wasn't in it for the love matches."

"Stokr?"

"Yes. I—" She paused. He felt her muscles tense beneath his hand and then—as if deliberately—release. Her chest rose and fell. "I was in it because I didn't want any more humans to die, I guess. Not from a bite, at least. Not if we could stop it."

He pressed his cheek against her hair. "Yeah?"

"The blood patches helped. I was eleven when HemoCorp invented those, did you know that? Octavia had just started working in synthetics. The blood patches were her brainchild. They seemed like a miracle at first. No more"—her voice hitched—"accidental killing. But it wasn't perfect. It didn't *prevent* the exsanguinations, not like Stokr, only reacted to a crisis. People didn't always have them on hand, and it was the vampires who needed them *most* who didn't have them. The ones who . . . the ones who assumed nothing bad would ever happen to them. Reckless and stupid. Young."

He remembered her that first day in the boardroom, when he'd told her about Ellery Klein. Her ferocity, her lethal speed. The way her fingers had trembled.

He remembered all the times she'd hesitated to let the Pillbugs get involved: her fears, her protectiveness. How she'd turned away from his wrist in the elevator—refusing to drink, even if it killed her.

He knew she wasn't done talking. He brushed his thumb along her collarbone, slow and soothing, and watched the ocean instead of her face.

"When I was sixteen," she said, "we killed a girl."

He kept on stroking her skin with his thumb. Refused to pause, to display shock. To hesitate.

He wouldn't do that to her.

"We . . . didn't mean to. It was an accident. Her name was Izzy." Sophronia's voice had gone raw; he could feel her delicate heartbeat fluttering beneath his palm. "We were in this vampire boarding school called Holbeck Priest. We weren't supposed to leave the grounds—to associate with the townie humans—but Del couldn't resist. She met Izzy at a playground, of all things. On the swings. Izzy introduced her to Skittles. Del adored her, and I was . . . jealous, a little bit. But it was hard to be jealous, because Izzy was so smart and interesting. Her mom was a French professor, and she was always talking about—I don't know, Liszt and ice-skating and—"

Her voice cracked. He wrapped his other arm around her waist, pulling her tighter against him.

When she spoke again, she'd gotten her voice back under control. "I was the one who invited Izzy to the party in Julian Vulpecula's dorm. It was all vampires. I *never* should have brought her. But Julian was—he and I, we . . ." She trailed off. Her chest rose jaggedly beneath his hand. "We were going to make a brilliant dynastic marriage. That's what everybody said. When he suggested that we test Izzy's blood to see which of us was a match, I didn't do anything to stop it."

He could picture her as she must have been then: tall, her brows drawn together in a scowl, taut with tension in the face of all that teenage recklessness.

But somehow the image wouldn't settle.

He remembered the way she'd looked on Nonna's doorstep. Her tiny hesitation before she'd sat down with the rest of them at the diner.

A crack. A fissure. A hint of yearning breaking through.

That, maybe, was how she'd been back then. Wanting to be one of them and not sure how to ask for it.

"Izzy cut the pad of her thumb," Sophronia went on evenly. "For each of us to test. Del wasn't a match. Julian wasn't either. That was . . . as far as we got. One of the other boys—René—lost control and bit her. It happens sometimes, especially with young vampires. That's why they keep us off at schools at that age, away from humans. Because sometimes, with the scent of blood in the air, they can't . . . they can't . . ."

"Soph," he murmured. "Sweetheart."

"We pulled him off her," she said. She reached up, wrapping her fingers around his forearm. "But Izzy just kept bleeding and bleeding. René didn't mean to, he was sorry, he was *so sorry*. Somebody ran for help, but . . . it was already too late. We didn't have a blood patch. And she died."

He brushed his thumb along her collarbone again.

He knew it intimately: that twisting knife of regret, the slow haunting of memory. The way the past sent barbed tendrils into the present, never quite letting you free.

From what he knew of her upbringing, it would have been difficult for her to let her guard down even then. Teenage Sophronia would have already had a lifetime in Vega-vampire training to remind her that emotions were a weapon to be used against her.

She'd invited a human—Izzy—into a circle of vampires she'd loved and trusted, and it had ended in Izzy's death.

And he knew her well enough by now to know that she would have blamed herself.

It seemed like a miracle, somehow, that she'd let him in all those weeks ago with Stokr. *She* seemed like a miracle: the way she kept on trying.

"That's what I used to think about," she whispered. "With Stokr. That what happened at Holbeck Priest didn't have to happen anymore."

He held on to her and breathed deep. Felt her chest rise and fall in the same rhythm as his own.

He smelled her and the ocean. Cinnamon-sugar donuts. Axle grease and seaweed and vampires and humans. Life plunging onward, sweet and painful and unstoppable.

And then, with his hand still pressed against her heart, he dropped his mouth to her ear. "We're not going to stop," he murmured. "We're going to figure this out, Soph. I promise. I won't ever, ever stop."

It felt dangerous to say it. He couldn't promise her that he would fix Stokr single-handedly, not really.

But he meant it differently. Not Stokr, but *this*. But *her*.

If she let him, he would never give her up.

"I talked to the analyst's husband last week," she said quietly.

He paused. "You did?" As far as he knew, the analyst's disappearance was a cold case—no one had found any evidence, any sign of where she'd gone. No one had even seen her enter HemoCorp that morning, except the two of them.

"I called him. I told him that we'd . . . put all the considerable resources of HemoCorp behind finding out what had happened to his wife. It was probably stupid of me to do. Octavia would be furious. If I even hinted that HemoCorp had some culpability in her death, the potential for lawsuits would be—"

"Soph."

His voice brought her to a halt.

He reached up to tuck her windblown hair behind her ear. "It was the right thing to do."

"I just kept thinking, with Izzy . . . Did anyone ever apologize to her family? I didn't. My parents wanted my involvement hushed up. René pled guilty to accidental manslaughter, and there wasn't a trial, and so I never saw . . . they wouldn't let me . . ."

She twisted in his arms. Her eyes were dark and blue and pained. Her hand lifted in the direction of the vampire-human family on the beach. "I can't . . . I don't know if I can ever . . ."

He caught her hand and warmed it between his. "What?"

"*Be* like that. Like them."

He looked out at the family, trying to see them as she did. "I don't know what you mean."

"Easy," she said. "Warm. A family."

His breath ruffled her hair. "Honey."

"It's not that I don't want—" Her voice cracked. "It's just—I don't see how I could—" Her shoulders had curled in, but her eyes were dry, her jaw tense with pain. "I keep thinking—what if I tried, and it turns out I'm just like my mother?"

Seagulls wheeled and screamed overhead. Rides were starting up behind them: He could hear the slow metallic grind, the clattering of gears.

He cupped her cheek, pink from the wind and his blood. "You're not."

"You don't know that, Casey. You didn't know her."

"I know *you*." God, he did. Her deep and terrible loyalty, her intensity, her exactingness—all of it was how she loved. With everything in her. With every part of her fragile, bottomless heart..

Her gaze shifted to the family. Back to him.

She searched his face, and the fear and hope in her expression nearly cut him off at the knees.

"It wouldn't be easy," she said quietly. "With me. I'd work too much. Want too much. Be afraid to say . . . what I felt."

He brushed his thumb across her mouth, then tucked his hand into her hair. "Nothing that's really worth it is easy, honey." He dropped his head. Kissed her once, slow and deep. And then a second time because he couldn't stop himself. "*You* are what I want. As you are. Sometimes, I feel like—"

He hesitated on the words. He wanted . . .

God, he wanted her. He wanted to tell her that sometimes she felt like the easiest thing in the world to him. That she made his past—the grief and pain and patience of being alive—feel worth it because all of it had led him here. Had made him for this moment, for this *person*, his edges fitting exactly to hers, his world bending around her as though she'd always been there.

Impossible, now, to imagine his house without her in it. His bed without her legs twined cool through his. His kitchen table without her there, a cat curled up in her lap as she looked up at him, helpless, smiling. Happy.

His phone buzzed in his pocket.

He bent, instead of answering it, to kiss her. But he'd barely set his mouth against hers when the vibration caught his attention again—not his phone, this time, but hers.

Again. Again.

He drew back. Her lips parted on an indrawn breath, and then she pulled out her phone to see what was going on that needed their attention so urgently at seven o'clock on a Saturday morning.

It was Del calling. Sophronia met his eyes, and he nodded at her to answer it, taking out his own phone as she did.

"Del? Is everything okay?"

"Soph." He could hear Del through the phone's speakers. Her voice was tight. "Have you talked to your dad?"

"My dad? No, why?"

"You haven't seen the news?"

"What news?"

Casey couldn't make out whatever Del said next.

There was a . . . humming . . . in his brain. A strange ice-cold vibration that deadened his hearing, that plunged through his body like poisoned darts.

His phone screen was filled with notifications: more and more pouring in as he watched. Alerts he'd set up for the word *Stokr*; news headlines; frantic texts from Mercedes and Brendan and George.

All of it familiar.

All of it impossible.

STOKR, he read, and BLOODBATH and BACK ONLINE and Casey I don't know what the fuck is going on, are you at HemoCorp??

TWO DEAD, he read. AND COUNTING.

CHAPTER 27

The executive-committee emergency alert had gone off an hour ago. It hadn't been sent to Sophronia.

She tried not to let that knowledge push into her chest like a shard of ice.

She and Casey had practically run to HemoCorp from the boardwalk. Casey had been frantically reading her everything he could find on his phone—the news, texts from the Pillbugs. Somehow, a new version of Stokr had been deployed to the app store for eager users to install. Not many people had noticed at first, but by 2:00 a.m., the tiny trickle of #stokr posts on social media had exploded into a fire hose.

Stokr was back. *Everyone* was talking about it.

It was a Friday night. Everywhere, all over the country, in bars and clubs and late-night coffee shops and backs of movie theaters, people logged in for the first time in months and matched and matched and matched.

And just like the last time, the matches didn't work. Worse than before—because this time Stokr's users hadn't known the app was coming back. They didn't have blood patches in their bags just in case.

They'd been gleeful. Defenseless.

This time, two humans had died before the app had gone offline again.

Her mind spun, dizzy and tractionless. She didn't know what the hell had happened. Casey had found the emergency meeting in her father's calendar. He'd sent frantic texts to Mercedes trying to figure out who'd deployed the APK—how they'd gotten around the guardrails he'd set up and why he hadn't been alerted when someone accessed the console—but Mercedes didn't know either.

No one had approved the app's release. There was no one *to* approve it, now that Sophronia had left DP&S and the Pillbugs had been reassigned.

And . . . no one had told her about the meeting.

It didn't bode well.

She shoved through the door to the conference room on the seventeenth floor. They were predictable—they always chose that one.

Everyone was inside, arrayed around the conference table. Octavia, Titus, Circinus. Kriti and Holmwood and the other humans on the executive committee.

Her father.

Despite the early hour and the fact that it was Saturday, each of them looked crisp, dressed for work. Not wind-flushed, cinnamon sugar and sand still lingering in the hollows of their palms.

"Dad," she got out. Her voice was breathless. "I just heard. What's going on? When was Stokr approved to go back online?"

"Sophronia." Her father was clipped, as always. Precise. Layered with cold and sediment. "It's good that you're here."

She had just a moment—one single shimmering instant—

to feel a flare of pride. Her father *had* wanted her there. He was glad she'd come.

And then he went on talking.

"I find you have anticipated my question, Sophronia. When was the Stokr restoration approved?" His mouth was tight. "And by whom?"

Her brows drew together. She looked down the table, to where Kriti looked back, her glasses on a chain around her neck, her lips pressed tightly together. To Titus: pale, weary, almost expressionless.

To Octavia, whose cool mask couldn't quite hide the fact that she was, the faintest bit, pleased.

"I don't know," Sophronia said. "I have no idea how a new version of the app got pushed out. I—"

"You have no idea?" Octavia repeated scornfully. "Please."

"You—" She tried to swallow. "You can't think that I had something to do with this."

"There was no decision made to turn Stokr back on," her father said. "Not from the executive committee, at least. The app was to remain shuttered."

"I know. I *agreed*—"

"Did you?" her father said. His voice was soft. Deathly. "I don't recall your agreement with any of my decisions regarding this product."

There was a terrible sensation in her chest, a weight crushing her lungs. "I . . . of course I wanted to keep the division open. I didn't want to reassign my team. But the most important thing to me has always been safety. Figuring out what went wrong with Stokr in the first place, not just getting it back online. All along I've been trying to find out the truth."

"Sophronia."

It was Titus this time. Not her father. His voice was gentle and tinged with terrible empathy.

"I know you wanted Stokr back," he said. "I would understand—all of us would understand—if you initiated the app's deployment. Not to hurt people. I don't believe that. But because you were under the impression that the program had been fixed."

She looked at Titus. Her father. Could they . . . Could they really *believe*—

"I didn't," she said. "I would never approve Stokr's restoration without talking to you."

"But if you wanted to prove to us that the app could be used safely—"

"No."

She felt sick. Obviously they had discussed this—and just as obviously, they'd come to one logical, if hideously wrong, conclusion.

They thought she had turned Stokr back on in some misguided attempt to prove that it was fixed.

The chaos—the deaths—

They thought all of it was her fault.

"I want to believe you," her father said. "Tell me, Sophronia. If you're not responsible for the app's restoration, who else could it have been?"

"I—" She looked helplessly around the table. "I don't know."

"Who would have had the technical knowledge? The necessary administrative access?"

Octavia's black-tipped nails clicked down against the table. "August. Is this pitiful attempt at subtlety necessary? We *know* who had the ability. Whether Sophronia was intentionally party to this fiasco or merely complicit is at this point irrelevant."

Sophronia blinked. Her lips parted.

Merely complicit? She didn't . . . she didn't know what . . . But no. She *did* know.

Octavia meant *Casey*.

"No," she whispered, but Casey was already talking, his voice firm.

"My team and I had nothing to do with this."

For the first time since they'd entered the conference room, she let herself look at him. His jaw was set, his curls tangled from the wind off the ocean, from their mad dash to HemoCorp. From her own hands.

She trusted him. Down to her bones. With all the vulnerable muscle of her vampire's heart.

It hadn't been one moment. It had been a thousand of them: whiskey and sour mix, a photo of a little boy with a goat in his arms. His father's old car, and two tuxedo cats, and his palm on her chest as they looked out over the ocean. *She's going to love you* and *You're okay, honey, I promise* and *I would never let you down.*

He wouldn't betray her. He hadn't played a part in this disaster.

Someone was setting them up.

"It wasn't Casey," she said. She looked her father in the eyes. "Or Casey's team. They've been by my side every step of the way. They didn't turn Stokr back on. They would never do that—not if there was still a chance that someone could get hurt."

"Sophronia." Titus's palms pressed into the table. He looked tortured; he looked like every word was a knife, twisting deep in his own gut. "Do you think it's possible that your judgment has been compromised by this human?"

"No. I don't think that. Just because I believe in Casey's

loyalty doesn't mean that my judgment is compromised. It means I know him."

Octavia breathed out: a quick exhalation that skirted derision. Almost a laugh. "Of course."

"Octavia," Titus bit out.

But Octavia ignored him. Her gaze shifted to August. "Your daughter," she said softly, "isn't the only one whose judgment is compromised. Look at her, August. Be serious. You have to have seen this coming for weeks. Since the day she stormed out of your office when you forced her out of DP&S."

"He didn't force me out," Sophronia snapped. "It was my choice to leave. My decision."

A half dozen pairs of eyes snapped to her, and she realized . . .

They hadn't known. They hadn't realized the transfer had been her choice.

Octavia's gaze sharpened. A hint of a smile touched her mouth. "I see," she murmured. "And you truly expect us to believe that decision wasn't based on your romantic entanglements? That this was another instance of your 'uncompromised judgment'?"

Sophronia swallowed. Hesitated. She had . . .

Of course her feelings for Casey had played a role in her transfer. That didn't mean she was wrong about him or about Stokr.

But Octavia's words seemed to reverberate through the conference room. Circinus's head tipped back in surprise, and Titus had his jaw clenched tight. His fangs pressed down so hard into his lower lip that she could see a tiny pinprick of blue-red blood.

Her father turned away from Octavia. Toward Sophronia.

His eyes passed slowly over her, head to foot, and she felt herself flush under his cool gaze.

She knew what she must look like. Her hair was wind tangled, her arms bare. Sugar crystals still clung stickily to her collarbone.

Even the heat that had risen to her face—it would be visible on her cheeks because of all the fresh human blood in her veins.

Casey's blood.

"Dad," she said, and to her abject horror, her voice wobbled. She gritted her teeth and steeled herself. Tried to make herself a wall. "I've been telling you for months, there's something else going on here."

"You are too emotionally invested in Stokr. How many times have I told you that such intemperate feelings make us weak—"

"They *don't*," she said. "Loving Stokr—believing in Stokr—isn't a weakness, Dad."

But it felt like one. The hot tears clogging her voice, the thundering of her pulse in her ears, the impossible desire to lean into Casey and feel his strength—

Here in this boardroom, all of it felt like a weakness. She needed to be icy, to be professional, to be *perfect* so they would believe her.

And she couldn't do it.

"Stokr has been nothing but a weakness," Octavia hissed. "Since the day we went public with it, HemoCorp has suffered." A hint of venom had crept into her voice. "Have you taken a look at the stock prices this morning, Sophronia? Because I have. I—"

"Is that really what you care about?" Sophronia demanded. "Shareholders? Two people *died*, Octavia."

"That's correct. Two deaths on *your* conscience. Because you wouldn't let this project go."

The conference room went airless.

Sophronia felt her lips part. She wanted . . . she wanted to say something. To protest. She wanted to breathe in, but she couldn't remember how.

Two deaths on your conscience. Because you wouldn't let this project go.

She'd dreaded exactly this for months now. She'd wondered, in the lonely doubtful hours of predawn, if she should stop investigating. Would the people she cared about be safer if she gave up? If she let the saboteur get away with what they'd done?

Always—always Octavia went right to the heart of Sophronia's fears.

And every time, Sophronia didn't know if she could believe it.

Her gaze flickered to her father.

But it was Casey who stepped forward. Pushed close enough to Octavia that the vampire had to look up to meet his gaze.

"That's bullshit," he said. His voice was low. Murderous. "It's a lie."

Sophronia felt her skin go to ice.

She wasn't close enough. She would never be quick enough, if Octavia lost control.

"Casey," she said. "Step back."

But he didn't listen—this intolerable human, with his big stupid heart and his ruinous courage.

"These deaths are *not* on Sophronia's conscience." His voice grated on the words. "She has done everything in her power to prevent this from happening. Her entire life has been devoted to stopping accidents exactly like this one. She would never do anything to put those humans at risk."

The words were a great shattering flood, razing the last of her walls, tearing her down to the studs.

He believed in her. He wasn't afraid to say it.

But then Octavia breathed a laugh, her chin lifted, and the sound made Sophronia's skin crawl.

"She would never do anything to put humans at risk?" Octavia repeated. "Quite a claim, Mr. Amato, when I can still see the marks she left in your neck."

Casey's jaw flexed. He let the silence between them settle for a long, taut moment, and when he spoke, his voice was firm.

"That's enough," he said. "That's more than goddamned enough."

Octavia stared at him, her gray eyes cool and challenging. She dropped her gaze deliberately to his throat, and then—

She curled her lip in a snarl, showing her fangs.

Sophronia was across the room. She shoved herself in front of Casey—she would *kill* Octavia if she touched him; she would bleed her dry if she put a fucking finger on his skin; she would—

"Sophronia," her father snapped. "Control yourself."

She took a breath—her chest heaved—her lips were parted, and her fangs brushed her lip, scalpel sharp.

She kept her eyes on Octavia even as she spoke to her father: a constant simmer, a low vibrating threat. "I'm fine."

"You're not," her father said. And then, on a painful breath: "I want you to take a leave of absence from HemoCorp."

Her chest compressed, squeezing the air from her lungs. Her gaze darted to her father, then back. "What?"

"Take leave. Indefinitely. Clear out your desk, Sophronia, and go home."

"No." She felt Casey's hand settle on her shoulder. "I can't just leave. I have to—"

"There's nothing that you have to do here, Sophronia." Her father's voice softened. He looked, for the space of one heartbeat, stricken. "I've let you take on too much at HemoCorp."

"Dad." The syllable was an agonized exhalation. "How can you say that?" She'd done everything he'd ever asked—she'd left DP&S—she'd been *perfect.*

"I don't mean too much at the company. I mean too much for *you*. I let you wrap your identity up in HemoCorp, the same way I did a lifetime ago. It's not—good, Sophronia. To be this way. I . . . have regrets." August's gaze shifted to Casey, his gray-purple lips held tight, as though at any moment they might twist into the shape of pain. "Both of you. Paid leave until I say otherwise."

"Dad—"

"Don't," he said quietly. "Don't argue. Don't make it worse."

She couldn't breathe. She couldn't *think*. HemoCorp was everything—family and memory and safety—and she loved it, and she couldn't bear to let it go.

She looked at her father: his pale-blue eyes, the sharp prominence of his nose. The curve of his mouth, a firm stroke of restraint and sorrow.

He wouldn't want her to make a scene. He wouldn't want her to beg.

And so she didn't.

She was ice. She was a wall. She was a Vega, and she was

the Queen of the Damned, and even if it killed her, she wasn't going to break in front of them.

She gave her father a brief, sharp nod. She let Casey slide his hand down her arm. And then she took his hand in hers and walked out of the conference room without looking back.

Out of HemoCorp.

CHAPTER 28

They were at Casey's house when Mercedes blew through the door and cracked everything wide open.

They'd had nine days off together. Nine nights and Casey had persuaded Sophronia to stay at his house for all of them.

He'd texted Del the moment they were home—a terse summary of what had happened in the boardroom.

Don't let her be alone, Del had sent back. I'll be there soon.

She'd appeared at his house two hours later with a suitcase full of Sophronia's things and a feathered wand for the cats. She hadn't said much to Sophronia, but the press of her head against Sophronia's shoulder, her arm wrapped around Sophronia's waist—it had been all gentle, wordless devotion. A whole lifetime's worth of love and comfort.

He'd had to take Sophronia back to HemoCorp the next day because she'd needed to pick up a few personal items from her office. At the front door, her ID card hadn't worked. She hadn't realized what was happening at first—neither of them had. Casey had thought it was some tech issue with the card, until he'd realized his didn't work either.

They were barred from the building.

He'd never seen her look like that before. A single flash of bare-faced shock. Of betrayal.

And then covered over by a mask of calm that he could see right through. That nearly broke when he took her hand.

She was devastated. Octavia's viciousness, her father's decision—all of it had shaken her down to her bones.

She didn't want to talk about it. He didn't think she *could* talk about it, not without crumbling in a way he knew she wouldn't want him to see. But she let him hold on to her: wrap his arms around her in the kitchen, press his lips against the back of her neck as she washed her untouched mugs of tea.

He was so glad she'd stayed.

He taught her about sphagnum moss and peat soil because she asked him to. She liked to have her hands in the dirt, liked to watch the physical evidence of her labor as they sat on the patio at sunset. He kept on finding her with a cat in her lap, and he hung up a hammock for her outside because he thought she and the cats would like it. She beat him at Monopoly, and he took her to bed, and when they were nothing but sweat and naked limbs, all bodies and hunger, he gave her everything she would let him give.

The Pillbugs and Del came by whenever they could. George had taught Sophronia and Del how to play *Baldur's Gate*, which Del had fallen hard for—that, plus she seemed to be using it as a convenient excuse for how often she came over to sit quietly next to her best friend. Brendan had found a candy shop that made extremely expensive alcohol-laced sugared jellies, which he presented to Sophronia so proudly that Casey felt a sudden and embarrassing urge to cry.

She was going to be okay. He would make it so.

On the ninth night, Del was over. She had a glass of Titus's wine in her hand, and she was waving it precariously while she filled in Sophronia on some arcane HemoCorp gossip that had gone down earlier that day.

You'll need to know this when you get back, she'd said.

Like it was a foregone conclusion. Like someday everything would go back to normal.

Casey was next to Sophronia on the couch. She had on shorts, which he loved, and his palm was wrapped around her thigh. He could feel the muscles there, flexing and releasing as she shifted closer to him. Her skin was cooler than he liked.

Later, when Del left, he would try to get her to drink from him again. She would protest—it was too soon; his blood hadn't had time to replenish. She could take a blood bag.

But he wanted her to drink from him. Right now, with the two of them locked out of HemoCorp and their investigation barely functional, his blood seemed like the best thing he had to offer her.

He couldn't bear to be helpless. Not with this. Not with her.

"I don't understand," Sophronia was saying. "Circinus is seeing one of the marketing vamps? And *she* was the one who was reassigned?"

"It's bullshit," Del said. Sophronia leaned over and tipped up the edge of Del's wineglass before it spilled sideways from the force of her outrage. "It's medieval. Are we *sure* some of these vampires aren't immortal? Because the ethics are giving Tudor court."

Casey rubbed his hand across his mouth to hide a smile. "Don't tell Brendan."

"Oh Abraham." Del laughed into the rim of her glass. "The other day he asked me to look at a daguerreotype he was *convinced* was Raymond Winterburn-Ross. It was from 1842. I really, really wonder where on the internet he found it."

Sophronia was laughing, too, just a little bit, soft and disused, and he was relishing it, wondering how to get her to laugh again, sending Del a quick, grateful glance—

The front door opened.

All three of them came to abrupt attention. They hadn't been expecting anyone.

But it was Mercedes, Casey realized, his shoulders easing. She had a key.

"Mer." He came to his feet, his fingers trailing past Sophronia's knee. "What's up? Everything good?"

Mercedes's face, he realized, was some mixture of shock and nerves and glee. Her hair—mint colored today—was standing on end. "You guys. Holy fucking shit, you guys."

Sophronia leaned forward, expression taut. "What happened?"

"It's—I don't even know where to—" Mercedes turned in a little frantic circle, like she couldn't decide whether to sit or run back out the door. "Should I wait for Brendan and George? I texted them, but I was only like two minutes away, so I came straight here, and—no. No, I shouldn't wait. What if—"

"Mercedes." Casey tried to make his voice gentle but firm, because Sophronia looked like she was about to leap off the couch and claw Mercedes's revelation from her brain. "What's going on?"

"Okay. Okay, okay." She flung herself onto the couch, her knee bumping Sophronia's, then seemed to notice Sophronia's tension. "You don't have to worry, I swear. It's good. I mean, I think it's good."

"Mercedes."

"Oh my God, I'm sorry. I'm freaking out." She yanked a tablet out of her bag and opened the now-familiar screen of Dr. LeBlanc's spyware program. "So remember how you guys left your phones in Soph's car when you abandoned it?"

"I do, yeah."

"I've been monitoring them. Absolutely nothing this whole time—I thought for sure Winterburn-Ross had just binned them or staked them or smashed them with a hammer or whatever."

"Staked them?" Del said dryly.

Mercedes waved a hand. "Don't act like he doesn't have a flair for the dramatic. Anyway, I set an alert in case anything happened with the phones, and it just went off about"—she checked the log on the program—"twenty-three minutes ago." She lifted her eyes to meet theirs, her expression fervent as a nun's. "Someone turned your phones back on."

"What?" Casey blinked. His mind spun.

All this time, Winterburn-Ross had held on to their phones. Why would he activate them now?

"I *know*. Luckily I was at work, and I had everything I needed right at my fucking fingertips. It only took me about forty-five seconds to activate Dr. LeBlanc's program. There was another device in the vicinity—two, actually—and so I—"

"Wait," Casey said. "Wait, that doesn't—what about the Faraday net? The cell network should have been blocked. You shouldn't have been able to—"

Mercedes shrugged. "I don't know. I'm guessing they had to take the phones outside the net in order to get them to turn on? Or temporarily disable the net for the same purpose? Either way, Casey, it *worked*. Dr. L.'s program worked exactly like it did at the HemoCorp executive summit. They had your phones turned back on for eleven minutes, and in that time, I was able to load the spyware onto the two devices that were in range."

"Mer," he breathed, "you're a genius."

She grinned at him. "I know."

Sophronia had a line between her brows, her shoulders thrown back. "I don't like this at all. Why would Winterburn-Ross reactivate our phones, when he went to so much trouble to shut them down with the Faraday net in the first place?"

"The net wasn't created just for our visit," Casey said. "He probably has it up as a precaution so that none of his employees can take photos or steal data from his house. He's paranoid in general, not about us specifically."

"And I'm positive he didn't know about Dr. L.'s program," Mercedes said. "One thousand percent."

"Why?" Sophronia asked. "How do you know?"

Mercedes's grin broadened. "Because he wouldn't have let himself get within a thousand feet of your phones if he knew."

Casey narrowed his eyes. "You mean—"

"Yup. One of the devices was Winterburn-Ross's personal cell phone. And now we have access to it."

Del let out a whoop, leaning across the couch to catch Mercedes around the shoulders. "You are an angel. A jewel beyond price. Holy shit—*Soph*—this could be the break we need."

Sophronia wasn't as gleeful as Del seemed to be. Her posture was still tight; Casey wrapped his hand around hers as she leaned forward to look at Mercedes's tablet. "What can we see on his phone? We can't read his emails, right? Or listen to his calls?"

Mercedes chewed on her lower lip, flicking through screens on the tablet. "No—just activity signatures. I can see every app and program he's accessed going back weeks."

"The program was intended to help us see who infiltrated the Stokr database," Casey said. "It doesn't have a keylogger or anything like that. It's bare-bones app activity—what the device is being used to do and when."

"We've got his call logs, though," Mercedes said. "Numbers that he's been texting."

Del set her wineglass down with a clunk onto the side table. "So we've got . . . what? More data to sort through? More analytics for the Pillbugs to run in their off time?"

"I can do it." Casey's heart beat hard—hopeful. This, finally, was something real he could do. He had all day now that he was on leave from HemoCorp. He could bury himself in the program's data until he had something to work with. Until he had something to tell Sophronia—some way to make everything right.

"Wait," Sophronia said slowly. One palm came down to press against her knee, and her other hand tightened on Casey's. "Check October 15. The day of the HemoCorp raid. Maybe we can see what Winterburn-Ross was doing while the raid happened. Maybe he called or texted someone while it was going down."

"Oh, that's good," Mercedes said. "Yes, absolutely. Doing it now—unless you want me to wait for George and Brendan?"

"Don't wait," Casey told her.

Mercedes nodded, eyes focused on the screen. "There's . . . yeah, okay. Holy shit. He was on the phone—basically the entire raid, he was on the phone. Same number. He made a call about five minutes before the raid started and then . . ." Her fingers flew. "He's called this number several times. He called it—oh shit." She looked up, dark eyes huge. "He called it last about three hours before Stokr went back online."

Casey felt Sophronia's fingers twitch in his grip. Her skin

was icy where it pressed against his. "Can we find out whose number it is?" she breathed.

"I don't—" Mercedes licked her lips. She tapped rapidly at the tablet. "I don't know. It's not . . . I don't recognize it. And when I search it, no name or address comes up. *Nothing* comes up."

"A burner phone," Del said. "That's what it's called, right? Anyone could be using it."

"Shit," Casey muttered.

Sophronia's pulse fluttered, visible at her throat. "Call it."

Mercedes looked up sharply. "What?"

"Call it. I want to hear who answers."

"Soph," Del said anxiously. "Are you sure that's—"

Sophronia's eyes were bright, bright blue, burning in the last shards of daylight. Agonized. "I have to know who it was. If it was . . ."

She trailed off.

She didn't have to finish. Casey knew exactly what she was afraid of.

Her father had been the one to shut Stokr down in the first place. And not just that—he'd done everything he could to put a stop to her investigation of the sabotage. He'd encouraged Sophronia to leave DP&S, and then he'd kicked them both out of HemoCorp.

She wanted to know if her father was behind this.

Mercedes had her hand raised to make the call, but Casey shook his head, stopping her in her tracks. "Wait. Don't. Not yet."

Sophronia's gaze flew to his face, and he reached out to find her other hand, to hold her long, tapered fingers in his.

"I know," he murmured. "I get it. But we have to be strategic about this. If we call this number and somebody answers, then we know who's behind everything that's happened. But we have no *proof*, Soph. No way to bring the saboteur to justice."

"How is this not proof?"

"Imagine what your dad would say. It's circumstantial. Anyone could've been talking to Winterburn-Ross during the raid. That doesn't mean they planned it together."

Her jaw tightened, but she didn't protest. She was so goddamned smart, so practical—even in her turmoil, she wasn't about to waste their best lead. "What do you think we should do?"

He freed one hand to rub absently at his jaw, staring at Mercedes's tablet as a plan swirled, split apart, then slowly coalesced in his mind. "What if we set a trap instead? Talk to whoever this is long enough to get hard evidence of their collusion with Winterburn-Ross?"

"How?"

"What if . . ." He slipped the tablet from Mercedes's hand to flick through the screens, confirming everything she'd told them. "What if we text this number, instead of calling?"

"How would that help? The moment this person gets a text from us—even from an unknown number—they're going to toss the burner immediately."

"Except the text wouldn't come from us." He looked from Sophronia to Mercedes and back again. "It would come from Winterburn-Ross."

Sophronia stared at him, and there was such fine, fragile trust on her face that it pulled at something deep inside him. "What do you mean?"

"Have you ever heard of number cloning? It's illegal, but . . . well, hell, so is plenty of other shit we've done at this point. If we go outside the US cell network, it's not hard. We send a text and make it look like it came from Winterburn-Ross's number. Say . . . say we've unlocked Sophronia's phone and found something suspicious on it. Something the saboteur can't just ignore."

Del was practically vibrating with excitement, her legs tucked up under her knees in the armchair. "*Yes.* And then we get whoever it is to admit their involvement. We'll have it in writing, Soph. There's no way your dad can deny it then."

Sophronia moistened her lips. Her fangs flashed, a quick glint of lethal white. "We could . . . we could tell them we have to meet in person. Get it all on video."

"Draw them out," Casey said. "Yes, Soph. Exactly."

She looked around the room—a slow, intense trail of focused blue. Her gaze passed over him, Mercedes, Del.

The people, he thought, that she trusted most in the world. The people she had chosen to believe in.

"Let's do it," she said. "How soon can we start?"

Mercedes ran a hand through her hair, her eyes on the tablet. When she looked back up, her expression had gone fierce and glitteringly focused.

"Now," she said. "We can send the text tonight."

CHAPTER 29

Sophronia sat in the back of Rick Tickle's catering van and tried to slow her pulse.

It was difficult. Her whole body hummed with anxiety—even Casey's familiar scent in her nose wasn't enough to calm her down. Her heart was beating so hard she could barely hear the humans', even though they were all pressed practically knee to knee in the van.

"Ten minutes," George murmured.

Sophronia's fangs bit down into her lower lip.

It had been about forty hours since Mercedes had texted the mystery number. George and Brendan hadn't even made it to Casey's house when they'd sent the first message.

They'd agonized over the language while Mercedes—after a quick call to Dr. LeBlanc for advice—had cloned Winterburn-Ross's cell phone number.

Eventually, Del had plucked the tablet out of Mercedes's hands and typed out the text. "Comms is what you pay me for, remember?"

"HemoCorp pays you," Sophronia had said reflexively and read the message over Del's shoulder.

My employees were able to reactivate your colleagues'

phones. I've found something you need to see regarding your role in our shared project.

"There," Del had said. "Winterburn-Ross is too paranoid to give anything away in writing. He wouldn't mention the raid directly or our names. But this way, we've invited our mystery traitor to implicate themselves."

They didn't have to wait long for a reply. In less than a minute, they'd had an answering text.

What did you find?

Sophronia's jaw had been so tense that she'd had to force the words out. "Not very incriminating."

"It's okay," Del had said. "It's a good sign. Whoever this is trusts Winterburn-Ross enough to keep talking."

She'd sent back: This conversation would be better had in person.

Fine. Where?

"How long do we need to set up?" Del had asked urgently. "Tomorrow?"

"Give us another day," Casey had said. "I want to do this right."

Incarnare Public Library, Del had sent. Wednesday at noon.

It was a good choice for the location—a two-minute walk from HemoCorp. It would be easy for all of them to watch and wait.

The reply came in seconds. I'll be there.

"Hang on," Sophronia had protested. "This isn't enough. They haven't admitted anything." If she wanted to convince her father that they'd found the traitor, they needed something concrete. Something beyond question.

Unless . . .

Her heart lurched.

Unless it *was* her dad on the other end of the phone.

"Give me a minute," Del had said distractedly. "I'm thinking."

Her fingers had flown over the tablet.

Be careful. They know you were involved.

I'll deal with it, came the reply. There was a moment of pause, and Sophronia held her breath, hoping against hope for more.

And then another text had appeared.

Remember: No blowback on Sophronia. That's always been part of the deal.

Brief. Terse.

Catastrophic.

At her side, Del had sucked in her breath. Casey's heart had sped up—Sophronia could hear it, hear the hiss and squeeze of valves as his blood rushed through his body.

"Is that enough?" Mercedes had asked. Her voice had been uncharacteristically anxious. "Do you think that's good enough? 'Part of the deal'—I mean, that certainly sounds incriminating . . ."

"I think it's enough," Del had said quietly. "Soph?"

They'd all looked at her.

Her head had hurt—a sick dizziness, like she needed blood. She couldn't talk around the hot stone lodged in her throat.

No blowback on Sophronia. That's always been part of the deal.

It sounded like August Vega. Underneath his cold command, he *did* care for her. She knew he did.

All this time, she'd been trying to understand him. His motive. Even if he did think Stokr was a vulnerability, or a humiliation too great to stand, why would he sabotage the app in such a dramatic and bloody fashion? Why not just push the executive committee to shutter it or shut down DP&S?

Could it have been for *her*?

It seemed suddenly, horribly possible that all his machinations had been some twisted effort to preserve the Vega dynasty's reputation. Perhaps he hadn't wanted to make his disapproval of his daughter's well-known pet project publicly known. Maybe that was why he had encouraged her to leave DP&S—because he'd known that Stokr was going to implode, and he wanted her insulated from the damage.

No blowback on Sophronia.

If she hadn't clung so hard to Stokr, been so insistent on staying the course of the investigation—if she hadn't shown up in the conference room covered in sugar and sand—her father's plan might even have worked.

"I think it's enough," she'd said to Del. She'd made her voice flat—emotionless—but her fingers stung, like her nerves were raw. Casey's hand wrapped around hers had felt hot. Burning.

"Okay," Del had said softly. "Wednesday at noon, Soph. All of this will be over."

But she didn't know how it could ever be over. Even now, parked a block away from the Incarnare Public Library, watching the street on a feed provided by George's drone, she still couldn't wrap her mind around what came next.

She knew she could stand up to her father. She knew she'd be able to confront him right there on the street. All of it roiled inside her: years of wanting to please him, of simmering resentment for the way he'd let her mother treat her. Her burning, potent, painful desire to resume control of Stokr—to go back to DP&S, to have her old life back, to make everything exactly the way it had always been.

But how could her life ever go back?

It couldn't. Not without August. She'd always wanted HemoCorp, above anything else in her life. But she hadn't wanted it like this: a trail of dead humans and her father responsible for all of it.

Some part of her still couldn't believe it. No matter what the text message had said.

Beside her, Casey reached out and wrapped his hand around her thigh.

She looked over. He had headphones on—all of them did—and his hair was a wild spill of curls beneath. His eyes were clear and patient and ready for whatever came next.

"You okay?" His voice was soft—soft enough that maybe the rest of the Pillbugs wouldn't hear.

She took a breath. Black pepper, green vines. Sweetness.

Murmured: "What if this doesn't work?"

There was barely any air behind the words—nothing more than a vibration as they passed her lips.

It didn't matter. He heard her anyway.

"It might not," he said. "If it doesn't, we'll keep trying."

She let herself look down at his hand. She could call to mind the image of his fingers on her hips, or intertwined with hers around an orchid pot, or curled into the sheets as she drew deep from his veins.

"If I had to bet, though," he said softly, "I'd bet on you. Every time."

She looked up at him. This, too, was as familiar now as the shape of his hand: the way he eased her. The way his warmth made her anxieties untangle and her fears ebb free.

When she opened her mouth, she found she wasn't quite sure what she meant to say. She wanted to tell him thank you.

She wanted to tell him she couldn't have gotten through the last few weeks without him.

She wanted to say that, these days, she could picture her life without HemoCorp. But she couldn't imagine a future without him.

Instead, George's voice cut in over their headphones. "Four minutes to noon. Stay alert."

"I am extremely fucking alert, George," Mercedes muttered.

Sophronia swallowed and fixed her eyes on the screen.

The time ticked down, closer and closer to noon. The six of them—she and Casey and Del and the Pillbugs—were close enough that she could hear every breath, feel every slight shift of weight. Each tiny movement sent her tension arcing higher.

Her gaze flicked from the screen to the back door of the van. Her muscles were taut, and some part of her wanted to throw herself out of the van instead of sitting in the dark. Step into the dazzling sunlight and *search*.

She wanted to be the first to find her father.

But when a familiar figure came into view on the screen—crisp charcoal suit, glistening shoes, gaze fixed on the black phone in his hand—it wasn't August.

It was Titus.

CHAPTER 30

Her breath caught. Her heart lurched.

Titus.

A lifetime of memories assaulted her, like waves pummeling her, knocking her back into the sand.

The internship he'd invented for her. The yellow legal pad he'd never failed to supply. *Make a carbon copy for my secretary. Your notes are twice as good as his.*

Her hand in his. Gold ribbon tied around a gift of cheap perfume.

His arm around her shoulders, two weeks before she'd graduated from Holbeck Priest. *Take a year or two before you come to HemoCorp. Give yourself time to be you, before you're the Vega heir.*

His familiar, gentle voice, speaking up for her, defending her—*always* defending her, even when her father kept silent.

August, he'd said. *Don't.*

Her throat constricted, tightening down and down, and for once the emotion collapsing her chest was easy to name. Heartbreak. Betrayal.

As they watched the screen, Titus came closer to the library's front door. But before he could pass through, he slowed, then stopped. His gaze was still fixed on his phone.

And then he turned away from the library and started to walk quickly in the opposite direction.

"What the hell," came Mercedes's voice in Sophronia's headphones. "Did someone tip him off?"

"Follow him with the drone," Casey said urgently. "Don't lose him, George. See if you can get in tight enough to read what's on that screen."

"Shit," George muttered. "I'm trying. I'm—"

But the drone was loud enough that Titus craned his neck, looking for the source of the whir as the device descended. His pace increased, almost a run, and Sophronia's chest throbbed: a sharp stab of fear and pain.

They were going to lose him. He was going to get away.

She gave in to the tense demand of her muscles and hurled herself at the van's back door.

"Sophronia, *don't—*"

It was Brendan's anxious protest in her ears, but she didn't listen. She yanked the headphones off and let them fall to the van's floor. The sun was bright and cool on her skin as she threw herself to the pavement and ran in the direction of Titus's retreating back. He must've heard her footsteps. His shoulders tensed, and his pace picked up.

She heard the Pillbugs scrambling to follow—their heartbeats, their breath—but she kept on running, a vampire's flat-out speed.

Titus tried to dart around a corner, but she was much too close. Nearly upon him now.

And then, abruptly, he slowed. Stopped.

And she knew even before he turned that he recognized the sound of her heartbeat. He knew it. As well as she knew his.

Finally, reluctantly, he wheeled around to face her. His

hand dropped to his side, his expression bleak with resignation.

"Sophronia," he said. His voice cracked.

"Titus." Her voice was shaking, too—emotion was a cliff, a wave she was afraid of being sucked under. She had no defenses left. "You . . . *you* sabotaged Stokr. You worked with Winterburn-Ross. Why would you—"

His complexion was gray, his mouth dark. "I didn't—"

"You *did*. We have proof that you did."

She sounded wrecked. She couldn't stop thinking of the tortured look on his face as he'd stared at her across the conference table, his hands pressed flat against the glossy surface. *Do you think it's possible that your judgment has been compromised by this human?*

He hadn't meant it. He'd been lying to undermine her. To make her doubt herself.

And she'd let him. She'd trusted him.

Because . . . why? Because he'd defended her? Was she really that weak—that starved for affection?

Her mother's voice hissed in her ears: *Once again you cannot control your pathetic desire to be just like the rest of them.*

"I didn't," Titus repeated, "ever want to hurt you. I'm so sorry, Sophronia."

"Why?" She tasted salt. "Why, Titus?"

"I needed HemoCorp. I needed . . . to be in control."

"*What?*" she demanded. It didn't make sense. "How would taking down Stokr give you—"

But before she could finish the sentence, the pieces assembled themselves in her mind: a cold tide of memory.

He's proud of what you've accomplished, Titus had told her at the summit. *Stay the course.*

Not to encourage her. To *manipulate* her. Because he wanted her to do exactly what she'd done—fight and fight for Stokr until she'd wrecked her own image, dragged her reputation through the mud.

She was the Vega heir. By publicly humiliating herself—by taking a starring role in the total collapse of the company's stock prices and shareholder trust—she wouldn't just lose her job.

She could destroy her position. Her father. Their name.

"Oh, child," Titus said hoarsely. "I'm sorry. I thought he'd be . . . I never dreamed he'd throw you out of HemoCorp. This wasn't how I meant for it to go."

She understood it now, all of it, clear and blazing. Titus had assumed her father would support her—that August Vega would throw his weight behind his heir and her pet project, and when Stokr burst into the headlines on a red blossom of death, he'd thought the executive committee would eliminate both Vegas from the company's leadership at once.

And Titus would have been next in line.

August, he'd said in the conference room, his face white with pain. *Don't.*

It hadn't been a plea for her sake. It had been for himself—pure ruthless dynastic maneuvering, the kind she had grown up enmeshed in. The kind her mother had tried, all her life, to teach her how to win.

By now the Pillbugs had caught up to them on the street. Del was with them—Sophronia could hear her heart, quicker and quieter than the humans', and when she darted a glance back at them, she could see that Del had positioned herself between the Pillbugs and Titus, a tiny fanged defense.

The drone buzzed above her head, and Sophronia realized that all this was being recorded. All of it was evidence; all this would be proof.

Titus's gaze had snapped to Del and the humans behind her. His fangs punched out against his lower lip, and Sophronia was so distracted by the sight—so ferociously alert to any threat to her humans—that she almost didn't see him slip the burner phone into his pocket.

"Who was it?" demanded Mercedes. "On the phone. Who texted you just now and told you not to do the meet? Was it Winterburn-Ross?"

For a moment, Sophronia didn't understand Mercedes's intensity. Her brain was still circling around Titus's betrayal, the sheer incomprehensible ruination of what she'd thought she'd known.

But then she did understand.

Who could've known that the texts they'd sent Titus were a trap?

Who but the six of them, sitting knee to knee in the van and watching Titus step out onto the street?

Casey, Mercedes, Brendan, George. Del.

Titus shook his head silently, refusing to answer Mercedes's question. Sophronia took a single step toward him, predator quick, her hand extended to seize the phone. But he bounded backward, and as he did, his lip curled up into a snarl. His fangs were fully extended, white and sharp.

She didn't . . .

He wouldn't hurt her. She didn't think he would. But still, she hesitated.

"Soph," Casey said urgently. "Stop. It doesn't matter."

"It does," she got out. Her voice was raw. "We have to know who—"

"We do know."

At the sound of his voice, she stepped back from Titus. Let her gaze dart to Casey and then back to the grim-faced vampire in front of her.

"Dr. LeBlanc's program," Mercedes breathed. She was staring at Casey. "You installed it on the burner phone while we were in the van."

"Pull it up," Casey said. "Check the logs."

Mercedes was already in motion, her fingers flying over her own device. It was bare seconds before she looked up.

At George.

George looked back, his hands locked around the controls of his drone. "I don't . . ." His dark eyes fell to the device in her hands. "I don't understand."

"You sent the text," she said, very low. "It's your number. You warned him."

George took a single reflexive step backward. He shook his head. "I didn't. I don't know what you're talking about."

"Give me your phone, then," she snapped. "Let me see your texts."

"I don't . . ." George fumbled with the controls of the drone. "I don't have it. I think—maybe I left it in the van? I haven't even looked at it all morning, I swear—"

Casey put his hand on Mercedes's arm. His voice, when he spoke, was very even. His gaze had shifted: away from George.

To Brendan.

"You took his phone," he said quietly. "Didn't you, Bren? Just now, in the van."

Sophronia's eyes shot to Brendan's face, shock pushing spikes of adrenaline into her veins, into her throbbing fangs.

Brendan looked sick. "Casey—"

"That's how you did it," Casey said. "That's how you did

all of this, isn't it? Stole George's phone to send the text so there wouldn't be any physical evidence tying Titus to you." He took a breath, harsh, through his nose. "Made me log into your workstation because you screwed up your multifactor authentication again. Only you didn't, did you? All those times you asked for my help—all those nights I covered for you when you fucked up the full-text index . . . What was your end game, Bren? For me to take the fall?"

"No." The word burst from Brendan's lips, agonized. "I didn't want you to get hurt. I didn't want *anyone* to get hurt. He said . . . he said the failures in the app would be local. He said we'd start at HemoCorp so everyone would have blood patches on hand. He said no one was going to die!"

"He lied to you," Casey said. "And two people are dead, and *still* you tried to save him—"

"No! I just—didn't want you to find out, that's all. But I didn't know if Mercedes had our office bugged, and none of you would leave me alone so I could warn him. I just wanted . . ." Emotion shredded his voice. "I just wanted all of this to *stop*."

"You've been trying to stop this?" repeated George. "Or stop *us*? The wiped access logs . . . and . . . and when the recording devices were destroyed . . . Was that *you*?"

"He said he'd protect you," Brendan said hoarsely. "He said he'd pay me and—and the only bad thing that would happen was that Stokr would go down. I'm . . . I didn't *know*—"

But Sophronia wasn't listening to George's revelation, to Mercedes's hissed, heartbroken retort.

Casey's words had hit her ears in a low buzz. They seemed to echo in her head, rebounding inside the bones of her skull.

All those times you asked for my help.

All those nights I covered for you.

She'd trusted Casey. He'd vouched for his team, and she'd watched them on the feeds, and she'd put *everything* in their hands . . .

And she'd been wrong. Two more people had died because she'd been wrong.

She felt nauseous. Dizzy. Her mind spun toward Titus, toward Casey, toward Julian Vulpecula's dorm and Izzy's blood on her hands, and she had *loved* them, Titus and Del and Izzy and Casey, and *this* was what happened; didn't she know by now that this was what happened when you let yourself *feel*—

She took a single step backward—away from Titus, away from all of them—but before she could go farther, her gaze caught on a figure coming fast down the street.

Too fast to be human.

Her father.

"I texted him," Del said breathlessly. "The minute we saw Titus on the screen. I thought—" Her voice wobbled on the words. "I hope it was okay, Soph. I thought you might need him."

But when August reached them on the street, he didn't turn to Sophronia. His eyes scraped across her, Del, the Pillbugs, then settled on Titus: his second-in-command, his longest-serving colleague at HemoCorp. His oldest friend.

In the end, it was Titus who spoke first. "I'm sorry," he said hoarsely. "About all of it. I had to, August."

"You should have come to me," August said. His voice was low, barely above a whisper. "Whatever you'd needed, I would have given it to you."

"I couldn't. I . . . couldn't."

August shook his head. His lips pressed tight: wordless and grim.

He was, first and always, a Vega. They didn't show emotion. And they didn't weep.

For a long, silent stretch, Sophronia wondered if Titus would try to argue—if he might turn to flee or bare his fangs. But he seemed to know he'd lost. He dropped his eyes, his head bowing, and turned his hands over, palms up.

Only then did August look to Sophronia. "I'll handle it from here."

"Dad—"

"Go home, Sophronia."

She took a breath, and it sounded like a sob.

She didn't let herself speak. She couldn't look at Del or Titus or Casey, and she could not—*could not*—fall apart.

She didn't wait to see what happened next. She spun and fled, and when agony tore at her throat, she fought it all back down.

CHAPTER 31

By the time Casey got to Sophronia's apartment, he was sick with worry.

She'd left the Pillbugs on the street—had turned and run and vanished, silent as a ghost. He'd wanted more than anything to chase after her, but he couldn't. He had to stay and deal with Brendan, debrief August Vega. Watch as the authorities carted Titus away.

He'd texted her a half dozen times and called another three. He'd resorted to texting Del, but she'd said the same thing.

Sophronia wasn't answering.

She'd been devastated when she'd seen Titus on the street. She hadn't been able to hide it.

And then when Brendan . . .

Casey couldn't catch his breath. He still couldn't wrap his mind around Brendan's betrayal, couldn't believe he hadn't put the pieces together sooner.

And when they'd all realized what Brendan had done, he'd seen the way Sophronia had looked at *him*.

He hated that she was alone right now. He wanted to talk, to explain. He didn't—

Fuck. He didn't want her to think that he had let her down.

The doorman knew Casey by now, but he still insisted on calling up to Sophronia's apartment. There was a long pause before he nodded, the phone at his ear, and then buzzed Casey up.

He found the door to her apartment unlocked when he stepped off the elevator. He let himself in.

"Soph?"

He knew she'd heard the door open and close—knew she'd heard *him*—but she didn't say anything.

Anxiety slid cold through his veins.

This is enough, he'd told himself, over and over. He could hold on hard enough for both of them because she kept on turning back to him.

But what if, this time, she didn't?

When he found her, she was in the kitchen. She was staring blankly down at an empty mug, her lips a deep, bruised-looking indigo.

Her kitchen was all stainless steel and pristine glass. Nothing like his. He'd been meaning to buy her a little herb planter for her window—he was pretty sure there was enough sun. He kept thinking about the satisfaction she'd taken in the simple, tactile pleasure of roots in soil, of water and the scent of lemon balm on his patio.

He hadn't had a chance to buy it. There hadn't been enough *time*—

His chest squeezed. Anxiety. Panic.

He shoved it back down.

"Soph," he said again.

She still didn't look up.

He stepped closer. He wanted to drag her into his arms, press his wrist to her mouth and tell her to drink. But he made himself take things slowly. He peeled her ice-cold hands from her mug so he could cradle her fingers between his. "Are you okay? I've been calling. Del said you weren't answering her, either, so I—"

She pulled her hands out from between his and let them drop to her sides. "I'm fine."

Her voice was flat. Emotionless.

It made the crushing pressure in his chest redouble.

But he forced himself to take a breath, to feel the pull of gravity, the solidity of the earth beneath his feet.

He knew her. He knew how hard it was for her to reveal even a hint of her vulnerability. He knew how Titus's betrayal would have shaken the foundation of her entire world.

He brushed his thumb across her knuckles just once and then drew back to give her space to breathe. "It's okay," he said quietly. "It's all right to be upset. I'm so sorry about Titus. About—everything."

The muscles of her throat flexed as she swallowed. She turned to the glossy counter and picked up the empty mug. Set it down again. Her eyes didn't meet his. "I'm fine, Casey."

He stepped a little closer. "Let me—do you have a blood bag, Soph? Or—if you wanted, you could—"

"I'm *fine*." Her voice snapped out, like ice cracking. "I'd like to be alone."

He pulled off his glasses to rub at his face. "I'm not going to leave you here by yourself. Will you let me call Del?"

"I don't need you to do anything for me."

The air in the room went thick. Choking.

He couldn't breathe. He couldn't—

He swallowed, a feeling like glass in his throat. He was

raw inside, heartbroken over Brendan and sick over his own mistakes, and he . . .

He wanted her to need him. He didn't know what it meant if she didn't.

"Soph," he said again. Helplessly.

"I asked you to leave."

He rubbed his hand across his mouth. "Don't do this. Don't shut me out. If you're upset with me, honey, then *talk to me*—"

She spun. *"Don't call me that."*

He swallowed again. His voice rasped. "Sophronia."

"What did you mean, Casey?"

"I don't—"

She looked at him now, fangs out, eyes blue as flame. "About Brendan. You said you . . . you said you covered for him. How much did you know?"

He stepped back, as shocked as if she'd slapped him. "I didn't know anything. How could you think that I—"

"You *said* you did. You said—"

"I *helped* him. He was mine—my junior engineer—I wasn't just going to let him . . . he messed up a few times, that's all. I didn't think he deserved to get fired."

"So you lied for him?"

"No! I just . . . I fixed things for him. Made it seem like nothing had happened."

A fine trembling was running through her. Her pulse was beating hard enough that he could see it, a scattershot blue throb beneath her skin. "I tr—"

The word cracked in half. She gasped for breath.

"Soph—"

"I *trusted* you."

Her cheeks were wet, and her voice sounded like death,

and the words might as well have eviscerated him, so hard did they land.

Memory was sticky and rain-cold, dragging him into black night, toward lights as bright as a scream. His mother's hands were in his, and he was helpless. Out of control.

He couldn't breathe. He tried to anchor himself. Tried to find Sophronia's fingertips, tried to remember she was safe. "Soph. I'm so goddamn sorry about Brendan, but I don't . . . you have to believe that I didn't . . ."

Her chest heaved, the way it had in the elevator, the way it had when she was dying. "I trusted you. I *believed* you. I let your team into the security system, and I fought to keep Stokr open, and I thought—I thought everything would be okay if we—"

"You weren't wrong to—"

"How many people have to die," she bit out, "before I finally *learn*?"

"Soph—"

"No." She took a step back. Her shoulder blades hit the wall behind her. "I can't do this right now."

He moved closer to her. Took her hands. "It's not your fault. It's—"

She yanked herself free. "Stop."

"I'm not—"

"I asked you to *leave*."

He knew it wasn't rational, the hot, panicked feeling in his body. It was just—it was just—

Leaving felt like abandoning her. Abandoning *them*. It felt like death.

He felt himself careening. Wet tires slick against asphalt. "Don't do this," he said. "Goddamn it, Sophronia, I need—"

He broke off. His chest rose and fell, and he tried to make himself stop.

But she pushed.

And he was already sliding.

"What?" she said. "What do you need?"

"More." He sucked in air. "All this time—I've been so fucking patient with you—I've waited and waited, and I haven't asked you for anything, but I can't—fuck, Soph. I need *more* from you than this."

He tried to stop the words even as they slipped free: hot shards, bloody and slicing and selfish, and all of it because he was so scared.

He didn't want to lose her. Sometimes he felt like he'd spent his life balanced on a wire, everything he did designed to prevent exactly this: standing helpless, useless, as his heart's blood slipped through his grasp.

Her jaw tightened. Her chin lifted. Her voice came out clear, as if each syllable were encased in ice. "If you've been waiting for some kinder, gentler person to emerge, Casey, then I am sorry to tell you that you've been waiting in vain. This is who I am."

"That's not what I meant, and you know it." He tried to cup her cheek—put his fingers in her hair—but that was wrong too. She reared back away from him: His skin was too hot, and her cheek was diamond-cold.

"There is no more." She bit the words off, fangs flashing. "I can't give you more, because I have nothing else inside me to give."

"That's not true. I know you, Soph."

"Obviously," she hissed, "you don't."

"Soph—"

She stepped away from him. When she spoke, her voice was flat. "I want you to go."

And he—

He didn't know what was right and what was wrong anymore. He'd fucked up with Brendan and here, too, with her. He'd told himself he'd be there to help her, to *comfort* her, and instead he was systematically tearing both of them to shreds.

Go, she'd said.

And maybe that was right. Maybe that was the only thing he could do.

"Okay," he said quietly. "Okay, Soph. If that's what you want."

But he didn't turn. Didn't step away. For the space of a dozen heartbeats, he only stood motionless, his eyes on her face. He . . .

Christ. He was still hoping she'd stop him.

She didn't. She broke his gaze, and eventually, he turned and left her there.

The only sound as he walked out the door was the throb of his own pulse.

CHAPTER 32

Everything went back to normal.

Sophronia had her office back, and Wendy. Del brought gummy worms. When Sophronia held her ID card to the door of the HemoCorp building, it opened.

She went running every night and every morning before work, and she didn't pass by the boardwalk, not ever, not even once.

Casey had called her phone three times and texted once, and she hadn't answered any of it.

She'd deleted the text as soon as she'd read it. And then, an hour later, she'd given in and searched the internet for how to recover it, her heartbeat thudding in her ears and her hands clumsy, her chest tight with something she *refused* to let herself feel.

I'm sorry, his text had said. I miss you. If you want to talk, I'm here.

She didn't reply.

Titus was gone from HemoCorp, and Brendan too. They'd both been charged. Titus had suborned Brendan over the summer, apparently, with promises to pay off his student loans and the rest of his debt. He'd told Brendan that no one would get hurt.

Somehow, over the last decade, Sophronia had forgotten the things her mother had taught her about the vampire dynasties. The lessons they learned in childhood: to fight for supremacy, to be ruthless, to bleed your enemies dry. As the head of the Fornax family, Titus was a master at those sorts of games. It had been a reflex as natural as breathing for him to manipulate Brendan.

It had been child's play, she thought, for Titus to manipulate *her*.

Her relationship with her father was more distant than ever.

She'd brought Titus up to August a single time, when he'd called her in for a meeting to tell her that he and the rest of the executive committee had decided to restore Stokr. She couldn't seem to let it go: the fact that, even now, they still didn't fully understand the extent of Titus's treachery. He'd refused to talk to anyone other than his lawyers.

She wondered, had Titus known she and Casey were going to Winterburn-Ross's compound?

Had the decision to try to kill them been, not Winterburn-Ross's, but Titus's?

Sometimes, when she thought of Titus—his wife and his family, his hand wrapped around hers—she still couldn't quite believe it.

But her father had responded to her tentative inquiry with a flat, frozen look. "I'll handle Titus," he'd said. "Focus on your new position."

And so she went back, as she always did, to her office at HemoCorp. Two days ago, the board had approved her promotion. She was the youngest member of the executive committee in the company's history.

She'd replaced Titus.

Sophronia had seen Casey only once since that day in her kitchen—in a meeting where he'd presented on the guardrails they'd developed for the new version of Stokr.

His hair was shorter. Beneath his glasses, his eyes looked bruised. His blood had long since left her body; he didn't smell like *hers* anymore.

And still, her skin ached for his.

You ok, sweetie? Del had texted her that afternoon, in the middle of Octavia's interminable presentation about R and D's wound-regeneration project.

Of course, Sophronia had sent back.

But she wasn't. When she slept, she had nightmares about Izzy's blood, and her mother's voice, and her own kitchen, the cold cruelty of her words an echo that wouldn't leave her ears. She'd started running instead of going to bed, sprinting until her thighs burned and the wind whipped tears and sweat from her face indiscriminately.

Vegas didn't cry. Not even at night, in the dark, when she was so lonely she couldn't breathe.

Casey didn't text her again, and she didn't text him either.

Softness, she told herself, was indistinguishable from weakness.

And if she thought about Casey—existing in defiance of everything she'd been taught, flourishing, like green leaves rising toward the sun—she forced herself to remember that it was impossible for her to survive like that. That no one, not even Casey, was safe enough to trust.

Not even herself.

CHAPTER 33

Inside the house in Parce Domine, Nonna fixed a tray of antipasto. Her bracelets glittered, cold sparks in the winter sun.

It was the first time Casey had seen her since the revelations of Titus's and Brendan's betrayal.

Since Soph.

Over the past two weeks, he and Mercedes and George had analyzed every piece of data they could get their hands on to find out exactly what Brendan had done to sabotage Stokr.

He'd been smart. As far as they could tell, he'd intentionally preserved a fired employee's login, then used it to deploy the app's faulty build. Later on, he'd used the access that Sophronia had given them to erase his own tracks and most of Titus's too. Casey could see how all of it had happened: a careful reconstruction of the worst mistakes he'd ever made.

But even after all the Pillbugs' work—the logs and data, the endless forensic analysis—he still wasn't satisfied.

Something still felt *wrong*. Unfinished.

To Casey's tooth-grinding frustration, they couldn't find any hard evidence on Raymond Winterburn-Ross. Titus, who was currently in custody awaiting trial, had refused to testify against his collaborators. The authorities seemed perfectly willing to look past the raid on HemoCorp, which hadn't resulted in any deaths, if they could nail Titus for the murder of the analyst and the accidental deaths of the two Stokr users.

Winterburn-Ross, it seemed, was going to get away clean.

It was the reason Casey had come to Parce Domine—the reason he let himself admit, at least. It seemed possible that Nonna or her friends might have heard some rumor about the paranoid billionaire.

But when he asked, she shook her head. She looked at him, eyes bright and searching, across the tray of antipasto. "I haven't," she said. "I'm sorry. I haven't heard a thing."

She moved from the island to the table. Set the tray in front of him.

Sat down beside him and patted his hand.

"Precious," she said, "tell me what's really the matter."

He looked down at the whorls and lines of the table's wood grain. The little glass cups of olives, shimmering green and black.

Nonna's familiar fingers: sparkling with rings, knotted at the knuckles. Beloved.

And, haltingly, he told her.

He made himself describe all the times Brendan had come to him, seemingly panicked over some minor error that had actually been calculated sabotage. He explained, on a rush of shame, how he'd helped Brendan—and had inadvertently let the sabotage go on unchecked.

He told Nonna everything that had happened in Sophronia's kitchen.

She was quiet for a while after that, her hand still resting on his. Her nails were unpainted; the shape of her nail beds was the same as his. The same as his father's.

"I know," he said. "I know I messed up."

"Oh, baby." She sighed and squeezed his hand. "You can't be everything for everyone, you know. It doesn't work like that."

"I'm—"

"You wanted to save Brendan and his job," she said. "Your heart was in the right place. Your heart always is. And it's not your fault that he deceived you—that's *his* fault. But . . ." She paused. Entwined their fingers. And then said, very gently, "You give away too much of yourself. You're allowed to say no to people sometimes. The world won't fall apart if you're not there to save it."

He took a breath and another. He watched the pattern of light and shade on her windowsill, the green leaves and glazed pots. Life pushing instinctively toward the sun.

"I'm proud of you," she said. "With Sophronia."

He breathed a laugh. "What?"

"I *am*. You told her what you wanted. You treated her like an equal partner, not a porcelain doll in need of rescuing."

"Nonna. I more or less gave her an ultimatum—"

"I wouldn't call it that—"

"*And* I did it about five minutes after she found out her beloved father figure had secretly been trying to destroy her life."

"Well." Nonna pursed her lips. "You certainly don't get points for timing."

Casey took off his glasses and pinched his nose.

Nonna patted his hand and smothered a laugh. "You can work on that part, baby. I have faith in you. In both of you."

She always did. He'd lost many things in his twenty-nine years on this earth—but never that unshakable faith. He knew how lucky he was.

He ate her antipasto and turned down the whiskey sour she pressed on him, and eventually he got up to drive home. Nonna walked him to the door, asking enough long and slightly rambling questions that he started to grow suspicious.

And when he finally got the door open, Sophronia was on the other side.

There was a moment—brief, endless—of frozen silence.

She was on the doorstep, surrounded by frothy ferns and bromeliads the color of blood. Her shirt was a crisp, meticulous white.

She had one hand raised as if to knock. The other held a plastic bag of whiskey and sour mix.

"Soph," he said. His heart had remembered how to beat; it was pounding so loudly in his ears that he could barely make out his own voice.

She was *here*. Why was she here?

"Casey," she said. Her lips parted, then closed. "I . . . Lola said you were in Monterey. I didn't—"

He looked down at Nonna, who was blinking innocently.

"Did I?" she said. "I must have gotten the weeks mixed up."

Sophronia thrust out the bag, like it might explode into a thousand pieces in her hands. "I—I'll just—"

He took it. His fingers brushed hers, and he wanted . . .

He wanted to grip her hands. He wanted to memorize the cool grain of her skin, the bones of her wrist, the curve of her cheek.

He hadn't forgotten. These last two weeks, he hadn't forgotten a single atom of her. He never would.

"I just . . ." She broke off again, and he knew it was because she'd heard the way her voice had trembled. "I was just going to drop this off."

"You drove two hours to drop off some sour mix?" Nonna demanded. "Don't be silly. Come in, baby. I bought another box of those Belgian fruit jellies you liked so much when you were here last weekend."

When you were . . .

His gaze flicked, startled, to Nonna and then back to Sophronia.

She'd been here? More than once?

She took a step back. There was dismay on her face and embarrassment, and it dawned on him that she loved Nonna, and she missed her.

He knew how little of that steadfast warmth she'd had in her life. Of course she would want to hold on to it.

"I can't," Sophronia said quietly. "I'm sorry, Lola, I . . . another time."

"You can stay," he told her. "If you want. I'm heading back to Incarnare anyway."

"No. No, I—"

"I just—"

They both broke off, and he couldn't help himself. He memorized her cheek, her mouth, her eyes. Permitted himself the terrible indulgence of *that* shade of blue: the one he knew by heart.

She was the one to break the silence. "Are you okay?" she asked. "I've been . . . I've really—"

She didn't seem to know how to finish. Her fingers twitched, like she wanted to reach for something—for him—but her hands stayed at her sides.

"Yeah," he said. "Yeah, Soph. I'm okay."

"I'm glad," she whispered.

She stood motionless on the doorstep. He knew the taut tension of her body so well: the hesitation, the yearning—not quite leaving, not quite asking to come in.

His girl. Sometimes she was enough to break his heart.

"Stay," he said. "I want you to."

He kissed Nonna's cheek then and handed her the bag of whiskey and sour mix. He breathed in—deep forest, cool shade—and then walked down the street to where his dad's ancient car was parked, half hidden behind a stand of pines.

Before he opened the door, he let himself look, just once, at Nonna's doorstep.

Sophronia was still there.

She hadn't left. She was still looking back.

•••

The voice note came that night.

Sophronia was still in her running clothes. Her sports bra was soaked with sweat, and her skin felt like ice, and still, she'd barely been able to make herself end her run and go inside.

She'd wanted to run and keep running, the December air like a knife in her lungs, cleaving away all the parts of herself that were soft, all the parts of her that were frigid, all the parts of her that hurt.

She'd brought the whiskey and the sour mix to Nonna because she'd thought that Nonna would like them. She had the gift right—the same bottles, the same brands—except Casey had brought chips too. She was sure he had; only she couldn't remember what kind they were. She kept trying to recall the name and thinking instead of a glass cup of jelly beans on the table and a little boy's photo on the wall, his cheeks pink from the sun.

When she'd seen him on the doorstep, she'd wanted to step straight into his arms. His scent had been in her nose, and her heart was in shreds, and—

Oh Abraham. It was dangerous to want anything this much.

She was still standing in her foyer after her run that night when her phone buzzed in her hand. When she looked down, she saw Casey's name.

She had their text thread open before she could stop herself. *I'm sorry* was still there, and *I miss you*.

And beneath that text, a voice message.

She stared at it for so long her eyes burned.

And then she took a breath and hit play. Casey's voice emerged from the phone, lower and scratchier than it had been that afternoon.

Hey, Soph. I keep typing texts and then reading them back and talking myself out of sending them so . . . trying it this way, I guess. I wanted to tell you—

His voice broke off, a pause long enough that she felt a pulse of fear. That *couldn't* be the end.

When his voice came back, it was even rougher.

I wanted to tell you I'm sorry. I fucked up with Brendan. I cared about him, and I wanted to be there for him, and I wanted . . . to be the hero, I guess. I wanted to fix everything for him so he never had to face what he'd done wrong. And I get it. If you can't move past that. I understand. But today . . .

On the recording, he took a breath, and so did she, lightheaded with the agony of hearing his voice.

I miss you. I feel like I've been walking around on life support and seeing you today fucking restarted my heart. And I don't want to push you too hard, honey. I promised myself I wouldn't. But I wanted to say . . .

I wanted to say that if you think there's a future for this—for us—I'd wait for you for the rest of my life.

She fumbled for the phone. The screen looked blurred—everything was fractured and refracted, light through water. Somehow she got her fingers to work and played the voice note again. A third time.

When it was done, she made herself breathe. She looked down at the screen, and as she did, the tears in her eyes spilled over, iridescent where they struck the glass.

Delete? her phone offered. *Save?*

Save, she chose.

Save.

CHAPTER 34

"So," Del said. "Twelve hours until we turn Stokr back on."

Sophronia glanced at Del's reflection in the hotel room's standing mirror, and then back down at the fan pattern on the carpet. "Yep."

Del continued to deliberately apply her plum lip stain. "And how are we feeling about that?"

"How do *you* feel? You're the one about to hold a live press conference defending HemoCorp's choices to approximately every journalist in North America."

Del finished with the stain and selected a lip oil. "I feel fine, thank you."

"Good. You should. You couldn't possibly be more prepared."

They were back in the Golden Palm, which was why the carpet looked so familiar. Del had arranged the location, along with every other minute detail of the event, from the time of day to the precise shape and design of her podium. She'd made Sophronia rehearse various antagonistic lines of questioning until she'd perfected every possible response, and she'd handcrafted the seating order for the HemoCorp executive committee on the stage.

Del tossed the lip oil back into her makeup bag with a sound of exasperation. "Seriously?"

Sophronia looked up. In the mirror, her hair lay sleek and just trimmed against the angle of her jaw. Her suit—Del had chosen it—was a rich, silky scarlet. "What?"

"You're not even going to *ask* if he's coming?"

"I"—Sophronia swallowed—"already asked Mercedes."

Casey wasn't coming to the press conference. None of the Pillbugs were.

It was a good idea. There was no need to put the individual engineers under public scrutiny. Better for everyone that the HemoCorp executive committee appear as a united front so that negative public attention didn't single out any employee individually.

But when she'd gotten Mercedes's reply, disappointment had nearly choked her.

Del zipped her makeup case and whirled. "Great. That's great. How does it feel, Soph?"

"How does what feel?"

Del had developed an uncharacteristic tendency to glare these past few days. "Getting everything you've ever wanted."

"I—"

"That's what this is, right? You're the youngest vampire ever in HemoCorp's executive committee. We're turning Stokr back on. Everything's going back to the way it's always been. And you're happy, aren't you? Living the dream?"

"I'm—"

"Or am I misunderstanding?" Del's voice rose. "Are you actually walking around HemoCorp like a tragic Victorian ghost because you're totally fucking miserable? Because the love of your life is three floors down *and you haven't even texted him*?"

"Del," she said thickly.

"Sweetie." Del put her hands on her hips. "You know I love you. And it is because I love you that I'm very gently asking: What in the sanguinary *fuck* are you thinking?"

Sophronia opened her mouth. Felt her breath emerge, shaky as a sob, and closed her mouth again. Gritted her teeth to hold everything in.

It had been five days since she'd seen Casey at his grandmother's house. Five days of playing his voice note, and pulling up his number in her phone, and never—not once—hitting call.

"I thought," she got out, "maybe after the press conference. Or once things settle down with Stokr, I could . . . he's probably really busy right now, and I—"

Del was staring daggers at her. She'd never seen Del's pale-green eyes look quite like that. "Really? You think he's too busy to take a call from you?"

"I . . ."

"Do you want Wendy to put in a calendar request, maybe? I'm sure I could get her to do it."

"No," Sophronia said hoarsely.

"Soph." Del settled herself on the hotel bed next to Sophronia, and then she wrapped one arm around Sophronia's waist. Like they were kids again, in the dorm at Holbeck Priest. "What's going on?"

"I'm—" She made herself say it, though it was difficult. Even with Del. "Scared."

"Sweetie." Del leaned her head onto Sophronia's shoulder; her blond curls tickled Sophronia's cheek. "Of what?"

"I wasn't . . . nice to him."

"Soph. Sweetie. He *likes* when you're mean. It makes him horny."

Her nose burned. Her eyes. "You weren't there. He was

so . . . he was so *sad*, Del. I knew it would hurt him when I pushed him away, and I did it anyway."

"Are you afraid he's not going to forgive you?"

She had to force the word out past the tightness in her throat. "No."

She knew he would.

I'd wait for you for the rest of my life.

"Then what, Soph?"

"I'm afraid," she whispered, "that he *will* forgive me. And that will be worse."

"Sweetie—"

"I didn't sound like myself." Her voice was so raw she could barely recognize it, and saying the words felt like cutting off her arm. Like giving away a part of herself she could never take back. "I sounded like my mom."

This was what kept her up at night. What froze her fingers every time she moved to text Casey back.

She'd been heartbroken and betrayed and afraid of falling apart, and when she'd opened her mouth, she'd heard her mother's voice.

I can't give you more, because I have nothing else inside me to give.

Del hugged her tighter. "Sweetie. You're not your mother."

"My dad—" She was crying in earnest now, her tears sliding down her cheek and into Del's hair. "He loved her. He never said anything. He kept . . . even when she was horrible, he always let her . . ."

"Soph."

"What if that's us? If that's *me*?" Her nails dug into her palms, and she only closed her fists tighter, trying to hold fast to what was real. "What if I keep on hurting Casey and he doesn't stop me?"

"You are not her," Del said fiercely. "You know how I know that?"

Sophronia's voice came out fractured. "How?"

"Because I love you, Soph. And I really fucking hated her."

The sound she made was somewhere between a laugh and a sob. "Del—"

"No. Listen for a second. Really listen, Soph, because I've known you more than half your life, and I'm not about to bullshit you."

She took a breath, slow and shaking.

And listened.

"You balance him," Del said. "Can you see that? He's a sweetheart, and he's too nice for his own good, and he likes to be needed—to a fault sometimes. That's *why* he screwed up with Brendan. But you don't let him do that. You are so damn careful with him—with his blood, with his family, with his horrible old car. Everything. You watch his back when he doesn't watch it himself."

"But I hurt him," she whispered. "I told him to go."

"You messed up," Del said. "You did. That's how it works, sweetie. You're both going to get things wrong, probably more than once. I say this from the perspective of someone who's been in about forty-five situationships, I know, but—whatever you learned from your parents, Soph, I learned the opposite from mine. I saw how it's supposed to work. You mess up, and you forgive each other, and it's worth it. Every single time, it's worth it because you love each other."

Sophronia breathed.

"You do love him," Del said, "don't you, Soph?"

She thought of Casey: his hands wrapped around hers, his wrist pressed to her mouth in an elevator. Two tuxedo cats, and his dad's ancient car, and his face turned to press a kiss into Nonna's hair.

His voice, scratchy and permanent in her phone's speakers.

His chest, flower inked and solid, rising and falling beneath her cheek.

"So much," she whispered.

"And you forgive him? For what he did with Brendan?"

"Of course."

Del's mouth quirked. She linked her fingers with Sophronia's. "Imagine for me, Soph, a world where he feels exactly the same way about you."

She almost could. She could see it in outline, at the corners of her vision, in shadows.

Casey's love, his devotion, his bone-deep generosity and his joy, and all of it *hers*—she could picture it, want it—and still the vision seemed impossibly far out of her reach.

But it was Casey. He made impossible things feel easy.

"What do I do?" she got out.

Del squeezed her hand. "It's not a test, Soph. Just—call him. Tell him how you feel."

She could see his face if she closed her eyes. Feel the gentle brush of his fingers over her cheek.

I love you, she would say, and *I'm sorry*.

And it *was* easy. As simple and familiar as the rhythm of Casey's heart.

"Come on," Del said. "Let me fix your face. And when we're done kicking ass at this press conference, I'll pull up his number in your phone and press call, if you want."

"Thank you," she said unsteadily. She pressed her cheek against Del's hair and willed Del to feel all the love and gratitude she had, quiet and deep within her fragile vampire's heart. "I don't know what I'd do without you."

"Yeah, yeah. Remember I'm your maid of honor, no matter how many celebrities Nonna introduces you to."

She laughed damply, and Del leaned in. She hugged Sophronia hard enough that Sophronia felt her ribs creak. And then—soft and wry and earnest—Del murmured: "Sweetie. I love you too."

CHAPTER 35

The Pillbugs had congregated at Casey's house for the press conference.

It was, technically, the middle of a workday, but Stokr was ready to go, and their new hire, Esha Gautam—hand selected by one of Dr. LeBlanc's cybersecurity buddies over at UC Saint Germain—was fully onboarded by now.

And, realistically, no one at HemoCorp cared what they were doing at this particular moment. The whole company was glued to their devices as they watched the public gossip spilling about Titus Fornax.

Casey had sent a text to the new Pillbugs group chat—plus Esha, minus Brendan—offering his house for the press conference watch party, and Mercedes had sent him a private text back.

Mercedes Obregón

6:06 pm

You sure you want to watch?

Casey Amato

6:06 pm

Yeah, of course.

I'm good, Mer.

It hadn't even been a lie. Of course he wanted to watch. He was hoping there would be something he could grab on to that would explain why Titus hadn't testified against Winterburn-Ross. He wanted to know what was going on behind the scenes, and the Vegas hadn't given him a crumb. And if he watched . . .

And if he watched the press conference, he could stare at the screen while Del talked and the whole time keep his eyes fixed on Sophronia.

Measure the hollow of her cheek and the tint of her lips. Watch the rise and fall of her chest, every flick of her long black lashes.

Tell himself it was enough just to know she was all right.

Well, anyway, the *good* part was a lie. Luckily Mercedes already knew he was a sad sack and didn't question him further—only showed up at his house with a handle of vodka for the viewing party as if that were a perfectly normal thing to do on a Wednesday at 2:00 p.m.

He hadn't heard from Soph since that day at Nonna's house. But he'd thought of her hands clutched tight around the plastic bag, and he'd run his fingertips over the seat belt in his car as he'd driven home, and he'd . . .

He'd sent the voice note before he could talk himself out of it. He wanted to tell her he was sorry, and he wanted to tell her he missed her. He'd seen her at Nonna's, and he'd felt a sudden flare of hope, so bright it hurt.

He wanted a future with her. He hadn't stopped wanting it.

He didn't think he ever would.

He blew out a breath, pulled off his glasses, and rubbed his face. He took a long sip of a drink that tasted a lot like undergrad and then, deliberately, clicked the TV on and found the press conference.

On the screen, the HemoCorp executive committee filed onto the stage, Del bringing up the rear. August Vega looked faintly funereal in his black suit and grim expression. Octavia looked characteristically sour, Kriti grave. Circinus looked like he was a hair's breadth from ripping the wireless mic off Del's white shirt so that he could opine about the Stokr situation to a captive audience.

And Soph—

He allowed himself the luxury of taking her in slowly. Her nails were red, and so was her suit. Her trousers had lots of buttons, which he figured was probably form over function because of how they drew attention to her taut, athletic waist.

Her eyes looked smoky and smudged and desperately serious, and Casey couldn't breathe for wanting her.

He came back to the present moment slowly. The cat pressing her head against his shoulder—the clink of Mercedes's glass—the sound of George's voice as he dropped tidbits of HemoCorp lore that Esha would need six months at least to be able to follow.

He watched Soph's mouth go pale as she pressed her lips together and found her seat on the stage.

Across from him, Esha took a sip of the drink and then tried to stifle a shudder. "I'm gonna, uh—" She started to put it on the ground, but in the face of Deckard's feline interest, got to her feet instead. "Maybe the sink?"

Casey tipped his head. "Just in there."

"Got it." She started to turn, then paused, angling back to

face the TV. "You know what? I didn't recognize that vampire at first, but—I *know* her."

Mercedes looked up from the drink she was staunchly pretending to enjoy. "Who? One of the HemoCorp execs?"

"I guess? If she's on the stage, she must be, right? I don't know her name."

Now George looked up too. "You know her, but you don't know her name?"

"Yeah." Esha's sweater fell down over her shoulder as she shrugged. "She went on a handful of dates with my thesis advisor, Dr. Uxbridge. The one who recommended me for this job. I used to wait tables and saw them together, like, at least four or five times this fall. Dr. Ux is super shy, though—I tried to bring it up, but he was too embarrassed to talk about it."

Something prickled along Casey's skin: some cool alert instinct that skimmed the edges of his nerves. "Who?" His gaze flicked to the TV, where Del was just starting to talk, and then back to Esha. "Which one?"

"The blond vampire. Not the one talking—the one sitting down, in the fancy green suit. The one who looks kind of pissed about something." Esha's mouth quirked. "I recognize her expression."

George blinked at the TV. "Octavia? Went on dates with your professor?"

Mercedes's brows rose. "*Another* human? Guess she has a type."

"Humans?" Esha asked.

"I meant nerdy computer science professors, but that too."

Very slowly, something began to shift inside Casey's head, like a great wooden mill grinding painfully into motion.

"All that complaining about Stokr," George was saying,

"and here she is dating half the computer science faculty on the West Coast."

"Ana said she went to a job fair at Portland U and Octavia was there," Mercedes added. "Honestly, that's some effort to find a suck buddy. You'd think she'd look a little happier about Stokr coming back—ought to make it easier for her to find whatever it is she's looking for."

Casey's voice came out so low it was almost inaudible. "What *is* she looking for?"

The Pillbugs went quiet enough that they could make out Del's voice, patiently outlining the review of vulnerabilities the Pillbugs had completed on the Stokr system with the assistance of a third-party cybersecurity firm.

George was staring at him. "What do you mean?"

Casey clicked the remote and turned Del's voice down to a whisper. "All this time—why has Octavia been so opposed to Stokr?"

Mercedes had frozen with her hand halfway through her tuft of mint-green hair. "Because she thinks it's cringe or whatever. Or claims to. Obviously *not* if she's prowling the entire West Coast for hot, nerdy human dates."

"Are we sure, though?" His gaze went back to the screen. "What happens to HemoCorp if Stokr goes down?"

"H-Corp loses credibility," Esha said promptly, as if it were an interview question. "And a hell of a lot of investor confidence, which this PR vamp is trying very hard right now to restore."

"But in the long run, if Stokr *is* a success, the investors will come back. What HemoCorp loses if Stokr starts thriving"—the wheel in his head was spinning faster, plucking pieces of memory and flinging them together in a smashing blaze of clarity—"is the med tech."

"What do you—"

"The blood patches," he said. "The hemostatic gels. If Stokr works—if it keeps working—there won't be a need for those products anymore."

"Casey," George said anxiously, "I don't understand what you're trying to say."

Titus and Brendan had sabotaged Stokr. Casey *knew* that was true—they'd been caught red-handed on the street in front of the Incarnare Public Library. Brendan had admitted it.

But some things had never entirely made sense. Somehow, in the back of his head, his mind had been puzzling them out, identifying the ill-fitting pieces.

Sending them cascading forward in a painful, accelerating blur.

"Why the raid at HemoCorp?" he said. He was on his feet, pacing, his gaze darting between Octavia on the screen and the Pillbugs in his living room. "It *never* made sense. They could have written the Stokr failures off as glitches before then, but the raid made that impossible. Why would they go to such extreme lengths at that point?"

"They uploaded something, remember?" Mercedes said. "They pushed a program that later became that final faulty build, most likely."

"But they had Brendan. He could've done it himself, at work, and covered his tracks the way he covered up everything else. There was no need for the raid, unless . . . unless the point wasn't the upload." He looked at the Pillbugs. George had paled; Mercedes was clutching her glass in both hands. "What was the outcome of the raid for our investigation? For *us*?"

"We"—Mercedes swallowed—"stopped suspecting Octavia."

"She gave herself an alibi. And sent us haring off after Winterburn-Ross."

"Wait," George said. "You think . . . you think Octavia was behind all this? But we *know* it was Titus. He was the one texting Winterburn-Ross."

"And how did we get Titus's burner number?" Casey demanded. "Straight from Winterburn-Ross. Do we really believe that with all his obsessive concern with security and secrecy, Winterburn-Ross let us into his cell phone by accident?"

Mercedes's dark eyes were fixed on his face. "What are you trying to say? That Winterburn-Ross let us access his phone on purpose? Why would he do that, Casey?"

Casey's eyes slid back to the screen, where Octavia sat on stage behind Del, her mouth pressed into a thin line. "Because someone told him to."

Octavia was devoted to R and D. Everyone knew it. The blood patches, the dermal grafts, the fibrin gels—all of it had been done under her direction. Outside of artificial blood, they were HemoCorp's flagship innovations and some of the company's primary sources of revenue.

The outcome of years of Octavia's dedication.

And Stokr could make all that obsolete.

What might she do to keep that from happening?

"What if she set Titus up?" Casey asked. "She's his sister-in-law, remember? She *knows* him—maybe even knows how to manipulate him. What if she pushed him toward Winterburn-Ross and then got Winterburn-Ross to expose Titus to us? What if she orchestrated all of this so that Titus would take the fall?"

"She didn't want Dr. LeBlanc for a date," George said. His eyes had sharpened; he, too, was staring at Octavia on the screen. "She wanted her *tech*."

"Dr. Uxbridge does cybersecurity too," Esha said. "And he's—sweet. Naive. I could absolutely see him giving up things he shouldn't to a smart and sexy vampire."

"Brendan told us it wasn't supposed to go this far," Mercedes murmured.

"Because Titus told him it wasn't," Casey said. "And all this time we've been assuming Titus lied to him, but . . . but what if Titus *wasn't* lying? What if he was just Octavia's pawn?"

"But we don't have any proof," George protested. "It's a good theory, I'll give you that, but how do we *know*? If Octavia's been behind this, she's been slick about it. Ten steps ahead of us this whole time."

Casey's gaze shot to Esha. "Can you call your professor? See what contact info Octavia was using when she met up with him?"

"Sure." Esha was already pulling out her phone. "I'll do it right now."

"Good." His gaze darted to the TV, where Del was still talking, and then he crossed to his bedroom and dug in his desk for a familiar ink-covered strip of paper.

When he reemerged, George and Mercedes were staring at him.

"What is that?" Mercedes asked.

"Remember when Soph and I went to Winterburn-Ross's compound and I accessed his network manually?"

"And you nearly got murdered? Yeah, I do, actually."

"I saw all of those emails to and from Kriti, but there was nothing about Stokr or the raid. I checked the call logs, and I didn't see any other contacts I knew from HemoCorp, but"—he gestured to the paper—"just in case. I made this."

"What *is* it?"

"I couldn't take a photo of the phone numbers I saw, because our phones were bricked. So, instead, I memorized them."

He'd never found a connection to any of their suspects. But now . . .

"Got the number," Esha said. "Dr. Ux just texted it to me. He asked me why, and I told him to turn on the press conference so—" She winced. "Possibly he's about to have a really bad day."

She held out the phone, and Casey took it, flattening the receipt so he could make out the numbers he'd scrawled there.

And at the very top of the page, he found a match.

"Holy fucking shit," Mercedes said.

"This is hard evidence," George breathed. "Right here. This is enough to prove that Octavia was talking to Winterburn-Ross this whole time."

"From a burner phone, probably," Casey said. "Just like Titus."

Mercedes looked up from the receipt, her expression bloodthirsty and delighted. "We're going to nail her ass to the wall. Do you realize that, Casey? Maybe Winterburn-Ross, too, if we can finally get something to stick to him. We're going to—"

But Casey's gaze had slid away from Mercedes and back to the TV screen. Del was taking questions from the audience now, explaining the timeline for the Stokr restoration, politely dismissing any suggestion that it was too soon.

Octavia's face had shifted from distaste to impassivity. Perhaps the very, very faintest bit pleased.

"But," Esha said, "if Octavia was behind the sabotage all along, then . . ."

Casey felt hot and cold at once as he looked at the screen. At the HemoCorp employees on stage and the journalists watching from the audience.

At Sophronia.

"Then this isn't over," he said.

It *wasn't* safe to turn Stokr back on.

Octavia wasn't done.

His heart pounded. His blood raced through his limbs, lighting up his nerve endings. His gaze shot to Mercedes.

"Go to HemoCorp," he bit out. "Do whatever you need to do to make sure the app doesn't go back online. Set the server room on fire if you have to."

He was halfway to the door already, his keys in his hand, metal digging into his palm.

"Wait," Mercedes demanded. "Where are *you* going?"

He clutched the keys tighter. Felt the cool impression of teeth.

He said, softly: "The press conference."

CHAPTER 36

They'd set a sixty-minute time limit, but at minute fifty-six, the journalists—and Del—were still going strong. Sophronia glanced at her watch and then up at Del, who was coolly reciting cybersecurity jargon like she'd personally designed the Stokr-restoration plan.

Del caught her eye. The corner of Del's purple-glossed mouth turned up, and she gave an infinitesimal nod.

She had things under control. Sophronia was so proud of her.

She went back to watching the audience, attempting to judge their reactions to Del's competent handling. The slouchy journalist in the graphic tee looked intensely skeptical—but on the other hand, the one with the candy-colored nails seemed vaguely starstruck, like maybe she wanted to get Del's number later. Sophronia's gaze skimmed the rows: analyzing heart-rates, watching the shift of shoulders and mouths.

She was watching intently enough that when the door to the ballroom burst open, she was the first to notice.

The first to throw herself to her feet.

There was a brief commotion—a clamor of voices, polite but firm—"I'm sorry, sir, but without a press pass, you can't—"

But whoever it was didn't listen. Journalists in the back of the room leapt from their chairs as someone struggled forward toward the stage.

She saw a glimpse of wild brown curls, half a head taller than the humans around him. The glint of his glasses. The throb of a heartbeat so familiar she heard it in her dreams.

Casey.

Everyone from HemoCorp was on their feet now. Octavia had her phone to her mouth, murmuring something. Del, the lapel mic still amplifying her voice, was trying to get everyone in the room to "calm down, for Abraham's sake. It's a HemoCorp employee, not some intruder off the street—"

It took Casey's voice, ringing firm and loud across the room, to bring the clamor of journalists to a halt.

"We can't turn Stokr back on," he said. The words were pitched so that everyone in the room could hear him, but his eyes were on Sophronia. "It's not safe."

The sound of the journalists swelled. Shutters popped; light burst in a dozen flares.

Sophronia heard her blood roar in her ears. Casey's face was set and desperately serious, his jaw clamped tight, and . . .

She believed him. Instantly. Utterly.

Down to her bones.

Del's amplified voice was the loudest thing in the room, echoing over the shouting journalists. "Casey. What are you—"

"It was Octavia."

A tiny, endless silence followed Casey's words. Even Sophronia's heart seemed to stop beating, tightening like a fist as her mind spun forward.

Octavia.

All along, it had been *Octavia*.

And in that brief and infinite hush, Sophronia heard another sound.

Vampire heartbeats. Closing fast.

Her gaze shot to the open doors, and somehow she already knew what she would see there. Six tall, slim vampires—dressed in black, holsters at their hips, ivory earpieces settled in their ears.

Headed for Casey.

She didn't remember moving. One second she was on the stage, and the next she was on the ground, running, putting her body between Casey and Winterburn-Ross's mercenaries.

They were vampires, too, and closer to Casey—but it didn't matter. She was faster than they were and lethal, and that was her heart, alone and vulnerable on the other side of the room.

It wasn't even close. She was in front of Casey before they'd cleared the door.

"Get back," she snarled. "Stay away from him."

Her fangs were out, her hands curled into claws.

Let them try to get to Casey—let them *fucking* try. Her throat burned for the taste of their blood.

"Who called for security?" August was demanding. "Those aren't HemoCorp vampires—"

Something flickered in Sophronia's peripheral vision, and her head whipped around, searching for threats.

But Casey lifted his hand and caught the tiny lapel mic Del had thrown to him, plucking it right out of the air.

He lifted the mic to his mouth. "Octavia Pavo was responsible for the Stokr sabotage. She set Titus up to take the fall."

The mic pushed his voice to the corners of the room. On stage, Octavia stood prey-still, frozen, her gaze flickering from Casey to the mercenaries to the open door.

"She's been working with Raymond Winterburn-Ross all along," Casey said. "She's been in contact with cybersecurity experts all over the West Coast. And I'm guessing if you check that phone she's holding, you'll see that she's the one who called these vamps in."

He was furious, Sophronia realized. Pissed as hell and stubborn and reckless and brave.

"What's the plan, Octavia?" he demanded. "There's a whole room of journalists in here, and I'm willing to bet at least one of them is live streaming this right now. You can order Winterburn-Ross's vamps to murder every single one of us, and you still won't get away clean. Not even vampires can hide if the whole world is watching."

Octavia was pale, her hands fisted at her sides. Even now—even now, that cool mask of calm didn't break.

She kicked off her shoes—the motion was a blur—and started to run.

Sophronia made her decision without realizing she'd made it.

She was between Octavia and the open door. She was quicker, though the older vampire was certainly stronger. She could stop Octavia from getting away.

But to do that, she'd have to step away from Casey's side. Leave him undefended in the face of six ruthless vampires.

It was no choice. Stopping Octavia or protecting Casey—

Her muscles didn't even twitch. She stood taut, fangs out, and watched as Octavia fled.

She didn't have to watch for long. Octavia didn't make it to the end of the stage. Del—little Del, almost human-looking Del—reached out, quick as a snake, and caught Octavia's wrist.

Octavia was moving so fast that she nearly dragged both of them to the ground. Del stumbled, holding Octavia back, as her nails—a vampire's nails, diamond hard, glossy pink and stiletto sharp—dug into Octavia's skin.

"Don't," Del hissed, "think you're getting away with this."

Her nails broke Octavia's skin. Blood welled.

And Octavia laughed.

She yanked hard, drawing Del closer through the force of Del's own grip. Octavia was half a foot taller, two decades older. So much stronger that Del skidded helplessly across the floor toward her.

Octavia moved so quickly Sophronia almost couldn't follow it. She spun Del around—Del's back collided with Octavia's chest. With her free hand, Octavia tangled her fingers in Del's blond curls and pulled hard, baring the side of Del's neck.

Octavia looked up. Her fangs were out, and her wrist was dripping, scattering blue-red drops along the floor, across Del's pristine white shirt.

"Get out," Octavia hissed. "All of you, get out. Clear the room, or I'll tear out her throat."

Sophronia stood on the balls of her feet, paralyzed, as a drop of Octavia's blood slid down Del's cheek.

She was too far. She could never get to Del in time.

Her heart throbbed once—searing, terror cracked—

And then Octavia was on the ground.

Sophronia's breath caught.

August Vega knelt over Octavia. Her arms were wrenched behind her back, caught in one of August's hands. His other hand, his grip deceptively gentle, was on her throat.

When he spoke, August's voice was a hiss—so soft that only another vampire could have made out his words. "Don't touch my girls."

Octavia twisted, trying to get away, but it was useless. August could break her spine with a twist of his wrist.

His thumb pressed into her pulse. Even from across the room, Sophronia heard the way Octavia's heart sped up, a crescendo of fear.

"Why?" he said, very quietly. "Was it about the tech? The blood patches?"

"Of course it was about the blood patches," Octavia snarled.

"For money?" August said icily. "You put my daughter in danger for *money*?"

"Not for money, you blind old fool. The two of you were going to destroy everything this company stood for." Her wrists slipped against her own blood; she writhed in the circle of August's fingers and thumb. "It was *my* legacy, and the two of you were throwing all of it away, and for *what*? For a joke. For *nothing*."

"No," Sophronia said. Her voice, too, was low, but she knew Octavia could hear her. "Not nothing."

"Get cuffs," her father snapped in the general direction of the crowd. "Steel, not zip ties. Don't forget what she can do."

Someone rushed to obey. Kriti moved toward Del, checked her for injuries, and wiped the blood from her face.

In her periphery, Sophronia saw Winterburn-Ross's mercenaries melt away, slipping silent and bloodless from the room.

She didn't care. Her eyes—her fingertips—then the sudden fearful grip of her palms—

All of it was on Casey.

"Are you all right?" Her fingers found his neck, his cheek, his hair; he was warm; he smelled like home. "Casey"—her voice cracked—"tell me you're okay, I can't—"

"I'm fine. Soph"—he was so close; his mouth found hers—"I'm fine. Oh fuck, honey—"

He muttered the words against her lips. His hands were on her waist, holding her to him, closer, closer. His whole body felt tense and hot, and she wanted to melt into him, drink deep from his vein, shelter him and hold him and take him inside her body.

"I'm sorry," she said, "Casey, I'm so sorry. I was going to call you as soon as the press conference was over and tell you—"

Somehow he was laughing against her mouth, relief drunk, horribly fond. "Oh, were you?"

"I had to—are you *laughing*?"

His fingers were knotted in her jacket, holding her fast. "God—a little—" He kissed her again, harder. "I'm just so relieved." He pulled back, a tiny whisper of space between them. His other hand came up to frame her jaw, and his lips parted to say something else, but she didn't let him.

"I love you," she said.

She heard his heart beat once, hard. Twice. The quick shaky inhale as his lungs worked.

"Soph," he said thickly.

"I love you. I'd quit my job a thousand times for you."

"You don't have to—"

"I would've killed those vampires if they touched you. I wouldn't—I can't—" She broke off. Her chest was heaving like she'd been running, and he still had his hand locked hard against her spine, holding her body fast against his. "I'm sorry," she said. "I'm so sorry about what I said."

"Don't," he murmured. He cupped her cheek. "I shouldn't have pushed you like that. It wasn't supposed to be an ultimatum."

"I *want* you to push me. I don't—" His face was blurred; tears slid down her cheeks and onto his hand. "Casey. I want you to tell me what you want. I don't want you to sacrifice *anything* for me. Not ever."

"Soph—"

"No, just—just listen. I want what you want, Casey. A future. A *life* with you. I want orchids at your house and . . . and video games and mean feral cats. I want to hold your hand on the boardwalk and look out at the ocean, and I want—*whatever* you want. Three kids on the beach. A family. Anything."

He held her gaze. His hand on her cheek was so gentle. "You," he said. "You, Soph."

Then he was kissing her again, warm and vital, his heart beating so hard she could feel it against her own ribs. He kissed her deeper, harder; his hand lodged tight in her hair, and she welcomed it all, a sigh catching in her throat as he licked at her fangs and—

He pulled back. His glasses were crooked. There was a wild glitter at the edge of her vision, but she didn't care. Didn't want to look at anything except his face.

"I love you," he murmured. "I've been in love with you for ages. Since that first day on the boardwalk, when you broke the railing under your fingers and still looked at me like . . ."

"Like I wanted to eat you?"

"Like you were afraid," he said, "and doing it anyway. I looked at you and thought, *I've never seen courage like that.*" He brushed her cheek with his thumb. "I think it every day. I can't seem to stop being dazzled by you."

He kissed her again, and she relished it: the slow care of him, the stubborn, gentle devotion.

It was hers. She could keep it.

Her eyes were closed, but the sparkle and flash seemed to go on and on, flecking the dark with stars, with fireworks.

Casey pulled back, but only to shift his mouth to her ear. "I don't want to stop kissing you," he murmured, "but I did want to remind you that there's an awful lot of press here."

She pressed her mouth against his neck and breathed him in and—

Oh. *Oh.*

The golden glitter flickering behind her eyelids was the pop and flash of roughly four dozen professional cameras.

She opened her eyes. Glanced once at the room full of journalists, then looked back at Casey: the strong angles of his cheekbones, his eyes, his wild hair. The familiar beloved curl of his smile.

She tugged his glasses off and held them loosely in one hand. Pulled his head back down with the other.

"Put it in the papers," she said to the room at large. "I don't mind."

Which was why, on the front page of several dozen news sites and at least two print papers the following morning, there was a picture of Sophronia Vega, EVP of regulatory affairs at HemoCorp Industries, tipped backward, her hair swinging free, as a HemoCorp software engineer kissed her breathless.

It was only a snapshot. A quick, fragmentary flash. Over in the time it took for the shutter to open and close.

And still, somehow, it was forever.

CHAPTER 37

It was three weeks before August Vega summoned them to his office.

Three sweet, golden weeks. They'd had Christmas at Lola's—the Harrisons had brought something called beef Wellington (*Whole Foods' best, precious*), and Sophronia had come up with enough signed Barbra Streisand memoirs for all of Lola's book club. Del had dropped by, and her parents had insisted on a video chat so they could finally set eyes on Casey.

It was cold enough that Sophronia wore Casey's UC Incarnare sweatshirt on the boardwalk. Cold enough that teenagers came laughing and screaming off the roller coaster: humans with wind-chapped cheeks and rangy vampires, arms slung around each other for warmth.

Sophronia watched them and thought of Del and Izzy. Of Stokr. Of the future, spooled out in front of her like the ocean, sometimes calm and sometimes swelling rough.

Of hope.

Sometimes it still surprised her that she hadn't recognized Octavia's true motive all along. Not disdain for Stokr but bitter, ferocious pride. Octavia's devotion to HemoCorp R and D had suffused every aspect of her life—maybe Sophronia should have predicted what she would do to keep her legacy alive.

But when she'd said all that to Casey, he'd shaken his head. Tucked her hair back behind her ear.

You wouldn't have seen it, he said. *Because you, honey, are a very good person. Stokr made the world safer. For you, that was the only thing that mattered.*

I love you, she'd said, and he'd kissed her hard and whispered back, *Love you. Always, Soph.*

She'd kept the words inside her heart.

Del was already in August's office when they arrived. Casey set his hand to Sophronia's lower back, and she leaned into it—into him—before they both sat down. It was a luxury she allowed herself, these days: to feel his strength. To share it.

August hadn't told them what the purpose of the meeting was. His admin had pushed the calendar update for the three of them, and when Sophronia had asked Del if she had any clue what was going on, she'd shaken her head.

By August's grim expression, Sophronia didn't think it could be good.

"Thank you for coming," he began. "I know you're all very busy. I've asked you here because I've come into possession of new information about the Stokr sabotage, and I believe that all of you deserve to know the truth."

Sophronia felt the throb of her fangs going tight in her mouth.

Any explanation Octavia might have made—any bitter gloating about how she'd outsmarted all of them—had been smothered into judicious silence by the team of expensive vampire lawyers the Pavo dynasty held on retainer. The Pillbugs had verified that she'd worked with at least four different cybersecurity experts across the country to access Stokr's servers and then hide her digital trail; a forensic analysis of her financial portfolio had helped them identify the creators of the faulty build that had been pushed when Stokr had unexpectedly gone live.

But the precise nature of how Octavia had manipulated Titus was still shrouded in mystery.

Or—Sophronia watched her father's face—it had been.

"First," August said, "I'd like to tell all of you that I'm sorry."

Sophronia blinked. In all her life, she'd never heard the words pass his lips. In the pale morning light, his eyes were heavy-lidded, deep in shadow.

"When you came to me and informed me that you believed Stokr had been sabotaged, I told you to let it go. Not because I did not believe you but because I had already suspected it."

Her lips parted. "But then why—"

"What I did not tell you—what I felt I could not tell you—was that I believed the saboteur to be Titus."

She sucked in a breath. Beside her, Del looked stunned, her lips indigo against the milky pallor of her skin.

"Titus had been behaving strangely for weeks. He skipped four meetings with his staff and asked his admin to adjust the calendar so that he could pretend he hadn't missed them. He left the office to take personal calls."

"How did you know all of this?" Casey asked.

August's mouth was a firm, flat line. "It's my company. I pay attention."

Sophronia suspected it was more than that—some complicated network of administrative gossip and security feeds, probably.

But also, Titus was August's oldest friend. If something had been wrong, August would have noticed.

"I intended to handle the situation quietly. I will admit that when you told me about your analyst, I was . . . disturbed." His fangs pressed tiny indents into his lower lip. "But for the friend I have known and loved all my life, I was willing to excuse what I supposed must have been an accidental death."

Sophronia swallowed. Her gaze flitted to Del, because . . . because . . .

She remembered Octavia's blood dripping down Del's cheek. She could understand her father's terrible loyalty.

"I did not realize how deeply Titus was committed to his course of action," August continued. "I never suspected he would go to someone as erratic as Raymond Winterburn-Ross—and in truth, I don't believe he would have, if Octavia had not planted the suggestion. I believe she thought Winterburn-Ross would be easy for her to handle." August's lips pressed together in an expression of distaste. "She always supposed she could outmaneuver everyone. She did not realize that Winterburn-Ross has long had motives of his own."

"I don't understand," Sophronia said. "If you believed that the sabotage was real, then why did you put us on leave? Why didn't you let us investigate?"

August placed his palms on the desk and looked down at his fingers. "I had thought . . ." He lifted his eyes and found Sophronia's face. "I had hoped to keep you safe, which meant as far from HemoCorp as possible. It is . . . not in my nature to speak directly. To reveal what I considered to be a vulnerability in the company."

She knew what he meant. He was the head of the Vega dynasty; his first instinct was to move cautiously, to take no risks. To scheme, rather than to tell the truth—even to his heir.

"But I underestimated your perseverance," August went on, "and I endangered you all." He looked from Sophronia to Del to Casey. Back to Sophronia. "I'm sorry to all of you. But to you, Sophronia, most of all."

Somehow, the words were a stinging sort of relief, like the lancing of a wound. She could remember his stark face in the conference room. Recall the devastation she'd felt that day with easy, blade-fresh clarity.

But she could understand, too, why her father had done what he'd done. She knew as well as he did the rules they'd both been taught.

Casey's hand found hers. Held on.

At her side, Del cleared a suspicious hoarseness from her voice. "You said there's something new? Something that you wanted us to know?"

"Yes. While Titus has been silent on the subject of his motivation, I have recently found myself in contact with a number of cybersecurity experts of—let us say, flexible morals."

"Abraham's fangs," Del said. "You mean you don't need Titus to explain himself, because you can get into his phone. His emails."

August betrayed no reaction, save a tiny shiver of his pale lashes. "I have new information. And I believe I know what prompted Titus's betrayal."

"I don't understand," Casey said. "We *know* why he sabotaged Stokr. He wanted HemoCorp. He believed that you would support Sophronia in her attempt to keep Stokr online, and then he could orchestrate a coup to have both of you ousted."

"Correct," August said. "But his bid for control of HemoCorp was never about power."

"What else could it be?" Del asked. "Why else would he want the company?"

August pressed his hands harder against the surface of the desk. There was some pain there, Sophronia saw, buried deep.

If he hadn't been a Vega, he might have looked heartbroken.

"Last March," August said, "Titus's daughter, Livia, came to him with a problem. Her teenage daughter—Valeria, Titus's only grandchild—had become fixated upon a group of . . . unsavory individuals. Valeria had discovered their existence via some conspiracy-oriented internet black holes, and—with the fervor only an adolescent can manage—attempted to infiltrate their group."

"What individuals are we talking about?" Sophronia asked.

"Enemies," August said flatly. "The Fornax family did everything they could to end Valeria's fascination, with precisely the opposite effect. And in July, these individuals kidnapped her."

"*What?*"

"Valeria has remained with this"—a tiny hesitation—"*group* for the past six months, and in that time, they have made exactly one demand in order to secure Valeria's return."

"What demand?" Del asked urgently.

Sophronia knew that Del remembered Valeria as well as she did. They'd known the delicate red-haired vampire child since the moment of her birth.

August's fangs flashed, and for a moment, he looked like exactly what he was—one of the most powerful vampires in the world. "Control of HemoCorp."

Sophronia leaned back. Gripped Casey's fingers harder.

Titus hadn't . . .

He hadn't wanted HemoCorp for itself. It *hadn't* been dynastic wrangling. He'd been trying to save his granddaughter.

"As far as I can tell," August went on, "Titus brought the situation to Octavia. I suspect he believed that loyalty to her sister—her own blood—would compel her to assist. To keep quiet." His jaw tightened. "He ought to have known better."

For her father, Sophronia thought, this would have been a betrayal beyond even the Stokr sabotage. Titus had been in trouble and had sought help not from August but from Octavia.

"However it happened," August said, "Titus told Octavia about Valeria's abduction and the kidnappers' demands. And Octavia, as is her wont, saw an opportunity for her own advancement. If she could use Titus's desperation to her advantage, then reveal his involvement in the Stokr sabotage at a critical moment, nothing would stand between her and control of her legacy at HemoCorp. Not you or me or Titus."

Sophronia swallowed against the hot sensation in her throat. "And . . . my analyst? Do you know—"

"Titus killed her. We were able to access the original security footage, which Brendan attempted to delete. I saw it myself. I'm sorry, Sophronia." His voice had gone gentle—gentler than she could remember hearing since she was a child. "He offered to pay her. A bribe. She said no. And he—"

Her father broke off. His eyes rested on her face.

"He believed he was protecting his family," August said. "No matter the cost."

Del pushed her curls off her forehead, taut and focused as she looked at August. "So Valeria—she's still with these bad guys, then? Do we know if she's all right?"

"I have seen photos of her," August said. "Grainy and distant. I believe she's being treated . . . humanely, let us say."

"I don't get this," Casey said. "I don't mean to—I'm sorry, August, but I don't understand who would fuck with you. With HemoCorp. Who would think they have a chance of winning a fight against some of the most powerful vampires in the world?"

August paused. He looked at the walls of the office, opaque and soundproof. He looked at Del and Casey and Sophronia.

He said: "Werewolves."

The room went very still. Sophronia stared blankly at her father: his severe cheekbones, the deathly earnestness of his mouth.

"W-what?" Del stuttered. "*Werewolves?*"

"Yes."

Sophronia couldn't wrap her mind around the words. Werewolves were a child's fairy tale. A dozen campy television shows. A story.

But vampires had been a story too. Abraham Stoker had built their legacy word by word, until the whole world had known their kind. Had feared them.

Del was shaking her head. "Werewolves aren't *real*, August. They're a myth. A conspiracy theory, like all the ones about vampires and garlic and silver crosses."

"I assure you," August said, "the werewolves are real. They maintain a number of distinct packs across the globe, including several here in California. Valeria spent three months attempting to infiltrate one such 'pack' before they took her."

"How do you"—Sophronia found she didn't know what to ask, where to begin—"how do you know about them? How long have you known that they exist?"

"The werewolves have long been an enemy of vampires," August said. "In my father's day, it was believed that the feud had ended—that their lust for power had been, finally, laid to rest." He looked across the desk at them, his gaze level. "It appears that we were wrong. This particular pack, it seems, is the group behind Beauchene Laboratory."

"Beauchene."

Del said the name like it was poison, and Sophronia looked over, surprised by the venom in her voice.

But Del, she remembered, had suspected the rival med-tech start-up from the first.

"I knew it," Del said softly. "I knew that if someone was trying to take HemoCorp down, it had to be Beauchene."

August inclined his head. "We believe that Valeria is being held captive at the Beauchene compound. Hidden within the pack."

"So what do we do?" Casey asked. His fingers were warm around Sophronia's. "What's our next move? I assume you're not planning to give in to their demands and sacrifice HemoCorp to get Valeria back."

"Of course not." August's jaw was sharp, his fangs white points against his lip. "I have called you in here today not just to apologize but to begin to enact a plan."

"What plan?" Sophronia asked.

But as she looked at her father across the desk, she realized she already knew what he was going to say.

August surveyed them slowly, patient as a knife. "We will retrieve Valeria ourselves."

ACKNOWLEDGMENTS

The first thing you should know about this book is that Lola Lovell is entirely based on my real-life Grammy, who was a runway model and the most fabulous, brilliant, mischievous person I've ever met. Miss you, GG. Forever delighted I got to immortalize you in fiction—wish you were here to see it.

The second thing you should know is that I am a literature professor who began drafting this book with exactly zero knowledge on the topics of apps or corporations. Huge, immense thanks are due to Melissa Kendall for holding my hand through every step of this book, from pitch to outline and then through multiple drafts, as well as to Eve Egelhof for answering a lot of questions like, "What are we calling PowerPoints these days?" Any technical errors remaining in this book are entirely my fault and can hopefully be excused by the fact that it's about vampires.

Thank you to my amazing editor, Lisa Bonvissuto, for helping to turn this book into the mystery-romance it always wanted to be! I'm so proud of what we've made together. And thank you to my wonderful agent, Jessica Alvarez, for helping to shape the earliest draft, and for all your support along the way. You are my favorite.

Thank you to the village at Berkley and PRH who helped

transform my Google doc into a real book, including Ariana Abad, Kalie Barnes-Young, Christine Legon, Alaina Christensen, Yahaira Lawrence, Laura Corless, and Devan Norman. Thank you to the incredible librarians and booksellers who've taken a chance on my books again and again—I love you beyond measure. Thank you to Blue Cypress Books for being the STARS of my LIFE, especially my best beloved Jodi Laidlaw.

Immense gratitude is due to my critique partners, Colleen Kelly, Kate Lane, Marianne Marston, Bella Barnes, and Jane Maguire, who helped this book take flight, as well as my life-saving author support group of Naina Kumar, Laura Piper Lee, Danica Nava, Ellie Palmer, and Jill Tew. Thank you to Esha, for letting me borrow your name and also write part of this book on your couch!

Thank you to my family: the best there is. I love you to the moon and back, always and forever. Special shout-out to my vampire-loving daughters—I'm really lucky I get to be your mom.

Scarlet Raven Photography

Alexandra Vasti is a British literature professor by day and *USA Today* bestselling romance writer by night. After finishing her PhD at Columbia University, she moved to New Orleans with her family. Her books have received starred reviews from *Publishers Weekly*, *Booklist*, *Library Journal*, *BookPage*, and *Kirkus Reviews* and have been featured in *The New York Times*, NPR, Entertainment Weekly, *People*, and elsewhere.

Visit Alexandra Vasti Online

AlexandraVasti